TAPESTRY

TAPESTRY

BELVA PLAIN

Delacorte
Press

Published by
Delacorte Press
The Bantam Doubleday Dell Publishing Group, Inc.
1 Dag Hammarskjold Plaza
New York, New York 10017

Library of Congress Cataloging in Publication Data
Plain, Belva.
Tapestry.

I. Title.
PS3566.L254T37   1988   813'.54   87-22346
ISBN 0-385-29630-4
ISBN 0-385-29656-8 Large-print edition
Manufactured in the United States of America

May 1988
10 9 8 7 6 5 4 3
BG

To my grandchildren

TAPESTRY

One

In the spring of the year 1920, Paul Werner sat in a private hospital on New York's Upper East Side, waiting for the birth of his first child. He was thirty-two years old, and after surviving the worst of the war in the trenches of France, had come home in good health. He was an attractive man, with a strong narrow frame and an aquiline face; when he was animated he looked younger than his years. Chiefly, though, his expression was thoughtful, courteous and listening; when his vivid blue eyes, so unusual in combination with olive skin, turned their full attention to anything or anyone, the effect was startling.

His future lay clearly marked before him; it always had been. Second in authority at the investment banking house founded by his late grandfather, he knew he was only a step away from the first position. Soon his father would retire, and Paul would be moving into the faintly shabby, spacious front room that looked out onto Wall Street. The family had deliberately maintained an atmosphere of quiet, unassuming prosperity. The elder Werner liked to compare their narrow little building, now wedged among skyscrapers, to a counting house in a Dickens novel. Its comfortable atmosphere suited Paul very well. An office was a place of business: one did not flaunt luxuries there; indeed, one did not flaunt them anywhere.

It would seem that Paul had everything. His wife, four years younger than he, was a gentle patrician girl whom he had known from childhood. Marian, affectionately called "Mimi," belonged to one of those families who, not necessarily related by blood, were a part of the tight, unbroken German-Jewish circle that had been prospering in the city since the Civil War. They went to the same schools, belonged to the same clubs, and summered at the same places in the Adirondacks or at the Jersey Shore. Paul's family and Mimi's had been especially close: Mimi and Paul had sat across a table from each other at birthdays and on holidays since they were old enough to eat with the adults. He had taken her to her first dance.

Now, after seven years of childless marriage, of numerous medical tests and monthly disappointments, at last she lay upstairs on the maternity floor. All his hopes lay with her. He wondered—for he was much given, perhaps too much given, to self-analysis—why his need to have children should be so consuming. Had it perhaps become so urgent because he had been marked by the terrible waste and slaughter of the war? But whatever the reason, it didn't matter. Simply, his need was there.

He sat now trying to concentrate on a magazine and, not succeeding, gazed out into the blank air at the center of the room. His long, slender feet were crossed at the ankles; he hadn't moved for half an hour. On the settee beside him lay his velvet-collared overcoat, his black leather briefcase and silver-knobbed umbrella. His agitation was concealed. Composure was a part of his nature and his training. One didn't allow whatever might be raging inside to reveal itself to the whole world. Only his eyes, alternately soft and sharply penetrating, could betray any message to those who knew him very well. There were not many who knew him very well.

When he glanced out of the window, he was surprised to see that the streetlamps had come on. The day had ebbed away; he had been here for hours, ever since they had summoned him to say that Mimi had gone to the hospital. The rain, which had been pouring before, had dwindled to a fine mist and the quiet street was deserted. There was hardly a sound indoors, either; in small private hospitals like this one there was no bustle. Now the quiet seemed eerie, and Paul shivered.

A first delivery could take an awfully long time. Everyone knew that. He had been prepared for it, and he told himself that he had also been prepared to see his wife suffer. It was expected and natural that women suffered. Yet her face had been so terrible, distorted, unrecognizable, wild! Her hair soaking wet on her forehead, and her screams, as she twisted and flung herself, lunging on the bed . . . They had put him out of her room.

She bore pain well, he thought, remembering the time she'd had a compound fracture of the arm. Yet childbirth was not to be compared with a broken arm, was it? So that the pain he had seen upstairs was not unusual? He didn't know. Certainly, though, the doctor knew. He was one of the best obstetricians in the city.

A young man came back to retrieve the coat and hat he had left on the chair across from Paul.

"A girl," he announced, answering Paul's question before it could be asked. "Seven pounds. A beautiful blonde."

Mirth seemed to bubble in the man's throat. He would go home now and sit down at the telephone to spread his happy news. Paul gave congratulations. The man had brought his wife in not two hours ago! When he went out again, the silence rang in Paul's ears.

He got up and began to pace the room. His legs ached from sitting. It was a dreary room, filled with imitation factory-made Chippendale, all in good enough taste but sterile. Tenth-rate landscapes on the walls. Hudson River school. Also imitation, of course. Well, what did he want in a hospital waiting room, for heaven's sake? An art exhibit?

He tried to focus his thoughts on art. He had always been open to new ideas, had bought Expressionists before they became as sought after as they were now; yet some of the wildest stuff that was being done today he couldn't look at. It reflected only what the war had done to the world: pulled things apart. It made you uneasy; the world before 1914 might have been a century ago, not just six years. His mind roved. Everything in the this postwar world was swelling larger. Debts, too, he thought soberly. Debt was a pit one must not fall into; that was one thing, anyway, on which he agreed with his father. There were others on which he did not agree.

Good God! What were they doing upstairs?

He pulled his thoughts back. What had he been thinking about? Oh, debts! No, no speculation, not for clients or himself. For the family, triple-A bonds and unmortgaged properties. Prepare for the biblical seven lean years that were bound to come.

Why didn't somebody come down and tell him something?

The people at the desks in the office across the hall didn't know anything, or said they didn't. Damn it all! He was just going to ask them again, to insist that they find out something, anything. Insist! He was crossing the hall when the elevator whirred, the door opened, and the doctor called out.

"Mr. Werner! Mr. Werner! It's all right. Your wife's fine." He laid his hand on Paul's arm. "We're very, very lucky tonight."

Lucky? Why? Was it to be a matter of luck, then? Had something gone wrong? Or almost gone wrong? Paul stood there, confused.

"My office is just down the hall. Come in. Sit down."

Yes, something has gone wrong. He wants to tell me.

"Very lucky," the doctor repeated. "We had to do a cesarean, Mr. Werner. Tried not to." He sighed, moving his hand, left, right, and back like a pendulum. "But it went well."

"A cesarean," Paul said. He felt cold.

"The problem was a transverse lie, lying crossways, that is." And again the doctor moved his hand; there was a small spot of blood on his white sleeve. "It's impossible to deliver a baby that way, you understand—"

I wish he would stop saying *you understand,* and get on with it.

Paul leaned forward as if to pull the words out of the other man's mouth.

"—and as the woman continues to labor in that situation, the uterus ruptures, with internal bleeding. An ordeal, Mr. Werner, if you want to call it that. Quite an ordeal."

"Yes," Paul said.

"But, thank God, she's come through. We've made the repairs and she's resting comfortably. Just came out of the anesthesia. I've been waiting up there until she did."

"Yes," Paul said.

"A very brave young woman, your wife."

Certificates and diplomas on the narrow wall at the end of the room behind the doctor's head testified to his knowledge and gave him authority. He's not much older than I am, Paul thought irrelevantly, reading the dates. *Arthur Bennet Lyons,* he read. One was in Latin; that gave authority too.

"Will," the doctor was saying. "There's no real proof, I know, but I'm convinced that a patient with a brave will can tilt things in the right direction. Your wife held on, Mr. Werner."

He's talking to fill a void, Paul thought. There's something else he doesn't want to get to; neither of us does. Yet he must know that I know what it is. And through lips so dry that they almost stuck together, he asked:

"The baby?"

"Dead. In that situation it always is. Inevitably."

"A normal baby?"

"Yes. A good-sized boy . . . I'm awfully sorry."

An old image flared in the eye of Paul's mind; like a bulb turned on or a match struck into total darkness, it flared and was quenched.

My son—my sons—and I go down to Conservatory Pond in the park, bringing the sailboats, the beautiful toy boats with mahogany hulls. A wind ruffles the water, the boats move outward with bellied sails and the strings go taut in our hands. I watch the boy—boys—laugh. Their baby teeth are like white seeds, like pebbles. We walk home, holding hands to cross the street. When they're older, we'll sail real boats out of Nantucket or the Cape. My son. Sons.

He came to himself. The doctor was doodling circles on a sheet of yellow paper.

"Would you like me to explain more clearly, draw you a diagram?"

"No, I'm sure you did everything anyone could do. May I see her now?"

The doctor's eyes were sympathetic. He looked old and tired.

"I don't see why not, for a minute or two."

Paul went upstairs. He felt like an intruder, passing between two rows of closed doors that seemed to frown reproach upon him as he broke the silence with his steps and his squeaking shoes. The place smelled of disinfectant and fear.

The door to his wife's room was ajar. In dim light he saw a

white bed in the center of the room; a long straight ridge lay on it; he saw a catafalque and a stone body.

A nurse, who had been sitting in a corner, stood up and rustled past him. "Come in. Your wife's been waiting for you." She went out and closed the door.

Lightly, gently, he kissed Mimi's forehead as if he feared that his touch would hurt her. She had come back from the dead!

"Are you terribly sad about the boy? Has it broken your heart?" she murmured.

"No. Well—yes, of course. But what matters is, you're here."

"They didn't let me see him."

Paul didn't answer.

"I'm sure they would have if I'd insisted. But I thought— this way I won't have to remember his face. This way—"

She turned into the pillow. Pity ran through Paul, watching her struggle for control.

"This way," she resumed, "it can be almost as if we hadn't had him at all, don't you see?"

"Yes, yes, I see."

They were both silent. Somewhere in the building, in some room tiled, cold and bare, as he imagined it to be, lay the child. Normal, the doctor had said. A good-sized boy. Eight days from now he would have been circumcised, given his name and the rabbi's blessing. In the living room, where the sun streams from the long windows, it would have been. After that, wine and cake in the dining room. All the relatives there, admiring. A good-sized boy. I can't grasp it, Paul thought. It doesn't make sense. Why should this have happened to us when everything was going so well?

Mimi was speaking.

"Paul, there'll be another, you know."

"You'd go through this again?"

"It wouldn't happen like this. Lightning doesn't strike twice."

That's not true, he thought. And yet a surge of hope, almost of elation, jumped at once into his throat. Yes, as soon as she was properly strong, there'd be another chance. Plenty of people had this kind of trouble and then went on to have as many children as they wanted. Of course they did. And a woman could have more than one cesarean. Look forward, not back!

She touched his hand with chilled fingers.

"You're cold," he said. "I'll go tell the nurse to get another blanket."

"No. Stay a minute."

He rubbed her hand between his. They smiled at each other. She looked normal. Who could believe it, after the way she had been only a few hours ago! Some pink had crept back into her fair, freckled skin; her long sandy hair had been brushed and the nurse had tied it back with a white ribbon.

"You frightened the life out of me," he said.

"Poor Paul! I'm sorry, I promise I won't do it again. What are you going to tell my parents and yours?"

"The truth, without letting them know how bad it was. I'll phone them all in Florida in the morning."

"You ought to go home. You must be exhausted. Have you had anything at all to eat?"

"I'm not hungry."

"But you have to eat! What time is it?"

"I don't know." He looked at his watch. "Almost ten."

"I know you won't wake the maids up, though you should. There's a whole roast chicken in the icebox, and a pudding. I had her make a lemon pudding this morning. Do fix something before you go to bed. I'm sure you won't take care of yourself at all while I'm here. You never do."

He laughed and kissed her forehead again. "How on earth did I ever get through the war without you to take care of me?"

"Oh, you!"

He stood up. "The doctor said only a few minutes. You have to rest. I'll be back first thing in the morning." At the door he remembered. "Is there anything you want me to bring you?"

"Only yourself."

He went out on tiptoe. Halfway down the corridor he was struck again with the thought that his dead baby lay somewhere in the building. He could ask. He had a right to see it. He wanted to. Also, he didn't want to . . .

Abruptly, there came a tremendous pressure in his chest. It surged and beat into his neck, burst and roared into his head. And he knew it for what it was: the pressure of something he wanted to forget. For a few hours this afternoon, and again up here with Mimi, it had subsided, but now it came back, expanding to fill him and take his breath away. And he had to grasp the wall to steady himself.

In a few moments he breathed naturally again. But he had to talk to someone! He had to!

Nobody, seeing the dignified young man in the fine dark suit, could have imagined his anguish as he stepped into the telephone booth.

I'll call Hennie, he thought. Who else in the world but Hennie?

Hennie Roth was not at home to receive the call. Having heard from the servants at the Werner house that Mimi was in the hospital, she had kept in touch all day. Hennie was Paul's aunt; more importantly, in a rare and special way, she was his most trusted friend, and had been since the days when he had sat on her lap and heard her read Grimms' fairy tales. Now, with her daughter-in-law, Leah, she sat in Paul's living room waiting for him to come home.

Still in her forties, she looked younger, not because of any beauty, for she was large-boned, tall, and too plainly dressed

—as now in her strict tan suit—but rather because of the vigor and enthusiasm that brought a certain charm to her long face, with its unfashionable coronet of brown hair.

Hennie had what her relatives called her "spiritual beauty." She was a fighter for social justice, as was her husband, Dan, a teacher and scientist, an idealist who had refused a fortune from one of his electronic inventions because the War Department had bought it. Both of them had spoken and marched for many causes; Hennie had marched for woman suffrage and in behalf of striking garment workers; she had even been arrested once while picketing a shirtwaist factory. They had worked for peace all their lives and, now that the war was over, still wrote and spoke for the League of Nations, for the National Council for the Prevention of War, and to anyone else who would listen.

They were, in short, the family mavericks.

And they had had their grief. Their son, their only child, had come home from the war without his legs; and after that, they had lost him; he had left a baby, Henry—little Hank, now four—and his widow, Leah. A slum child, orphaned at the age of eight, Leah had been adopted by Hennie and Dan. From them she had learned all that they had to teach, had married their son, and had now traveled beyond them into a world they had no wish to enter. For Leah was ambitious; gifted with a sense of fashion, she had already opened her own luxurious establishment on Madison Avenue. Remarried to an equally ambitious young lawyer and accountant, she lived with him and Hank near the Metropolitan Museum in Georgian elegance, in the handsome private house with marble fireplaces and circular stairs that Dan's money had bought for his wounded son. What he would not touch for himself, Dan had accepted for his son.

Leah bore no mark of early deprivation. Her glossy brown hair was coiffed short in the newest style; her narrow gold and diamond bracelets glittered at the pleated cuffs of her pale blue woolen sleeves; her alert, inquisitive round eyes surveyed Paul's lovely room with expert appraisal as she waited.

No two women could have been more unlike than Hennie and Leah; yet they loved each other as mothers and daughters, when they are fortunate, can love.

Restless now, Hennie got up and went to stand at the window, pushing aside the silk curtains to strain and peer through the dark mist, as though she could hurry Paul home.

"Do you suppose anything can be wrong?" she asked. "It's taken all day and no word. I don't know why I have such a feeling that there must be." Hennie was a worrier.

Leah, who was not, said cheerfully, "No, it's a first baby. They don't all have as easy a time as I did. You remember, Hank practically fell out," she finished, with some complacency.

"They've waited so long," Hennie fretted. "It would be awful for Paul if anything were to go wrong with this baby. Awful for Marian, too, of course."

When they heard the key in the lock, they both sprang up and Hennie came toward Paul with outstretched hands.

"It's all over. Marian's fine. She almost wasn't, but she's fine."

"Oh, thank heaven for that!"

"The baby's dead. A boy."

Paul was thinking of how clearly he could remember Hennie's Freddy. He'd been six years old and they'd taken him to the hospital to see the new baby. The arms and legs had waved. . . . A dead baby must look like one of those life-size dolls one saw in expensive toy stores. Waxy. Would the eyes be open or shut? He felt sudden nausea.

Hennie had turned away. She was twisting the wedding ring on her blunt finger.

Leah said softly, "It's awful, Paul. Awful. But you'll have another. You must think of that. And Mimi must. Not right away. But soon. You will."

They wanted to help him.

"Yes," Hennie added, "a neighbor of ours, when we lived downtown, lost two in a row. Then she went on to have three more!"

Funny, that was what he had told himself, there in Mimi's room tonight, and had felt so heartened . . . until that other thought had knocked the breath out of him. Now Leah was here, and he wouldn't be able to talk to Hennie about it.

"I suppose I could say, at least we never knew him."

"Ah, yes, that's true," Hennie said.

Poor Hennie! You didn't rear a son to fight in the war you so violently hated that you had spent years of your life trying to prevent it, only to lose him because of it—

Then he thought: There's no comparison between her poor Freddy and this. Yet comparisons weren't the point, were they?

"Have you had anything to eat? I asked your cook to fix a plate in case you wanted anything."

"Thanks, but I don't."

Hennie didn't urge him, for which he was grateful. Mimi was always coaxing him to eat, to wear his galoshes, to take a sweater, to lie down and rest.

Hennie wanted to know whether he had been able to see Marian.

"Yes. She's taking it very bravely."

"You must get her away as soon as she's able," Leah exclaimed. "A trip abroad will do marvels for her. Do some shopping in Paris, then the Riviera—or perhaps Biarritz a little later in the summer."

Paul felt an inward smile. How well she had learned, this young Leah, about life's pretty toys and prizes!

"And start another baby," she added boldly.

She went out to the hall and returned with a package wrapped in navy blue satin paper, smartly tied with a scarlet bow.

"My new logo." LÉA, complete with accent, sprawled across the top of the box. "It's a bed jacket for Mimi. Don't forget to bring it to her tomorrow. I rushed the monogram."

"It's absolutely beautiful," Hennie assured him. "I saw it. An extravagance."

Paul murmured the appropriate thanks.

"Is there anything we can do for you, Paul? Do you want us to leave you alone or go home?" Hennie asked.

He didn't want to be alone just yet. "No, stay. Unless you're tired."

"We'll stay a little, then. Dan won't be in before midnight anyway."

They resumed their seats on either side of the fireplace. Between them, on a low marble table, lay a shallow bowl of gardenias, giving off the strong sweet smell that Paul hated. For no good reason it made him think of funerals, and he would have moved them into the pantry, except that Mimi loved gardenias, and it didn't seem right to get rid of them just because she wasn't there.

"Dan's downtown, speaking about the League of Nations," Hennie said, "otherwise you know he'd be here."

"How's he feeling?"

"Oh, angina comes and goes. He takes his nitroglycerin when he's misbehaved, gone out in the wind or something else that he's not supposed to do."

"Shouldn't he give up teaching? High school kids can wear you out."

"It's his life. That and his lab. Especially now that he's got that new little place for himself on Canal Street. He's working on two or three inventions, something about a bladeless steam turbine. He just couldn't give it all up."

"Hennie—you're not worried about money?"

"We never were, were we? You know us. We don't need much."

"Well, if you—well, this is a day for straight talk. If anything should happen to Dan, I want you to know I'll take care of you. You're never to go without, do you hear?"

Leah interposed. "You don't think Ben and I would let her go without?"

"I can go without almost anything except Dan." Tears sprang to Hennie's eyes. She raised her voice. "I worry. He's too outspoken for these times! They're hunting Bolsheviks at every peace meeting, dragging decent people off to jail for simply speaking the truth! You'd think we were back in seventeenth-century Salem hunting witches! And I don't mind telling you, I'm terrified. Dan talks too much."

Paul shook his head. "With that bad heart, he can't afford to take risks. I'll speak to him."

"It won't do any good. You know how stubborn he is. . . . Oh, I shouldn't bother you with my troubles after the day you've had!"

"You never trouble me," he said.

And he wanted so much to tell her about the pressure that had almost torn him apart a little while ago. He wished he could tell her everything; he hadn't told her "everything" since that afternoon before his wedding, when he had come to her in his anguish.

"Alfie telephoned," Leah was saying, "the minute he heard that Mimi had gone to the hospital."

Uncle Alfie was another generous soul. Now that he had made his fortune in real estate, his life's pleasure was to give, whether money, advice, or vacations at his country place. Softhearted, he would be teary over Paul's dead baby.

Hennie added, "Mama called too. She was awfully worried."

Grandmother Angelique, going toward eighty, had been looking forward to being a great-grandmother again. She, too, would be genuinely sorry.

At least I am blessed with a family who cares, Paul thought.

"Now I'm really going," said Hennie. "Good night, Paul dear. Do try to get some sleep."

"I'll have the doorman call a cab for you."

"No, I'll walk. I've an umbrella and it's only a few blocks."

Only a few blocks—and a world of distance—from this apartment or from Leah's house to the East River and Dan's walk-up flat. And yet the simple places in which Hennie and Dan had lived had always been, and were still now, a kind of other home for Paul. He, who so cherished the beauty that dazzles the eye, could surely find none in those sparsely furnished rooms, but it was another kind of beauty that he found there, something that spoke to the other side of his soul. He went with the two women to the elevator and kissed Hennie's cheek with extra tenderness.

When he walked back to the apartment, the telephone was ringing.

Back in the waiting room, he sat with the intern who had been sent downstairs to talk to him.

"She began to hemorrhage about an hour after you left there. We called Dr. Lyons and couldn't get him right away. He'd left for home, and must have stopped off somewhere. We made several calls and just missed him each time, but finally—"

"Yes, yes," Paul interrupted furiously. Why couldn't the fellow get to the point? "You got him. And then? And now?"

Flushing, the young man spoke faster. "The internal bleeding resumed and—"

"Hemorrhage, you're saying?"

"Yes. I stopped it as best I could, using—"

"How is she now? Now?"

"Well, Dr. Lyons operated. He's still upstairs. I believe she's back in her room."

Another trip through the silent corridors. Again his shoe

squeaked. It didn't seem to squeak anyplace but here. Dr. Lyons was just leaving the room when Paul reached it.

"Oh, Mr. Werner. Come into the solarium for a minute. Your wife's not quite awake yet."

Weak lamplight quivered at the end of the hall. They sat down on the kind of wicker chairs that belong on a summer porch. A sense of unreality shook Paul, here in this place, past midnight.

"You operated? What happened?"

"It was a bad time. There'd been too much tearing after all. We couldn't seem to stop the bleeding. So there was no choice but to do a hysterectomy."

"Hysterectomy! My God! You had to?"

"I wouldn't have done it if I hadn't had to." The voice was gently reproachful; the eyes were circled black, like an owl's.

Paul took out a handkerchief and scrubbed his wet palms.

"A nasty combination of events, Mr. Werner. Nasty. Just about everything that could have gone wrong, did go wrong."

"But she—there's no danger now?"

"I'd say she's probably out of the woods. Barring infection, heaven forbid. We'll just keep our fingers crossed."

The end of the road. Miles and miles through wastelands and over mountains; then the weather clears, it's all blue and silver, you're almost where you want to go, until you come to the blank wall, hundreds of feet high, all stone, and the road stops.

"How will this affect her? All through her life, I mean?"

"Well, naturally, it's pretty sad to have a hysterectomy this young, but it shouldn't keep her from having a normal life, from being a woman in every respect."

Sex, he meant. There'd be no difference. Except—no children.

Words slipped out of Paul's mouth. "You have children, Doctor? Boys?"

"Three—a girl and two boys."

"I'm sorry. I don't know why I asked that."

"That's all right, Mr. Werner."

They stood up, hesitating in the gloom.

"Is there anything else you'd want me to explain to you? We could go downstairs to my office. I have books and diagrams that might make things clearer."

"Diagrams."

"Well, some people want them and they're entitled to them."

"I don't," Paul said. The sweat was pouring again on his palms. What questions? What difference now?

"You can always call me if there's anything else you want to know. Call me anytime or come in."

Paul remembered civility. "You've had a hard day, Doctor. Go home and rest."

"Not as hard as that girl of yours has had. And you've had."

Poor Mimi. Poor Mimi.

"I think you can see her now. She'll be waking up, but she'll be groggy, so don't stay more than a minute. Then go home and have a brandy. Two brandies." Dr. Lyons winked. "Even if it is against the law."

Again she lay like stone on the catafalque, and again the nurse rustled tactfully away. He stood above her. She was as pale as the sheet that was drawn around her neck. Her cheeks seemed to have sunk since the last time he'd seen her just a few hours before, making her proud, arched nose more prominent. He touched her spread hair.

"Mimi," he whispered.

To have been as happy as she had been only yesterday, to have anticipated everything; to have suffered all that hellish pain and end with nothing!

No child now, or ever.

It was wrong, it was unfair, it was cruel. What had either one of them done to be punished like this? His anger boiled.

She opened her eyes. "Paul?"

"I'm here, don't be afraid."

Her lips barely opened, so that he had to bend down to hear her.

"Not . . . only sleepy."

"I know. You've had a little operation. You're fine though, the doctor says. Can you hear me?"

"Yes. Sleepy."

He stood there, stroking her hair. He felt powerless. He wasn't used to feeling powerless. One planned things with care, one took precautions, was reasonable, industrious, and considerate. Then a whirlwind came and one was nothing more than a scrap, after all, blown ahead of the wind.

She stirred. He bent down, thinking she had said something, and spoke her name, but she had only sighed. Then he remembered he was to stay just for a minute, and took another look at her, listened to her even breathing, and went out.

He walked home. There were no cabs on the avenue, and anyway, he needed to walk off the turbulence inside him. It had begun to rain heavily and he had forgotten his umbrella, but he didn't care. He could have walked the length of Manhattan and back.

The night elevator operator looked at him with curiosity. "You've got yourself soaked, Mr. Werner." Then as the elevator rose, "I hope everything will turn out fine for the missus."

"Thanks, Tom."

He wants to know what happened, Paul thought. It's a natural curiosity. This is a situation that, when it becomes known, will arouse excitement and sympathy in equal amounts. The possibility of tragedy always does. Accidents. Deaths. Crimes. All those uncomplicated sorrows.

But what if the sorrow is not uncomplicated? What if there are other hidden factors? Guilt, for instance? And the pressure came back, along with the roaring in his ears.

He turned on a lamp and sat down in his front hall, holding

his head in his hands. This time, though, he felt no urge to seek out Hennie. This time he knew there would be no use in confiding, after all. Perhaps, too, given the terrible events of the day, he would be too miserably ashamed to confide, even to Hennie, whose mind was so open, who made no judgments. Yes, he would be ashamed.

He hadn't been ashamed that other time; he'd been so desperate, so torn apart before the wedding, torn between Mimi and Anna . . .

Into his parents' house she had come as a maid, only another in a stream of young foreign girls who stayed awhile, married, and left; there had been nothing different except that he had fallen in love with her, and she with him, in a way that he had not thought possible before or since.

But he had married Mimi. He had been promised to her. . . .

He stood up. Always, always that face before his eyes! When would it go away and leave him?

He had thought, during the glad months of Mimi's pregnancy, that he was teaching himself at last to say a final farewell to Anna. He had been—how absurdly!—trying to convince himself that she might possibly have been some sort of aberration, one of those sexual delights that can beset and confuse a man or woman, and ultimately will vanish; that it was only Mimi who was real and right and would last.

Absurd indeed.

And today in that hospital, he had been filled with a new horror. What if it had been Anna, he had thought, whose life was slipping away upstairs? The thought had shattered him. Would he have had an instant's care for the loss of the baby, for the children they would never have? No, much as he longed for a child, a son, he would have gone on his knees and begged for Anna's life. What worth could any child, could ten children, have, compared with her?

And today what had he mourned for, what was he mourning for now? For his wife, whom he had almost lost or might yet lose? No, not for her, but only for the child, for the children he would never have.

"God help me," he said aloud, thrusting his fist into his palm.

Then he began to walk around the apartment. He went from one fine room to the other and back again.

Only a few months ago, they had moved into this much larger apartment to have space for a growing family. They weren't even finished with the furnishing of it; he almost tripped over a roll of carpet that hadn't yet been laid. He'd been so pleased with the arrangement of the possessions that he treasured; the glimmer of sunshine on the Monet landscape over the mantel, the antique English table in the dining room, the crystal horse on its pedestal, a wedding gift from his German cousin, Joachim, who had remembered his love of horses. He was even growing used to Mimi's experiment with art deco in her little sitting room, with its unfamiliar angles, its inlaid ivory-and-shagreen table at which she worked on correspondence for her charities. But what good now were all these things?

He paced the hall, not knowing what he was looking for, not looking for anything. In the library, he stood gazing absently at the array of awards and plaques that Mimi, so foolishly proud of him, had hung on the wall behind his desk. Everywhere his name, Paul Aaron Werner, was written in black ink on white paper or in brass letters on brown wood; his charities, the hospitals and orphanages on whose boards he served commended him. The American Joint Distribution Committee honored him for his work in filling the $7 million New York City quota "for relief of suffering in the war-ravaged ghettos of Central Europe." Solid citizen, he thought with irony, condemning himself.

He picked up a framed snapshot of Hank at the age of three, sitting on a park bench one day when Paul had taken him on an outing. Such a merry little face! Bold like Dan's. And yet a little like his father, with a softness around the mouth. The dead Freddy had left something of himself behind, anyway. To have a boy like that . . .

Try not to be bitter, Paul. It's useless and it's ugly.

On the opposite wall he came face-to-face with his wife in a silver frame. The photograph was a duplicate of the one he kept at the office. She had an air of sensitive refinement, showing her characteristic somewhat prim and wistful smile. Her long neck was framed in an Elizabethan collar of starched lace; she wore lace because he liked it, she did everything because he liked it. And he could have wept for her, for himself, for everything.

Then he crossed the hall. The door to the nursery was ajar, so that light fell over the canopied bassinet. That old wives' warning about buying nothing for a baby until it was safely born, a warning at which both Marian and he had scoffed, made sense after all. He slammed the nursery door. Tomorrow he'd call some charity and get all the stuff out of the house.

At last he went into the kitchen. Take a brandy, the doctor had said. He'd laid in a nice supply just before Prohibition went into effect. He'd thought to save the brandy for some celebration, although what possible celebration there would be now, he didn't know. So he poured a generous, wasteful glass. Maybe it would help him sleep. And, sipping it slowly, he went to stand at a living room window, looking out into the night. Here and there, in houses up and down the street, a light went on: some student studying late for an examination, someone struck by sudden sickness, or a lover come home late, after having loved?

For a long time Paul stood waiting for sleep to tranquilize him. At last, near dawn, he went in to the wide, solitary bed and closed his eyes.

Two

The year was 1923, with the Red Scare still continuing. Never before in these United States had there been suppression so severe, not even during the worst moments of the Civil War. The Military Intelligence Bureau had drawn up a list entitled "Who's Who in Pacifism" and given it to the newspapers and the courts; Jane Addams and Lillian Wald were among the eminent personalities on this list of supposed public enemies. The Reverend John Haynes Holmes was arrested for speaking his mind on a street corner. Not long ago the president of Dartmouth College had accused Attorney General Palmer of concocting imaginary dangers to further his own political ambitions; it was said by many in a position to know that he was angling for the presidency. All over the country, petitions were being circulated and speeches given, while the arrests went on.

Dan Roth was to speak one evening at a little hall on the Lower East Side. He felt that he had been still too long, deferring to Hennie's fears for his health. For herself she had no fears at all; she spoke out whenever she was invited, attacking and giving names; her caution was only for him. But this time she had not been able to hold him back. Unfortunately, too, she had come down with the flu that morning, and could not even be with him.

A varied crowd had assembled in the little hall. There was the usual mixture of intellectual and academic types, neatly but soberly dressed, along with a swelling of labor union people.

A sprinkling of Communists as well, Paul thought, surveying the dingy, poorly lighted room.

This was not his usual sort of gathering, although certainly he was against war and in favor of free speech! Perhaps, though, it occurred to him, he wasn't courageous enough to be an agitator. On the other hand, perhaps these impassioned harangues delivered to people who already held your point of view were just so much wasted breath. He wasn't sure. He had come because Hennie had asked him to. Obviously she wanted him to help fill the hall.

Also, he had come because he had wanted to get out of the house, this being ladies' bridge night and Mimi's turn to be hostess. One night a week, among a certain group of friends, the husbands met for cards and on the same night their wives met in some other house. Paul, it seemed, was the only husband who didn't play, a fact that annoyed Mimi considerably. He had no interest in cards, couldn't remember who had dealt what card and didn't care. Ordinarily he had no problem with ladies' night but simply went into his library to read. Lately, though, there had been times when the feminine gathering grated on his nerves. The women seemed so trivial, with their idle gossiping. . . . At the same time he felt ashamed of himself for so harshly condemning an innocent amusement. What else, after all, did Mimi have to do except to make a life for herself among her friends, with their charity luncheons and their bridge games? His feelings were confused.

Suddenly he recognized Leah and Uncle Alfie's Meg across the room. It was vacation week, he realized, so Meg was down from Wellesley. That's an odd friendship, he thought, watching the two heads nod and bob. A smart chinchilla beret perched on Leah's glossy hair, while Meg's face was framed by a wide felt brim; the hat was schoolgirlish, yet pretty and becoming. Meg was a big girl with strong jaw and cheekbones; comfortable in sweaters and plaid skirts, she glowed in cold weather, when her fine skin shone pink. There was something in her trusting, wholesome face that had always touched Paul with a kind of pity. Of late, though, there had been change: Leah was teaching her how to dress. Her mother, having a fetish about refinement, had always dressed her badly.

Paul, too, liked to take some credit for having "rescued" Meg, since it was through his urging that Alfie and Emily had finally allowed her to go away to college. They would have kept her at home, dependent and infantile, forever. She'll have a hard time with them when she tries to marry, he thought.

He got up and took the vacant seat beside them.

"What a surprise! A family turnout!" Leah said. She could sound faintly mocking without meaning to mock at all.

"What brings you here?" Paul bantered back. "Shouldn't think this sort of thing was your first interest."

Leah grinned. "You know very well it's not. But I couldn't disappoint Hennie."

Meg said earnestly, "I wanted to come. There's been so much talk at school about what's going on in the country. Even Radcliffe has been attacked as radical because they had a debate about labor unions! Can you imagine? So when Dad said at dinner tonight that he'd heard that Uncle Dan was to speak, I decided to come."

"Your father's not here, though," Paul said somewhat mischievously.

Now Meg laughed. "Oh, you know Dad doesn't think people should get themselves involved in government business! You've got enough to do to mind your own affairs."

She has her mother's symmetrical English face, Paul thought, but her smile is Alfie's. She ought to use it more. He wondered whether she went out much with men, and rather thought not.

Then Dan came out onto the platform, along with the chairman of the meeting, who was to introduce him. Promptly the buzz of talk ceased, and there was a general expectant settling of chairs.

The chairman had a bushy head and a foreign accent. He spoke in orotund phrases: "This distinguished scientist, this devoted teacher, a man of conscience who had come here tonight, calling us all to heed . . ." et cetera, while Dan, who was obviously embarrassed, sat stiffly with his hands clutching the arms of the wooden chair.

The years had changed Dan very little. There was just a threading of silver in his thick hair; his expression was vivid; his suit, Paul saw with a smile, was still carelessly rumpled. And settling back, Paul prepared himself to let his mind wander. He knew so well what Dan was going to say that he could have given the speech himself. There was, after all, only one point of view that any right-thinking citizen could take.

"What we are here for," Dan began at last, "what we have to do is prevent the next war. In the next war, let me tell you now, there won't be any front lines or any safe rear quarters where the tax dodgers, corrupt politicians and militarists can go on living in comfort, while the young are slaughtered. . . . What we have to do is to silence those people who would silence us . . . the very kind of people who get rich out of war. . . ."

Paul felt himself wince. Not everyone who made money

during the war had been a militarist. Not his father, who had simply made loans to the Allies when they needed money; wars cost money. God knew his father never wanted a war, nor Paul in it. Yet wealth had flowed. Were they to give it all away? Well, they always had given a good deal of it away and still did.

Always, in Dan's presence, he was made to feel apologetic, not by Dan but by his own self.

Dan said, "Now they attack the settlement houses! 'Hotbeds of Communism in America,' they say. Well, I should like to inform him that these dangerous ladies come from what he would call our best families. Oh, these dangerous ladies, subverting the immigrant with lessons in cooking and English and child care—"

There was laughter from the audience.

"Yes, of course you laugh! You see the absurdity of it. Now they condemn the International Conference of Women for Peace. You recall when they met in Zurich to influence the makers of the Versailles Treaty? Well, I say it is too bad those women didn't have more influence, because the treaty contains the seeds of the next war, unless we here do something about it."

Dan's voice rose. The room was absolutely still. He knows how to rouse them, he's an orator, Paul thought, and then was worried because Dan was using too much energy and too much emotion. He would be needing his pills before he was through.

Dan held his arms aloft, crying, "Yes, I say, it's these false patriots who are the menace! Their mouths are filled with bitter lies. Every prediction they ever made was wrong and a lie and, what is more, they know it. The May Day parades these last couple of years at which, we were told, there were to be bombings and assassinations: Were there any?"

A murmur went through the room: No, no.

"They would like to extend, to renew the war powers and

the Espionage laws. They flout the constitutional guarantees of free speech and a free press. Innocent people have been arrested and railroaded through their hearings. This outrage—these outrages—"

Dan caught his breath. He was shouting now as he grasped the podium and Paul, alarmed, thought: We shouldn't have let him come.

"Listen to what Clarence Darrow has to say about what is going on!"

Dan took out a sheet of paper, put on his glasses, and—three men in dark suits leapt up on the platform. At the same instant the doors at the rear of the hall were flung open, slamming against the walls. A stream of sallow light from the lobby poured in and a dozen policemen came trotting down the aisle in double time.

"What in blazes—" Paul began.

A gasp went through the audience, followed by faint screams and a scramble to see what was happening.

"Cossacks!" someone yelled.

The police had taken their stand with folded arms at the foot of the stage, glowering back at the crowd. A woman wailed, and then, as suddenly as the commotion had erupted, it ceased and the room fell still.

One of the dark-suited men produced a badge. "You are Leo—" and then some difficult name, probably mispronounced.

"I am." The moderator, who was half a head shorter than his interrogator, stood his ground. "I am," he repeated with defiance.

Meg had seized Paul's arm. "What is it? What's happening?"

"Department of Justice, U.S. marshals," Paul whispered. His eyes were on Dan, who had sat down, huddled on his chair. A heart attack coming on, or simply terrified? Paul's own heart drummed.

"Leo"—again the blurred name— "you are under arrest. You are a member of the Communist Labor Party and a threat to the established peace and order of the United States. I order you to identify among those present any and all active members of your organization."

"Absolutely not," said Leo.

"It would be a great deal simpler than having us make a personal search of everyone in this room for identification."

Indignant shouts broke out. "This is America! Where do you think you are? Show your warrants!"

A second marshal stepped to the edge of the platform. "Less noise here, please." Firm and correct, he might have been speaking before some conservative forum. Obviously, he had been instructed to permit no violence. The arrested were just quietly to be whisked away.

"We are in possession of warrants to search the premises and the persons present. It will be to your benefit to comply willingly. Will all on the left side of the center aisle please line up on that wall, those on the right do the same."

Paul looked about. Leah and Meg were in the seats closest to the aisle, next to an exit. Men and women, some silent with fright, others cursing with anger, were shoving and being shoved to the wall. Paul pushed Leah, who resisted. "Get out. Slip out. Fast." He pushed Meg, whose face was crinkled, ready for tears. "Get out, both of you! Fast, I said! Dammit!" he cried, steering them through the rising frenzy of the crowd. He slid them safely through the door, just as a policeman, having suddenly become aware of the open door, came rushing up to block it.

The men on the platform were now interrogating Dan.

"I'm not a member of any organization. Never have been," Paul heard him say.

They were asking him to turn his pockets inside out. They were examining his wallet. There would be nothing subversive there, that was a certainty. Still, what had he just been saying? Paul tried to recollect what he had been hearing only a few minutes before. But whatever Dan had said, it had been his right to say it. Or it always had been, in this country. . . . Dan and Leo were now alone on the platform except for one policeman; must that mean that Dan, too, was under arrest?

The men from the Justice Department were now beginning to examine the people lined up against the walls. Carefully, quietly, they looked through pockets and wallets, briefcases and pocketbooks. There were mild protests of innocence and ignorance, tears from some of the women and muttered fury from some of the men, all of which the examiners ignored as, methodically, they proceeded to separate the crowd.

Many were dismissed, sent up the center aisle and out of the building. It will take a couple of hours to go through everyone here, Paul thought, resigning himself.

Then suddenly, he was called out of turn and asked to show the contents of his pockets. He wondered whether he could possibly be under suspicion for something. Or was it that they thought he looked out of place here? His clothing, which was merely his habitual business dress, did set him apart. Complying, he withdrew the contents of his pockets: a Dunhill pipe and tobacco pouch, a monogrammed cigarette case, a pair of gray suede gloves, and a gold house key on a gold chain, last year's birthday present from Marian.

"Your wallet, please, sir?"

Yes, it must be the clothes; the workmen in the line had not been addressed as "sir." The wallet, of black pin seal, contained the following: two hundred dollars in new bills—he liked new, clean, unwrinkled bills—his business card, and an identification paper giving his home address on Fifth Avenue.

His examiner replaced everything with care. "And what were you doing here, sir, tonight?" There was a slight emphasis, as of surprise, on the word *you.*

Paul felt his indignation mount. An American citizen, being asked what he was doing! But it was only common sense to deal prudently with an opponent who had the upper hand. For Dan's sake, if not for his own.

"I came to hear my uncle speak. Daniel Roth. He's been a peace activist, no Communist, I guarantee you!"

The man smiled slightly. "Guarantee?" he repeated. He was a young man, surely not more than twenty-five, and very polite.

"Oh, yes," Paul said. "He's a schoolteacher, idealistic—" And searching for anything that might help Dan, he explained, "Lost a son in the war, you see, and that's why he's so mixed up in this peace business. But that's all it is. And he's got a heart condition. You aren't going to hold him, are you?"

"I really can't discuss that," the young man answered. "But you certainly may leave, sir. In fact, you must leave now. Out through the main door, please." And he proceeded to the next in line.

Out through the main entrance. Of course! So he wouldn't be able to go down the front to where Dan was still sitting. Only when the cold air hit him, did Paul realize that his body was burning, as with a fever.

There were not many people on the sidewalk. Those who had been released had scurried as fast and as far away as they could. Under a streetlamp in the corner, he saw Leah and Meg.

"My God," Leah cried, "you took forever! What's going on in there?"

"You've read enough about it. They're looking for Communists."

"Well, why are they holding Dan? Are they holding him? Where is he?"

"Sitting up front with that other fellow, the one who made the introduction. I think they are probably going to hold him. I'm not sure," Paul said.

"They won't put him in jail, will they?" Meg was aghast.

"I don't know. There's nothing we can do till we know. I wish you two would go home," Paul said impatiently. "This may take half the night. I'll find a cab for you."

"I'm not going," Leah said. "You don't really think I could go home and sleep without knowing what was happening to Dan?"

Meg murmured, "Hennie will be frantic."

His heart, Paul thought, and wondered just how much pressure Dan could stand.

The others were thinking the same.

"I hope he has his medicine with him," Leah said.

A few more people emerged from the hall, glanced cautiously toward the three under the lamplight, lowered their eyes and went rapidly down the street. Like frightened rabbits, Paul thought, but aren't we all? He felt the rage rising again. It was blowing up cold. They walked to the next corner and back. There was nothing to say, nothing to do but walk and wait.

Presently, three black vans drew up and stopped in the alley at the side door through which Paul had pushed Leah and Meg.

"What are they?" Meg asked.

"Police vans. And," seeing their faces, Paul added kindly, "if they do take him away—if they should—we'll get bail and take him right home. So that's all that will happen."

The street was strangely deserted. The news must have spread through the neighborhood and people were staying indoors out of sight.

Now the side door opened. Police came out first and made an aisle between the door and the van. Over their shoulders one could see a few men and women being hurried toward the van. Paul thought he saw Dan, but couldn't be sure. He felt Leah's hand on his back.

"Let me through—they can't do this, let me through, Paul, dammit—"

He blocked her. "Stop it! This is serious! Keep out of it, don't be a fool."

He addressed the nearest policeman. "How far is the precinct house? Can we walk?"

"Ten blocks, down the avenue and one west."

There wasn't a taxicab in sight. "Hurry," Paul said.

The three walked. Behind them now others were walking, almost running, to be first to see their people. No one spoke; the only sound was the scurry and slap of feet on the sidewalk.

The vans had arrived at the station ahead of the walkers, and the space in front of the high desk was filled with police and prisoners. They must have been making arrests all over the city. The crowd was pressed against the grimy walls, and the scuffed chairs along the walls were overturned. Up in front, Paul saw the same three cool young men in dark suits presenting their warrants to the man behind the desk. His eyes searched desperately for Dan and found him, pressed in a corner against a spittoon.

Roughly, he pushed men aside. "You all right, Dan?"

"I'm all right, I just took my medicine."

"You need a chair, I'll get one, you can't just—"

"No. I'm worried about Hennie, that's all."

"Hennie will be all right. We'll get bail for you as soon as they set it. This is crazy. What have they got against you?"

Dan said wearily, "They didn't distinguish me from Leo. He is a member of the Communist Labor Party, though God knows I'm not. But they wouldn't believe me on account of my speech."

"Bastards," Paul said.

"Hey, you haven't got Leah and Meg with you?"

"I didn't bring them. I met them there."

Dan grinned. "Alfie will have a fit that Meg was there." The grin turned into a grimace and his hand went to his chest.

"Is it bad?" Paul was frantic. "I'll rush this through, get you to a doctor, they can't do this, keep you standing here—"

Dan put out the other hand, restraining him. "No, it'll pass. Just get home to Hennie."

Ignoring him, Paul pushed his way back through the jostling crowd, to a policeman.

"Officer, there's a sick man here. He's got a bad heart. Is there any way he might be called up fast, so I can get bail? That will be no problem for me."

The policeman's placid middle-aged face took on an expression of wonder. "Bail? There's no bail in these cases, mister. These are *federal* cases, didn't you know? Department of Justice."

"No bail?" Paul heard his own voice rise sharply. "I never heard of such a thing!"

"Well, you're hearing it now." And the man turned away.

Paul was in a state of shock. A bystander who had overheard explained, "Oh, yes, my brother was taken last month. He's still in a federal penitentiary."

"I don't understand," Paul repeated. He felt helpless; it flashed across his mind that he wasn't used to feeling helpless, and he wasn't going to accept it. His name was Paul Werner; he knew where to go and how to get what he wanted; he had been doing it all his life.

One of the marshals was approaching. Paul pulled him by the sleeve.

"Is it true that bail won't be set?"

"Yes."

"This is a crime! You have a completely innocent man here, a sick man. I demand bail!"

The man surveyed Paul from foot to head, pausing at his necktie. "You can demand what you want, that's your privilege. See your lawyer in the morning."

"In the morning?" Paul cried. "I can get him now! Right now!"

"It won't do any good. The prisoners are being taken to the Tombs overnight, and nothing at all will be done until the morning. I'm sorry. Take your hand off, please." For Paul had not released his sleeve.

"Jesus," Paul said.

He made his way back to Dan, who was standing with Leah and Meg.

"It's an outrage, Dan. You have to be kept overnight. The bastards."

Dan said only, "I rather expected so."

"I swear to you we'll have you out first thing in the morning! Dan, you'll manage, won't you?"

His cheeks looked blue and Paul was sick with fear for him. So they stood, the two young women speechless with fright, holding Dan by the arms, as if leaning on him or helping him to lean on them. No one spoke. The gabble and the swarming in the close, fetid air was sickening. Half an hour later, Dan's name was called and they had to let him go. He was taken to the desk, there was a brief buzz of talk, some statements were written down on some official papers, and then Dan Roth, remanded to the Tombs, was led away.

Now the two women let their tears fall. "I'll get right home to Ben. He's a smart lawyer," Leah said. "He'll find a way to wiggle out of this."

Meg said, "I'll go to Hennie's. And I'm not," she added, with some defiance, "going back to college until this is over."

In spite of all, Paul had to smile at that. Little Meg was becoming a person.

Ben Marcus sat in his office overlooking Grand Central Station. His accountancy and law diplomas, in fine mahogany frames, were ranged behind the mahogany desk. From this seventeenth floor, he could see the rivers east and west; north lay the green oblong rug that was Central Park. Its lakes and ponds looked as if someone had dropped a couple of Tiffany diamonds on the rug, he was thinking now as he waited for the family to gather.

This was the morning of the third day since Dan's arrest and he was still being held in the Tombs.

Well named, Ben said to himself, with a shudder; it was as dank as one imagined a medieval dungeon must have been. Fear hovered in the corridors. Thieves and derelicts of every description, the scum—and the tragedies—of the city, suffered and cursed and yelled and wept and beat with their fists upon the walls. God help them! he thought, for although Ben was above all a keenly practical and ambitious man, he was also a kindly one, and had imagination. He could be haunted for days afterward whenever he had to go into a prison cell, which was now very seldom, since in his practice he dealt with corporative balance sheets and contracts rather than with street crime. He shuddered again.

What in the name of creation possessed a man like Dan Roth to get himself into a fix like this? The times were very dangerous for anyone who had what one might call "liberal" tendencies; surely the politic thing to do was to keep quiet until the times changed, which assuredly they would.

But Dan was an odd one. Likeable, but odd. Stubborn as all get out. Irritating, sometimes, with his holy attitudes, especially when he gave his opinions about the upbringing of Leah's boy. For example, he was a nut about the public school system. Hank was seven, and Leah wanted to put him into a good private school, which made sense. There certainly was money enough! Dan's money, Ben thought, shaking his head.

What an unusual lot he had married into! No two of them alike, and yet tight together as glue. Having grown up without relatives, he valued that.

Take Hennie and Dan—well, they were in a class by themselves. How people could be satisfied with never getting ahead, was beyond Ben. As far back as he could remember, when he had been a little kid in the Bronx, he had made plans to get ahead.

Alfie, now, Hennie's brother, made a lot more sense, even though, in spite of his marked success, he never seemed quite grown up. A funny thing to say about a corpulent man of forty-five! Maybe it was his explosive laugh, all that expansive good nature, that kept him boyish. One wondered about his marriage, too, a marriage in which he seemed to be content, as did Emily; yet they didn't seem to have much in common. They had started with a religious handicap, his Jewish parents and her gentile parents having been equally opposed to the marriage. She was sedate, while he was convivial. She was cultured, while he never opened a book. Of course, he had made a great deal of money and that had a way of smoothing the bumps. Certainly it helped their social climb—and a lot of nonsense that was!—although because of Alfie's being Jewish, the climb would have its limits. Even the great parties at Laurel Hill wouldn't help that much, Ben thought as he recalled the handsome spread in the green New Jersey countryside, the lavishly remodeled farmhouse with its wings, the pool and tennis courts, and the herd of fawn Jerseys in the barn.

It might be nice to have a place like that someday, he reflected, if Leah wanted it, that is. She loved the city, so she probably wouldn't, and that was all right with him. Anything Leah wanted was all right with him. He chuckled. He'd gotten the gem of the family, all right!

He made a second's comparison with Paul's wife, the proper Marian. Straight as a broomstick, and about as lovable. He wondered how Paul really felt about her. Wouldn't be surprised if he kept a pretty little person somewhere! Wouldn't blame him. But one could never get close enough to Paul to know anything about him. Still, one liked him. Respected him. He had—what was the best word? Authority. And it wasn't all because of his inherited position, although heaven knew that helped. No, it was the strength in him. Funny, Ben thought, I find myself deferring to him lots of times, not minding it, and I don't defer easily.

Yet today they are coming to me; neither Alfie nor Paul has been able to get anywhere.

He stood up and moved closer to the window. He had a narrow, foxy red-brown head and quick humorous eyes. Now, as he studied the view, placing the museum in the park, gauging the location of his house, so close to the park, those eyes brightened with pleasure. He had come far! And he was going farther; he was no pauper, no hanger-on among his wife's rich relatives; he could hold his own among them.

Now he heard them come in, heard Paul's and Alfie's voices.

Paul looked haggard. "Nothing," he said. He threw up his hands. "I was down there again yesterday afternoon. He's holding up, but he looks terrible. I don't know how long he can last."

Alfie confirmed that. "He hasn't eaten or slept. It could break your heart. Hennie went yesterday. She can hardly stand up. Dan said she's not to come again."

There was a reflective silence. Ben, doodling on a pad, frowned over a new thought.

"Oh," Alfie said, "I see you've redecorated! New carpets. Nice. Very nice."

Paul threw him a look and turned to Ben. "I spent last evening with my lawyer. Of course, he's wills and trusts, but he knows plenty of people. He's tried here in the city. He was on the phone all day with Washington. That's the sum of it, and it looks bad."

Chastised, Alfie made amends. "I even called my stockbroker. A very wealthy man, top family, Son of the American Revolution, and all that. I must say, with all the money he's made out of me, I thought he'd be a little more cooperative, but he seemed to feel that people like Dan deserve what they get. I don't know. . . ." Alfie looked puzzled. His voice trailed off.

Ben drummed on the pad with his pencil. "So it looks as if we're exactly nowhere, doesn't it?"

"I'm afraid so," Paul said. "You know, I've had the feeling, since the moment those men jumped onto the platform where Dan was speaking, that this isn't real. I keep thinking of Alice in Wonderland. Curiouser and curiouser. The police station, and the cell. Dan Roth sitting in a cell on a dirty cot. For what? What's he done, for God's sake? God damn it! I feel like going down there and blowing the place up and taking Dan out!"

Ben had never seen Paul like this, and he regarded him with interest. Paul's tie was askew; he was still wearing his topcoat and had dropped his hat on the floor.

Alfie, who had probably never seen Paul so agitated either, asked almost timidly what legal proceedings were next.

"He'll stand before the magistrate's court in a few days," Paul answered. "The docket's full, that's why it's taking so long. And then a federal prison. I don't know for how long. It'll kill him," he finished. "Kill him."

There was another silence in the room, until Ben said, "A stone wall."

Paul sighed. "I've asked everywhere I could think of. The banking community, bar association men, my congressman and senators. Everybody I could dredge out of my memory. And my father has too. I must say he's done his best, and you can imagine how much he disapproves of the sort of mess Dan can get into." He managed a rueful smile.

"I can imagine," Ben said. He'd met the old gentleman only two or three times, but it hadn't been hard to size him up: stiff collar, Prussian moustache, high button shoes.

"Well, what are we going to do?" Alfie's cry was almost a wail.

"I'll tell you what," Ben said. "I've been thinking of something. I don't know whether it would work. I don't know."

As a matter of fact, he had been thinking since early the previous day, but for reasons of his own had been hesitant.

"There's a man, a client who's come to me recently. I don't know him all that well—yet. But he's got connections. There's a man who really has got marvelous connections."

"Well, why didn't you call him right away? What are you waiting for, if he's so marvelous?" Paul asked almost angrily.

"I'll tell you. It may cost money."

Paul and Alfie spoke at once. "For Christ's sake, Ben, what difference does that make?"

"On the other hand, it may cost nothing."

"What's all the mystery? Get hold of him," Paul commanded. "I'll admit I've used up all my resources. I don't care who the man is, I want Dan out of there before he dies of a heart attack, or Hennie has an emotional collapse!"

Ben stood up. "It's nine-thirty. He's got an office not far from here. I'll just run over. This is too big to handle on the phone. Where are you both going?"

"We'll be going down to see Dan. After that, Hennie," Paul said, straightening his necktie.

"Hennie is still at my house. Leah wouldn't let her stay alone in the apartment." Ben was already halfway to the door. "I'll call you at my house the moment I hear anything. If I hear anything."

Paul had read through the *Times* and *The Wall Street Journal;* his head had begun to ache with the strain of idle waiting. Momentarily alone in the library, he could hear the life of the house, in the dining room where the women had been having coffee all afternoon, and upstairs where Hank had come home from school with two little boys. Their shrill voices were cheerful, Paul thought, as he heard them whooping down the stairwell. His eyes wandered around the room from the Steinway to the pale silk curtains, the gilded mantel clock and the muted pinks in the Oriental rug—all bought by Dan when he made a gift of the house to his son.

And now he sat in the Tombs. A queer business, among many queer things in this queer world.

Leah had added to the quiet luxury. She had begun to collect art, consulting Paul about her purchases. She was making a great deal of money herself. She had enlarged her shop, which was frequently mentioned in *Vogue* and *Harper's Bazaar*. Ben was making money, too, rising with surprising speed for a young lawyer who had no family connections. That spacious office this morning . . . and Leah had new jewelry . . . Paul had an eye for such things and recognized quality: a small fine emerald ring, excellent pearls with a diamond clasp . . . Well, it was none of his business.

Restlessly, he got up and crossed the hall to the dining room. Leah, Emily, Marian, Meg, and Paul's mother hovered around Hennie, who sat without speaking. Her hands were locked tightly in her lap and her face was gray.

"We're trying to get her to eat something," Marian said. "She's had nothing but tea all day."

They all talked at once. "She still has fever, better not to eat. She should lie down. Do go upstairs and take a little nap, Hennie. We'll call you the minute there's anything, you know we will."

But Hennie only shook her head, took another sip of tea, sighed, and locked her hands together again.

I don't know what we'll do with her, Paul thought as a possibility ran through his mind. Given what had been happening lately, it might even be a probability. Dan might receive a very stiff sentence, and how would they care for Hennie? And, as always, he felt that sense of blood linkage among his relatives, something, he knew, that was often remarked upon by outsiders because it was regrettably being lost in this century. He wondered why he felt it so strongly; his own parents didn't feel it as strongly as he did.

Alfie came in, looking despondent. "I've been on the phone again with Ben's office. He hasn't come back and hasn't called in. Could something good be happening?"

No one answered, and Alfie followed Paul back across the hall.

"Dan and his socialist politics," Alfie grumbled. "But I have to say this much: He's sincere about it and always was."

"He's not a political Socialist," Paul argued, having a penchant for absolute accuracy. "He never was in politics."

"Same thing," Alfie replied, glumly. "This Red Scare business—it will all pass. Sticking your neck out, what does it get you? And I'll tell you something: Margaretta had no business being there. She ought to be back in college right now, but I can't budge her."

"Meg's grown. She has her own mind, Alfie."

"Oh, I know, I know. Of course, I understand she's crazy about Hennie, always was even when she was a little kid. You know, in many ways I think Meg seems to be more like her Aunt Hennie than like her mother."

The afternoon grew shorter. The women, having apparently consumed their limit in coffee and tea, drifted in from the dining room and sat down. They picked up sections of Paul's discarded newspaper and conversation ebbed; they had run out of it. Someone turned lamps on, and this reminder that the day had almost gone, with still no word, was depressing.

Presently Hank and his friends came rushing down the stairs. When he had seen his friends out at the front door, Hank came back. His entrance stirred them all to life.

Uninhibited and boastful, he had to display his writing sample, his arithmetic paper, his drawings, and all his second-grade prowess. He did it with the ease of a child who is used to grown-ups and expects to be listened to. He has Dan's charm, Paul thought, while Hank, curled on the sofa next to

Hennie, spread his artwork on her lap and brought to her face the first relief from the blank, awful trance that had lain upon it all through these last three days. And Paul felt loving thankfulness, observing the little scene. It could have been so different for the child: either a household without a father at all, or else, if Freddy's fate had been different, a sorrowful home with a troubled father and an unhappy mother striving, as he knew Leah would have striven, to conceal her unhappiness. Yes, poor Freddy's tragic end had not been without its benefit for his child, who now had a cheerful home, two parents, and in Ben a father who, it was plain, was good for him.

These thoughts were interrupted when Alfie, who had been using the telephone in the library, came back and called everyone to attention.

"I've just talked to Ben's office. The secretary said he's on his way home. She didn't know anything more than that. He left almost half an hour ago, she said."

A general sigh moved around the room. And then in the midst of the sigh, the downstairs bell rang; they heard a maid run from the rear of the house to answer the door; heard voices, several voices . . . Everyone stood up.

They were all standing when Ben came into the room, wearing a wide, triumphant grin. Then Dan came rushing to Hennie. And a third man followed, to wait at the door unnoticed in the tumult.

"Oh, my God!" For the first time, Hennie broke and wept, while Dan held her and Hank pulled at him and everyone else crowded around.

"What happened?"

"How do you feel?"

"Are you all right?"

"Oh, Ben, what a miracle!"

"How did you do it?"

"Dan, sit down! Are you hungry? Let me get you a drink."

With his free arm, Dan waved them all away. The other arm held Hennie firmly around the waist.

"I'm fine. I'm all right. Not hungry. But you can get me a brandy."

Meg rushed away for the brandy.

"Now let the man sit down," Ben said. He was in command, and enjoying it. "Let him rest, I'll do the talking. This is the man we must all thank. This is Donal Powers, who knew what to do." And he motioned to the man on the threshold, who had been quietly watching the happy commotion. Mr. Powers made a gracious gesture.

"My pleasure to do a favor for Ben's family. My pleasure."

Introductions were made; Mr. Powers was surrounded; everyone had to shake his hand and marvel that he had been able to do what no one else had been able to do. Everyone thanked him again and again, while Hennie kissed him and cried.

In a second, the dismal vapor of the afternoon had been dispelled. A holiday atmosphere now filled the room; everything glittered. Champagne was brought in; a maid appeared with plates of all the little extras that go with it, hot stuffed mushrooms and crabmeat cups, and everyone was invited to stay for supper.

"It's last-minute, but we'll manage to throw something together. You won't go hungry," Leah cried gaily. This was what she loved, being the dispenser of hospitality, the center of celebration. She did it well, too.

But Paul withdrew. He removed himself from the babble of pleasure. It was a mental trick of his, seldom used, and then only when he was tired—as he now was after these days of trial—or when his mind was troubled.

He was aware of his own mixed feelings. Gratitude—of course he was grateful! There was something else, though, that he felt, something quite—well, not quite nice. He felt, to a certain extent, humiliated. Always, young as he was, he had been the one in the family who knew how to manage, to arrange things. Today was the first time he had failed.

His respected name, which ought to have been influential enough to vouch for Dan, even in the face of the crazy fanaticism of the times, had not been. But this other man's, this stranger's name, had been. Why?

Puzzled, Paul observed him. He was no more than thirty, dark and well built. Women, no doubt, would find him handsome. He was impeccable, as if he had just come out of the shower. His cashmere jacket fitted his shoulders in a way that only English tailors knew how to fit them. He wore handmade shoes. His demeanor was correct as a funeral director's, he carefully moved and carefully spoke, always with that small, gracious inclination of the head. Yet, for all this gentility, Powers had what Paul recognized as an untamed air. He had known enough powerful men to know what he was looking at. Powers! Well named, he thought.

Who was he? Whom did he know? Well, time would tell. It told most things eventually.

The supper was a buffet. Paul filled his plate and carried it into the library, finding the only vacant chair directly opposite where Powers was sitting, talking to Ben. Even though Paul was unable to hear what they were saying, he could see that Ben was deferential. Powers had a commanding mouth; one could imagine the lips drawn under in anger. His eyes were long-lashed and feminine, but there was nothing else remotely feminine about him. Women would love those eyes.

Briefly, the eyes met Paul's and looked away. He knows I am trying to figure out who he is, Paul thought. And a few minutes later, when Ben got up, Powers came over to Paul.

"I understand you're in banking. *The* Werner."

"Yes," Paul said, not liking the emphasis.

"This must have been quite an experience, having an uncle arrested. An unusual occurrence in a family like yours." The eyes were amused.

"Dan is an unusual man," Paul answered, rather stiffly.

"So I heard. Ben told me something. An inventor, isn't he?"

Paul didn't feel like talking about Dan. Yet surely it was natural for the man to be curious about someone whom he had rescued, so he explained briefly.

"He must have made a pile of money," Powers said.

"He did. But he didn't keep a cent of it, because it was war money. Radio transmission used at sea."

"Ben's told me about this house. Quite a place! And right off Fifth Avenue."

"Yes. Dan gave it to the boy. To Hank."

"While grandpa lives in a tenement." Scorn was obvious.

"It's comfortable and clean," Paul said, controlling himself. "And they are happy in it."

"Well, you meet all kinds, don't you?" Powers said.

"Indeed you do."

And Powers, not defeated, but wanting apparently to conclude on an easy note, said calmly, "He's a nice old codger, though. I'm glad I could help him out."

"I'm glad you could too."

"By the way, who's the girl in the red dress?"

"That's my cousin, Meg. Meg DeRivera."

"I seem to have missed her before. I think I'll go over and introduce myself."

What does he want with Meg? Paul wondered as Powers walked away. Meg's surely not *his* sort . . . and he turned his attention to little Hank, who well knew that he could always get attention from Cousin Paul.

Much later, an hour or more, after he had gone up to Hank's room and been shown all his toys, Paul came downstairs again, still trailed by the little boy. He went into the living room, out of which there now came the sound of singing.

Meg was at the piano. She had no great talent, but played well enough to accompany herself in Fanny Brice's "Secondhand Rose." Donal Powers was standing in the curve of the piano, watching her.

Her red dress was the color of ripe cherries. It had a French look and came, undoubtedly, from Leah's place. She looked flushed and happy. Of course, everyone in the room was happy tonight. But was there not something special, different, unusual, in her animation?

"You aren't listening, Cousin Paul," Hank complained.

"Oh," Paul said, "it's all that food and being sleepy." He was thinking, Why, she is lovely! And saw for the first time that Meg could be radiant.

Quite clearly, something had happened during this last hour. She had stopped playing; her hands were just drifting over the keys making tinkling sounds, while her face was upturned to whatever Donal Powers was saying.

Paul was standing next to Alfie when Powers came over with Meg beside him.

"I hope," he said, "I have your permission to take this young lady out to dinner tomorrow, Mr. DeRivera."

Alfie was flustered. "Why, if you're sure you—very kind, yes—you've been so kind," he said, unaware of the awkwardness of his response. "You've gone to so much trouble for us," he went on, more awkwardly still.

Powers's smile dismissed him. "No trouble at all. It's a disgrace, holding such a harmless gentleman in jail."

Paul winced inwardly. Dan, the stalwart warrior, would hardly relish being thought of as "harmless"! However, Dan hadn't heard.

Alfie thought of something. "Meg really ought to be going back to college tomorrow."

"It's Saturday," Donal Powers reminded him. "She can take an early train Sunday morning. I won't keep her out too late."

"Yes, Dad. I don't have any Saturday classes this semester."

"Well," Alfie said.

Donal Powers looked at Meg. The look was mischievous,

triumphant, intimate. And in the instant, Paul saw what was happening, what had already happened. It was an unmistakable sexual attraction, as if the very air were scented with it. There was something palpable between those two, like sudden heat. It had happened almost as rapidly between himself and Anna. The signs were clear: the girl's flushed cheeks, high voice, and averted eyes; the man's frank stare; the sudden silence. He recognized them all.

"I don't even know who he is," Alfie complained later. "But in the circumstances, I couldn't very well refuse, could I?"

Ben assured him that Meg was in responsible hands. "He's a decent man, you've nothing to worry about." He became enthusiastic. "It's really remarkable, another remarkable American story. Absolutely self-made. Grew up poor as the devil in Hell's Kitchen. Turned himself into a polished gentleman, as you saw."

"But what does he do?" insisted Alfie.

"Oh, a lot of things. He's an entrepreneur, an investor. Owns a couple of restaurants, mostly."

For some reason Paul doubted that.

Ben continued, "He's a big investor in real estate, too. Has contacts everywhere. Always mixed up in politics. Either party, it doesn't matter. Politics makes strange bedfellows." Like Alfie, Ben was apt to use clichés. "I believe, though I'm not sure and I'm not about to ask, that he got Dan out through somebody in the Department of Justice. The main thing is, Dan's home. And none the worse for the experience, it seems."

For Dan, still close to Hennie, was laughing.

That I wouldn't say, thought Paul; it must have been unforgettable, especially for a man who suffers with angina. Dan was haggard and his cheeks were colored an ominous dark blue-gray.

"Better get him home to rest," Paul warned, and then told

Dan, "I've had the car with me all day, ready for you. It's downstairs. Marian and I can take you now."

"Always the optimist," Hennie said gratefully.

Outside in the foggy night, the Holmes Protective man, a private detective hired by the homeowners of the street to guard their treasures and comforts, was pacing up and down the sidewalk. As always, turning eastward toward the humble street where Dan and Hennie lived, Paul was struck by the contrast. You had to be made of very different stuff to turn your back on these treasures and comforts, when you could have possessed them.

Dan was exhausted; he sat without speaking, holding fast to his wife's hand. As soon as he had delivered them to their home, Paul sighed.

"All's well that ends well."

"It would end a good deal better if he didn't have four flights to climb with that heart of his," Marian replied. "It gets to be absurd, this pose of poverty and wanting nothing."

"If there's anything you can't accuse either of those two of, it's posing."

"Well, the whole business these last few days has been ridiculous, anyway. Just gone too far."

Some unusual perversity in Paul drove him to argue, to pretend that he hadn't understood. "Who went too far? The police. Of course they did."

"I didn't mean the police, I meant Dan." Mimi was exasperated. "He opens his mouth and asks for trouble. Asks for it! He knew perfectly well it was risky, and although the authorities may be quite wrong, any sensible person would keep his mouth shut."

"That's just what Alfie says."

"Well, Alfie happens to be right. All this agitation! It's so— so Russian."

"Now that's absurd. And anyway, Dan isn't a Russian."

"He acts like one. You know I like him well enough, but the truth is the truth."

Paul's urge to argue died as abruptly as it had risen. He felt suddenly, now that the crisis was past, the full strain of events, from the shocking moment when the police had seized Dan on the platform to the moment he had walked into Leah's house this afternoon.

It had begun to rain; an oily film slid over the pavement; the windshield wipers creaked. He leaned forward, concentrating on the car, while Mimi resumed complaint.

"I always think it's so odd that there are such extremes among us Jews. People like—oh, people at our temple, or at the club, and then people like Hennie and Dan."

He had to argue again. "Without realizing it, you've fallen into the trap of anti-Semitism. Why shouldn't we differ among ourselves? Nobody finds it strange that an *Oxford don* and an *Appalachian hillbilly* are both Anglo-Saxon."

"Well, all right, then, it's not strange. Let's just say that some of us embarrass the rest of us. Let's leave Dan out; he's too close to home. Take that other man who was arrested with him. He probably came to this country ten years ago, survived on the charity of families like ours, and now that he's getting somewhere, has to go around making speeches and attracting attention, instead of being satisfied to make a living out of whatever he's doing. The garment industry, most likely," she finished with disdain. "It's always been full of troublemakers."

"Why scorn the garment industry? You think well enough of Leah, don't you?"

"Of course I do. I'm fond enough of her, although I must say I liked her better before she got so prosperous and important. And yet you do know perfectly well that she would be entirely out of place at the Harmonie or at Century, don't you?"

"Indeed she would."

At the Century Country Club, you had to be of German stock. No one said so; it certainly was not in the bylaws, but that's the way it was, all the same, and everyone knew it. Although he was a member, he seldom went there and wasn't about to challenge their customs. If that's the way they wanted things, it was their business. One could exercise oneself over far greater injustices in this world, and Paul did. Social affairs he left to Mimi anyway. He was not a club man. He had no time.

Mimi got out at the apartment house and he garaged the car. Walking back, he felt himself frowning and relaxed his facial muscles. Of course, like himself, Mimi had been reared in a certain "milieu." It formed you and you could never escape it entirely; he was aware that he had not done so, and moreover had no burning wish to do so. It was a decent, refined, and comfortable milieu. But he had a different set of mind from his wife's. Had she always been what she was now? He couldn't recall that she had ever taken this—he reflected—this hard attitude, or been as absorbed with class and snobbery as she was now. He tried to understand. She suffered. She was still so young, just thirty, and had lost that vital organ, the womb. She had been robbed; perhaps she felt mutilated. Perhaps it was like a man's being emasculated? He couldn't know.

He resolved to be very patient with her, not to get into any more of these pointless, peevish tiffs.

Yet things kept happening that tried him and irked him. The way she talked in public about what she called her "ordeal." Of course, it had been one; the doctor himself on that dreadful night had used the same word. But why did she have to keep recalling the pathetic stillborn boy? Sometimes, after dinner, when the men were divided from the women at opposite ends of somebody's long drawing room, he could hear her voice, repeating her tale of suffering endured, with a kind of pride in her tone as though she were waiting for praise of her heroism. He would wince; she was boring people, making herself foolish. Once he had intercepted glances between two other women who, having quite normally brought forth one or more healthy children, were regarding Mimi with pity and scorn as they preened themselves, with equal foolishness, on their own fortunate good health.

He let himself into the apartment and went down the hall to their bedroom. She was sitting in front of her dressing table; she had a hairbrush in her hand, but it lay on her lap and her head was bowed; he caught a glimpse of her doleful face in the mirror before, hearing him come in, she straightened and began to brush her hair.

He said suddenly, without having planned to say it, "Mimi, I ask you again: Why don't we adopt?"

She looked at him through the mirror. "And I tell you again: No. If I can't have my own, I don't want any substitutes. I suppose I'm just one of those people born to have nothing, not supposed to have anything in this life. Nothing. I have nothing."

He saw that she was not aware of her words' recklessness, nor of their irony. The room was warm; the perfume with which she sprayed herself before going to bed still hung in the air; the white satin quilt was turned down and a little pile of books lay on the bedside table. She had not yet hung up her sable-trimmed suit, which lay on the chaise longue.

Yet these were only possessions and comforts; was it not to her credit, when you thought about it, that they weren't enough to assuage her pain? Any more than they were able to assuage his own?

And because he needed suddenly to hide his face, he opened the closet door and pretended to search for something. If Mimi knew what he knew and had anguished over all this past year, ever since that unforgettable, blustery spring afternoon when he had at last met Anna again and learned . . . what he had learned!

He had a child! He had a little girl!

It was unreal, and yet it was true. She had been born of their one and only union; her name was Iris; she was a pair of huge eyes in a blurred photograph. And that was all, and that was all she ever would be, or ever could be. . . . His daughter. His. Brought up and nurtured by another man, by the innocent husband . . . because it had to be that way . . . because he had promised never, never to try to see either Anna or the child.

To wreck her marriage, after what she had already suffered, was not to be thought of. And yet sometimes his longing was unbearable.

He collected himself. "You going to bed now, Mimi?"

"Yes, I'm tired." Then swiftly, the familiar look of anxiety crossed her face, as if she were controlling tears. "Paul, I shouldn't have said what I did about having nothing. I didn't mean it the way it must have sounded."

He saw how real her distress was, and answered kindly, "I know you didn't. I knew it while you were saying it."

"I know I have an awful lot to be thankful for. I have you, and this home and—and everything."

"You were feeling blue, that's all it was."

"Yes, blue. And bitter, which isn't anything to be proud of. But I just cannot help it sometimes."

He patted her shoulder. "Forget it. You've a right to a mood. Get some sleep and it will be all gone by morning."

"Are you going to sleep too?"

"I'm not quite ready yet. I think I'll go fiddle with the radio for a while."

The Freed-Eiseman, his latest toy, was in the library. Having adjusted the earphones, he waited for the miracle. It came: the far-distant, slightly tinny sound of music, a jazz band. For a while he listened and marveled again, trying to comprehend the wonder of sound that was able to fly into his room from the outer air. Dan had once tried to explain it to him, but it was still not clear; Paul's was not a scientific mind.

Then, swiftly, he grew tired of listening. It occurred to him that he was too often and too swiftly tired of whatever he was doing, except when he was working at the office. Here at home, he, who had once been able to read for hours, immersing himself, grew restless after half an hour and had to get up and walk about or look aimlessly out of the window. It's Mimi, he thought. Marian and I. Then it struck him that, very often now, he thought of his wife as "Marian" rather than "Mimi," a name that seemed to come from another time, the time of her girlhood, and from a different personality. Marian-Mimi-Marian. Confusing.

And remembering "Mimi," he thought: She was so trusting. She is still. She trusts me, depends upon me. His thoughts about her and his resentment made him feel guilty.

But things kept cropping up, small things. Her voice when complaining, and she complained often about services. The cook just never learned to make proper toast; the delivery that had been promised for two o'clock didn't come until half past. Her voice had developed a whine.

No doubt, though, he had habits that must irritate her. He knew, for instance, that she couldn't stand the noise he made when he bit into an apple. He had seen her glance at him and tighten her lips to keep from saying something.

Still, these annoyances must be quite normal, mustn't they? Probably most couples, maybe all couples, developed such differences in the course of their years.

If only those were the sole differences between him and Marian! Then: Hold on, Paul, hold on. She's a good woman, a good wife. Compliant. Willing. Even in bed, he thought wryly. Obedient, although she didn't like it. She would never admit that she didn't. He had asked her once and she had flushed, replying, "Why, of course! Of course I do, Paul. What a question!"

A stupid question, and stupid of him to have asked, when he already knew the answer, when it was so plain.

And when he reflected upon the attentions that she could still bestow, waiting on him, catering to his wants until he felt stifled, he wished, and then was ashamed of the wish, that she would not love him so much. All that devotion! It passed for love, but was it love? Love without passion? But perhaps that was the most unselfish kind? Or was there a contradiction? Could she unconsciously sense his true feelings? Did he rebuff her in any way? He didn't mean to. Would she—could she—be different with some other man, passionate as he would be if he could have Anna?

He thought not.

Unanswerable questions nagged him, and he sat dully. Tired. He was so tired.

He had been thinking off and on for the last few months about Europe. He hadn't seen the real Europe—the time in the trenches didn't count—since that summer of 1912 when he had gone over with poor Freddy and shown him all the old splendid places, and met their cousin Joachim, fourth cousin or third cousin once removed or something like that, and talked about their ancestors. Such a *German* he'd been! And yet they had liked each other, and it would be good to see him again. He'd been wounded in the war, but he was well now, he wrote, and married; he'd sent a photo of his pretty wife with their little girl.

Yes, it would be interesting, it would be good to see him.

Then he thought of the ship. To be on a ship again! To hear once more the long deep blast of the horn as we move downriver, out through the Ambrose Channel, past the Light, and into the open, rolling, vacant sea. . . .

Suddenly he knew he had to go, had to get away.

Marian was reading in bed.

"How would you like to go to Europe?" he asked, being fairly sure that she would not.

She put the book down. "What? Why now?"

"I really should see some people who used to do a lot of investing with us before the war. Pick up the pieces."

"Can't it wait? I'd be miserably seasick on the North Atlantic this time of year."

"I really should. With this inflation in Germany, everything's unsettled, and we've some loans outstanding there. In London, too. Father thinks I should go."

His father hadn't mentioned it, but most certainly he would approve, would even be enthusiastic. The more Paul thought about it as the seconds passed, the more important it actually seemed for him to tend to business abroad.

"How long will you need to be gone?"

"Well, a week each way for the voyage and other travel, with probably two, maybe three weeks over there."

"Oh, dear! We'd be coming back in November and it's so horribly cold."

Paul waited.

Marian's wrinkled forehead looked plaintive. Then she said, "Oh, Paul, would it be too awful if I let you go alone? Do you really have to go just now?" she repeated.

And he repeated, "Clients. Business."

"Well . . . I could go down to Aunt Flora's new place in Florida."

"You really have been wanting to see it, haven't you?"

"I had thought we might go together this winter."

He had no love for Florida, especially for Palm Beach, where he felt unwelcome in spite of all the denials on the part of Marian's family and friends, who had abandoned Miami as being "too Jewish." It was pleasant, he admitted, to wake up after an overnight trip and find the train stopped among palms washed in sunlight. But the life there bored him, the golf and cocktails and dinner, golf and cocktails and dinner again, with bridge thrown in, one day after the other.

"We'll go together another time," he promised.

"I do feel so guilty," she sighed, with a pleading look. "Poor Paul, with a silly wife who gets seasick and can't stand the cold, so that he has to go all alone. Oh, I do feel guilty."

"Guilty? Of course not!" he said soothingly.

"I'm sorry I said that before about having nothing. It's not true, of course. I have so much . . . I have you. It's just that I feel discouraged sometimes, wondering how you must feel about a wife who can't give you a child, when you want one so badly."

Her tone, beseeching, called forth his answer. "You mustn't talk like that." He patted her cheek. "You have me, I have you, and we're here together. Let's not go feeling sorry for ourselves. Agreed?"

She gave him an obedient smile.

"There, that's better! That's more like you, Mimi. Tell you what, you just go on down to Aunt Flora's, have a good time in the sun, and I'll be home before you know it." He bent and kissed her.

Later in bed, when Marian was already asleep, he lay thinking that, in a way, it would be a lonesome voyage. One ought to have a companion on shipboard, walking the deck, breathing the pure air, and eating the marvelous food together. Even Hennie would have been a companion of some sort. She'd been wanting to go to Europe to a meeting of the Women's International League for Peace and Freedom, but Dan's health was too precarious for her to leave him. So he would just walk the deck alone.

Yet, the way things were, maybe some time alone would do him good.

Three

"At last I meet the American cousin," said Joachim's wife, Elisabeth.

Regarding him frankly from across the table, she sat with her chin in her hands, a somewhat plump young woman, with an upswept mass of very blond hair fastened in a topknot. Her round, lively face made the word *adorable* come to Paul's mind, although it was a sentimental word that he seldom used.

He had arrived in Munich at midafternoon to find coffee and a spread of yeast cakes waiting for him in the alcove at the end of the dark Gothic dining room. Now, only a few hours later, they were back in that room, this time at one end of the long main table, eating an enormous dinner: vegetable soup with dumplings, potatoes, red cabbage, sauerbraten, fruit conserve, turnips, pickles, homemade bread, wine, and a black cherry pudding. Solid, heavy nourishment. Germans, Paul remembered having thought before, are always eating.

"Too bad you didn't bring your wife," Elisabeth remarked.

"Well, except for visiting you, this has been a business trip. It was a rough voyage and London was all foggy," he said lightly, adding, "Marian isn't well, she has sinus trouble. I couldn't postpone the trip," he repeated, "so many threads to pick up that the war tore out." He was making unnecessary explanations, and stopped.

Joachim sighed. "The war tore out a lot of threads."

"To think that you two fought each other," Elisabeth exclaimed. "It's crazy, all of it! Did you know that Joachim got the Iron Cross? He captured ten Frenchmen. Ten poor souls like himself."

Joachim reprimanded gently, "Let's not talk about it. Paul and I got through the war talk in our first ten minutes, riding here from the station. Now let's just talk of good things."

"Of course," Elisabeth agreed.

Paul observed, "This is a beautiful apartment."

He had known what to expect the moment they had driven past the wrought-iron gates into the courtyard, having been in many buildings like this one in Rome and Paris and all over the Continent. You entered the public hall, floored with marble, and on a red carpet mounted the central staircase to the private apartments. This one had fourteen rooms.

From where Paul was sitting, he could see past velvet portieres into a room filled with French Empire furniture; the drawing room fireplace was faced with Delft tile; through the opposite doors he could see the conservatory, in which settees and little tables stood among palms and frothing ferns. Above his head a cascade of crystal icicles hung from the chandelier, which brightened a table long enough, Paul estimated, to seat twenty-four.

"The apartment belongs to my parents-in-law," Joachim said. "They've moved to the country. At my age I certainly couldn't afford anything like this."

"My father and my uncle Cohen own three department stores, but they have real estate, too," Elisabeth explained.

"Excuse me, Elisabeth, but then you are Jewish?" Paul asked her.

Joachim laughed. "What did you think? I know you are thinking she doesn't 'look Jewish,' whatever that means."

"Whatever that means," Paul repeated.

It was true. How many "real" Germans were as blond as they liked to imagine themselves? If you knew anything about Europe's history, you knew it was age-old wandering; Romans in England left from their seed dark eyes and arched noses; Teutons in Italy left a legacy of blue eyes; Vikings left their red hair everywhere from Poland to France. And as to the Jews, two thousand years out of Jerusalem, how many copulations, willing and mostly unwilling, had produced their variety?

His mind, as he ate the pudding, began to wander. Traveling, as well as the hours-long effort to speak German for the sake of Elisabeth, who knew no English, had tired him. He was suddenly aware that Joachim was telling him something.

"If we can manage to hold on to the properties, we'll survive the inflation. It can't go on forever, it simply can't."

Paul was jolted awake. This dinner—what it must have cost them! While he had been eating with good appetite, they had been skimping; they had taken barely a spoonful of pudding on either of their plates. He felt embarrassed, ashamed of his own thoughtlessness, and quickly declined when the maid offered a second helping. Thoughtless. He had read in the newspaper, on the train, that a single restaurant dinner now cost almost two million marks. Yes, the table was set with fine cutwork linen and the chairs were upholstered satin, printed in Napoleon's gold bees, but you couldn't eat the linen or the satin.

Joachim inquired whether he was cold. "We are somewhat short of coal," he said, cheerfully enough. "We try to put the heat up for you. People say that Americans live in hothouses."

"Oh, not for me, please," Paul protested.

"I can get you a shawl. In the evening the heat goes down. We men are not ashamed to sit with a woolen shawl over our jackets."

"I'm fine, I'm fine," Paul insisted.

"Well, we Germans have lived through worse than a little cold," Joachim said. "What we have lived through! And we will survive. We always do."

Paul felt that he was expected to respond to this optimism. "Yes, with patience," he said. It was a banal remark. And he added, "This war will go down in history written large as the fall of Rome. What folly! But then, all war is folly."

"And the folly of the peace." Joachim's tone was surprisingly sharp. Quite suddenly it altered the jovial atmosphere. He leaned toward Paul. "Your president, with his Fourteen Points. He promised we would not be dismembered or punished. He promised justice. And what happened when we came to Versailles? There was no justice. We lost our colonies, we lost Silesia, we were dismembered. The Armistice was a swindle!" He rapped the plate with his spoon. "But you will be sorry, all of you Allies, when the Russian bear comes to full power! It will be the strongest on earth. Murderers! Look what they did to their royal family! And only Churchill, among all of your leaders, has sense enough to see what they are. It's they whom you should ruin, not us Germans!"

Elisabeth met Paul's glance. He saw that she was embarrassed.

"He gets so emotional, my poor man. I tell him, what's the use? What's done is done. Save your breath."

"We are a great and civilized nation," Joachim said, as if he had not heard. "And say what you will, the treaty that has been imposed upon us is a swindle. It is not what we were promised!"

It was true that even his own secretary of state had said that Wilson had betrayed his principles, Paul reflected. He himself had felt some of Joachim's doubt; the demand for reparations was ruinous. But hearing these things from this—this *German* was another thing.

"Our economy is being strangled," Joachim went on, breathing heavily and staring reproachfully at his empty plate.

Quietly, Paul answered, "With a balanced budget, this suffering could have been avoided. But your right-wing industrialists wouldn't let the government raise taxes; they're getting rich on the ruin of the mark."

Joachim raised his face. It looked wounded. "Excuse me, but that sounds like nonsense."

"You forget, I understand currency. I'm a banker."

"Paul is right." Elisabeth spoke eagerly. Her pale eyes shone. "The right wing doesn't want the republic to work. That's why they killed Walter Rathenau—such a brilliant man, a friend of my father's—because he was trying to make the Weimar government work. And also because he was a Jew. That's why."

"You exaggerate," Joachim said. "You have always had an exaggerated fear of anti-Semitism. You see it everywhere. It's foolish and it's bad for your health, Elisabeth." His anger having exploded and died, he pushed his chair back. "Come, let's have our coffee in the drawing room," and for the second time that evening, he added, "We must talk of happier things. This is no occasion for such serious talk. Go, darling, tell Jeanne to bring Regina in to say good night."

The silver coffee service stood on a table between the windows. Elisabeth poured coffee into Meissen cups. They were very old and very precious, Paul saw. Lately, he had been learning about porcelains. There were more little cakes, iced petit fours; he wanted to refuse them, but did not, for they had so obviously been prepared in his honor. So he ate, exclaiming over the cups and the cakes. This was safer ground than politics.

Then the child was brought in. Two years old and readied for bed, in her ruffled pink robe and little slippers, with her apple face flushed from her bath, she was enchanting. She held a doll upside down and insisted that everybody, including Paul, must kiss it good night. Her dark eyes, resembling neither parent's, gleamed with intelligence and mischief. When the parents called the nursemaid back to take her away, Paul understood that they were caught between a wish to show her off before him and a fear of boring him with their adoration.

"Regina is learning French. The governess is French," said Elisabeth. "We want her to know many languages. She must grow up to be a citizen of Europe."

Joachim smiled. "My Elisabeth is a visionary. Regina is a citizen of Germany and that's good enough. However, it's not a bad idea to know languages."

Then Joachim told two anecdotes about his little girl, quoting her comical remarks, which reminded Paul that he, too, could produce an anecdote, so he told about the day he had taken Hank to Central Park and Hank had asked a bald man what had happened to his hair.

"He's a tough little fellow, smart and strong," he concluded, and was suddenly aware that he had been speaking as though Hank were his child. Feeling rather foolish, he explained, "You see—I've felt a special concern for him because of Freddy."

"You told me you have pictures," Joachim said.

"Snapshots. They're not very good, but they'll give you some idea of your American relatives."

He drew an envelope from his breast pocket and laid a sheaf of photos fanwise on the table. "Here, these are my parents. Here's Hennie, that's my mother's sister, the one who is very political. She's on every peace committee you might think of."

"Wonderful!" exclaimed Elisabeth. "I'd like to know her. Yes, she has a serious face." For Hennie, who had always been uneasy in front of a camera, was staring soberly into its eye.

"And here's my uncle Alfred, Alfie we call him, standing on the porch of his country house. That's Meg with him, his daughter; this was taken a few years ago, she's quite grown up now, away at college, the university, as you say." A thought fled across Paul's mind, something uncomfortable, and for a second he strove to place it . . . oh, it was Meg with that Powers fellow the day he brought Dan home . . . and he resumed, "Here's Hank. He's seven now. He's with his grandfather Dan. Don't they look alike? And now here's Leah. I took her picture the day she opened her new shop, the light's not very good, but—"

Leah had been caught in the middle of a laugh, showing her even teeth; a collar of silk petals circled her neat head.

"Oh, isn't she pretty!" Elisabeth cried.

"She really isn't. She's very fashionable and bright and friendly, so that one likes to look at her. And one likes her, too," Paul added hastily. "Everyone does."

"This is so nice," Elisabeth said. "I'm beginning to know these people. Now let's see the most important one, your wife."

Paul shuffled through the snapshots. He looked again in the envelope. "I don't seem to see it." He looked on the floor. "Could I have dropped it someplace?" He was flustered. Was it possible that he hadn't brought it with him? He tried to recall the evening when he had packed his bags and selected the photos. He could remember clearly how he had sorted through the box into which they had been tossed helter-skelter, and had selected the best ones to take along. Could he really have omitted Marian? He felt heat rising to his face.

"You must have dropped it," Elisabeth said. "I'm sure you've been showing it all over London and Berlin."

"I must have. I'll send you one when I get home. Now tell me about all of you," he said hurriedly. "Your sister's married, Joachim?"

"Yes. They live in Berlin."

And Joachim went on to tell about the distinguished family of which she was now a member, collateral descendants of Moses Mendelssohn. They had been prominent in the Kaiser's circle, an honor accorded, as Paul must know, to very few Jews. And so forth.

Presently Elisabeth got up and excused herself. "Good night. It's early yet, but I'm suddenly quite sleepy." She kissed Joachim on the lips; the kiss lingered a moment longer than a perfunctory one and Joachim's arms held her a moment longer than in a perfunctory embrace.

"She's pregnant," he explained, when she had left the room. "She gets tired at the end of the day."

"She's charming, Joachim."

"We were engaged all through the war. She is what kept me going. And still does." Joachim's eyes were moist and shining. "I cannot imagine life without her," he said simply.

Paul looked away. "You're very lucky," he murmured, and, swallowing a lump that seemed to be forming in his throat, heard himself say, "My wife had an operation. We can't have any children."

Joachim shook his head. "No children," he repeated.

Something about the other man's moist eyes and the way he had kissed his wife gave Paul a crazy desire to confide, *I, too, have a woman I don't want to live without. On my wedding night I thought of her while I lay with my wife.*

He stifled the desire. Joachim was looking at him curiously.

"You're tired too," he said. "It's been a long day on the train. Come to bed." He stood up. "I'm sorry if I got too excited about the war and all that business. Forgive me." He laid his arm around Paul's shoulders. "It will take a little longer before we can all calm down and forget it."

It was pleasant to have no responsibilities for the next few days. After completing the business calls he had to make in the city, Paul was free. In the evenings, his hosts took him about: one night to the National Theatre, and on another to the Hofbrauhaus, a vast, dim columned hall in which hundreds sang and swayed and drank. A cathedral of beer, Paul thought, disturbed by a rowdy quality that he would have found hard to describe.

Always in foreign cities, he loved to walk alone, satisfying his curiosity, getting the pulse of a place. Landing in Hamburg, the first thing he had observed was the silence in the commercial streets, with their vacant shops and factories. Cars in show windows had no tires; five years after the war, there was still no rubber in Germany. And there were so many amputees, so many shabby men wearing the jackets of their uniforms because they obviously couldn't afford new clothes. And everywhere there was the silence.

Here in Munich, the food stores were fairly empty; he had read, before leaving America, that there was a shortage of soap in Germany, and so had brought a supply for the family. As soon as he got home, he would send them a package of canned goods.

In desperation, people were selling their valuables. Joachim had told him about an art dealer in the Schwabing section who handled a good many distress sales. On the second morning, Paul went there, and recognized it as the building in which, on one halcyon summer day before the war, he had bought Expressionists, two Kirchners and a Beckmann. To his surprise, the old proprietor remembered him, too.

"We don't get—excuse me—too many Americans who know as much about paintings as you do," he said.

Paul let the slur—if it had been a slur—go by. The man's

jacket was seedy and his eyes were sorrowful; quite possibly he was hungry.

"We have some good things from the finest homes," he assured Paul hopefully.

Paul walked around the little gallery. There were a few Postimpressionists. One, a small Cézanne view of a road cut through yellow fields in evening light, was very much like the one that he and Anna had seen at the Armory Show, where he had taken her that first winter, the very first time they had gone anywhere together.

"A lovely piece," the old man said, seeing him hesitate.

"Yes, lovely."

But something else had caught his eye. A woman, copper-haired and enormously pregnant, lay nude against a pile of red and violet, jewel-bright Persian pillows.

"You don't want that, Herr—Werner, you said? It's only an imitation of Gustav Klimt. The artist was wounded and I feel sorry for him, but that's not a painting for a man of taste like you."

"Yes, I know it's a copy." The woman had a trace of a smile on her lips and in the corners of her eyes; this gave to the well-bred face an expression both secretive and hopeful.

The longer he looked at her, the more the woman "spoke" to him. She didn't really look like Anna, except for the hair. And Marian would certainly find her offensive in her nudity, with that huge belly, so relaxed, so pleased with herself. Well, he would just hang it in his dressing room and she wouldn't have to look at it.

"I really want this," he said, and feeling a need to explain, added, "I buy whatever appeals, good or not so good."

Having made arrangements for shipping, he went out into the morning, feeling the contentment that comes with getting something one wants. He stopped to buy a newspaper and walked on away from the center of the city. The day was gray and still, except for sparrow twitter. In this section, all was orderly. Here Germany, although vanquished, was undamaged, and looking through tall wrought-iron gates at fine villas and formal flowerbeds, bare now in November, he felt a rush of anger. In France, the villages had been shattered and the houses burned; he had a vivid recollection of a street, the usual single street in the usual village, with the houses strung like beads on either side; there had been an empty baby carriage in front of a house half blown away, and a dead dog lying next to it with a ribbon in its hair.

And yet, a moment later, when two young women passed him, wheeling baby carriages he thought: It isn't their fault. All those atrocity reports are propaganda; these young Germans are no different from any on the other side.

He looked at his watch and, finding that it was early, sat down to observe the view. Green tiled roofs ascended the rise. In summer they would be hidden in an ocean of trees. The scene was a gentle one and pleased him. He felt relaxed. Then he opened the newspaper, the *Völkischer Beobachter,* and began to read.

"We must abrogate the Treaty of Versailles." Well, Joachim would certainly agree to that! "Germany must be unified with all German-speaking peoples, the Sudetenland and the Austrians, into a strong Nationalist Greater Germany." Very possibly Joachim would like that, too. "This republic is a disaster. We need a dictator who will restore order." Paul read on. "There are no morals in the cities . . . the foreigners, the Jews have bastardized us . . . they have dirtied the soul of the people . . . it is the common wisdom of the peasant that has made us and has kept us healthy."

Paul put the paper down. What—what filth! Rot! He picked it up and read it again. Was this perhaps some monstrous, crazy joke, a satire, a parody?

No, it was desperately and passionately in earnest. "The November criminals," he read, "most of them Jews, who made the republic—"

Not even true. Most of them were not Jews, although it was to their credit, it was a brand of honor, that some of them were. And he sat quite still, looking out upon the friendly landscape, while his pulse beat audibly in his ears. After a while he got up and still with that pounding pulse and core of cold fear in his chest, he walked slowly back to lunch.

He presented Joachim with the paper. "I can hardly believe what I read in here."

Joachim seemed to be amused. "Good Lord! Whatever made you buy a rag like that?"

"I didn't know. How would I know? I wanted a paper."

"A stupid rag. A gossip sheet."

"That's what you call it?"

"Certainly. A lot of down-and-outers, that's all. They're bitter and they have to blame somebody."

"They're not all down-and-outers," Elisabeth interjected. "I've been listening to some women at my hairdresser's. Very wealthy women. They've been contributing, or talking about friends who contribute. They say this fellow Hitler has very influential friends, some of them in the army, too."

"Nonsense! He's a Socialist," Joachim argued. "He talks about profit sharing, doing away with land rents. Why should wealthy people support ideas like those?"

"Because nothing will come of them if he ever gets power. He doesn't mean them and they know it," Elisabeth said.

Joachim buttered his bread. "It will all pass as soon as they have jobs," he assured them, "when the factories open and things pick up. In the meantime, it's stupid to pay attention to such drivel."

Neither Paul nor Elisabeth replied.

Letters came via American Express. As usual, Paul's father had last-minute instructions, calls for him to make in Hamburg before taking his ship home. From Hennie came a cheerful letter telling him that it was hard to keep Dan indoors, the weather was terribly cold, fortunately the Red Scare was over with and real American decency had prevailed. She enclosed a note from Hank, who sent his love in printed letters, three words and his name.

Meg wrote in some distress. She had been seeing Donal Powers, but her parents didn't like him. Her father thought he was "fast," which Meg didn't understand, because he had visited Laurel Hill and was such a gentleman. Her plea leapt from the page: When you get home, will you talk to them?

She's gone on him, Paul thought, and felt sorry for women, who had to wait passively, hoping to be chosen; to be unmarried at twenty-five was a humiliation and at thirty, a disaster. So Meg, a senior at college, was already starting to worry. Poor girl! Nothing came easily to her. Was it possible that Powers was *serious?* Or that Meg herself knew enough to be serious? And, puzzled by indefinable misgivings, Paul frowned. Then, reading her childish postscript, he had to smile again. "If it's not too much trouble, will you bring me a Black Forest cuckoo clock? I'll pay you for it."

"Good news from home? That's nice," said Joachim, who had been waiting while Paul read his mail. "I'll tell you what, you've only a couple of days left, so I'm not going to work tomorrow. We'll have a morning walk and then lunch with an old friend who wants to see you."

They walked along the banks of the River Isar. It was another day of winter thaw. A little wind swayed through the bare trees and the sky was like blue water.

"You should see it when the chestnuts bloom, the great white flowers. And the lindens, and the swans in summer. It's a beautiful city." Joachim spoke dreamily. "A beautiful country."

"Everyone thinks his country is beautiful," Paul said kindly.

Innocence beamed in his cousin's face. A good-hearted fellow, so simple in spite of all his culture and graduate degrees! He could do with a little worldly skepticism. His young wife was far more clever than he, although he undoubtedly didn't know it. So he would finish, one could safely predict, in some prosperous enterprise owned by his wife's family, where he would work honestly and well.

In European fashion, Joachim linked his arm with Paul's. "Think, if your great-grandmother hadn't gone to America, you might have grown up right here on one of these streets too."

A thought struck Paul: We affect the future of those who come after us almost as much as we affect our own. And then: But there is no one coming after me.

"Today is the anniversary of the proclamation of the Weimar Republic," Joachim said. "There'll be parades in town. I'm not sure what time. Anyway, we have to head toward town for lunch."

Crossing the Hofgarten, between rows of formal clipped greens, Paul felt the palatial nineteenth-century atmosphere. Presently, they heard brassy, martial music.

"The parade already?" Joachim was puzzled. "Come, they'll be around here. We'll get a better view farther in."

Pleased as a little boy, he hurried, urging Paul with him until, turning a corner into an open street, they came abruptly upon a crowd that must have been collecting for some time. The two men, caught up in it, were pushed on farther as it streamed toward the mounting blare of the music. From every side street came people in swarms, converging.

There were men and women, young and old, family people carrying little children, all running now with an air of excitement, an air of holiday jubilation, toward some central destination. Some of them were even singing.

The music was upon them. Surely by accident, Joachim and Paul had been shoved to a perfect vantage point along the curb, where they had a clear view of the approaching parade. Down it came, and it was an astonishing sight.

A column of men in brown shirts wound as far back as one could see. They carried guns. Light flashed on their bayonets. Their arms and feet swung together in cadence. Their banners swayed; red, white, and black, they were, with the swastika prominent on high, as on the bands around each man's upper arm. Paul, recognizing the hooked cross, an ancient design, out of Egypt and China and Hindu India, could only wonder what it meant. And why the weapons?

They were singing. "Germany wake up" or "Arise," went the refrain, or something like that. Then, as the sections wound past, segmented like some long, creeping insect, he distinguished out of the general roar of voices a sprightly refrain: "When Jewish blood spurts from the knife."

With his mouth dropped open, Joachim stood and stared. Paul grasped his arm.

"Let's get the hell out of here. Which way can we go?"

Now it was he who propelled the other along. But the throng behind them was surging forward again toward the marchers. Elated by the triumphant bugles and drums, gleeful and cheering, it rushed to march with the columns. Joachim and Paul were moved along with it, swept into a surge of violent energy. Paul stumbled and fortunately caught himself. To fall here would be fatal; one would be trampled by these people who, in their frenzy, would be as indifferent to a single human being as a herd of stampeding beasts would be.

The march emerged into a square. The marching mass melded into the mass already there, as it forced its way through a crush of human beings. In the center of the square, on a platform, another brown-shirted man was speaking. His threatening tone and threatening gestures now willed the people into silent attention.

"Streicher," Joachim whispered into Paul's ear. "His picture was in that paper you bought."

Joachim's eyes were bright with excitement and curiosity. Paul saw no fear in them. But he himself was terrified and not ashamed of it.

"How do we get out of here? For Christ's sake, you know these streets. I don't!" he whispered back.

He tried to turn around, to press his way out, but it was impossible; no one would move to let him through. So they were forced to stay and hear the speaker to a finish.

Happily for Paul, who knew by now what the man must be saying, he was able to hear almost none of it. The raucous voice, bawling in a foreign language, was a considerable distance away; besides, despite the attentiveness of the listeners there were crowd sounds, coughs and shuffling feet. There were intermittent shouts of approval, which he tried to shut out of his mind, to concentrate on the moment when the dispersing mass would set him free.

The end came at last, a peroration with a raised arm salute. The crowd moved, probably without even knowing where it was going. It simply melted out of the square, while Joachim and Paul, propelled ahead, found themselves entangled with a remnant of armed and uniformed marchers, squeezed into an old narrow street beyond the square.

Paul was tall enough to see above most of the heads in front of him. So it was that he realized, before Joachim could, that they were headed into a trap. At the end of the street, there waited a phalanx of police with guns at the ready.

"My God!" he heard himself cry, and tried to push his cousin toward the side of a building just as chaos broke out.

Some of the marchers attempted to flee in panic when they recognized the situation. Some, in defiance, beat drums and upheld the swastika banners, while others, with guns leveled to fire, headed straight toward the leveled guns of the police.

Shots crackled, sounding far away. People who didn't know expected them to sound enormous, but actually they made a toy explosion like firecrackers: all this went through Paul's head as he flattened himself, wanting to crawl through the stone wall of the house to shelter. For a second, his heart stopped: Am I to die, then, on this street in a strange city, for no reason at all?

Then he saw a man fall, and another; then a policeman fell, and the defiant ones, routed and hysterical in their terror, turned and fled. More shots crackled. More men fell. Others stepped over them. Almost none stopped to raise the fallen.

There was a piercing whistle and *ping!* A ricochet: Joachim fell.

He fell queerly, just slid and slumped against the wall. Panic, a giant hand, closed in Paul's chest. In a few seconds this had happened, a few seconds. Death in a crazy instant, on a mild morning.

He knelt, staring at Joachim. He rummaged for a handkerchief. Joachim's dapper breast-pocket handkerchief was bloodied, while Paul's own had been used. He took his jacket off, removed his clean shirt and tore off a sleeve to make a clumsy bandage, thinking, He's dead, I don't know what I'm doing. . . .

As suddenly as it had begun, the firing ceased. Now came the shattered cries of the wounded and the sound of feet scurrying to save themselves. No one even stopped to look at the two men on the sidewalk.

Paul searched up and down the street. At the far end there was a flurry of movement; the injured were being cared for by their comrades at that end and hastily carried out of sight. But here where Joachim lay, a sudden, almost eerie stillness had followed the commotion. Doors and windows were shut. He tried to think coherently.

To pick him up and try to carry him? But carry him where? To leave him and look for someone? Then Joachim vomited. His eyes flickered, he opened them and retched. Then he sank back. After a minute or two he gave Paul a twisted smile.

"Not dead! You thought I was."

Relief surged through Paul; he had been on the verge of tears.

"A flesh wound. That's what it is," he whispered. Yet how could he be sure? It was a head wound, after all.

"There's a doctor . . . a friend . . . two streets over . . . I'm awfully weak," Joachim murmured.

"I'll help you. Can you walk at all? Lean on me."

"Wait. I feel faint."

"We can't wait too long. I'll pull you up."

And Paul had a shock of recollection: One night he'd crept from no-man's land with a wounded man on his back, only to find, when at last he reached the trench, the man was dead. Five years ago that happened, and here he was caught up again in madness.

"Lean on me. We'll take a few steps at a time."

So, unaided, they crept, pausing and resting, through the unreal city.

Dr. Ilse Hirschfeld, a small woman in her early thirties, behaved as though there were nothing strange in the sudden appearance at her office door of two disheveled gentlemen, one with a bloodied head, staggering, while the other, trying to hold him upright, gasped out their story. Slight as she was, she at once took half Joachim's weight from Paul's sagging back, and together they got him to a couch.

Relieved of responsibility, Paul took a seat in a corner while the doctor went to work. She was quick and also silent; the silence gave Paul a sense of calmness. He watched her slim fingers—which he imagined must be cool to the touch—examine and cleanse the wound; the ticking of a clock was steady and reassuring; he began to feel his own heartbeat slow down and strength run back along his shaking arms and legs.

At last she dressed the wound, took Joachim's pulse and blood pressure, and gave a shot of brandy to him and another to Paul.

"Ah, Joachim Nathansohn, luck was with you today," she exclaimed. "Another fraction of an inch, my friend . . ." Her wide, unmarked forehead was creased, for an instant, by a frown. "What were you doing on the street with all those savages, anyway?"

"We were caught," Paul said quickly. "We didn't know."

"So. We shall all be caught in one way or another if we're not careful. However, one problem at a time." She poured another drink into a small glass and gave it to Joachim. "You need this. You'll be all right. I want you to lie down for a while, and when I think you're ready to go home, I'll tell you. Your friend may stay here with you if he wishes."

Joachim made apology. "Excuse me, I didn't introduce you. Paul Werner, my cousin from America. And Dr. Hirschfeld."

"Joachim, this isn't a party. Lie down. How do you do, Herr Werner?" She closed the door and left them.

Paul laid his head back on the chair. He had begun to feel a touch of hysterical humor. I do seem to walk right into trouble, don't I? Dan last month at home, and now after I cross an ocean to get away, comes this business! I suppose it's just that the world is still not settled after the war. The ocean stays restless long after the storm has passed over. . . .

"A remarkable woman," Joachim said after a while. "Do you think she's good-looking?"

The question seemed completely incongruous in the circumstances, and Paul had to laugh. "You must be feeling a lot better. Yes, when you consider that she's absolutely unadorned in her white coat."

"Elisabeth says she has classic features. Personally, I prefer more curls and ruffles."

Paul was curious. "Is she married?"

"She's a widow. Came from Russian Poland with her little boy. Didn't want to live under communism. She's built up a good practice here, mostly with women, but some men too. They say she's excellent, but I myself, you know, I don't feel I have the same confidence in a woman. Although for a flesh wound like this, she will do very nicely."

Paul made no comment.

The door opened and the doctor appeared again. She was smiling this time. "You want to hear the news? It came over the radio just now. Also some friends called me. Göring, the fat one, was wounded. Hitler, the brave one, saved himself by falling down, and the rest of them ran away. And that's the end of the big revolt," she finished scornfully.

"I don't understand what it was all about," Joachim said.

"Don't understand? Why, they're supposed to be saving the country from communism, though they're just as bad, God knows. I ran away from it and just in time, too. But I don't want to live under these maniacs either." Her hands searched and refastened Joachim's bandage. "You can go home. I'll call a taxi for you. By the way, I wouldn't let the baby see this until the blood stops seeping and you can change the bandage. It'll frighten her."

"I hate to walk in on Elisabeth like this. And when she finds out how it happened! She's such an alarmist."

"Elisabeth," Dr. Hirschfeld told him sternly, "is a realist. There's a difference."

"I fear so for the future," Elisabeth said. She was knitting a sweater while sitting close, leaning against her husband on the sofa.

It occurred to Paul that Marian would be embarrassed by such intimacy.

"*Liebchen,* as I always say, with you every cold is pneumonia."

"My God, you went for a walk and you could have been brought back to me dead."

"You forget, I could have died any day during my four years in the army. But I didn't." Joachim turned to Paul, dismissing the subject. "I'm annoyed that we missed a good lunch with Franz, that's what I'm annoyed about." He was making light of the horror, not only for his wife's sake, but partly too for his own; Joachim did not want to think that the sweetness of life could be spoiled.

Elisabeth, however, was not to be dismissed. "Do you realize that in Berlin at the students' elections more than half the vote went to Nazi candidates? And that in the universities they still read that crazy lie, *The Protocols of the Elders of Zion?*"

"Ach, who reads it, who buys it?"

"They've sold thousands and thousands of copies, Joachim."

"Ach, we're being scared out of our wits by a pack of gangsters. Don't you have them in America, Paul? I read about Chicago and Prohibition."

"It's not the same." Paul knew he sounded lame, but he felt in no mood for complicated explanations.

"And if anyone thinks," Elisabeth went on, "that Jews will be the only sufferers from this violence, he's wrong. We will only be the first and the most, but plenty of other blood will be spilled too."

Joachim was irritated. "So what do you propose doing?"

"That we take it seriously and try to stop it or else leave the country before something comes of it. Go to Palestine or someplace. Are there many Zionists in America?" she asked Paul.

"I don't think so. I don't know any myself."

Joachim laughed. "Does Paul look like a Zionist, for goodness' sake?"

Elisabeth flushed. "What does a Zionist look like? It is the one thing we argue about," she said seriously to Paul, and put her knitting away.

"Our friends all tease her," Joachim said. "Elisabeth, my pretty blonde, with a gun in one hand and a hoe in the other."

"It happens I don't want to go there," Elisabeth said, "but I can understand those who do. Yes, I can. I have some very good friends who are Zionists. My friends, not Joachim's."

Joachim was scornful. "Poles, naturally. Immigrants! Not Germans. Ach, enough! We shall go on as we always have, you with your babies"—he leaned down and kissed her forehead—"and your poor wounded hero." He laughed again. "Sorry your visit had to end with this mess, Paul. Listen. Why don't we have a little celebration to clear the atmosphere? I'll dress myself up with a fresh bandage, get concert tickets and make dinner reservations for tomorrow night. How does that sound?"

"Fine, provided that you let me be the host. Otherwise, no."

"If you want it like that," Joachim agreed. "I've already learned that you're a man who gets his way."

"Wonderful!" said Elisabeth, and suggested that it would be nice to invite Ilse Hirschfeld. "She's always so thoughtful. And she doesn't get out very much, I'm afraid. You have no objection, Paul?"

"None at all," Paul said.

Often Paul found himself examining people, especially women, as though he were studying a painting, reaching toward the meaning under the surface. More and more as the evening progressed, this woman interested him; her type, in spite of his considerable experience, was new.

"Classic," Joachim had said. Her face was very white and her straight, shining hair, parted in the center, was very black. Her dark blue dress was plain, adorned only by a heavy twist of pearls around her throat. She wore pearls in her ears and no rings on her narrow hands. This total simplicity extended to her manner. One saw that she had no wiles. Her black eyes, faintly Asiatic, made straight contact; her full mouth opened wide in unaffected laughter.

Conversation, during the supper after the concert, was general if one-sided, for inevitably it was Joachim who commanded. Only a few facts about Ilse emerged: that her boy was ten years old, that she was a serious tennis player, and that she was studying endocrinology in the hope eventually of specializing.

They had not yet had coffee when Ilse looked at her watch. "It's late and you're looking tired, Elisabeth. Why don't we leave now?" And when Elisabeth protested, she scolded, "You needn't be so polite. I'm your doctor, after all."

Joachim promptly stood up. "Yes, listen to your doctor. She had a miscarriage last time," he explained to Paul, "and she mustn't get tired. But you two stay, have your coffee and pastries—they're delicious here. You can get a taxi right at the door."

When the two had departed, Ilse remarked about Elisabeth, "She's a darling. A sweet, intelligent woman." There was a pause. "But he adores her."

Paul, silently filling in what had been left out—*and far more intelligent than he*—betrayed his thought with an unintentional smile. And Ilse, apparently aware of what she herself had unintentionally revealed, smiled also. The two smiles, meeting, collapsed into mutual laughter.

"I'm very fond of him all the same," Paul said, after a minute.

"And so am I. Do you know, he has no nerves? I really believe he's forgotten how close he came to death just yesterday."

"Forgotten! I wouldn't be surprised to have a dream about it when I'm eighty."

Abruptly, Ilse turned somber. "I wonder where it's all heading. This kind of violence can mean nothing much, or it can grow into a reign of terror, as I saw in Russia."

"My grandparents were in Paris in 1894 when Dreyfus was convicted. They used to tell about the jeering mobs. But, after all, that was France, they always said, not their beloved Germany. I wonder what they would say if they could see what I saw yesterday."

Ilse, not replying, finished her coffee. Holding the cup between both hands, she sipped it thoughtfully for a minute and then abruptly changed the subject. "How about a liqueur?"

"Of course. What shall it be?"

"Not here. I meant at my house. That is, if you'd like to."

"I would like to, very much."

It had been a long time since Paul had felt the bright anticipation of going home with a stranger and having a drink together to bring an evening to a festive close. He had, truly, no thought beyond just that.

Ilse's little parlor was, like her, without pretense. The room could have been in Dan and Hennie's house. People who lived in rooms like this one were obviously not concerned with owning things.

Books, not leather-bound sets or handsome bindings, but books for reading, lay about among journals and magazines. A bag of knitting stood by the sofa and under a table lay a pair of ice skates. Snapshots were stuck into the frame of a mirror. He was looking at them when Ilse came back from the kitchen carrying a small tray with a bottle and glasses.

"That one's my son," she told him.

"He has your eyes, hasn't he?"

"Yes, but he's like his father. Filled with ideals. He wants to improve everything."

"At ten?"

"Oh, yes! Right now he's heard so much about Palestine, and he wants to go there."

"Would you go?"

"No, no. I've seen enough turbulence. My husband was killed on the Russian front. I'm settled here. No more upheavals, if I can help it at least."

She took a seat opposite, curled her feet beneath her, and

warmed the glass between her palms. The sunny liquid tilted under the lamplight. Then she sighed.

"This is very, very pleasant for me, Paul. May I call you Paul?"

"Of course. But you surprise me. Germans are so formal."

"You forget, I'm not German."

"Sorry, I did forget. Well, this is very pleasant for me, too, Ilse."

"But different for you. You're married. A quiet drink together in a warm room on a chilly night is no novelty to you, while to me, it is."

He thought, Marian doesn't drink and she goes to bed long before I do. He said instead, "I shouldn't think it hard for you to find a companion."

"Oh, it's very hard. So many men were lost in the war. There aren't enough to go around. And I'm thirty-two, I can't compete with the nineteen-year-olds. Not that I even want to," she added quickly.

She was a contradiction. The exotic eyes were sensual and promising, while the easy, comfortable posture and plain dress were domestic.

"You look puzzled," she said, startling him.

"I am, a little. You're hard to figure out."

"Why am I?"

He felt a soft compassion for her, but pity—she was far too strong to be pitied—seemed unnecessary.

"You haven't answered."

"I can't. Why don't you tell me something about yourself, so I won't be so puzzled?"

"It's boring to talk about oneself."

"Not if someone wants to listen," he said gently.

"All right, I'll make it short. I had a husband, David. We were very much in love. We were wonderful in every way together, in body and mind. We were one. Nobody else existed. . . . When I lost him, I lost the world. Do you understand?"

"Of course," Paul said.

"Not of course." Ilse shook her head. "Not all marriages—or love affairs—not even most are like that. I can always recognize, at least I imagine I can, one of those rare pairs who are really perfect together. I think you have to have known something like that yourself to see it in others."

Her quiet words cut and probed. She seemed to be waiting for an answer, but he could say nothing. And she went on, "I keep looking for what I had, which is probably foolish. Still, one has needs . . . I've had a few men here and there, I'm not ashamed to say. The sex can be good enough, but there's no feeling for the *person.* I'm always sorry afterward because I know what it could be."

Although she had made no move at all in that direction, he was becoming aware of her powerful sexuality. Or was it only his own that was stirring? He felt confusion.

She frowned. "Why am I talking like this to a stranger? I never have before."

"I don't know. Why are you?" he asked.

"Oh," she said, "perhaps because there comes a moment when you need to speak out just once, and it's better to talk to someone you'll never see again. Also—" She stopped.

"Also?"

"Because—you won't be angry, I hope—because you seem kind, and sad."

He was offended. The impression he always gave, so he was told, was of authority and vigor.

"Sad!" he cried.

"Elisabeth says so too. Or maybe not sad, but lonesome."

"I am not sad, and I am not lonesome, regardless of Elisabeth or anyone." Women! Gossiping about him, invading his privacy!

"You *are* angry . . . I'm truly sorry. I speak too frankly. David always told me to be careful about that."

She got up to fill his glass, but he laid his palm over it, and she moved back across the room to replace the bottle. Her slender skirt was tight, spanning the curve of her hips; he saw that her legs were very long, the long, strong legs of an athletic woman. And again there came that stirring, a contradiction and a fusion of reluctance, surprise, and anger.

She was leaning against the bookcase. The lamplight struck across her face, making an art photograph of the eyes, all the rest receding into shadow; the extraordinary, barely slanted, jet and brilliant eyes were all he saw, and they were fastened on his own.

For a minute, a long minute, the eyes held as if, having discovered, they were considering something. It was Ilse who broke the silence, repeating, "You are angry."

He rose half out of the chair and sank back. "No."

"My trouble is," she said, "that I don't know how to talk properly to a normal man anymore. Most of the men I see are either bitterly unemployed or crippled. It makes a difference. You don't flirt, you can't dance with a man who has no legs."

She moved; the lamplight blazed first on a glistening mouth, then shifted down to a white cleavage between dark mounds of concealing cloth. He became suddenly conscious of his heartbeat and knew he had better leave.

"Do you want to go? Say so if you do."

"No," he said.

"Well, then, what shall we do? Would you like to dance?"

He was hypnotized. It came to him that if she were to ask whether he'd like to jump out of the window, he would say yes.

"Yes. Dance," he said.

She put on a record. The music scratched, while a male voice quavered in English, "Rose Marie, I love you, I'm always dreaming of you."

Paul got to his feet and took her in dancing position. Tightly held, they moved around the little room. Her body was hot against his, as if she had a fever. He was trembling.

"My son loves American records. He saves his allowance for them."

He didn't answer. Her fingers moved on the back of his neck. Her legs moved against his thighs.

He heard her say, "This awful music. It's absurd. I'll turn it off."

She reached behind her and the music squealed to a stop. Still they stood, not disengaging. Afterward he was not sure whether it was she who first turned her mouth up to his, or he who had bent down to find hers, but in any case it did not matter; the long kiss led to the bedroom.

He remembered that she had murmured something about her son's being away on a weekend visit. He remembered her voice, urging him who needed no urging, and the clamor within him, all the pulses, and the perfect culmination.

Her head was lying on his shoulder when her whisper awoke him.

"It's after midnight. They'll be wondering about you."

"I'm wondering about myself." He laughed. "Believe me, I didn't plan this."

"Nor did I. Shall we just blame it on fate?"

"Why 'blame it'? I'd rather thank fate."

"Yes." She kissed his neck. "It was quite, quite wonderful."

He was trembling again. "It wasn't enough."

This time she pulled away and got out of bed. "We can't. You have to go back. But I have an idea. Tomorrow's Saturday and I can take the day off. I can borrow a car, we can go to the country and get you back in time for Elisabeth's big Sunday dinner. If you want to, that is."

"You know I want to."

"Can you make an excuse?"

"Yes. Business. A client has invited me overnight. Herr von

Mädler, it will be, if I'm asked. I handle his American investments."

"Tomorrow, then. Be here as early as you like. We'll have the whole day."

What had struck him? he asked himself, and answered: sex, purely and simply. Unbelievably, he had forgotten what sex could be. The tepid couplings with Marian had become habit. This joy, this marvel, he had not felt since—since Anna.

They had been hiking and eating and driving all day. Now, just before dusk, they passed through a village street between a row of medieval houses with mullioned windows and pots that, in summer, would be filled with geraniums. They crossed a wooden bridge over a stream and turned up a slope where, in a barnyard, a troop of dachshunds was barking at an old, patient horse.

"Why, I've been here before!" Paul exclaimed. "This is the place I've been telling you about. We bought a dachshund puppy at that farm. And there's the inn where I stayed with Joachim that summer before the war."

It might have been the same room, he thought later. The windows faced the dark hill behind the building. The four-poster bed was curtained, and a comforting fire burned in the porcelain stove.

"Shall it be early dinner and bed?" Ilse wanted to know. "Or bed first and late dinner?"

"Bed now, late dinner, and bed again," Paul answered.

So, in the great, soft feather bed they made love, slept, and woke to the rumble of a wagon, the clink of harness, and homecoming voices on the road. For a while they lay and talked about whatever came into their heads: Beethoven versus Mozart, impressionism versus abstract painting, dogs versus cats, and French cooking versus Italian. After a while they got up and dressed again for dinner.

They were the only city folk at the inn; the dining room

was deserted, and they ate at leisure. Facing Ilse across the little table, Paul reflected how strange it was to be feeling so relaxed with a woman whom he had first met only three days before. His other casual liaisons, on business trips, had answered a physical need alone; he hadn't ever felt pleasure in being with the lady afterward.

Her voice interrupted his thought. "You've done something very important for me, Paul."

"I have?"

"Yes. You remember what I said about feeling the *person*? And that I never did after David? Well, it's happened with you."

"I'm glad," he said genuinely. And knowing that, quite naturally, she was expecting to hear from him, he said, "It was the same for me."

She raised her eyebrows. "The same? Then you've been missing someone too?"

Missing the warmth that my wife doesn't have, or missing something even more, before and beyond it. . . .

"In a way," he said guardedly. And aware of the need for explanation, he added, "My wife's a good woman. I could never hurt her in any way."

Ilse put out her hand to cover his. The touch was gentle, almost maternal. "You would never hurt anyone, I think, if you could help it."

The naked kindness of her touch moved something in his chest. And something burst open. At once he recognized the need to reveal himself that he'd had only once before, when Hennie had come to his house on the night Marian lost their baby, the need he had stifled then and ever since. Now, here, in this foreign room with this foreign woman, it overflowed.

He began to speak rapidly and very low. "I had someone once, who was to me what your David was to you. She was the most beautiful woman I've ever seen. . . . Excuse me, I didn't mean . . . you're very lovely, too."

She smiled. "You don't have to treat me like that. I'm not beautiful and I know it."

He lowered his eyes to the wineglass and fondled it for a moment, reflecting, letting the past emerge from behind its curtain.

"She was Polish, not an educated woman like you, but with us, to use your words, it was as if we were one mind and two halves of one body. I didn't marry her, as I should have done." He stopped. He had been about to say, "We have a child, a little girl whom I have never seen and cannot see." But the words, sharp as pins, were too painful in his mouth and he could not speak them. Instead, he finished his short tale. "We're parted, permanently parted. And yet, she will be with me for the rest of my life."

He raised his eyes from the wineglass to meet Ilse's intense gaze.

"It must be very hard for your wife, then," she said.

It was not the response he might have expected. And he replied, "I don't think so. She doesn't know. You're the only person I've ever told, from the day I married her."

"You don't think she must feel it, even though she doesn't know it?"

Paul shook his head. "I'm very good to her," he insisted.

"Yes, you would be. But surely you must be depriving her of something."

"Nothing that she misses. Marian is—she's the salt of the earth. But cool, like salt. She's not like you."

"Or like the other one. . . . Now I understand the sadness in you, Paul. You see, Elisabeth and I were right. We saw it."

He drew back. Something, some male need to be invulnerable, reasserted itself. He had perhaps said too much.

A silence followed. A coal fell with a clink in the stove; somewhere upstairs a door closed. Still neither spoke. In such stillness moods are volatile: rapture, enchantment, or melancholy can absorb each other.

But no doubts or melancholy must tinge his last hours with this extraordinary woman. . . . And he stood up so abruptly that his chair fell with a clatter. "Come! Enough! Let's go to bed."

The morning was cold, with snow in the clouds waiting to fall. In the close warmth of the tiny car with their thighs and shoulders touching, their spirits varied and flowed. They chattered and laughed and fell still. Once they even sang a silly ballad. The nearer they came to the city, the greater grew Paul's sense of the unreality of the last few days' events. He glanced over at the woman who had moved him to so much delight. If only that quality, that magic, could be transferred to the good and faithful woman he had married! How changed would their nights become, how different a man would he be in the mornings! He glanced again at Ilse, who was looking straight ahead with a thoughtful expression. He must remember her carefully, the serenity of her forehead, the curious upward slant of her eyes, the lower lip's delicate protrusion—

She turned to him. "I want to tell you something before we leave each other, Paul. You've taught me something. You didn't mean to, but you did. Do you want to know what?"

"Yes, my dear. Tell me."

"That I can go on now to a life after David. That another man can give me what he gave."

He was too moved to answer.

"Only, I have to find him . . . I wish he could be you."

The right reply to that would be: And I wish so too. But it would not be a truthful answer. If anyone could take a permanent place in his life, it could only be Anna. . . . And because that was so, he would not sully the beauty and honesty of these hours with Ilse by lying. Instead, he put out his hand, took hers, which was lying on her lap, and held it warmly.

"We won't ever see each other again," Ilse said, "so I'm going to say something that may make you angry once more."

He smiled. "Go ahead."

"All right. I think you should try to forget that other woman. You didn't tell me her name . . . I think you should forget her as if she had died like my David, since you can never have her." She turned her face up to Paul's. "You're not angry with me yet?"

"I don't want to be angry this morning, Ilse dear. I've never been a man who enjoys being angry anyway."

"Well, then I'll finish. I lay awake this morning while you were still asleep and I watched you. I could love you, Paul. But I won't, because you have to go home. I know you don't love your wife, not in the real way. But you ought to love someone, not a fantasy, not a woman-who-might-have-been. You must find someone, Paul. You really must. And that's all I have to say."

He saw that her eyes had brightened with tears. You're wonderful, he thought, wonderful. And yet, you don't understand. If you could move beyond your David because of me, I'm glad for you. . . . But in spite of all you gave me, you still don't understand about Anna.

He leaned over and kissed her cheek. "You're lovely, Ilse, and I'll never forget you. A 'queen among women.' Isn't there something in the Bible like that, or is it Shakespeare?"

She dried her eyes and resumed a gay voice. "I'll be sure to look it up. Now watch the turns. Next left. You can stop here and walk around the corner to the house, so Joachim won't see you with me and be scandalized."

So they parted.

Joachim said, "I wish you could stay over Christmas. We'd show you a really good time. We go down to the country and tramp through the snow. Friends come in and sing carols in front of the fire . . . but I forgot, you don't approve."

"No," Paul said. "My parents did the same. I didn't approve then."

Joachim said easily, "It's a German thing. Tradition. It may seem silly, but tradition is comforting. Year after year, the food and gifts, the music and the fragrance."

Paul answered quietly. "It's a deep religious holiday. Don't you think it insults believers when you make it into a light entertainment?"

"My dear fellow, I'm the last one to make light of it! On the contrary, I respect it. But each can take from it what he will."

Paul let that go. Again there was no use in argument. "I'll come back some summer," he promised.

"Do you remember how we went walking through the Odenwald?"

Yes, he remembered. The villages with their peaked roofs and red geraniums. The cherry orchards, and the pine hills rising. It had been such an innocent time for him, when he was loving the last of his total freedom and also looking forward to his marriage.

"Yes, some summer," he repeated.

"Good! Bring your wife next time and don't wait eleven years!"

The last he saw as the train pulled away was Joachim's waving arm; the other arm was laid around Elisabeth's waist.

How different they were from one another! And yet they pulled so well together. This was what living ought to be. . . .

The weather had turned abruptly cold and the sky had a wintery look as the train sped northward. It passed through somber Teutonic towns and cities; their granite was the color of bone in the thin light; their massive Romanesque brick piles were blood-brown. An ominous sense of doom lay gloomily on all these places. It lay like a heavy hand on Paul's head. Closing his eyes to shut the dreary landscape away, he tried to doze.

The only relief during the whole somber journey came when, after buying a newspaper at a station stop, he learned that Adolf Hitler had been caught and arrested.

In Hamburg, he made his business calls and then went for a walk. Passing the American Express office, he stopped to inquire for mail, although he expected none the day before his sailing date. But there was a letter from Marian. It was short and he scanned it quickly.

"Paul dear, I have been sitting here all afternoon thinking about us. I know how you have felt these past years about not having children . . . I've watched you with Hank . . . you would be a wonderful father . . . I know how many children there are who need a home and I wish I could be like you, and could be happy to adopt a child . . . I wish I could, but I just don't want a baby who isn't my own, and I suppose that's wrong, and I'm sorry, but then I tell myself that there are many people who feel as I do . . . It wouldn't be right to take a baby into your life when you truly don't want to . . . I keep hoping you will get used to the idea of living without a child. Please, please try. Let's not spoil our lives because of it. We're still young, and there is so much in life that we can do. . . ." There was more, much more, in the same vein.

He put the letter in his pocket and kept on walking. Clearly, he saw her seated at the little art deco desk in her sitting room, writing in her even backhand on the pale gray notepaper. Something had struck her deeply, very, very painfully, to cause such an emotional—for her—appeal. It might have been a book or a play, or maybe just the quiet of the house without him in it.

The pity of it! He knew that he himself was in an extraordinarily emotional state; surely he had had enough reason these last few days. Yet the pity was not to be denied.

And he walked on. Down a broad avenue, he came upon a statue of the late unlamented Kaiser, corpulent and arrogant, on a proud horse. The horse was a nobler creature than his master, who, centered on self, had sent millions to their deaths and paved the way for the sickness that was eating away at his country.

Paul sat down on a stone bench to read his wife's letter once more. Her arms reached out, asking for peace. Had he too, like the man on the horse, been centered only on self? Wanting and wanting . . .

So he sat, while it grew darker and a foggy chill crept under his coat. He thought of Joachim and Elisabeth, with their baby, in their home. He thought of Ilse's warm body and warm voice telling him: *You must find someone, you must find love.*

Find love! How easy it was to say! She didn't know. Her situation was not at all like his own.

And he thought again of Marian. The letter, the summons and appeal, weighed like a solid thing in his pocket. *Let's not spoil our lives.* Poor, willing soul . . .

What was he thinking of? Like any responsible adult, he must go back and take up where he had left off. Anyway, where else had he to go but home?

The Monday night theater audience, in formal dress, paraded up and down the aisles and greeted and clustered in the lobby during the intermission of *All God's Chillun Got Wings.* Conversations were animated and opinions strong; Eugene O'Neill could be counted on to provide material for strong opinions.

It was Ben and Leah's anniversary and Marian had suggested taking them to the theater. "What else can we give them?" she had asked, remarking that they seemed to have or to be acquiring everything.

Paul had not been sure whether Marian's remark had meant disapproval or had been merely a statement of fact. Leah's little coterie of friends and customers, two groups that frequently overlapped, had gathered around her in the lobby. She attracted attention; her dress was very plain black silk, cut to display white shoulders and her marvelous breasts; its simplicity emphasized the magnificence of her diamond-and-ruby earrings, Ben's most recent and most sumptuous gift. They blazed as she tossed her head. She wore no other jewels. Clever of her, Paul thought.

People came up to speak to Marian for other reasons, because they knew her or had probably always known her. They were all active in the same charities; Marian's name was on the important committees, and she was respected for it. She liked to say, had indeed with some disdain said that very night as they were getting dressed, that people who were sure of themselves didn't need to be fashion plates, didn't need to keep displaying new clothes.

Old family, old clothes, Paul reflected with a sudden flash of amusement. Just like Alfie's Emily. Not that Marian didn't look well enough in a dress two seasons old.

He caught her eye, and she pulled him aside. "Look! Look over there! Isn't that—do I imagine it, or isn't that the maid you had when—no, I guess it was just before we were married—"

"What?" he said dumbly.

"Over there! The tall, red-haired woman going down the aisle. I swear it looks like her. The maid your parents had."

"I don't remember," he said.

"Well, I do. She was very striking."

A red-haired woman was moving down to the front of the theater. Paul craned his neck to see, but she was obscured and he wasn't able to see her face. Why would she be here in this place? Why wouldn't she be here? This was the sort of play she would like.

The curtain rose; figures moved on the stage and voices spoke words, but he neither saw nor heard them. He was totally unsettled. And he had really been settling himself quite well all this last month, ever since he had returned from Europe with another new and strong resolve to straighten his thinking, start fresh, wipe the slate, let the past die.

With a feeling almost near to resentment he had erased Ilse's admonition about the need to love. Well, Ilse was an ocean away, and almost surely he would never see her again; the brief idyll—for it had indeed been an idyll—would fade, if it had not already faded. He felt no guilt about it, for no one had been harmed. He had come home to his wife, to welcome and to work.

Consciously, he had straightened his shoulders, as if to put himself in command of himself, as if he were back in the army, responsible and committed. No more starry dreams! No more looking backward toward what might have been . . . toward Anna. Finished. Hopeless. Accept it. And so he had done, and the month had gone very well; Marian was happy to have him home, friends had been calling, things were going smoothly at the office; his resolve was holding fast.

And now here he was, rigid in his seat, straining toward the footlights in the hope that a stray beam might reveal the red-haired woman! What would he do, what would he say, if she should turn out to be Anna? His hammering heart was apparently unaware of all his resolve. It kept on hammering until the play was over, and the red-haired woman disappeared in the crowd.

"How did you like it?" Marian asked when the play was over.

"Good. Yes, very fine."

She shrugged. "I didn't. Too sociological. All this underdog business. One gets tired of hearing it."

"I don't know," he answered, since an answer was expected.

"Well, that's what it was all about, wasn't it? Let's take them for a drink," she whispered. "After all, it's their anniversary."

He would gladly have gone home, but evidently Ben and Leah welcomed further celebration, so they went instead to the St. Regis, where a handsome young crowd was dancing to society music. Paul played the host. Leah's new ruby earrings glittered at his shoulder as they danced.

"By the way," she asked, "has Alfie asked you yet to talk to Meg?"

"No, what about?"

"He's going to. About Donal. He and Emily are fairly out of their wits."

"What do they want of me, for Pete's sake?"

"Obviously, they don't like the man, and since Meg worships you—"

"Oh," Paul said, embarrassed.

"Well, she does and you know it. They think she'll listen to you. They're going to ask you to just drop in casually on Meg in Boston. You do go there fairly often, don't you?"

"Yes, but I don't like subterfuges. And I don't know anything factual about the man except what he did for Dan."

When the music stopped, they rejoined Marian and Ben at the table.

Marian was curious. "You look like conspirators. What's the secret?"

"Nothing really. Or rather, yes, we've been talking about Meg and Donal Powers," Leah answered.

"Perhaps we shouldn't—" Ben began, and stopped, looking uncomfortable.

"For goodness' sake, we're family!" Leah said. "We can talk. Besides, I'll bet anything Paul suspects."

"Suspects what?" asked Marian. "Something about Mr. Powers?"

"All right, he's a bootlegger," Ben admitted. "That's what all the excitement's about."

"Oh, my!" said Marian. "He seemed such a gentleman!"

"He is a gentleman," Ben said. "He's honorable. He pays his bills and he keeps his word, which is more than can be said for a lot of people in high places. Right, Paul?"

"Well, yes, in a way," Paul said. Of course, it was far more complicated than that. And he thought of Meg's pathetic letter.

"You did suspect something, Paul, didn't you?" Leah asked.

"Well, I was somewhat puzzled about him. Where his influence came from. I daresay it wouldn't have been hard to figure out if I'd put my mind to it, which I didn't," Paul said.

Suddenly, Ben became agitated. He leaned across the table, whispering, although the music had started again and no one could possibly have overheard. "Remember, *I* never told you anything. Have I got your word, all of you?"

Leah admonished him. "Of course you have. Don't be ridiculous."

"*I'm* not responsible," Ben argued. "I keep the man's accounts and work on his investments. I'm his accountant and his lawyer, that's all."

"I don't know, though," Leah worried. "You are aiding him to break the law, aren't you?"

"It's a stupid law and won't last. Everybody knows that. And I'm not aiding him, I just told you. No need to worry." Ben patted her hand. "Just keep quiet, that's all. I shouldn't have told you. That was wrong of me in the first place." He seemed to have reassured himself, as he sat back and lit a cigarette. "Donal's no criminal, for heaven's sake! Meg won't come to any harm with him. She's probably having more fun than she ever had in her whole life." And, as no one made any comment to that, he added, "Besides, this whole business is stupid. The man hasn't asked her to marry him and I don't think he even wants to get married. Let's dance again, Marian."

Leah drew her chair closer to Paul's. "Let's talk. I'm awfully fond of little Meg. Why do I call her 'little' when she's as tall as I am?"

"Why did we all used to think of you as 'little Leah'?" And he gave an oblique glance toward her marvelous breasts, which stretched the thin black silk and gave off a warm perfume, vaguely Oriental.

"I really am afraid she's in love with the man."

"She is," Paul said. "She wrote to me."

"Oh, damn! Love! This is her first experience, and she's probably scared stiff that she'll never have another. Oh," she said, indignantly, almost contemptuously, "to bring a child up like that! In a vacuum. Keeping her out there in those woods like a pioneer woman, shy as a rabbit or—what do you call those little animals, the fat things she loves that come to eat grass?"

Paul had to laugh. "Woodchucks."

"Yes, and the one with the long nose that hangs upside down?"

"An opossum," he said, still laughing.

"Well, it was all wrong of them. They're odd people, Alfie and Emily. They don't belong anywhere, don't let themselves belong. In the country, a few of the more liberal gentiles tolerate Alfie because of Emily, while in the city, Alfie does business with Jews, but he keeps away from the Jewish community. The two of them are really in the middle of nothing, and that's what they've done to Meg."

It was a clever observation. Leah, seeing things clearly and unembellished, seldom shrank from telling exactly what she saw.

"We don't really know Meg, do we?" Paul reflected. "Draw

the curtain away and maybe there's a gypsy inside, for all we know. Although I doubt it," he added.

What fools men and women were for pairing off as foolishly as they did, when any onlooker could tell that the pairing wouldn't work! How blindly they stumbled! But, if he were asked, he supposed he would have to talk to Meg. Would he, after all, want any daughter or sister of his to marry a man who stood outside the law, even though the law was an absurdity?

On the other hand, people always wanted to pull lovers apart when they found them "unsuitable." And he thought again of poor Meg's despairing letter. Donal, her parents said, was unsuitable for her. But Anna, Paul thought, had also been "unsuitable" for him! Who, then, was to know, to judge, to look into the future, or into the human heart?

Four

"It's so romantic," Meg's roommate said, "I mean, the way your parents hate him and all that."

The girls on the floor had come into the room that Sunday afternoon where Meg was dressing for the arrival of Donal Powers, who had come up from New York.

"Why don't they like him?" someone asked.

Her roommate answered before Meg could. "Because he's Catholic."

"Well, mine wouldn't like that either," said the first girl, who had made one of Boston's most publicized debuts at the Copley Plaza; she lived on Beacon Hill in a house that belonged to her great-grandparents; it had wavy, lavender-tinted windowpanes and was filled with so many old possessions—portraits and Sheraton chairs and Paul Revere bowls—it seemed as though no one had had to buy anything at all for the past few generations. It was the kind of house Meg's mother would love to live in and might well have lived in if she had married someone other than Meg's father.

"He's awfully good-looking," her roommate said loyally, not because she was usually that loyal and generous, but because she had just become engaged and was feeling benevolent toward the world.

Donal had driven up once before in the dead of winter, had stayed overnight in Boston and met Meg there; they had gone to Locke-Ober for dinner and he had driven her back to the college. Naturally, he had attracted attention, and the attention had spilled over onto Meg, who now had a man of her own and could therefore command a respect that she had never received before. For three years at Wellesley, she had been a person in the background, a position to which she had long been accustomed. A good scholar, but not one of the small brilliant vanguard who were going on to become doctors or lawyers; a good swimmer and tennis player, but not remarkably good; she had never been much of anything until Donal came.

A woman without a man was a shadow. It was his life that reflected on her, and if he was an older man, no college boy, and obviously affluent and worldly in his manner, why then the reflected light was very bright indeed.

When the girls left, Meg still had an hour to wait. She dressed carefully, lingering before the mirror. She had finally had her first permanent wave; it had been an ordeal, sitting there, attached to the machine with the wires dangling from the ceiling, and she had really been scared, but the result had been worth the ordeal, as Leah had assured her it would be. Her fine hair, instead of being severely drawn back, now dipped and curved about her forehead, and a little stray curl kept coming loose at the temples. The careless effect was becoming and she let it stay.

She selected a red dress: it would bring good luck, being almost the shade of the one she had been wearing on the day they met. She would never give that one away, no matter how old it got. She remembered, too, the day she had bought it and the feel of the broadcloth, silky as slipper satin. Leah had reached up to adjust the collar.

"Stand straight, don't crouch," she had admonished Meg. "You're tall, so be tall!"

Emily had doubted. "That red is terribly conspicuous, don't you think?"

And Leah had retorted, "What's wrong with being conspicuous?"

For once her father had stood his ground against Emily, who had come home complaining about Leah.

"Her taste is simply not of the best. It's too nouveau. After all, where would she have acquired a refined taste, coming from where she did?"

And Meg had recognized the unconscious anti-Semitism that her mother, being truly unconscious of it, would have refuted with outrage.

But Alfie admired Leah because, like him, she was self-made. She hadn't fussed about with college. You had to hand it to her. Independent: lets nothing stand in her way. And so on.

Yet he denied such independence to his daughter. And he would certainly not have approved as much of Leah if he could have known some of the things Leah talked about with his daughter.

They had gone to tea one afternoon after the shop had closed. It had been during Meg's first year away at college, and, so Meg guessed, Leah had probably been thinking, rightly thinking, that there were many things Meg needed to know about. So they had talked, or rather, Leah had talked and Meg had listened. She could recall even now the feel of the afternoon, warm and cheerful and intimate at the small table.

"When you're married," Leah had begun, and Meg had interrupted, "But what if I never am?"

That was the secret fear of most girls, except for the beauties or the real "personalities." Never to be chosen, never to be loved! Meg had dreams of standing alone in a vast room, where everyone was talking, paired off and passing her by . . .

"What if I never am?"

Leah had been confident. "Oh, you will be! You must never think that way. And when you are," she had told Meg, "you must remember always that a man wants a passionate woman. Even if you are dying to fall asleep, you must never say no. Even if you don't like it, you must pretend you do. That's the way it is for women. But then, who knows? You may love it and there won't be any need to pretend." And she had laughed, so that Meg had known she was one who loved it.

A certain fear had stirred in her, a sinking in her chest. Leah had looked at her keenly. "I frightened you. I didn't mean to." And she had taken hold of Meg's hand. "You'll be all right, you know, you'll be fine."

Meg's fingers stopped now as she fastened the buttons at the back of her neck. How would it be? She had no idea. It was so strange. You read things, not very much, because books couldn't actually say; they could merely hint, and you had to fill in the rest with imagination. Would it not be awkward? No, of course not; the bodies had been designed to fit together. She felt warm all the way through from thinking about it; a little tremble went through her like a shiver, but warm.

Donal had never kissed her, only held her hand when they were at the theater, and sometimes in the car while he held the wheel with the other hand. And the way the two palms had clasped, flat against each other, had made her think that was the way their bodies would be, and thinking that, she had felt that same warm shiver, and wondered whether he was feeling it too.

He was very formal, very respectful. Perhaps he only liked her mind. Perhaps he had another girl for the other thing? That happened sometimes, so she had heard. But would he come all this way just to talk to her and hold her hand?

She hadn't seen him in a month, although he had called often on the telephone. They had had a marvelous weekend in New York, hearing Martinelli sing at the Metropolitan one night, and the other night they had heard Eleonora Duse doing Ibsen's *Lady from the Sea* in Italian, which neither of them understood. But her voice had been so beautiful! And looking at Duse, one felt inspired to be beautiful, so that one sat up straighter and used one's hands more delicately. Walking down the aisle during the intermission with Donal's hand on her elbow, Meg had not been shy about being looked at, had even wanted to be looked at, which was strange, because all her life as far back as she could remember, she had dreaded and hated it.

"Come read your poem," her father would say to the guests assembled after dinner. "Meg has written the most beautiful poem," and when she had hesitated, her mother, putting on her strict face, had made her. Yet they had meant well, especially her father had. He was so foolishly proud of her, proud now of her high marks at the college he hadn't wanted her to go to. They had never understood why she was so afraid of being looked at, and she couldn't have told them because she didn't know herself.

But no more. Away from home it was different. With Leah or Paul, and now with Donal, it was different.

Oh, if he were to ask her to marry him, nothing would stop her!

Nothing her parents could say or do. Had they not defied their own parents? They never talked about it, but Aunt Hennie had told her how Emily had been in tears at their wedding, a runaway drab affair at City Hall because her parents refused to come to it. Yes, it had taken courage. Oh, nowadays there were more mixed marriages, even conversions, especially among the fashionable people Cousin Marian knew. The Jewish partner, almost always the man, converted, but it hadn't been fashionable when Alfie and Emily had married; it had been shocking and rare.

And now they didn't want Donal Powers because he came from an Irish slum. They had hoped for a stylish marriage, her father forgetting who he was himself. She knew as well as if she had been told in so many words what they wanted for her: a tawny-haired, gray-eyed husband, who was properly connected, who would provide for her a membership in the clubs that had turned Alfie down.

They would be surprised to know how much she had understood when she was still very young.

"There are rumors that the country club wants to buy a piece of our land," her mother had remarked one day.

And Uncle Dan had answered, "Does that mean Alfie will be able to join?"

He hadn't fooled Meg with that straight face of his; she had recognized sarcasm. Because, of course, they knew that for all Alfie's favors and jovial hospitality, they would still never accept him in the club.

How ridiculous it was, and somehow sad, that anyone could care so much about things like that!

Donal had no such stirrings. He was what he was. You had only to look at him to recognize his cool pride. Truly, he was a man. He made you feel strong. You were strong when you were with him. . . .

She looked at the clock. In half an hour he would be here. The car would come around the curve and stop at the door. Time crawled, as it had been crawling all winter. In the evenings, thinking he might telephone, she had sat with her mind only half on her work; paper rustled, the chair creaked, and the alarm clock moved with a steady click and tick, until she was summoned to the telephone in the hall, or not summoned. New Year's to midterms, midterms to spring vacation; time crawled as the hands crawled around the clock's innocent blank white face.

"It's nice that you don't smoke," Donal told her. "I don't like the way young women have been taking up smoking since the war. I like the old ways. Places like this, too. I'm glad you brought me here."

"You couldn't get anyplace much older and still be in America," Meg said.

The inn at which they were having a midday Sunday dinner, in itself a tradition, was an eighteenth-century farmhouse. An ancient musket was slung below the mantel, which was decorated with bayberry candles in pewter candlesticks. Their table faced this hearth, and the fire warmed their feet. The menu offered hearty food, chowder, roast beef, brown bread, and Boston beans. No mistaking that they were in the heart of New England!

Meg, thinking of Donal as an urban person, had been afraid that he might look askance at all the pine-and-maple rusticity, but it was he who had suggested that they spend the day in the country rather than in Boston. So she had guided him down rural roads through Lexington and Concord and then brought him here, where the food was known to be very good; he had said he was hungry.

"Yes, I like it," he repeated. "They're a nice class of people here too."

The others in the room were couples and families with well-behaved children; all were dressed in good country tweeds. Until this moment, Meg hadn't thought to notice that Donal also wore a tweed jacket and knickerbockers; it was the first time she had seen him dressed that way, and she thought, Why, he does everything right! He planned this, he watches everything; a city suit would have been out of place in this setting.

"You know, I didn't think you'd like this kind of place," she said.

"You don't know very much about me, Meg," he answered.

His eyes examined her steadily. She was the first to look away; she had a sense of something imminent.

"I guess I don't."

"Well, then, it's time I told you more about myself."

He paused. Directly in their view at the next table, an elderly man—very correct with pince-nez and gray moustache —drew a silver flask from his pocket. Quickly he slid it under the tablecloth, while with the other hand he slid a glass of soda water under the cloth. Then, having effected the mixture, he replaced the glass on the table and the flask in his pocket.

Donal looked amused. "A criminal act," he said, shaking his head.

"My father does it too," Meg told him. "I always think it seems silly, because the fact is, he really doesn't like whisky. He hardly ever touched it until Prohibition came in. It's funny, too, he always stays within the speed limit, he's so particular about the law."

"This adds a little spice to life, a little daring," Donal said.

"You never do it?"

"What? Carry a flask? No, I have all I want at home. I'm not much of a drinker anyway. Like your father." He paused again, moved a piece of beef around his plate, and said, "Your father doesn't approve of me. No, you mustn't be embarrassed. It has nothing to do with you. With us."

"He's really a very kind man. Softhearted," she apologized.

"I saw that, but he still doesn't like me." And he waited for her to answer.

"I don't know," she faltered.

"But of course you do," he said gently. "He must have talked about it . . . do you know what I do?"

"What you do?"

"Yes. For a living. I deal in liquor. I import it. Illegally."

She did not know how she was supposed to feel. Shocked, probably. But her father had said many times that he suspected as much. Yet it did not register as anything important. She was only conscious of his hand resting on the table as he leaned nearer across the table, talking to her in an intense low tone.

"I'm what's known as a bootlegger. Does that seem dreadful to you?"

"No," she said. "Actually not."

"This law won't last forever, you know. There's no way in the world that you're going to tell people they can't have a drink, any more than you can tell them they can't make love. Alcohol is a part of every civilization known to man."

"I know."

"Well, then. Isn't it better to provide people with stuff that won't poison or blind them like the stuff they call hooch, doctored up and colored with caramel to fool them? So I bring in the pure product, right from the distillery in Canada. I bring it into New Jersey. It's an import business, that's all it is."

Thoughts ran through Meg's mind. When Dad knows this for a positive fact . . .

"Are you upset, Meg? You look upset."

"No," she lied.

Her parents would really make a fuss, enough to drive him away, perhaps.

"It's all hypocrisy. You can be sure that the politicians who put this law through stocked up their own cellars first, with enough to last for years. Your upper classes"—and Donal's head nodded in the direction of the table opposite "—get all they want at their expensive clubs. I own a couple of those clubs myself. Judges come there, senators come there. I'm confiding in you, Meg. I'm trusting you."

There was great confusion within her. She was elated and she was frightened, but also she felt responsible; she felt womanly.

"I feel that my hands are morally clean. I never owned a firetrap tenement or a sweatshop."

"You sound like my uncle Dan when you say that."

Donal smiled. "He's an idealist, isn't he? I don't know that I'm quite like him."

"It was wonderful what you did for him."

"No trouble. I just knew the right people. That's what it's all about, Meg. Knowing the right people. I learned that young. I had to."

"Ben told us you came up the hard way."

"True. But why am I bothering your head with all this?"

"You aren't bothering my head. You can tell me."

"All right. Let's have dessert and get back in the car. Maybe we can go for a walk someplace, and we'll talk some more."

He started the car, drove for a short way, and turned down a dirt road, little more than a lane wide enough for another car to pass from the opposite direction.

And again, Meg felt a sense of imminence, a tension that needed to be broken. "This is a nice car," she remarked, for lack of anything better to say.

"It's well made. I always wanted one like it. I love having *things*," he said. "Good things. Grown-up toys."

That, Meg understood well enough, having witnessed all her life her father's joy in his possessions.

"You should learn how to drive. This would be a good little car for a woman. In the city I have a man to drive me. It saves time."

The landscape was frozen. Wind roared in the bare elms that lined the road. The sun went in and out as clouds sped across the cold sky. In barnyards, cows in their shaggy winter coats clustered together for warmth.

"Is it too cold to walk?" asked Donal.

"No, I like it. I'm a country person."

On the dark northern side of the road, under spruce and fir, a thin film of ice lay in the ditches; water gurgled beneath it. There wasn't a house to be seen in any direction.

"Take my arm," Donal said. He pulled her hand through his arm, and thrust the joined hands into his pocket. "Shall I begin?"

"Please."

"All right. I grew up in what's called Hell's Kitchen, a few steps off of Eleventh Avenue, on the top floor of a tenement house, a cold-water flat." He spoke severely, almost as if he were making an accusation.

"My mother had me, then never any more, because a tumor killed her. Maybe if there had been money for a proper doctor, it wouldn't have happened, I don't know. So, like you, I'm an only child. That was a rare thing in my neighborhood. I want a big family, a house full of children.

"My father—he was a longshoreman—was killed on the docks when a crate fell on top of him. So I had to go to work, quit school after the eighth grade. I had a second cousin who owned a bar. He was an old man and he had no sons, so I went to work for him. He promised to leave the bar to me when he died and he kept his promise. I had the place until Prohibition came in."

Donal was looking straight ahead, still with that severe expression. And Meg thought that other men, except Cousin Paul, looked like boys compared with him.

"You meet a lot of people in that business and I made useful contacts, all kinds. I met a young priest over here from Ireland, who took an interest in me. He knew a good deal about music, knew a good deal about almost everything. He took me to a concert. I hadn't known there were such places. Carnegie

Hall was light years away from Eleventh Avenue . . . but I got hooked. Can you believe it? I even remember the program to this day. Richard Strauss's *Ein Heldenleben,* A Hero's Life. Father Mooney was his name. He's back in Ireland now, and we still write to each other. He taught me to read. I mean really read. History and English literature. I swear I learned more from him than I ever would have learned if I had gone on through school. I had a lot to learn, too. Grammar and diction and table manners."

He pulled their joined hands from his pocket and stood still. "I've never told all this to anyone else. Pride, I guess." He laughed. "Or just not anyone's business. I'm naturally secretive. But enough about me. What are you studying?"

"History and government."

"Government! You think a professor on some pretty campus or in a town like this can know what it's really like? Or that books can tell you how corrupt it is?"

"Well, I've read Lincoln Steffens's *Shame of the Cities*—"

"All right, then, that's part of it. I've read it too. Let me tell you, everyone has his hand out. And I mean everyone. Judges, cops—they're all alike. Both parties. I give campaign money to Republicans and Democrats, it doesn't matter. They all come to me when they run short. I pay the cops to protect my trucks so they won't be hijacked between the boat and the warehouse. I pay the judges . . . does that frighten you? It shouldn't. It's just the way the world is. Always has been."

She was mesmerized.

"Now I'll tell you the rest. I'm a softhearted man. I give money away practically without counting it. I make money and I give it away. The Salvation Army knows me, you can ask them. And the Boys' Clubs, so kids will have a place to go instead of hanging around the streets. And the orphanages and the Red Cross during the war. You can ask them about me. I wasn't able to serve because I had flat feet. Crazy! Flat feet! I can outwalk anybody. And the flophouses: I keep soup kitchens there on the Bowery where the poor drunks flop. The temperance people, so holier-than-thou, blame drunkenness on drink when they ought to blame it on poverty. Sometimes a drink is the only comfort a man has. I hope you don't think I'm boasting, Meg. It's only that I want you to know all about me, good or bad. Come on, let's walk. It's too cold to keep standing."

Trees closed in. They were walking through a second-growth woodlot of sumac, birch, and cedar. A rabbit crossed the path at their feet and stopped to stare at them out of black, unblinking eyes, then scurried away and disappeared into the dry, warm cover of fallen leaves. Above their heads, there was a squawking in the trees.

Donal looked up. "What are those? Ravens?"

"No. Crows."

"I don't know anything about country things. You'll have to teach me."

She didn't know what to say. They stood still again.

"We'll have plenty of time for you to teach me."

In that first moment, his meaning seemed clear . . . she had so dearly hoped, and here it was . . . and yet, had it been too foolish of her to hope? Could he possibly mean what she thought he meant? He was, after all, so different from her . . . What could he want with her? A woman like Leah, clever and confident, would be better for him. . . .

"Won't we?" he asked.

He put his hands on her shoulders, turning her toward him, but her eyes, puzzled, confused, fearful of being misread and thus making her ridiculous before him, looked stubbornly away. Raising her chin, he forced her to look up at him.

"You know I'm crazy about you, Meg. You do know it."

She could only murmur, "I . . . didn't."

"But I've known it. I only waited to tell you until I could be sure you felt the same."

He took her head between his hands; in a flashing second

she saw his face coming down toward hers; his eyes were closing, curling their black lashes over the delicate, white lids. He kissed her; her lips opened to meet his while her arms, knowing what to do, went up around his neck, pulling him to her as his arms pulled her to him. So they stood, pressed together in the dry thicket, in the wind.

Heat ran through her, spreading from some secret pit; it was marvelous, mounting and mounting so that she wanted it never to end. She was dizzied, as when once or twice she had drunk wine; this had to lead to something further; it was unbearable, standing here minute after minute, melting into each other.

They pulled apart and stared.

"Well, Meg. That's it, isn't it? Did you ever think, when you lay in bed dreaming about a man, that it could be so wonderful?"

"No," she said, and thought at the same time, astonished, he sees through me, has seen through me, and I am not ashamed.

His mouth twitched with amusement. "Oh, you're a darling! Oh, I've had in my mind somebody like you. Vague thoughts—how could they be anything but vague? I'd never met anyone like you. Where would I? Not the women *I* knew. And still there was something in me that understood about gentle girls, ladies, warm and innocent and good and loving. Maybe it came from reading about them in Father Mooney's great books, I don't know." Donal laughed. "I walked into the room that day we brought your uncle home, and when I saw you standing there, so tall and quiet, with your serene sweet face, I recognized you, Meg. I knew you. And I knew enough to go slowly with you, not to frighten you. I haven't frightened you, Meg, have I?"

She put her hands up to his face, touching, stroking with light fingers the three parallel lines in the forehead, the faint crinkle at the corners of the beautiful eyes and the hollow of the cheeks.

He caught her fingertips and kissed them. "Let's get out of here. The place is too deserted. I can't be alone with you in deserted places until we're married."

They walked back to the car. He didn't ask me, she thought. He told me. *Until we're married.* He moves directly to where he wants to go.

The wind rose higher, lashing and whipping the trees. Lonely houses and barns were battened down against the storm. Through the bleak landscape, the car moved, humming; she was in a safe, warm little world that had nothing to do with the perilous world around it. And with a little shiver of delight, she glanced over at Donal, thinking, *Why, I belong here now! I belong to him! Am I the same person I was yesterday? An hour ago?*

He felt her glance. "What is it? You don't say anything . . . but it's my fault, I haven't given you a chance, have I?"

"I'm thinking. I don't know what to think. It doesn't seem real."

"It's real, all right. You're not afraid of anything, Meg? About who I am? What I do?"

"It doesn't matter."

As he had said, the real crimes were to house people in dirty firetraps, to underpay them in miserable factories. Meg had not grown up around Uncle Dan and Aunt Hennie without learning something! Add to that what she had learned in government classes, and how could one possibly be horrified over a simple traffic in whiskey?

"You're so beautiful, Meg," he said. "It's a pity you don't think you are."

"What makes you say that?"

"Leah told me. We were talking about you. Don't be angry at her. She's a true friend to you. Get out your mirror and look at yourself."

"Now?"

"Yes, now."

She saw that her eyes were enormous; their gray held a glisten of lavender. Her mouth was full and moist. This was an unfamiliar face. Could it have changed so much in just one afternoon?

"Margaretta," Donal said. "It suits you. A lady's name."

"It's a stuffy name. It belonged to my mother's grandmother and I hate it."

"Then I'll never use it, if you hate it. I'll do everything to please you." He put a hand over hers. "I'm really very soft inside, Meg."

The words, which touched her with sudden pity (How hard his life has been, how he has fought his way!) and the pressure of his hand, which brought back the burning, the body heat that she had felt through their layers of woolen cloth, combined into a surge of feeling that ended with a little cry like a sob.

Her cry alarmed him. "What is it, what's wrong?"

She said the first thing that came into her head. "You'll be going back to New York—"

"But only for a few days. I want us to be married next week. Or the week after at the latest."

Now reality rushed back. "But my parents, my father—"

"Meg, I'm not even going to ask your father. You know as well as I do what the answer would be, and I'm not going to humble myself, not going to explain or argue or plead when I know it won't do any good. No, we'll be married and then we'll tell them. When it's done, they'll accept it and put a good face on it."

He was right, of course. It did make sense to avoid a nasty hopeless argument and her mother's tearful lecture: *You hardly know him . . . we had hoped . . . good family . . .* It would be hopeless. And this was irresistible. An elopement. Romeo and Juliet.

She thought of something else. "But graduation. I have to graduate. They'll be heartbroken if I don't. The way I begged to come here! They didn't want me to. They gave in really because of Cousin Paul, and now if I don't finish—"

"You'll finish! We'll be married, but no one will know it until June, that's all. You'll hide the wedding ring. I'm going to buy you another little ring, so you'll have something of mine to wear in the meantime. You can tell the girls in the dorm that it's your engagement ring." He grinned. "You'll like that, won't you?"

"So fast, so soon," she said, shaking her head in wonder.

"Why not? There's never any time like the present. I've always worked on that theory." He drew the car over to the side of the road. "Before I take you back, shall we say a week from Saturday?"

"Where—where will it be?"

"Around here. A civil marriage."

"But aren't you a Catholic?"

"I'm not much of a one anymore, I'm afraid. And you're not Catholic, so a civil marriage will do nicely. Of course, children have to have some religion. I'll leave that to you."

Children. The word tied them together again, as when they had stood in each other's arms in the woods.

"You'll need a pass for the weekend, an invitation from a relative."

"I'll talk to the housemother. I'll think of something."

He grinned again. "No need. I've already done it."

They registered at the Ritz-Carlton in Boston. Over his shoulder, she watched him sign in firm letters, double-sized, *Mr. and Mrs. Donal Powers.* On her left hand, the wedding ring, a wide band of diamonds, bulked under her glove; the right hand wore a small sapphire surrounded by more modest diamonds. Her fingers, rubbing against each other, assured her that she was awake.

In a hall mirror, as they followed the bellboy to their room, she saw herself; the gentian-blue wool suit did look bridelike.

"Good God!" her roommate had said, "it looks like a bride's going-away suit!"

"I couldn't resist the blue," she had answered quietly. Wouldn't it be a conversation piece for them all when they found out the truth!

Donal tipped the bellboy and locked the door. The windows faced the Common, where people were strolling as though it were just an ordinary day. He raised the shades to the top and the room went bright with sunshine, so that the bed was illumined like a throne.

"We're too high up for anyone to look in, and I want to look at you. See all there is to see."

He pulled the spread from the bed. "We've only got a day and a half, so let's make the most of every hour."

She kept being surprised at herself. Her daydreams had been different; in them, she had been hesitant, wondering and awkward. But she was none of these now. Instead, she went into the bathroom; with steady hands she removed her clothes and put on a nightgown; took the pins from her hair and let it fall to her shoulders; felt her heart, which was pounding, and went back into the bedroom.

Next to the bed, he waited for her, wearing a dark silk robe. His eyes widened with pleasure.

"You're not afraid," he said.

"No. Did you think I would be? I always used to think I would be."

"You didn't know yourself. You've wanted this ever since you first had any idea what it was. Come here."

He reached out and pulled the nightgown back over her head. Then he let his robe drop and they fell upon the bed together.

At the very same hour, in New York, Paul was hanging up the telephone. "Alfie thinks it's really serious," he told Marian. "He says that if the man proposes, he's sure Meg will accept. Probably in the summer, right after graduation."

"What does he want of you?"

"Well, he has an idea Meg might listen to me. He wants me to 'put all the cards on the table,' 'talk to her like a Dutch uncle,' you know how Alfie is. And he thinks that you and I might know some suitable young man to come to the rescue." There came a sudden recollection of Donal Powers's amused, sardonic gaze. "As a matter of fact, I was expecting to be in Boston next month, but I could move it up . . . will you make a reservation for lunch or tea or something with Meg, week after next? We'll stay at the Ritz. I think you should come along. Maybe you can talk to her, give her a woman's point of view." Paul grumbled. "I don't know why I get saddled with advice to the lovelorn."

"You get saddled with everything in your family," Marian said with a sigh. Fine lines creased her forehead. "I worry about you, Paul. You ought to think more about your health. You're overworked and you'll end up with high blood pressure before you know it."

"No, no, I'm fine. Strong as a horse."

Meg sat with her back to the windows, so that wisps of her hair, escaped from its smooth-tied length, were blond in the light. She had always seemed older than her age; *matronly* was the word, Paul thought, as though whatever might have been spontaneous in her was being held down—as it had been. But now, this minute, she was radiant. And he remembered having been shocked by that same radiance on the night Donal brought Dan home.

"You haven't had much experience, known many men," he said, trying to be tactful.

"How many do you have to know when you're sure?" Meg replied. There was a tremulous brightness in her eyes.

He pursued the subject ineffectually. "You're very young."

"Most people are very young when they fall in love, aren't they?"

"Yes, but to take the first one without waiting—" Paul began, and was interrupted.

"You both took the first one. I remember your wedding, being a flower girl—"

Now Marian interrupted. "We had known each other a long time. And what's more important, our families had known each other. We knew what we were getting."

"I think that's terribly snobbish," said Meg, sitting up straighter. "I'm sorry, but I don't see what families have to do with it at all."

Yes, she had changed. The way she sat . . . the way she moved her hands . . . there was a ring on her right hand, a very blue sapphire, which Paul had not seen her wear before.

"I can't live without him," she said now.

Paul sighed. After more than an hour of careful, reasoned argument, he had gotten nowhere. He knew he was beaten. Alfie was beaten.

"I won't live without him," she said shamelessly.

Marian had a look of distaste. Her lips were tightly closed, giving her face a look of forced patience.

"I know he sells liquor. He's told me all about it. Why not? The best people are breaking this stupid law. It won't last anyway."

Marian opened her lips. "May we ask, has he proposed to you definitely, formally?"

"Why, of course!" Meg's eyebrows rose. "Why else would I be speaking like this?"

Rebuked again, Marian flushed. It occurred to Paul that perhaps he should have brought Hennie instead. Soft and motherly as she was, Meg might have listened to her; she had always loved Hennie. Though probably it wouldn't have mattered. The girl was in the delirium of first love. She was either making a terrible mistake, or else this was to be her lasting love, the real one. Who was to say?

He called for the check. The two women went to the ladies' room while he waited. Loneliness chilled him as he sat there by himself, surrounded by the discreet murmur, the refined ritual of teatime. Two couples at a table nearby were talking, or rather the women were talking; the men seemed satisfied to let their wives keep up the chatter. Inane chatter. They were women of middle age, with gray hair marcelled in iron wavelets. Sexless women, not like that glowing, perhaps foolish, girl who "won't live without him."

He met Meg and Marian in the lobby.

"Well, it was good to see you anyway, Meg. Don't be angry with us, will you? We mean well."

She kissed him. "It's all right, Cousin Paul. I still love you. I always will."

They watched her get into a taxicab and then went up to their room. Marian took her hat off and flopped into a chair; the air sighed out of the cushion.

"A silly infatuation," she said. "I do think you might have been more forceful, though."

"I didn't want to blacken the man completely, once I saw that she intends to go through with it. You can say just so much, then there's a point of no return that you reach, and she'd never speak to us again."

"How much do you really know about this Powers?"

"I'll talk to Ben again. I don't think he can tell me too much, or wants to. But I've made other inquiries. He's known in political circles and in business. He's immensely rich and will be richer, although that certainly doesn't matter to Meg. I doubt she even knows it."

"She had a handsome ring. Did you notice?"

"I noticed. Who knows? He might be very good for her, in spite of all. Since that's what she wants."

He thought, I'm talking nonsense. But she was so glowing, so trusting and happy . . . Powers is tough, he gets what he wants . . . and he wants our Meg because she stands for something he never had.

"Well, maybe it will work. He may be very good for her," he repeated.

"I don't see her with him at all. The girl's simply mesmerized."

Well, yes, he knew about that . . .

"She'll live to regret it if she does marry him," Marian said. "A physical attraction and nothing more. Disgusting. As if that were all there is in life."

Paul wanted to say, "You don't know the first thing about passion," but didn't answer, and picked up the newspaper instead.

There was a small item. "Adolf Hitler sentenced to five years in Landsberg prison," he read. He'd never serve out the time. They were making a hero out of him already. They hadn't seen the last of that "funny little man," as Joachim called him.

A wave of melancholy came over him now, after this fruitless day, here in this stiff, unfriendly room, with the overnight cases on the floor and Marian gazing somberly out of the window.

"I think I'll take a walk," he said. "Look in at some galleries on Newbury Street." Always pictures, whenever he was upset. "Want to come?" he asked. Annoyed with her, he yet felt sorry to leave her sitting here alone.

"No, it's too blustery. Boston's always so cold. I wish we could start home now."

"Too late. We'll take the first train in the morning."

"I'm sorry we came. It was a fool's errand."

"Not really," he said calmly. "At least we tried."

"You're not going without a hat, are you? You lose half your body heat when your head is cold, Paul."

He put on his hat and went downstairs. The shops were full of gay things, spring clothes, flowers and books and pictures. At a gallery window he stopped to look at a drawing of a horse leaning over a rail fence; the head was wonderful, with an expression in the large, sad eyes that only a man who knew horses and loved them could have put onto paper. He thought idly that Alfie would like it, not because he would appreciate the art, but because it would make what he'd call a "nice piece," a rural scene for the library at Laurel Hill, where he played at being a farmer. Good old Alfie! He was due for some pain when Meg brought Donal Powers home!

Loving . . . Meg and that man. And he with Marian, who clung and believed that she loved, while not knowing what love could be.

Still, was it her fault if she was made that way? Some listen to Beethoven and are moved to tears, some hear only the technical quality of the performance, and still others don't want to listen at all.

He walked back toward the hotel. I know I came home from Europe resolved to make it work, he said to himself. In a way, I suppose, one might say it is working; this is all, very likely, that most people ever get.

And yet, absurd as it was, he had been envious of Meg, of little Meg, this afternoon. To want like that, and to be getting what one wanted!

Five

The boy Hank lay at the edge of the pool, with the sun burning nicely on skin that had been chilled after a long cold swim. One hand still trailed in the water, while he lay comfortably, letting his thoughts drift. It was nice here at Cousin Meg's house. He had been coming to the pool every summer, ever since Cousin Meg got married. It wasn't city like his own house, and not country either, like Uncle Alfie's, which was wonderful, with horses and hikes up through the woods and a waterfall and fishing in the lake. This was in New Jersey about halfway between Uncle Alfie's and the city, on a wide curving street with big houses, far apart on lawns as green as the billiard table that Cousin Donal kept in a special room. There was a shady porch with striped awnings; there were flowers and little tables under umbrellas where Cousin Meg served cookies and lemonade. The pool had a hedge around it and the water was blue because the bottom was painted. There was a brightness over everything on a day like this, and he was happy because summer was just starting.

His eyes traveled across the lawn to where the nursemaid rocked the baby carriage in which Tommy was asleep. Timmy, who was a year older, was sitting in the playpen. Beyond them, the driveway was filled with cars, shiny as black glass. Expensive cars, he thought, wanting to know more about cars. There were always men coming and going at this house, at least whenever he came on a Saturday or school holiday with Ben. Business associates of Cousin Donal's. He knew about that, because Ben talked pretty freely to him and didn't treat him as if he were a child who couldn't be trusted.

He loved being with Ben. It was a year or more ago that he had stopped calling him "Daddy." He didn't know why he had; it just seemed more manly to call him Ben, and Ben didn't mind at all, although his mother thought it wasn't proper. Ben had said, No, he's ten years old, he's almost a man, it's okay.

Grandpa Dan didn't treat him like a little boy either, but his grown-up way was different. It was more like teaching, as when he would say serious things, explaining carefully, "You're old enough to understand." He loved being with Dan in his laboratory, watching him move about with all his tubes and flasks and wires, his fitting and measuring; he'd seen how connected wires buzzed and sizzled into sparks, and wheels spun around. He'd listened as Dan told about electrical charges in the universe, and how sounds could travel under the ocean or through the air. He could see how you could get so curious about science that you would always want to know more and more.

Often they would go out to lunch together and meet Dan's friends, who would shake his hand and say, *My, he is the spitting image of you, Dan.* Hank could see that Dan was a kind of special person to those men. Dan's downtown friends were poor people, not hungry-poor, but certainly different from the people Ben knew.

Funny how he loved them both, and they were so different.

Once in the park, a boy stole his roller skates. Ben had been very angry. *I'd wring his neck if I caught him,* he'd said. But Dan said, "Of course, it's wrong to steal, but you have to try to understand. Where I teach, there are boys who can't ever have a pair of roller skates, and so when they see some lying around and nobody looking, why you see, the temptation's just too great."

It made you wonder who was right.

His mother and grandmother treated him like the little boy, like the child he had been two or three years before. They probably thought that as long as a boy was only up to their shoulders, he was still a little child. But his head was filled with things they didn't know he thought about.

There were secrets . . . they had told him that his father had been wounded in the war and had later fallen down stairs and died. He always felt, although he had no reason to think, that there was more to it, something he hadn't been told.

And so many secrets about money! Why was money so important that people talked about it that much? Grandpa Dan said it was disgusting and that was what was wrong with the world. He could see that his grandfather didn't care very much about it. Where he lived, you had to walk up *four* flights of stairs, and the halls smelled of cabbage. When the weather was warm, men sat on the front stoop in their undershirts. So he was puzzled when once he heard the cook say to the woman who came to clean, "The boy is very rich, you know. This house is his, and it all came from the grandfather."

He had asked his mother about it. "But is it true that Grandpa Dan gave everything to me?"

"Yes, it's true."

"Why did he?"

"Because he loves you."

"Didn't he want any for himself?"

"No, he didn't."

And then Ben, who had been there, said, "Tell him, Leah, he's old enough."

So that was how he had found out about the invention; the War Department had bought it, and Dan wouldn't take the money for himself since it was being used for war, and war was the thing he hated most.

In school, the teachers all said there would be no more wars, because the last one had been fought to end wars. Anyway, that war seemed to be a long time ago; it blended in his mind with Washington and Valley Forge. He had said that once to Cousin Paul, who had laughed and answered: "I was in it, you know, so it couldn't have been that long ago."

Paul didn't like to talk about the war. Once Hank had asked him whether he had killed any Germans, and Paul had just said very gently, "I don't know. And that's a question you mustn't ever ask," which was unusual for Paul, who always liked to answer questions.

He rolled over now on his stomach. The front of him was getting hot. Besides, he wanted a view of the house. He was hoping Cousin Meg would bring out the lemonade and maybe some cake.

Grandpa and Cousin Paul didn't like his coming to this house. He could tell by their faces and by their not saying anything whenever he told them he had been here. He knew why, too. They liked Cousin Meg, but they didn't like Donal, and he knew why they didn't. It was because of Donal's business, that you weren't supposed to talk about. But Hank knew all about it. Ben never said anything directly, but he didn't make much effort to hide it either. Lots of times, when they stopped off here on the way back from fishing at the shore, he would let Hank come into the room where the men were all talking. He'd sit in the corner with the funny paper and listen.

So he knew all about how the whisky came from Canada across Lake Erie, down through country that was so empty that there was nobody to see the trucks being loaded. He knew how some of it came directly from Scotland and England; the ships would sail as if they were heading for those two little French islands off the coast of Canada, but they never landed there. Instead, they went straight through to New Jersey, where speedboats raced out past the three-mile limit to unload the ships. Donal's company owned thirty ships.

Only once had Ben observed that Hank, finished with the funny paper, had been sitting very still and paying close attention. Later, when they were alone, Ben had said, "You must never repeat anything you hear—" and Hank had interrupted to say that of course he wouldn't; did Ben think he couldn't be trusted? And Ben had said, "I know you can, but it's your mother I'm thinking about. Women imagine things, they exaggerate. You know how women are, Son." Hank liked the manliness of that, being one with Ben in strength.

But his mother knew plenty already. They had been talking in the car. They must have thought Hank couldn't hear.

"I'm just an accountant, a glorified bookkeeper, Leah. I've nothing to do with anything."

"You know better than to tell me that," she had answered.

"In a few years the country will get rid of Prohibition and Donal will have a legitimate business. Ten businesses, the way he's going. And I'll be his adviser, on easy street."

"Your street is easy enough now without that."

"No, it's not. What am I making? Except for the fees I'm entitled to?"

"I don't like it. It worries me."

"Come on! I'm completely legitimate. Anyway, I'm not Donal's keeper."

It was all very interesting. And confusing, too.

He liked to watch the people in his family. They were all so different from each other, and yet all seemed to come together in him. He wondered, looking at them, what he was going to be when he grew up. He knew he didn't want to be like Donal, even though Donal was always nice to him, kidding him and giving him presents. But for some reason, Donal scared him. He would never want Donal to be angry at him. . . . Maybe it would be good to grow up like Grandpa Dan, sort of *noble*. Or jolly, like Uncle Alfie. Or very smart like Cousin Paul; he noticed that whenever anybody had a problem, like finding a surgeon for Ben's elbow operation or finding an apartment where Dan wouldn't have so many stairs to climb, they always asked Paul's opinion. So maybe he'd like most of all to be like Paul.

Sometimes, though, he thought he wouldn't want to be like any of them, but only like himself, different, separate and unconnected; quite free, like an Arctic explorer or an aviator—

"You must have been bored to death out here by yourself," said Cousin Meg. She was carrying a tray with the pitcher of lemonade and a plate of cookies.

He scrambled up while she put the tray on a table under one of the umbrellas.

"Oh, chocolate chip this time," he said.

She sat down and watched him eat. She looked nice in her pink summer dress.

"You might have time for another swim before you go home. Why don't you bring a friend when you come again? You can use the pool whenever you want to, you know."

"Mother says not to make a nuisance of myself."

"You could never do that, Hank. I enjoy company when I swim, anyway. But the baby's been teething and cranky today. That's the only reason I didn't go in with you."

He followed her glance across the lawn, where the nurse

was lifting one baby out of the playpen. The carriage with the other one had already been wheeled away. He thought, She has another baby inside her already. She was beginning to bulge.

He'd heard somebody once—he couldn't remember who— say something about people breeding like rabbits. And he munched slowly on another cookie, keeping his eyes away from the bulge under the pink dress where another baby was growing, the third in four years. He felt himself blushing, because it was only this past spring that he'd found out from one of his friends how the baby got in there. It was queer to think that Donal did that to her. The last time he'd been here, he'd gone up to the nursery and passed their bedroom, where the bed stood on a platform and the spread had lace around it. And he'd thought: That's where they do it.

Donal gave her a present each time she had a baby. The first time it was a bracelet that his mother said was gorgeous. *Gorgeous* was one of his mother's favorite words. *Generous* was another. Donal was generous. They were building an addition on the house now, more bedrooms and a playroom. They would need it with all those babies. The house was supposed to be English. *Fake,* said Paul, fake half-timbering; no self-respecting English house ever looked like that. *Ostentatious,* Paul said. It means showing off, his mother told him when he asked, and wanted to know where he had heard it. But he hadn't told her, because he had been doing what they called "eavesdropping" on Paul. Anyway, he didn't agree. He liked the house.

"You're looking at this?" Meg asked. He had actually been seeing the house behind her, but she thought he was looking at the locket that hung on a chain around her neck. It was a big diamond heart.

"Donal gave it to me when Tom was born."

"It's pretty," he told her, not caring.

"He's just so good to me," Meg said. "Just so good."

She sighed. He noticed that she sighed a lot. . . . Then there was a long silence that began to be uncomfortable. He felt that he ought to say something or do something besides eating cookies. This was his fifth, and they were large ones, the soft kind with big chips.

Finally, he thought of something to say. "There were two parakeets in our yard yesterday morning. Dead."

"Oh, poor things! Escaped from someone's cage, I suppose."

He had found them when he went to put the dog out. Buff and yellow they were, with their bright tails fanned out and their tiny claws curled.

"The world was full of seeds, but they didn't know where to get them. Didn't know how to take care of themselves. That's the most important thing, Hank, to know how to take care of yourself," Meg said.

He wondered why she was telling him this.

"I hate to go to the zoo," he said. "People always want to take you. They always think children want to go to the zoo."

And he thought of the lions pacing with lowered heads, back and forth and back and forth, looking so sad.

"I know," Meg said. "I always think caged animals must be wondering why they're caged. Their eyes are so . . ." She paused. "I always think, if they could cry, they would."

It was an odd conversation. A moment ago he had been embarrassed because there was nothing to say; now here they were, talking so easily together. And he had a queer thought: She's not like anyone else in this house. He couldn't have explained the thought, for it was just something that darted through his head and, an instant later, was gone.

Ben came out just then with Donal and their friends. They were all in dark city clothes; they all looked alike and they all got into their black cars and drove away. But Ben came across the lawn.

"Hey! I'm going to get my suit out of the car and jump in with you, show you how to do a half twist," he called.

"I'm ready," Hank answered, and splashed back into the cold pool, letting the water wash away all heavy thoughts and secrets. He felt happy again because the summer was just beginning.

Six

Paul picked his way through the hectic heart of the financial district and entered his private world. The discreet, low building, with its double doors and its polished brass, was now in his charge, his mother's death the year before having driven his father into final retirement.

All was in order as he strode through the main floor on his way to the private elevator in the rear. But then, it always was. On either side of the carpeted aisles sat the ranks of his "bright young men," fresh from the Ivy League, fresh in their white shirts and good dark suits. A few early clients were already in consultation. Through a door on the left Paul's glance fell on the private sitting room, in which special customers and ladies made their private transactions. Already a small fire flickered under the marble mantel, while above it, Paul's grandfather, in Lincolnesque whiskers and solemn broadcloth, fingered his watch chain. A tea table stood in front of the long leather Chesterfield sofa; at four o'clock the bowl of chrysanthemums would be moved aside and replaced by Wedgwood cups on a silver tray.

This was the proper way to run a banking service. Always Paul thought of his work as a service, ranging from investment advisory accounts for individuals to managing a bond issue in the many millions. In either case, you were oiling the industrial machine, keeping the nation at work. There were responsibilities in it, and great dignity.

Upstairs at his monumental desk in the square front room, he sat down to read the morning's mail. At the top of the pile two letters with foreign postmarks caught his attention. One was in Joachim's familiar writing. Garrulous and exuberant on paper as much as in person, Joachim could be depended upon for a letter every fifth or sixth week. The second envelope, from Elisabeth Nathansohn, would contain a thank-you note for his Hanukkah presents to the children. He was about to open Joachim's when his secretary came in.

"There's a Mr. Donal Powers on the telephone. He would like to make an appointment with you."

"What's it about? When does he want it?"

"He didn't say what about. He said, at your convenience. You have nothing this morning until eleven, so you could see him."

"All right. Have him come over." He added quickly, returning the courtesy, "If that's convenient for him."

What could Donal Powers want? It was doubtful that he would want financial advice, for surely he had his own sources. Anyway, to judge from the few remarks that Alfie had dropped—very few, since one could be quite certain that his son-in-law didn't confide in Alfie—Powers managed most of his affairs himself. He could probably take my job, Paul thought, and handle it as well as I do. The man's mind was an engine in absolute working order, all gears and pistons smoothly synchronized.

Donal and Paul met very seldom, which Paul regretted only

because he would have liked to see more of Meg. But her marriage had changed things. Donal had taken her into a different world. There was no common meeting place anymore. There was not even time. When she was not at home with babies, she was out in that different world of Donal's.

One met Meg and Donal, then, only at duty affairs: Alfie's birthday party or a visit to Dan when he was recovering from a heart attack. Donal never failed to appear at the proper places at the proper time; in all things, he was correct. He had even made a generous contribution to the temple in memory of Paul's mother.

And yet, surrounding him, a vague dark presence like oncoming shadows, stood what, in the eye of Paul's mind, could only be written in capital letters: THE MOB.

One strained, one made an effort to reconcile the image of the conservative gentleman in the English suit and striped tie with what one read in the newspapers about assaults, hijackings, and extortion. Ben, of course, maintained that the newspapers exaggerated, that the liquor traffic was for the most part a respectable although illicit trade, run like an ordinary business, nothing to get so excited about.

Paul neither argued the matter nor pried. The only thing he would have liked to know was whether Meg was contented. *I won't live without him* . . . Donal looked like a man who knew exactly how to satisfy women—at any rate, he knew how to make them pregnant. Meg had her third and fourth last summer, twin girls, Lucy and Loretta. The children had all saints' names, which was odd, since Donal was certainly not a religious man.

Meg looked well, only a little tired around the eyes: four babies in four years, after all, and quite possibly another on the way. But the face was as sweetly wholesome as ever, and the manner was the same, despite the new jewels and the chauffeur-driven Isotta-Fraschini. So it might well be turning out as she had been so sure it would.

Paul wondered how much she could know of whatever there was to be known, and what she thought of it. He had no way of finding out. If there should be any trouble in paradise, neither her parents in their pride, nor Ben and Leah for a different reason, would have revealed it to him, that he knew. And that was assuming Meg would let them know about it in the first place! He rather suspected that she wouldn't.

He went back to his mail.

In his angular European script, Joachim covered three pages.

"We moved to Berlin last month and have a beautiful apartment, better than the one you saw in Munich. I am developing the import side of our business and keep very busy. You wouldn't recognize Germany. In the five years since 1923 we have gone from despair to a flourishing prosperity. The inflation, such a terrible medicine at the time, turned out to be the best cure. It wiped out our debts and now we are rebuilding. You should see the theaters and sports arenas and all the new housing. Unemployment is almost wiped out, the factories are humming; it is a miracle, Paul, a German miracle. You remember, when you were here, I told you it would happen! A little patience I said and you will see. . . ."

A little patience and a generous lot of American money. He opened Elisabeth's letter.

"We thought that you and Marian would have come to visit us before now. You would find us changed. You wouldn't have to wear a shawl to keep warm in our apartment this time. And, of course, I am happy that we can live more easily and give the children everything they need. One worried so during the inflation that they might not be getting enough protein. But Regina has her second teeth now and they are perfect, thank God. She is such a bright, lovely child. But I worry. I can't talk about it at home. Joachim thinks I'm neurotic when I say I'm worried. I can't forget that terrible day when he was shot. So I think you will understand and will not mind if I spill my thoughts out to you. You needn't answer if you don't want to. Do you know this man Hitler, as soon as he served his short prison term, has come out a hero? Prominent people are giving him huge sums. Little by little, in spite of all, this evil grows—"

"Mr. Powers is here," said Miss Briggs.

Donal was waiting on the threshold. Paul stood up. They shook hands. There were amenities to be gone through: the offer of a seat away from the window's glare, the offer of coffee, which was declined, and the usual inquiries about the family.

"I hope Marian is feeling better?"

For just a second, Paul was puzzled. "Her sinus trouble, you mean?"

"Am I mistaken? I thought Meg said something, or maybe it was Ben—"

Of course. A report would have come from Leah, to whom Meg had stayed close. Marian, although she liked to criticize Leah's taste, still shopped at her place.

"No, it's an old story, nothing serious. Just New York's damp winters. Fortunately, she can always escape to Florida."

The words were barely out of his mouth before they echoed back to Paul's ears: they were words of discontent, revealing too much. Annoyed with himself, he raised the pitch of his voice to inquire cheerfully about Meg and the children.

"Oh, fine. Fine. All well. Kids keep Meg busy."

"Must be nice to have two girls after two boys."

Paul wondered how long one could keep a dialogue rolling along like this, with neither one really caring about what was being said. A long time, probably.

"They're nice babies, but I'm hoping for another boy or two."

More thoughts swirled in Paul's head. Flashes like the perilous lights of a migraine: the waxen, white, dead boy he had never seen and who had been his; the enormous dark eyes—had they been troubled or only serious?—in the small face of a strange little girl whom he knew only from a photograph, and who was his.

He collected himself, making an inane remark. "Well, boys are nice too."

Donal extended his cigarette case to Paul. It was solid gold and monogrammed, but otherwise quite plain. Good taste.

"No, thanks. I've taken to pipes lately."

Donal leaned back. "Speaking of boys, that fellow Hank is growing some, isn't he? Tall for his age. I forget how old he is."

"Thirteen in the spring."

"He certainly thinks the world of you."

We are leading into something, Paul thought. "I'm glad of that," he answered simply.

"He comes out to our place now and then with Ben. Saturdays mostly. So I've gotten to know him, know how he feels about you. And you about him, of course."

Paul waited, not helping.

"I understand you take care of his financial affairs."

Ah, here it was! But why?

Paul replied evenly. "I'm a co-trustee, along with the bank that has the trust, until he reaches twenty-one. That's all I am."

"I take that to mean that any change in the investments, buying or selling securities, has to be agreed upon by the bank's trust department and by you?"

"That's right."

"That's what they told me."

Paul sat forward. "Who told you?"

"The people at the trust department at the bank. Ben had happened to mention the name of the bank, and then one day when I ran across an interesting proposition, it occurred to me that I might be doing young Hank a big favor to bring him into the deal."

Ben didn't just happen to mention anything. You asked him. A hot little spark of anger flashed in Paul's chest and was prudently quenched.

"You have no objections, I hope?"

"You haven't explained what it's all about."

"Of course. Here it is. I invest in a variety of enterprises, oil, rubber, real estate . . . I diversify. I've got a fairly big piece of National Electronics. And they've been buying companies like Richmont Dynamo, for instance, and a couple of others that you're probably familiar with."

Paul nodded. Now they were approaching the heart of the matter.

"Well, Richmont's interested in taking over an outfit called Finn Weber."

Now they were almost touching the heart of the matter.

"Finn Weber has an interesting history. One of their biggest money-makers, I learned, was Dan Roth's invention years ago. Got them their first War Department contract. Of course, I'm telling you what you already know."

"Of course," Paul said.

"They're a lively outfit. They've brought younger blood in since the war, really outgrown themselves. Even reached out overseas with some important connections. The fact is, I see such a future there that I've just got hold of a large piece of their stock—this is highly confidential—with the idea of buying Richmont away."

They had touched the heart of the matter: Hank's vote.

"Why?" asked Paul.

"Because I see Richmont holding them back. They'll do better on their own, and you'll see why in a minute when I tell you about their foreign connections. Not that I'm giving up National either; they've got too many other things going for them, you understand."

Paul understood. It was playing it both ways.

"Now I'll get to the point. You're probably there ahead of me, though."

"I'm there. The stockholders' meeting is next week and you want Hank's shares voted your way. You need Hank's shares."

"I do. Of course, I could get my people to run around and buy up all the odd lots, but that would take time, and this way we could vote the thing through with a lot less trouble."

"So you went to the bank," Paul said, swallowing his indignation. Gall! What gall! "Why didn't you come to me, since you knew I was a trustee too?"

"You were out of town all last week, weren't you? And time, as you can see, is of the essence." Donal's look was unfazed. "So I talked to Mr. Walcott in the trust department."

"And what did he say?"

"Oh, that they had faith in Finn Weber's present management. That they had certainly proven themselves. They've had stock splits and amazing growth. But if the management favored the move, they really had no reason to object. The matter had also to be discussed with you, naturally."

"I don't like to upset applecarts," Paul said. "Just as they told you, Finn Weber has been making money. Hank's got more than he needs by far, and it's all secure. Why tamper with it?"

"Tamper? No. I'm talking about taking over the company and doubling—tripling—its value. Here's the way it is. There's a firm in Germany that's looking for certain things they make, certain patented electronic gear. Actually—and I've got a couple of electrical engineers quietly looking into it —the thing they're especially interested in is some sort of long-distance detection device that's an offshoot, an improvement on Dan Roth's old original patent. Interesting, isn't it?"

"Very," Paul said.

"Well, to make a long story short, I'd like to own—or rather I'd like Hank and me to own Finn Weber before these Germans start buying, and they're going to buy big. So far, I've been holding them off."

Donal ground out the cigarette, mashing it round and round the ashtray, as though he were killing it. Paul watched the strong, manicured fingers for a moment or two before he spoke.

"Where are those Germans of yours going to get all this money?"

"Oh, they've got plenty! You surely know what's been happening in Germany the last couple of years? Starting in about twenty-five, everything has boomed. Last spring, when Meg and I went over, I was amazed at what I saw. Do you know that they're right back to where they were before the war, and then some? Production is 122 percent of what it was in 1913. The people are satisfied, well dressed and well fed. . . . The restaurants are the finest anywhere. We went all over. Frankly, I found Berlin more exciting than Paris. The cafés— the parks, the music and theater—"

Donal's voice was rich in timbre and softly modulated. It is one of his assets, Paul thought, and corrected himself: one of his many assets. A woman might let herself be hypnotized by that voice.

"And the paintings," Donal said. "I know very little about art, I'm sorry to say, but they tell me that some of the best work is being done in Germany today. The galleries are certainly crowded enough. A dream of a place for a collector like you, I should think."

"So we're agreed that Germany is prosperous. But do you know why?"

Donal laughed. "Any fool knows why, or ought to. Loans!

They owe billions. Speaking of fools, the creditors are mostly Americans. Naturally. I wouldn't invest a cent in Germany! I'd only sell to them for cash."

"You think they're going to crash, then?" asked Paul, who knew that they inevitably must.

"No question about it." The reply was prompt and sure. "Then a new government will take over, repudiate the debts, and build the nation back. Probably go to war again someday. They'll wreck all Europe." He shrugged. "However, that's not our affair. Certainly not now while things are rosy."

The cynicism was revolting. If Joachim should hear him—

"I can't give permission to vote Hank's stock your way," Paul said clearly.

Donal stared at him. "Just like that? The answer is no, just like that?"

"It's not something I want to get involved in. As I've said, Finn Weber is doing well enough. I'm satisfied, and I don't want to have dealings with Germany anyway."

"I don't see why not."

"They want this stuff for rearmament. The country is quietly, secretly rearming. Even now, under this republic. Oh, they'll say they're buying it for civilian purposes, but they don't fool you, do they?"

"They don't. But what if they do want it for armament?" Donal flung the question. "They're going to get what they want, if not here, then somewhere else."

"Let it be somewhere else, then." Paul's glance fell to the pile of letters on the desk. He saw himself standing again on that narrow street, squeezed against the sun-hot wall of the building; Joachim was slumped on the sidewalk with blood pouring over his face.

"Evil," he repeated. "That's what you will be selling. Not electrical equipment, but evil."

"You exaggerate," Donal said. His smile had long faded. "I find all this ridiculous, if you don't mind my saying so."

Paul shrugged. "That's the way it is, ridiculous or not."

"I don't think Leah and Ben will be pleased to hear this."

Paul didn't restrain his anger this time. "It's none of Ben's business. I'm Hank's trustee, he isn't. And Leah, although she may possibly not agree—I can't say—will at least understand. Dan Roth didn't take one cent from his work because our War Department had bought it, and that hardly compares with making money out of foreign rearmament."

"Dan Roth and his scruples! You can buy a seat in the park with his scruples. Or a seat in the Tombs." And from the fine eyes, with their feminine lashes, there gleamed black scorn.

As if Paul needed to be reminded that it had been Donal Powers and not Paul Werner, of the distinguished banking house, who had rescued the little teacher, the scientist, the naive and simple dreamer, from the cell!

"The company's going to sell to the German outfit, make no mistake," Donal said. "So Hank will profit anyhow. The pity is he could profit a whole lot more if you didn't stand in his way. If you weren't so—"

"Pigheaded?" Paul suggested.

"You said it. I didn't."

"I never favored acquisitions. 'Friendly takeovers.' They are very seldom friendly, and this one surely isn't."

Donal stood up. "Is this your final word?"

"It's my final word. Sorry."

"Very well. I'll be going. I've got my work cut out for me, I see, and time's wasting."

Paul stood up too. "I take it you're going to buy up a majority of the stock?"

"What the hell do you think I'm going to do?"

"I think you are. But Hank's shares are not for sale."

"I didn't think they were," Donal said impatiently, as if to say, *What do you take me for?*

No fool, God knows, Paul was thinking. Also, a man who

doesn't like being thwarted and will not forget who thwarted him.

"Remember about Dan's heart," he continued. "When you do sell to the Germans, I hope you won't let word leak out to him."

Again the eyes flashed scorn. "I always keep my business under my hat."

"Good. That's a good place for it."

Donal took his time, putting on his overcoat and gloves. Then he said, "Sorry if I blew up. I don't make a habit of it."

Paul took the cue. Appearances were to be preserved. It was better that way.

"Quite all right. You didn't really blow up. Give my love to Meg. Doesn't she ever come into the city?"

"She's here today, shopping." Donal bowed slightly. "Regards at home."

The door closed, making a delicate click. I shouldn't like to be there when he throws appearances to the winds, Paul thought.

From the window he watched Donal stride down the street through the gusting rain. *That man is my enemy,* he thought.

The same gusting rain slid down the windowpanes under the single name, written in gilded brass script: *Léa.* On the other side of the panes two mannequins, in white linen and straw hats heaped with daisies, announced the start of the resort season.

Meg stood for a moment looking out at the passersby as they struggled and hunched themselves against a wind that turned their umbrellas inside out. Then she went back to the full-length mirror.

Leah circled her, considered every angle, with her round eyes narrowed in concentration, and said finally, "Yes, this is the one. It's for you. It has enough dash, but it's sweet too."

A woman in a black velvet evening gown looked back out

of the window at Meg. The skirt stopped at the knees. A wide belt of pink crystal beads had been appliquéd to the dress and formed the design of a large flat bow in front.

"You need black velvet shoes, you know," Leah said. "And a pink beaded bag."

Meg sighed. "Who has time to run around looking for all those things? I've got four children. Oh, people say 'relax, you've got a nurse,' but they're my children and I can't just—" and aware of sounding plaintive, she stopped.

"I can pick up the purse for you. I saw one last week," Leah said promptly. "Shall I have it sent?"

"Oh, please do. Now, am I finished?"

"Except for a hat to go with the green suit. Come on back to the dressing room."

Clothes hung against the silver brocade walls of the little room and lay over the back of the silver brocade chairs.

"I seem to have bought the place out," Meg remarked to the air, Leah having disappeared.

When she returned, she had in her hands a pile of velour hoods, the plain shapes out of which hats were cut and fitted.

"I've brought you a model to try for style. We made this for a customer in bois de rose, but it would be stunning in moss green for your suit. Try it on."

Again, as Meg obeyed, the face looked back at her. Her eyes sank into dark hollows under the cloche brim, which came down to the level of her eyebrows. Her cheeks had grown thinner. With each baby they had grown thinner.

"I don't know that it's so becoming," she murmured. "One looks as though one had no forehead in these hats."

"You look lovely. You need to get used to it," Leah replied positively. She stroked a green hood. "Feel the fabric; isn't it exquisite? Silky as fur. French, of course."

Leah really loved all these clothes. So much enthusiasm! So much energy! You wondered where it all came from.

"So, we'll baste the hat and you can have a fitting next

week. While you're getting the velvet shoes, why don't you get yourself a pair of bronze kid pumps? You know the kind with square buckles? They'd be marvelous with green. And amber beads, long ones, right to the skirt hem."

Meg removed the hat to reveal a short bob, saying only, "One goes to all the trouble of a permanent wave just to have a hat flatten it out."

"What can you do? *C'est la vie!*"

Meg had to smile. Leah liked to dot her remarks with her newly acquired French.

"Now I really am finished," she said, pulling the velvet over her head and handing it to Leah. "Let me get dressed and get out of here."

Leah draped a pile of dresses over her arm. "You're sure you don't want to think again about the charmeuse?"

"No, I'm taking the velvet, that's enough."

"You go to so many places. Theater and nightclubs. You can't wear the same thing too often." Leah hesitated. "Those people—the women you're with—have tons of clothes."

Nightclubs. Speakeasies, you mean. Jazz. Blues. Harlem. Hard-eyed men and smooth; men of few words. Their subservient women, expensively decorated. Three o'clock in the morning. Sleeping in the car on the way home.

I'm bored by it too, a lot of the time, Donal conceded. But it's business. You have to put in an appearance. Be one of the guys.

"I'm not those women," Meg said now.

Leah gave her a gentle look. "Meg, dear, I'm not putting any pressure on you."

"Goodness, I know that! I didn't mean—"

"It's just that Donal phoned yesterday and gave me a list of what you were to buy. Three suits, two evening gowns, a wrap, a sport coat for the races, and—here, I wrote it all down. His idea, not mine."

"I'm sure I don't know why I need all these clothes, when I'll only be pregnant again in a couple of months."

Leah appeared to ignore this observation. Instead she called a saleswoman. "Lottie, will you have these wrapped and carried out to Mrs. Powers's car? It's a maroon car, just to the left of our door. Oh, and by the way, make sure the alterations on the Lemming order are finished before anyone goes home—she's packing for Europe and must have the delivery before ten tomorrow. And tell Annette to duplicate this bois de rose for Mrs. Powers—here's the green hood—not that one, this moss color. Thanks."

Meg got back into her clothes. "You know, I admire you so much, Leah. You've built up this place, you've made a name for yourself, doing what you like doing. It must be wonderful. I read that mention of you in *Vogue,* when you were at the Paris openings."

Leah shrugged, making light of her pleasure in the admiration. "I've always loved clothes, ever since I was a poor kid. True, I've worked hard, I still work hard, and I've been lucky. Ben's money didn't hurt at all, at least until I could get started on my own."

"Even so. This place . . ." and Meg waved her arm toward the salon in which, through the open door of the dressing room, beige carpet, silk-covered chairs, and a spray of burnt-orange lilies in a black porcelain vase were visible. "You've created all this without anything but public high school, while I went to private schools and college, where I got almost all A's, too, and I don't do a thing."

"Not do a thing? You call four babies not doing anything?"

"I don't mean it the way it sounds. Of course, they're wonderful. The boys are darling. They're into everything, especially Tommy. You know how two-year-olds are. And the babies are getting so pretty, they already have Donal's dark wavy hair . . ."

"What do you mean, then, if you don't mean it the way it sounds?"

Meg sat down. She couldn't have described the weakness

that went through her sometimes. It was a kind of draining, a kind of—could the word *dread* describe it? And she sighed, as though there were something inside that could not be contained.

"I don't know. I know I wouldn't want to go into business and leave them all day. Anyway, I'm not like you, I couldn't run a business. Not," she apologized, fearing to have said something hurtful, "that it isn't all right for you. You only have one child." She paused. There was something she wanted to know and, timidly, she ventured it. "Was it that you couldn't have any more, Leah? Do you mind my asking?"

"I don't mind, and the answer is I don't want any more."

As simply as that a woman could say: I don't want any more. Meg had to pursue it. "You never thought it wrong not to want to?"

"Well, it's my body and my life, isn't it?" Leah sat down and stared at Meg. Two vertical frown lines appeared at the root of her nose. "So that's your problem, is it? Do you want to tell me about it?"

The subject was too intimate. It was between husband and wife alone. The moment you let a third person into the circle of that intimacy, you destroyed the perfection of the marriage. Her marriage to Donal had been flawless; their love had defied everyone, hadn't it? No stranger must ever be permitted to pry into that perfect circle.

"There's not much to tell. Forget what I've said. It's childish of me to complain when I have so much. I guess I'm just tired. People say foolish things when they're tired."

"It seems pretty clear that what's tiring you is the thought of being pregnant again." Leah's frank gaze was kindly.

Meg didn't answer.

"Well, isn't it? Raise your head. Do raise your head and look at me."

Thus focused, Meg whispered, "I guess so."

"Then why do it?"

"Donal wants to." There, now she had said it. Her first disloyalty.

"Oh, the devil with what Donal wants! He doesn't have to walk around with a big belly for nine months!"

Meg started up. "Leah . . . people will hear us."

Leah shoved the door shut with her foot. "There isn't a customer in the place, the girls are all in the workrooms, and besides your voice is so low that my ears have to strain to hear you. Listen, do you mean to tell me he won't use anything?"

Heat prickled up Meg's back. "Oh, no! He wouldn't dream of it!"

"Why? I could understand if it were a question of religion. But he never goes to church, does he?"

"No." Meg's voice was almost a whisper.

"So what's this all about?"

Again she had to sigh. "There are just certain things he clings to. Habit, I suppose. Customs."

"Customs! Habit!"

"Some conviction, too, probably. Birth control is something he won't even talk about, except to say that his grandmother had nine."

"Lord! He doesn't expect you to have nine, does he?"

"I don't know. I suppose I could have. I'm very fertile." And in a small, bleak voice, she repeated. "I suppose I could have."

"What you need is a diaphragm," Leah said.

"Oh, no, I couldn't do that. I wouldn't even know where to go for one."

"Meg, you're a babe in the woods. Listen, there's an awfully nice obstetrician who comes in here now and then with his wife. As a matter of fact, he's the man who took care of Marian that time. I'll give you his address or, if you'd like, I'll make an appointment for you, all in absolute confidence, nothing to fear."

But fear was running up and down Meg's body. "What if he were to find it at home in a drawer?"

"You mean to say he goes through all your things?"

"No, but it could happen."

"You're making difficulties. You can do it."

"I don't dare. Honestly, Leah, I don't dare."

"What's the matter? Are you afraid of him?"

She knew what Leah was thinking, that she was a fool and a weakling. But you had to be born like Leah to act like Leah. One was made in a way that determined what one was capable of doing.

There was a silence. And Leah said, "Go get the shoes. You might try Altman's." She kissed Meg's cheek. "You'll work things out. Eventually you will."

Meg rode down Fifth Avenue with Leah's glossy boxes on the backseat beside her. In front, the chauffeur's head and shoulders loomed out of the falling dusk and the falling sleet that had followed the rain. The thought of the velvet shoes depressed her. Which were the others that Leah had recommended? Bronze kid. She had no interest in them.

"Roy," she said, "never mind Altman's. We'll go home instead."

She laid her head back on the seat before remembering that the man could see her through the rearview mirror. She sat upright again; it was undignified for the madam to loll. Shades of Emily, she thought, with faintly bitter humor. She didn't miss Emily. . . .

Sometimes she missed Alfie, though. Often she did. Right now she did. "Come on, kid, buck up," he'd say if he were there, and the funny thing was, she probably would "buck up." He could laugh about almost anything, her father could. She wished he would visit more often; he had never said so, but she knew he preferred to have her do the visiting. He still didn't feel comfortable in Donal's house, that was why, although he was surely impressed by it and liked to tell people about it, and about the Isotta-Fraschini.

The car arrived at the ferry slip and jolted on board. The engines started up and the boat, lurching over a swell, began to move across the Hudson.

"You can get out and stretch, Roy, if you want," Meg said. "I don't mind."

"Too cold, ma'am, thank you." He turned around to her. "In a couple of years they'll have finished the tunnel under the river. Beats me how they'll be able to keep the water out of the tunnel. A wonder, ain't it?"

"It surely is. A wonder."

In a couple of years, how many children will I have?

Sleet glittered in the long paths of light that poured out of the downstairs windows. On the second floor a bedroom window was bright; Donal was home early. The children heard the front door open and came running. Whenever Donal came in, they expected a present, while from their mother they expected only a hug, wide-armed enough to hold them both.

"What have you been doing?" Meg asked when she had released her boys, although she knew the answer. The sweet smell of fresh bread had seeped into the hall. They had been "helping" in the kitchen.

"We made bread," Tim said. "And cupcakes. I made the icing. I let Tom lick it."

The boys had glossy white skin. Their eyelids and delicate nostrils were almost transparent. They were both quick, agile as monkeys, and yet their knees were always bruised. In one second, the very second in which you looked away, they could disappear; you had to search for them then, calling frantically through the house until you found them in the cellar or the garage or in a neighbor's yard far down the street. They were alert and tough and purposeful. Like their father.

"I licked it," Tom repeated. He repeated everything after his brother.

The boys followed Meg into the kitchen. How cozy it was! There was a tureen of pea soup on the table, which was set for the children's supper. Kitty, the nursemaid, was slicing bread. The cook and she must have been talking the afternoon away; there were signs of mirth around their eyes. The sight of these two sturdy, friendly working women was somehow heartening to Meg.

She asked about the twins. "Sleeping," Kitty said. "Good as angels."

"I wish we didn't have to go out tonight," Meg said, observing the good, thick soup. It was a night to be indoors, the cook agreed.

In the nursery, a night-light threw a milky arc up from the baseboard, barely bright enough for her to see the babies, each in her pink point d'esprit crib. She bent over through the semidark. Lucy's mouth was slightly open, the lower lip still wet with milk. Meg was the only one, except for Kitty, who knew that the two girls were not exactly alike. For a few moments, she listened to their soft breathing, and then went to the bedroom, where Donal lay on the sofa, reading the paper.

He had had his shower. His hair was wet, with comb ridges stiff between the thick waves. Under the red silk dressing gown, he was naked.

"You went shopping, I see. You didn't get very much," he said, counting Leah's boxes.

"Wait till you see the bill. You won't say that's not very much."

"I've never complained. Not that her prices aren't sky-high." He laughed. "More power to her, though. She gets away with it."

Meg took off her coat, hung it in the closet and searched for this evening's clothes. Behind her, over the rattle of hangers, she heard him.

"I never can figure out why a wife of Ben's has to work. He certainly makes enough . . . the fees I pay him . . . she ought to be home having children. Only one kid! And that one not even his."

She pulled her dress over her head. Her voice came out muffled.

"Oh, I'm tired! I hate shopping. Do we really have to go out tonight? All the way back to the city?"

"All you have to do is move from the seat in the car to a seat at a table. What's so hard about that?"

"These charity dinners. We go to so many of them."

Donal enjoyed them. He could sit patiently through all the boring speeches in anticipation of the moment when his name, included in a list of distinguished long-time benefactors, would be called out and he would rise to acknowledge with a slight bow, a self-deprecating smile, the recognition of his gift. Naturally, he knew that he was only tolerated there because of his gift. He laughed about that.

"Wear your diamond earrings," he said now. "The drops, not the studs."

"They're much too formal. People are never that dressy at this dinner."

"I know, but I don't care. That prissy snob Marian will be there and I want her to see the earrings."

Surprised at such childishness, which was not at all like him, Meg came to the defense of Marian, not so much for the sake of Marian—who really was, to tell the truth, more than a little "prissy"—as for the sake of Paul.

"She's not really a snob. She's just quiet and unhappy."

"What's she got to be unhappy about? She lives on the fat of the land."

"That's not all there is."

"No? Try living on the lean and you'll find out."

Meg was silent. Peeling her stockings off, she examined the small cluster of thin, blue-red veins on the side of one knee. The twins had done that.

"On the other hand," Donal said, "it may be pretty tough having to live with Paul."

"With Paul? Why, any woman would give her eyeteeth for him!"

"You think so? I had a run-in with him this morning. Oh, he's quite the gentleman, all right, but no more than I am. I know how to play that game too. I play all the games. He hates my guts and, I don't mind telling you, I hate his."

Meg was aghast. "You had a fight with Paul?"

"Well, we didn't come to fisticuffs, but I had a proposition, a perfectly decent proposition that anybody'd jump at, an acquisition—it's too complicated to explain—exchanging stocks in one company for another. Leah's kid would have made a bundle, and he turned it down." Donal stood up and leaned his elbow on the mantelpiece. "Pure and holy! Wouldn't touch it because it's weaponry, might be used in another war, he says. Bah! Never mind, I'll get there without him. Donal Powers will get along without Paul Werner. Pure and holy. Who does he think he is?"

"I don't think he thinks he's anybody."

"That shows what you know. The man's loaded with conceit."

"Never!" Meg said hotly. "I've known Paul all my life. You'll go far to see anyone as—as respected, as—"

"You're taking his side? I'm your husband! Remember?"

"I'm not taking sides. I only said that he's respected."

"And I'm not?"

"I didn't say that."

"You meant it. You think I don't know what passes through your mind? I read you like a book, Meg. All right, I sell liquor! Booze! I sell to the highest in the land. Your mother's stuffy D.A.R. ladies—"

"Leave my mother out, please." There was anger in her, not because of her mother or even because of Paul. She was just— angry.

Donal chuckled. "I'm laughing. Those proper biddies, with their bootlegger! Wouldn't invite me to dinner in their homes —not that I want to go, Lord, no—but I've seen them tipple at the clubs, the proper biddies."

"I don't see anything so funny," Meg said stiffly.

He stopped laughing, tilted his head and narrowed his eyes, examining her. "The trouble with you is you have no sense of humor."

"I won't deny that. It's a lack. They left it out when they made me. But the trouble with you is—" And she regarded him; still he stood, resting an elbow on the mantel, so nonchalant, so sure of himself. He must have dealt with Paul and been infuriated because for once it hadn't worked. "The trouble with you is, you always have to have your own way. Everything *your* way."

Donal blinked and opened his eyes wide in a show of amazement. "I don't believe what I'm hearing. *My* way? Name one thing you've ever wanted that you didn't get! A house? You pick it. A week in Bermuda? We go. Anything you want and you know it."

"It's what I don't want," she said, very low. "But I get it anyway."

"Oh," he said.

"Yes, 'oh.' You know what I mean. I've told you often enough."

"Birth control again. We're back to that."

She lifted her chin. "Yes. Birth control."

"And I've told you often enough, no." He took a step toward her. "I told you when I married you that I wanted a large family. You can't say you weren't told."

"How large is large? We have four children and I adore them, but they're enough. How many do you want anyway?"

"As many as come."

She sneered. "As many as the Lord sends?"

"If you want to put it that way."

"You don't believe that, Donal. You're not a believer."

"Different people have different beliefs. Principles. And one of mine is, no birth control. Except rhythm."

"You don't even adhere to that. You take me whenever you want me."

"Yes, and you love it, too."

"Do you want me to go on having children until I drop?"

"You won't drop. You're healthy as a horse." He took her by the shoulders. His palms, clasping the rounded flesh, were hot.

"Didn't they wear this kind of chemise at the Folies-Bergère, except that theirs were black? Black lace, weren't they?" and as she refused to answer, "weren't they?"

"I don't remember. Leave me alone."

"Yes, you do. You remember everything. When we went back to the hotel, in our room, when we—"

Her voice shook, quavering. "Leave me alone."

Backed up, pressed against the footboard of the bed, she was losing her balance. With one hand she braced herself, while the other, made into a fist, struck Donal's chest.

"Strong. Strong. Go on, fight me. I love it when you fight me."

She was on the edge of tears. "Donal, no, I'm angry. Can't you see how angry I am?"

He slid the frail silk straps down over her arms; the soft loose garment dropped to the floor. Tipping her lightly off balance, he pushed her down on the bed, onto the quilt that lay folded at its foot. He was laughing, chuckling into her shoulder.

"Come on now, Meg, you're not angry. You can't ever stay angry at me."

She struggled. "I can, I can."

He was still laughing. "But I know what to do. I always know, don't I?"

The struggle was silly. It was like trying to push aside a rock.

"Please, please not now."

"Yes, now." The laughter ceased. "Why, most certainly now. Little Meg, that's it. Yes, little Meg."

"You loved it . . ." she heard him whisper, felt the slither of the quilt when he laid it over her and tucked it gently on her feet. "Take a nap. There's time. I'm going in to the boys."

Her mind was wide awake. Again, he had proved how he could do what he wanted with her. Dammit! he could. And she frowned with effort, trying to trace back to the start, on the very first day at Leah's house. . . . They had all been fussing over Dan, where he sat in the big wing chair, and she had been standing aside in the curve of the piano, and Donal had gone straight over to her. *I didn't get your name, he'd said. That's a beautiful color for a cold day. You look like a Christmas rose.* She'd been so ignorant then, a Victorian holdover. Too ignorant to know what it was that she wanted of him. But he had known.

He knew everything about her. Perhaps it was supposed to be like that. The man led and the woman, secure in his care, followed. When you looked around at the world, it seemed to be the way things were.

Five years, she thought, and was back in her room at college, dreaming out of the window, seeing beyond the colors of the campus, sky, trees, or umbrellas glistening in the rain, into a future that was in some ways what it had turned out to be, and in some ways inevitably not. So how could one foresee?

Voices floated from downstairs. Donal was playing with the boys. He would have taken up the Oriental runner in the long hall and they would be playing ninepins, a baby version that he had bought them.

He led two separate lives. He never talked about his business, but things filtered through the screen of secrecy all the same. There were telephone conversations, overheard from an adjoining room. Things were said when colleagues came with papers or messages. When there was a crisis, she knew of it, as when a convoy of trucks had been ambushed on the road. She knew, and kept the knowledge to herself, that numbered accounts had been opened in Switzerland—as they were for many so-called respectable businesses. But the amount of money, the sheer ease and flow of it, astounded her, even though in her father's house she had been accustomed to the best of everything. Yet her parents, her mother especially, had paid attention to the prices of things and had kept careful checkbooks. Never had there been so much cash lying freely in a man's pocket.

Guilt beset her. This bed in which she lay, this house and the help who kept it, the clothes she had bought this afternoon, all came to her in a way she did not want to think about.

Then she rationalized: Donal wasn't harming anybody. . . . True, he wasn't out working for causes, as were Dan and Hennie. He affected scorn for their kind of "do-gooders." "All talk," he would say, "beating the air and getting no place." But with his charities, not just the public ones that gave him a touch of grudging prestige, but the private gifts out of his generous pocket, was he not in a way a do-gooder himself?

Suddenly she remembered Paul. She would have to do something about him and Donal. She couldn't lose Paul. . . .

Donal was coming down the hall. She got up quickly and switched on the light at the dressing table. The Cartier box with the earrings lay there; he had taken them out of the safe for her. They were magnificent, splendid as sun on dew, she thought, letting them lie on her palm. She leaned toward the mirror and fastened one in her ears. Her face was flushed, not weary as it had looked in Leah's mirror. That was what love-making did. She fastened the other earring. They swung half-way down her neck, and were sensational, and all wrong for the occasion. But he had ordered her to wear them.

Seven

Early in the spring of the year 1929, Paul's father died. Since the death of his wife, the elder Werner had faded and seemed actually to grow smaller. Paul wondered whether his parents had had a deeper attachment to each other than he had supposed. But such analysis was superfluous; it was enough to regret that one had not done more, said more, or left some things unsaid. That was always true after a death, no matter how tranquil the relationship had been. These were his thoughts during one of those days on which the possessions of the dead must be sorted and disposed of.

Two shelves in a back hall closet were piled with photographs. Here they were, the whole family, having an outing at Uncle Alfie's place sometime before the war. The women were sitting on the porch steps and the men were standing behind them. Here was a somewhat thinner Alfie, beaming as usual. Here was his father, sedately buttoned up in a city suit, and here he was himself, wearing his Yale blazer. Right in front of him sat Marian; apparently his mother had invited her for the weekend, laying her plans even then when Marian was barely sixteen.

And holding the browning snapshot to the light, he examined the face he had forgotten, the face of Marian in early youth. Proud and cool she was; could he have foreseen the dry, neutered woman she had become, fussing over a stain on her white kid gloves?

She called to him now. "Paul, come help me with these things, they're heavy."

He followed her voice into his father's dressing room, where she was emptying another closet.

"All these boxes! We'll just have to call someone—Paul!"

For he had stopped still and was staring at a picture on the farther wall.

She looked over his shoulder. "Duval. That's valuable, isn't it?"

"Yes, fairly so."

It was a watercolor of a little girl with huge eyes. She was sitting with a copybook on her lap, and the tip of a pencil in her mouth. "The Multiplication Tables," he read on the label. A sentimental title. A sentimental piece. But the eyes . . . They were the eyes he had memorized.

Is this how you look now, Iris?

"Why on earth are you staring like that, Paul?"

"I'm not staring, just looking."

"But you look shocked, as if you had recognized somebody."

"I was only thinking, it's odd that I never saw it before. Father must have just hidden it here to fill a space between the windows." He managed to laugh. "Somebody must have given it to him. He'd never have bought it. One thing my parents didn't have was any taste for art."

"I liked your parents," Marian said. She paused, and when

he did not reply, added with a certain wistfulness, "Funny . . . they liked me, too."

"Why funny?" he said lightly. "Why shouldn't they? You're a likable person."

"Funny because you don't like me the way you once did, and they still did up to the end."

He felt a pain around his heart. A sad conversation loomed, one that would lead nowhere.

"I don't know why you say that, Marian."

"You do know. Don't you think it's time we talked?"

"What about?" he said, staying calm.

"About ourselves. I'm not attractive to you anymore."

Her neck, poked forward, brought to his mind the sudden image of a goose's neck; the image was pathetic. He flinched from it in shame. Her mouth twisted. *Lord, don't let her cry. Poor soul, don't let her cry.*

"That's silly," he said gently. And repeated, "I don't know why you say that."

"Because . . . you haven't made love to me." She turned her face away and he saw what humiliation these words had cost her.

For a few seconds he didn't know how to answer. He made quick calculations: two months maybe, or more. Now that the firm had a branch in Chicago, he was there almost every month. Often there were one or two casual women—never yet a repeat of Ilsa, he thought ruefully—but eager and decent women nevertheless, who needed, as he did, whatever was missing in their lives. He certainly wasn't taking anything away from Marian that she wanted, except not to feel humiliated.

"You don't really care about it that much," he said, still gently.

"But you must," she said. "It's different for men, I know."

Ignorance! A most revealing, pitiable ignorance! And yet there must be millions of women like her.

"Come, sit down," he said, taking her by the arm. "We've done enough for today." He led her into the living room. "You see," he said, "a man doesn't always need what you may think. It's not anything to do with you. I work hard and I'm getting older."

Getting older! And he not yet forty! If she could understand the longings in him, she would know how absurd a remark *that* was. Older!

She smiled weakly. "Perhaps I'm too sensitive. I guess I am. I've been reading things . . . there's so much being written. Perhaps I'm neurotic, I sometimes think I am. Do you think I'm neurotic, Paul?"

"I think you shouldn't think so much about yourself." He patted her hand. "As long as you're happy. You've a busy life." He was spewing words without meaning; it was like pouring a soothing syrup. "All your charities, and you've so many friends."

"You don't even like my friends."

She was reminding him, he knew, of the bitter argument they'd had a while ago, one of the very few really angry arguments they'd ever had. As usual, she had wanted him to go to Florida for a month, this time with a group of friends, and he had refused to go. The friends were agreeable people, but not the kind with whom he cared to spend a whole month. They'd be playing cards all day and, again as usual, would consider him clearly unsociable because he wouldn't. So there had been an argument, and he had said things he was later sorry about. He had said that her friends were dull and they bored him, and he couldn't stand their cold, frozen faces. He remembered exactly what he had said.

"I do like some of them, most of them," he told her now. "But anyway, that's not the point. You have a right to like whom you like, and I have the same. We needn't argue about it."

"There's a little house in Palm Beach on the ocean that I could buy. I'd love it and I can afford it," Marian said.

"You said 'I.' You don't mean 'we'?"

"Well, you don't want to go."

"That doesn't matter. I can still buy the house for you."

"Would you really do that?"

"I would buy you anything you want, Marian."

"You *are* good to me, Paul." Her eyes were wet. "You won't mind my going down by myself, then?"

"No. I guess I can manage to take a little time off for a winter visit, too."

She was silent. The silence hummed in the dead room, with sheets flung over the chairs and dust already gathered on the tabletops. Then she asked him surprisingly, "Are you unhappy, Paul? I sometimes think, I don't know why, that you're not a happy man."

"No," he said. "Of course I'm not unhappy. I'm a very lucky man. I think we're both lucky."

"But things do turn out so differently from what one expects when one is sixteen or twenty-one."

"Yes," he said, persisting in cheerfulness, "and sometimes they turn out a lot better."

She was making an effort to match his smile. For an instant, standing there in the dimming afternoon, he saw her face under the bridal veil and her face on the hospital bed after that dreadful surgery. He thought, you suffer, and I want to be kind to you, and I will be kind to you, but we are strangers.

He put his arm around her shoulders and kissed her cheek. "Come, dear. This is enough for today. Let's lock up and go home."

Later that evening, he sat up alone smoking his pipe, watching the smoke rise and disappear. It had been a melancholy day, sorting his father's things, having the conversation with Marian, and finding that picture.

Iris. It was not a name one heard very often, but it was

pretty enough. He wondered why Anna had chosen it. It made him think of a tall woman dressed in lavender, with an Edwardian sway and slenderness, and a dark, sleek head.

Iris.

He went to bed and saw the name hovering in the air above him. He knew nothing about her, having kept his promise and stayed away. But she was his. His. Had he no rights at all?

Turning in the wide bed, his leg brushed Marian's. Peacefully asleep now, she was unaware of the heat and turmoil on his side of the bed.

I cannot endure this another day. I have to find out and damn the consequences.

He waited in the morning until half past nine, an hour when surely a man would have left his house for work. Pausing for a minute with a heart that leapt around in his chest, he finally took the receiver off the hook.

"Number, please," the operator said.

He heard the telephone ring. He imagined the room in which it rang. A hall, probably. Those West Side apartments had large square foyers, as big as a room. Most people kept the telephone on a table there. The table would have a lamp; a pinkish light would shine through a pleated silk shade; a shelf under the table would hold the telephone book; there would be Oriental scatter rugs on the floor with spaces in between, so that a woman's heels would move without a sound over the rugs and click on the bare floor in the spaces. She would be in the library, for Anna, with her love of books, would by now have collected enough of them to fill some library shelves.

Or maybe the child would answer? All this went through Paul's head in the few seconds it took for the receiver to be lifted at the other end.

"Hello?" The voice was hers.

His lips moved without making a sound.

"Hello? Who is it?" Questioning, a trifle impatient.

"Anna," he said.

"Oh!"

"I had to talk to you."

"Oh," she whispered, "you promised me. What if—if someone else had answered the phone, or was in the room now? You promised."

"I know. I'm sorry. I won't do it again. But I had to, this time."

She said anxiously, "Why? Is anything wrong? You're not ill?"

"No. But terribly troubled. Anna, I want to see the child."

"Oh, my God! What are you saying?"

"I'm saying that she's nine years old and I don't know her." He forced himself to speak very quietly, very reasonably. "I don't know one thing about her, and it's not fair to me, Anna. It's cruel."

He heard her sigh. "My heart's broken for you. But how can it be any different?"

"In a different world where we might all be honest with each other, we would tell the truth. I could claim my own daughter and provide for her."

"Oh, my dear, that's an impossible world! A fairy tale. What's the use of talking about it?"

"We come back to that word again. It seems as if everything that involves you and me has always been impossible, as if there were some conspiracy against us."

"That's not sensible," she said gently.

"Sensible be damned! Listen, I want to see Iris. I want to talk to her. You owe it to me and I'm going to insist on it."

"Paul! Are you crazy? Do you want to destroy the child? What is she to think?"

"What, do you really think I would destroy either one of you? I can't believe you could have such a thought! All I'm asking for is a casual meeting. She'll have no idea who I am."

"But she'll tell her father. She tells him everything, including what she had for lunch. And you know he's always had vague suspicions about you and me. I don't have to tell you again, do I?"

"Listen here, we'll meet accidentally, you'll report it all quite honestly at home. How could anyone object to that? Take Iris to Schrafft's or some such place for lunch next Saturday. Don't you ever do that?"

"Not often."

"But you could once, couldn't you?" Paul insisted.

"I suppose so," she said fearfully.

"All right, then. You'll come in and I'll already be there. I'll walk up to you, greet you with great surprise, and insist that you let me buy your lunch. It will be all my doing, all perfectly natural and open."

She didn't answer.

He said desperately, "It will be completely innocent! And Iris can tell it all at home just like that. Is it too much to ask for an hour in an ice-cream parlor so that my daughter can be a little more to me than a name and a face in an old photo? Please, Anna. Please."

"Oh, my God," she said. "It'll be so hard to sit there with the two of you." There was a long silence.

"Hello?" he said. "Are you there?"

"I'm here, Paul. I'm here. . . . All right, I'll do it. Just once. I see that I must."

His heart was racing. Surely under her graceful composure, hers must be too.

"This is Iris," she said, and to the child, "Mr. Werner is an old friend. I knew him before you were born."

The child was staring up at Paul. She had a small, peaked, earnest face, an old face, not a pretty one, except for the dark and curiously prominent eyes. He smiled and was given a shy smile in return. Something struck him, something familiar in the face: wide cheekbones and a conspicuous cleft in the chin.

Also, the startling, outsized eyes, like the ones in the picture the other day. . . . And like his mother's. He was looking at his mother's face!

She was dressed the way children were dressed in London, in tweed with a velvet collar. Anna's coat was a violet woolen, thick and soft as cashmere; she wore a fur hat and gold in her ears. Her husband was evidently faring well in the building boom. He didn't want to be reminded of the husband. All this passed through Paul's head in the first few seconds.

They found a table and took their coats off. Anna's dress was dusty pink. She removed her hat, saying that it felt too hot, and revealed what he had been waiting for, the hair with the myriad reds of grained mahogany. She no longer wore it as long as he remembered it, but it was still massed, curving below her cheeks.

"You broke a rule," he said lightly. Someone had to open the conversation. "Redheads are never supposed to wear pink, are they?"

"On the contrary, they should. A woman taught me that in Paris, where Joseph bought me an evening dress, a pink one."

Joseph again . . .

It was necessary to keep up a dialogue. No, they weren't building houses anymore like the old ones off Central Park West, those fine old brownstones. Yes, the election had been tense with a Catholic running for president. Yes, things looked bad in Germany; Paul's cousin had written about the National Socialists, who were gaining every year.

He was too conscious of the passing minutes. This was an occasion that would not recur, he knew that. And how much could one prolong the eating of a sandwich and a dish of ice cream? And he was aware, while talking about inconsequential things, that Iris was searching him. She would remember every word. He must be very careful to let nothing slip.

Suddenly she spoke. "Do you know my father, Mr. Werner?"

"I think," Paul said quietly, "I saw him once. A long time ago, that was."

The workman in the cap, going down through the basement entrance, the servants' entrance. Anna murmuring an embarrassed introduction. The cap being tipped.

Paul took a long drink of water, while Anna fumbled in her pocketbook. They had run out of small talk.

"Tell me about your school," he ventured, adding fatuously, "I have a young cousin, a little older than you. He likes to come to me with his school problems, what courses to take, things like that."

The girl gave a small shrug, a delicate gesture. "I don't really have any problems except with math. Daddy has to help me with it. He never even went to college, but he can figure almost anything right in his head."

"Very few of us are perfect in everything, so I wouldn't worry about the math." Another fatuous remark, when what he wanted to say was: Let me look at you, stare at you, take your features apart one by one. Let me ask you whether you're ever very unhappy and why. Tell me what you want to do when you grow up. Tell me whether there's anything you want very badly and let me give it to you. Let me tell you who you are.

Anna had recovered herself. "Iris is a very good student, and a good pianist. She works hard. You may be hearing her at a concert someday." And she gave the girl a fond look.

"No, Mama, you don't understand," Iris said impatiently. "I'll never be good enough for that. I keep telling you, but you and Daddy keep saying it and it's really silly."

She has a sharp little tongue when she wants to, Paul thought. Well, good. Stand up for yourself. And he asked, "How do you know you won't be good enough, Iris?"

"Because I can tell. I'll probably be just a piano teacher."

"Do you feel bad about that?"

Again there came that delicate shrug. "Well, anyone would

like to be famous, but I know I won't be, so I don't think about it."

What extraordinary judgment for a nine-year-old! "Very well put," Paul said. "It's not always easy to see oneself. In fact, I'm not sure that I've done it yet."

Iris laughed, showing the braces on her teeth. She was going to be an interesting personality. In a vague way, she reminded Paul of Meg at the same age; although there was no physical resemblance between Meg's big-boned awkwardness and this girl's thin, dark fragility, there was the same mixture of childish shyness and adult perception.

When she had scraped up the last of the ice cream, Iris went to the ladies' room.

"How sweet she is," Paul said as soon as she was out of hearing.

"She doesn't think so. She's convinced that she's homely."

"You must do something about that."

"Well, we do. But you must admit she's not a beauty."

"She'll be distinguished-looking when she's older."

"She's much too serious."

"Does she have many friends? Tell me everything, quickly before she comes back. Is she healthy? She looks pale."

"She's healthy. A nervous type of child, but perfectly well. As for paleness—well, you aren't exactly rosy, are you?"

He laughed. "Oh, Anna, this is the most wonderful thing, in spite of all! Our child . . . Tell me, does she love you very much? It's not every girl who has a mother like you."

"We have no big troubles. But she's closer to Joseph. He adores her. She's the heart of his heart, he says."

Of course. Fathers and daughters. That's the way it is, Paul. Fathers and daughters.

Anna cried out, "I wonder sometimes whether my feelings ever come through to her. Because when I look at her, oh, I try to put the past away and act as if she were—"

"His and yours," Paul said steadily.

"Oh, I try. But now that I've seen you together, it will be harder."

"I had to do this, Anna. You're never out of my mind. Don't you understand that, my darling?"

He could barely hear her answer. "It was a mistake."

"Day and night, you're with me. You spoiled me for other women, charming women. . . . There's only you."

Her head was bent and her eyes cast down so that her eyelashes lay on her cheeks. He had forgotten how thick they were and tipped in gold. He remembered, though, the infinitesimal bump on the bridge of her nose, which so offended her, and how once she had taken his hand and made him feel it. And he remembered walking together in the winter, and how he had been always aware of her coat, a smart, cheap gray wool not nearly warm enough. He had wanted to give her things, but had not dared to; in his mind he had dressed her in velvet and put diamonds on her fingers. Now he saw that she did wear a diamond, a large one, emerald-cut, the gift of the man who lay beside her and enjoyed her body. White as milk, her flesh . . .

How little he knew about her anymore!

"Years," he said. "Time spins away. Does it seem long to you or short?"

"Both, depending on the way I feel that day."

"I think of you as my wife, my real wife, my child's mother. You should be with me, really with me, all the time. You know that, don't you?"

"Darling Paul, don't. It's too late."

Hopelessness lay on him like a heavy hand. His fists, lying on the table, were clenched. "Is this the way it's to be for us forever?"

When she turned her face up to him, her collar spread open; her bare throat asked for pity. "Oh, don't, I'll start to cry. For God's sake, don't do this to me."

"All right. I'll be good."

"You promised. Don't make it harder."

They sat for a moment in silence, making an island of somber quiet in a sea of clatter and chatter.

"There you are, Iris. Ready? Mr. Werner has to go back to work." Anna spoke blithely. "We must tell Daddy what a nice time we had."

He marveled: How does she do it? Lies, lies . . . She lives with a lie and is cheerful, or has to pretend to be. Where does the courage come from?

They shook hands. Thanks were spoken, polite and casual thanks. And he watched them walk away, the tall, graceful woman and the girl who would soon be as tall as her mother. He watched them as far as he could see, until the crowds on the street absorbed and hid them, these two whom he loved, who were his, who were part of him and would be as long as they all remained on earth together.

He went back downtown to the office and closed the door. Miss Briggs had come in, although it was Saturday, to clear up a backlog. She had left a pile of papers on his desk for his signature. He read them without understanding what he read, and gave up, to sit and stare and think.

So it had happened, and only God knew whether he would ever see them again. Just across the park they lived, a bird's short flight from where he lived. There Anna did her daily chores, there Iris went to school. And he knew, quite clearly he knew, that their painful presence so near and so far was a fact he would have to accept, exactly as if he had been born lame or born the king of England.

But in another way, it was not a fact; it was a debt. He hadn't married her, and there lay the wrong. There lay the lifelong debt on which the interest would be forever owing. Out of his memory, his heart and soul, he would have to pay. It was a fixed charge on his life and there was no use struggling against it because it would always be there, coming due again and again and again.

Miss Briggs tapped on the door. "I'm sorry to disturb you, but there's an urgent call from London."

"Put it through," he replied.

Stocks and bonds, debentures, and loans and gold. The whole lot was worth little more in the sum of things than a heap of dust.

He picked up the transatlantic call.

Later, much later, he went home. He was in no hurry, for it was Marian's turn to have her card club, and he had no wish to greet the women today. Instead he left the subway and walked the rest of the way through the park. It came to him that if it hadn't been for Central Park, the city would often have been unbearable. What tensions had he not walked off, or tried to walk off, in the park!

Children were still sailing their boats and still circling the Ramble on their two-wheeled skates. A tiny girl, pushing a doll carriage, sang to her doll. He stopped for a moment and tried to recall the voice of Iris, but the sound had vanished. For so long he had wanted a son! He had even sometimes pretended when they walked together that Hank was his boy. Now it seemed to him that there was nothing to compare with having a daughter, buying dresses and books for her, taking her to Europe maybe, or out west, through the Rockies . . .

The card tables had already been put away, the women were long gone, and Marian was sitting by herself.

"Where on earth have you been all afternoon?" she asked.

"I had to see a client at the office."

"It's a shame that people can't leave you alone on a Saturday afternoon. It really is." Marian's mouth had her familiar, set look of patience. "You work much too hard. Between the bank and all your charities, you're hardly ever home."

"But I don't mind. I like what I do."

"I was hoping you'd be here to say hello to my friends."

"I'm sure they didn't mind, Marian."

"Well, I minded. You said you'd be home early."

She was in one of her moods. To be fair, they came seldom. He supposed she might be having another miserable sinus attack.

He asked mildly, "Have you got a headache?"

"As a matter of fact, I have. And one reason is, I don't get enough sleep. You get up so early, and then I can't fall back."

"I'm sorry. I do try to be quiet."

"Would you mind—now don't take this the wrong way, Paul—but I've been thinking, maybe if we had twin beds, it would be better. You see, it isn't so much that you make noise, it's that I feel you getting out of the bed, and that wakes me up. Would you care?"

He could have answered: Why should I care? But he said only, "Not at all, if it will make you rest better."

"You mean you don't care at all?" There were tears in her voice.

"Marian, I want to please you. If you can sleep better—"

"Another man would be disappointed, to say the least, that his wife wanted to move out of his bed."

"And if I were disappointed, what would you do?"

"Why, I would just give up the idea."

"But wouldn't that be foolish, when it's a matter of your getting the proper rest at night?"

She did not answer, and he went on, speaking quietly and reasonably. "Marian, if I said no, I will not allow you to change the bed, you would say that I didn't care about your health. I've said yes, change the bed, and you accuse me too."

She stood up and went to the window. Something was roiling within her. Maybe she wanted him to be possessive and jealous, to give the appearance, at least, of that miraculous closeness we call love. Once, very briefly, he had thought they had it. He remembered that summer when they were very young, when he had been in Europe on business for his father, and had written to her from London and Paris, missing her and wishing that she were there with him. That had been before they were married.

That had been before Anna.

She turned suddenly about. "If only you loved me!" she cried.

"I do love you, Marian. Why do you say these things? I do love you."

And in his way, he did. He would do anything for her, to guard and keep her, as he would for any of the women in his family, for Hennie or for Meg, and as he had done for his mother.

The inverted V, as her eyebrows drew together, looked painful. She was twisting her wedding ring.

"Sometimes I feel, I think, I'm useless. Am I useless, Paul?"

This humble appeal, coming from Marian, was especially distressing because it was so at odds with the patrician hauteur of her face. Nature's accident, it was.

"Oh," he said, "whatever, whatever could have put such a thought into your head? I suppose it's because we have no children, and some silly women have set you thinking that there's no other purpose in life. Is that it?"

She cast her eyes down. "In a way. Maybe."

"Well, they're abysmally stupid! Is a woman no more than a fertile womb?"

She gave a weak smile.

"You're a valuable citizen in the city. When I think of the things you do for the community! Useless! I defy anyone to say that to me about you—including you. Don't you dare," he threatened in mock indignation, "don't you dare talk like that about yourself, do you hear?"

The smile grew a bit stronger. And he beheld her: an immaculate woman, not unpleasing, with a formal appearance even in her underwear. Such a good, well-meaning woman! And he felt a piercing pity because he could give her no more than he had given, because of the wrong he had done when he married her. Yet if he had not married her, that would have wronged her too. Round and round.

"You know," he said, "we really are being very silly about this business. All because you asked for twin beds and I said yes."

She said doubtfully, "Maybe you're right . . . I suppose I do make mountains out of molehills sometimes, don't I?"

"Don't we all? Come, aren't we invited somewhere to dinner?"

"To the Foxes'. They're having a few people in."

"Well, that's nice." He heard how amiable he sounded. "I always enjoy them," and added, "I hope it's early. I didn't eat much lunch."

"I'll get you a sandwich to hold you." She smiled, quite brightly. "I'm sorry. It was just my beastly headache."

Battering at clouds, that's what it was, for neither one had any real grievance against the other. They were such a decent, civilized pair! They would have a pleasant dinner that evening with their friends, talk about them on the way home, and go to sleep.

Tomorrow would be another day.

Eight

Today was a good kind of day, traveling around with Ben in the new Packard coupe with a rumble seat, having lunch, then stopping for an ice-cream sundae at a place on Ben's route and ending with a night baseball game. Hank had felt cooped up all winter in school; now in this first bright week of summer vacation, he was ready to celebrate.

It was coming close to noon by the time they crossed to the New Jersey side of the river.

"Hungry?" Ben inquired.

"Yup."

Ben grinned. "I shouldn't ask. You've got two hollow legs."

It was true. The older he got, the hungrier he got.

"Growing like a weed," Ben said, glancing at him with approval. "Thirteen years old and tall as I am. You're going to be like Grandpa Dan."

Well, Hank knew that. He probably heard it five times a week.

"Where are we going to eat?"

"Tony's. Suit you all right?"

"Suits me fine." His mouth was already watering with the taste of meatballs or clams oregano or spaghetti carbonara, and after that a couple of desserts.

Tony's was across the street from the courthouse. The food was the best ever. Lawyers and judges, flashy, diamond-fingered politicians and union bosses gathered there to transact their various affairs.

The place really belonged not to jovial, swarthy Tony but to Donal Powers. Hank, knowing that, also knew enough not to mention it.

They were early. The tables, covered with clean white cloths, were set and ready for the lunch crowd with baskets of breadsticks and a container of grated Parmesan cheese in the center of each. A garlic-scented breeze blew out whenever the kitchen door swung open. Ben greeted Tony and took a table in the rear.

"Bring us a platter of antipasto for starters, Tony. What'll it be today, Hank?"

"Spaghetti with clam sauce and a Coke."

"Two Cokes," Ben said.

Whisky and wine were for the bosses in the back room at night, not now in broad daylight, in full view of the street across from City Hall.

The clam sauce was rich and smooth. They both ate steadily without much talking, pausing only to sop up the sauce with the good bread. Ben winked at Hank.

"No women around, so we don't have to make conversation. Just eat."

Hank laughed. They always teased his mother, making bets that she couldn't keep still for five minutes straight. Sometimes she won, but you could see it was a painful effort for her.

"Mind moving over here for a minute?" Tony beckoned to

Ben. "You don't mind, Hank; just a little private conversation. Business."

Ben took his plate and sat down two tables away. The two men spoke in low tones with their backs to Hank; nevertheless, he was able to catch a phrase now and then.

". . . padlocked last week . . . no, can't prove who, but the boys have an idea . . . sure, we lost two days . . . the prosecutor."

This was no unusual occurrence. Hank had overheard such accounts before and, anyway, in the newspapers he read about them everyday. Everybody knew that mix-ups occurred. Somebody failed to pay somebody, and the place was closed up, most often for only a couple of days.

Hank wasn't shocked. Prohibition was a farce. Even Grandpa Dan, whose respect for the law was religious, said that it was, that it wouldn't last, that taking a drink of liquor was no sin—although he himself drank none—and that rather than to go about locking up restaurants, the authorities might better go about locking up factories where underpaid men were sweated like slaves.

The dialogue between Tony and Ben was lasting too long. The restaurant began to fill, men came up to Ben, and still he talked, while Hank sat alone waiting. Bored with the wait, he ordered a second dessert. You couldn't get a coconut cream pie like Tony's anywhere else in the world, he guessed. He ordered a third piece and, although he was feeling too full, kept raising the fork, more slowly now, not wanting to waste a bite, while musing on a fly that had buried itself in the sugarbowl. Then he overheard more pieces of Ben's conversation.

"I'm a little worried. Not too much."

He guessed it must have something to do with the income tax, not Ben's own, but Donal's tax. He wasn't sure when he had heard them, but somehow or other, he could recall some pieces of talk during the weeks just past, something about

Internal Revenue and going to court and Ben being the accountant.

Then he gagged. The last forkful of pie had stuck somewhere in the back of his throat and wouldn't go down; his stomach lurched; cold perspiration wet his forehead and his palms; he stood up and rushed to the men's room, making a clatter of overturned chairs as he ran.

Ben came up behind where he stood vomiting into the toilet. Ben held his straining head, while the lunch came up, a mess of clam sauce, pasta, meat, and coconut cream pie. It was agony. His knees buckled. When he was finished, too weak to stand, he braced himself against the door of the cubicle and trembled.

"Whew!" Ben said. "How much did you eat, for Christ's sake? You puked up enough for a horse."

"I don't know. Three pieces of pie," Hank mumbled. "It came on me all of a sudden."

"Shouldn't wonder. Here, rinse your mouth and go lie down. You look green."

Tony stuck his head in at the door. "Kid sick?"

"Ate too much. Tell you what, I've got to run across to the courthouse for a couple of minutes. Can he lie down in the office? By the time I get back, he'll be okay—now that he's puked it all up."

"Sure. Come on back here, Hank."

Hank had never been in the office. He'd only had quick glimpses of it when the heavy steel door opened to let somebody in or out. In his misery now, as he followed Tony, he had an impression of a chilly place, concrete and bare, with a large battered desk, a safe, and a few wooden kitchen chairs. Across the room in the rear, a curtain hung on a rod. Tony pushed it aside to reveal a cot with a blanket folded at the foot.

"Here, lie down, kid," he said, covered Hank with the blanket, and drew the curtain.

The blanket was thick and warm enough to stop the shivering. He lay quite still, feeling the warmth. Ahead and above, close to the ceiling, were two small windows with strong bars. It was like being in a cell, except for the curtain that separated the dim little space from the rest of the room. He wondered why the windows were barred. He began to feel eased, now that his stomach had been relieved. With ease came embarrassment over the mess he had made. He was thankful he hadn't got any on his clothes, otherwise he would have had to go home and change; no, Ben would just have gone down the street and bought him some clothes . . . he was sleepy . . . he closed his eyes . . .

When he opened them, he heard voices from the other side of the curtain. One was Tony's.

"Nah, the kid's asleep. He got sick. Wouldn't know what we're talking about anyway. Just a kid."

"Okay. If you say so."

Then a third voice. "So, I was telling you, the big guy's worried."

"Bad as that?" Tony sounded surprised.

"Yeah. Why not?"

"I didn't figure he would be."

There was a long pause. A chair scraped on the concrete, making a cold vibration down Hank's spine. Someone struck a match.

"Ben worries him."

"You're kidding. Ben does?"

"Yeah. He'll be subpoenaed."

"So?" That was Tony again. "What about it?"

"Don't be a jerk." The voice was exasperated. "He won't know how to handle it, that's what about it."

"Ben can handle anything. Why do you think the big guy's kept him around, coddled like a baby?"

"Because he's smart with figures, that's all. Can keep them in his head. But he's liable to scare on the stand."

Hank wanted to let them hear his indignation. Ben scared? What are you talking about? Ben's not afraid of anybody! But he kept still. They would be very angry if they knew he wasn't asleep.

One of the men, not Tony, inquired now, "What's his program today?"

"The usual Wednesday route."

"He's over at the courthouse now. Be back any minute," Tony said. "You see the big guy this morning?"

The third man said quickly, "What's it your business? What do you need to know for?"

"Oh, nothing, nothing," Tony apologized. "Only asked."

"So don't ask. Just keep the spaghetti coming and keep your mouth shut."

"Of course, of course," Tony said.

Chairs scraped. They were leaving.

"Unlock the door. See you around."

The door closed, its weight making a muffled thud, and then the lock clicked.

Hank closed his eyes. What was all that about? he wondered. All that talk about the big guy. What big guy?

When the curtain was drawn back, the rings clinked so that he could pretend to have just been awakened. He opened his eyes, yawned widely and stretched.

"I guess I slept," he said, smiling up at Tony.

"I guess you did. Feeling better?"

"All right now, thanks. It was awful, though."

"Well, don't overdo the pie next time. Come on out and wait for your dad."

Ben was just coming in. "Hank! Feeling okay again, are you? Sure, you look like yourself. Okay, I just have to make one phone call and then we'll be off. It's a great day out."

Ben sat down at the desk to use the telephone. He had a hat on, pushed far back on his head, and his forehead was sweating. Hank noticed things like that. He watched people.

"Donal? Okay, I went over all the books again. . . . I don't know yet. . . . I'm a little worried, sure. Why not? Well, naturally . . . The Treasury guy is pretty sharp, you know."

Then Ben fell silent and listened. The voice at the other end of the wire sounded, from where Hank sat, like radio static. It went on for quite a while. Finally it stopped and Ben spoke again.

"But I've told you, Donal. I thought I made myself pretty clear. I just don't want to be in this business anymore. It's as simple as that. Nothing against you—for God's sake, you know that! You've been good to me, and I appreciate everything, you know that too. What? What? What did you say? Oh, you can't mean that, Donal!"

Static sounded again across the room. Yet, unintelligible as the words were, Hank was sure that they were furious.

"I know I like the money." Ben's free hand, gripping the desk, showed white knuckles. "I never said I didn't, did I? But I'm a professional. I've got two degrees and I want to use them to do bigger things, stretch my mind. There's nothing wrong about that, is there? It shouldn't be hard to understand— What? What did you say?"

A fierce croaking sounded from the telephone. Ben sat up straight and threw his hat on the floor.

"Now listen, Donal. I don't deserve this from you. I've given you the best that's in me, we've played fair and square with each other, and you know it. That's no way to talk to me. Don't I have the right to quit, for God's sake? Shake hands, part friends, go my own way? For Christ's sake, Donal, be reasonable . . . Yeah . . . Yeah, I said I'd stick with you till this is over. How many times do I have to tell you? Did you think I'd walk out on you in the middle of a mess? Listen to me, as God is my witness, I'll see you through this and give you my best with all I've got, the way I've always done. After it, though, I'm through. I really am, and nothing's going to change my mind."

The voice that answered on the other end was quieter now. With the receiver at his ear, Ben began to nod as though in approval.

"Why, yes," he said. The frown between his eyes eased away. "That makes more sense. This has nothing to do with our friendship, just because I go my own way. Sure, Donal. Well, I feel better hearing that. Today? The Acorn, that's my first stop. Then Rainbow Inn for a quick look at the books. Oh, I'll have time. There's no traffic that far out. It won't take more than thirty minutes at the Rainbow. There's nobody there in the middle of the afternoon. Okay. Take care, Donal."

"Did you have a fight with Donal?" Hank asked.

"Well, sort of. But he calmed down. It's okay. Don't worry, kid. You look worried."

"I didn't think you and he ever fought. Are you really not going to work for him anymore?"

"No, I've had enough. It's time for a change. A nice change. It'll do us all good. Come on, kid."

The fine car hummed as it rolled down the highway. Hank watched Ben's hands make the slight turn of the wheel that brought the car around the curve at forty miles an hour. He had already memorized the movements of the shift and knew, in advance of a looming hill, how Ben was going to slide into second gear while his foot depressed the clutch. In just five years, he would have his own driver's license. He couldn't wait.

They turned off down the main street of a neat little town, past the usual row of Woolworth's, the A&P, a gas station, a school, and, at the corner, the police station. Diagonally across from the latter was the Acorn. Hank had been there before. It was a simple place with sawdust on the floor; the specialty was steaks and chops. On the second floor was the room where they shot craps late at night with the shades drawn. Ben hadn't made a secret of it.

"People like to gamble," he'd said. "I personally never do, it's not in my nature and I hope it won't be in yours. No," he'd said, "I'll correct that. I don't hope, I know it won't. Not with your background and the education you're getting. But as long as so many people like to, just the way they like to drink, they might as well make whatever money's to be made out of it. At least, that's the way they figure it."

He stopped the car. "I'll just hop out and pick up some papers. You can wait."

In a minute or two he reappeared with a ledger under his arm. "My night's work. Sometimes I'd rather go over this stuff in comfort at home. Well, here we go! Out to the sticks. A grand day for it."

It was really beautiful here. There were almost no cars and they could speed along as if they were flying. The fields were so quiet! White little country houses looked as if they were asleep. There were swings on the front porches, but no one was in them. Hank supposed they were all far out of sight, working in the fields; planting, mostly, this time of year. The little he knew about farms he had learned at Uncle Alfie's place.

"We'll almost be passing Uncle Alfie's, won't we?"

"Not far. If we had time, I'd take the detour, but then we wouldn't make it to the ballgame tonight."

"My father died at Uncle Alfie's house, didn't he?" Hank knew quite well that his father had died there, but something made him want to talk about it.

"That's right," Ben said.

"Did you know my father very well?"

"A little."

"Were you there when he died?"

"Yes." Ben took a hand off the wheel and laid it on Hank's arm. "What do you want to talk about that for? Dead is dead and it's a wonderful day. Think positively."

"That's what Grandpa says."

"Well, he's right. Dan has a good outlook on life, although I don't always agree with him."

"I know, why don't you?"

"Well, sometimes I think he tends to be too serious."

"Like taking me to see *Journey's End*?"

"Well, yes. To my way of thinking you're too young to be thinking about the trenches and the killing."

But he hadn't been too young. He had thought very deeply afterward about the awful cruelty—the *stupid* cruelty—and it had made him decide not only that he would never fight, no matter what, but that when he grew up he would do whatever he could to keep men from doing such awful things to each other.

"Didn't you have a better time when we saw Douglas Fairbanks in *The Thief of Baghdad*?"

"I liked that too. You can't compare them, Ben."

Ben glanced at him and smiled. "What a nice kid you are! I'm glad you're my kid, even if you're like your grandfather. No, I have no worries about you, at least. None at all."

No worries about you, at least. Then he did have other worries, even though he had denied them.

The frown came back between Ben's eyes as if, suddenly, in the midst of happy talk, he had remembered something.

They rode on in silence. For a time Hank kept his thoughts to himself. Finally he had to speak.

"When I was lying down before," he said, "they thought I was asleep. They said you were worried or scared or something."

Ben was startled. "Who said?"

"Some men. They were talking to Tony. They said something about you going to court, that you'd be scared. I was pretty darn angry to hear that."

Ben seemed to be thinking. Then he asked whether Hank could remember anything else.

Hank shook his head. "No, but they had no right to say that about you."

"Well, people shoot their mouths off sometimes without its meaning much. You have any idea who they were?"

"I was behind the curtain."

"Of course. You wouldn't have known them anyway." Ben bit his lip and frowned again, deepening the parallel creases in his forehead. After a while he straightened his face and looked over to Hank. "Listen to me. I've always trusted you. And you're old enough to understand. Or if you're not old enough yet, you will be some day. What I want is your promise not to talk to anybody—anybody at all—about what you heard today."

"About those men?"

"About them, or about my talk with Donal. It's nobody's business. I can trust you, can't I?"

Hank felt solemn and prideful and grown up. "Of course you can, Ben."

"Swell! So now let's drop it. You've got a reading list for the summer, haven't you?"

"Yeah, a long one."

"Well, that's a private school for you! I'm glad I got my way. In that school and with your marks, you'll walk right into any Ivy League place you choose. Still want to be a doctor, do you?"

Hank nodded. "Or something else in science, physics maybe or electrical engineering."

"There you go! Like your grandpa again. Well, we're almost there."

They were in a region of rich estates. The two-lane blacktop road swerved between cut stone walls, thick privet hedges, and whitewashed fences. Long bluestone gravel drives led to where fine houses stood on top of a rise or lay among meadows and paddocks. Horses and dairy herds grazed in the sunshine.

Ben whistled. "Some neighborhood, eh?"

The blacktop road crossed a highway. At the junction, set back on a perfect lawn among beds of perfect flowers, lay a long, low house with verandas and striped yellow awnings. A small sign at the corner of the lane said RAINBOW INN. Otherwise there was nothing to indicate that this was not a gentleman's country estate.

This time, they both got out of the car and went inside.

"An ice-cold Coke will settle your stomach," Ben said.

"My stomach's fine now."

It was dusky in the great hall, after the glare outdoors. One needed a few moments to accustom one's eyes to it, and then it all came clear: the polished parquet floor, the mirrors, the walnut staircase rising to the second-floor casino, and the dining rooms on either side of the hall, where the double doors, flung open, revealed the bouquets on the tables, the paintings, and the velvet-backed chairs.

A man in a tuxedo jacket came hurrying from somewhere in the rear. Otherwise the place was vacant.

"Mr. Marcus! Good afternoon! Good to see you! I haven't seen you in a long time, young gentleman—I'm sorry, I don't remember your name."

"This is Hank, Andre. How's everything?"

Andre kissed his fingertips. Frenchmen did that. This man was no Tony in shirt sleeves.

"Perfect, Mr. Marcus, the best month we've had. Three times last week we had a state governor at the tables upstairs, from three other states, I mean. Can you imagine? And then there is our friend who comes regularly, they say he will be our next senator—who knows?"

"Well, you're doing a good job, Andre. The best food, top entertainment, what more can one ask?"

"Nothing much, Mr. Marcus. Except good liquor. You forgot to mention good liquor."

"That I take for granted here. You're not running short?"

"No, we're in good shape. I suppose you want to step back into the office?"

"Yes, please. I won't be long."

A car came roaring up the driveway; with a dreadful screech of brakes, it scattered the gravel and halted with a jolt in front of the open door. Ben turned to squint into the light.

"Now what kind of a way is that—" he began.

Two men jumped out and bounded up the shallow steps to where Ben stood, a silhouette framed by the pillars on either side of the door. From behind Ben, near the staircase, Hank peered curiously around him. He thought he saw that the men had bandannas tied around their faces. Afterward, he wasn't sure whether they really had had, or whether he had imagined it. Everything happened so fast. But he did remember and would never forget the dreadful rattle of guns, which, although he had never heard a gun fired, he instantly recognized. He heard a cry, Ben's awful cry, and saw him fall backward to strike the floor. He saw the men scamper down the steps, heard the car doors slam, the spurt of gravel, the squeal, the roar . . . over.

And all was silence. He didn't move, couldn't move. Then people came running down the stairs, up some other stairs and from the kitchen; feet scuffled; a man in a chef's hat screamed and screamed. Andre knelt with his face in his hands, where Ben lay. It seemed as if a hundred people had begun to babble at once.

Oh, my God! Shot to pieces—

Sprayed . . . look at the walls!

Good Christ! . . .

Did anyone get the license?

The police!

Don't touch him—

Hank walked to the front. He felt nothing, because it wasn't real. It couldn't have happened. Didn't happen.

Somebody tried to pull him away. "Come back here, sonny. Don't look."

"That's his kid."

The eyes were open. Ben's twinkly eyes under the red-brown brows. His mouth was open with the lips drawn back to show the teeth and the gums. The mouth of a dead animal, the fox that had died of some sickness at Uncle Alfie's place. He was dead. Ben was dead. Of course. What else, with the blood all over his new linen jacket and his polka-dotted bow tie. His hands were flung out, palms up, on the floor.

But a minute ago he was telling me to drink a Coke, it would settle my stomach.

Why?

How?

And then he heard himself howl, heard his own terrible howling and bawling, and couldn't stop in spite of all the rushing people and cold water and gentle words and hands. Couldn't stop. Everything whirled; pinwheels burst before his eyes; they made him sit down, they talked and talked, but he didn't understand what they were saying.

Then, after a while, a long time, he couldn't have said how long, he began to recognize things. He saw a uniform, not a navy blue policeman's coat, but gray, the color of dust. A man's voice said, "We're state police, son. And we'll take care of you. Let's step outside to the air. Here, we'll go this way."

With his arms around Hank's shoulders, the man led him to a side door. Though Ben must still be lying there, where they would have had to step over him. The man sat Hank down in a chair, one of those fancy iron chairs at a table under an umbrella. Two more police came over and sat. Quiet now, Hank put his face into his hands.

"We need to telephone to somebody," the first man said. "Your mother—"

"No!" Hank cried. "Not my mother. You can't just call her and tell her—"

"Who else then? Can you think?"

"My Uncle Alfie lives near here. About fifteen miles, I guess. His name's Alfred DeRivera. The number's in the phone book, I don't remember—"

"That's okay. Joe, you make the call. I'm going to stay here with—what's your name, son?"

"Hank."

"You're a brave boy, Hank. I'm not going to leave you until your uncle comes. And if you want to cry, don't hold back, just go ahead. It'll be better for you."

But the sobbing was over; only still tears stood in his eyes, dazzling his sight. Numbly he sat, watching two small gray birds hop in the grass. The afternoon had turned hot and windless. The horizontal branches of the trees lay still on the heavy air. And the life had gone out of the day, out of the world. Numb he was, until after a long, long time he heard the sound of a familiar voice and saw Alfie, sweating and red, come running to take him in his arms.

The funeral was a public event. On the sidewalk outside the funeral parlor, a small crowd jostled and craned to see the coffin emerge, to count the widow's tears, and to speculate about the death. The newspapers had given moderate publicity to the event under the heading SUSPECTED GANGSTER KILLING IN NEW JERSEY.

Paul thought with distaste that there certainly were flowers enough for a gangster's funeral. An indecent profusion of them took up a separate car behind the hearse. He stood for a moment, holding Hank by the hand. Cameras flashed and he suspected that government men must be there surveying the crowd.

Donal, evidently, had the same thought. "It's a disgrace. Rumormongers," he muttered, coming up behind Paul. "Fault of the newspapers, making a mystery out of a clear-cut case."

Some columnists had conjectured that Ben Marcus had

been "gotten out of the way," lest he talk too carelessly under subpoena in a forthcoming trial for income tax evasion.

Paul repeated, "Clear-cut?"

"Of course. A simple payroll robbery. They thought he was carrying cash. He often did."

"They didn't rob him. They ran away," Paul said.

"They lost their nerve when they saw he wasn't alone. That's simple."

Paul was motioned into a car before he could reply. It had been thought better that Hank ride to the cemetery with him and Marian, rather than with Dan and Hennie and Leah, for fear that Leah might break down again on the way; she had been hysterical all the day before, and the boy had seen too much already.

The short black procession pressed through heavy traffic toward the East River. It crossed over onto bleak Long Island flats, strewn with warehouses, factories, gridiron streets of drab identical dwellings and cemeteries; the whole sweltered under the dull sky, while hot wind blew grit and soot through the open windows of the car. They rode in silence, while Paul watched Hank warily.

The boy still touched his heart. Halfway between manhood and childhood he was, a man in his gray trousers and navy jacket and well-polished shoes, with the start of a dark down on his upper lip; a child with the braces on his teeth and the sweet candor of his smile. He would have touched any caring heart.

His head was bent as though he were praying. Poor fellow, perhaps he was.

They were all in shock, but to Paul, the horror of his own particular shock was that it could not be shared; indeed, he could scarcely allow himself to think it through. He wondered whether anyone else in the family could be harboring the same bizarre thoughts.

Could Donal—would Donal—have ordered such a deed to

help himself out of a tight spot? The first question was *could* he? Yes, of course. It would be naive to think otherwise. There were plenty of henchmen, a hierarchy ranging from truck drivers at the bottom to specialized lawyers at the top. A telephone call, a word, and almost anything could be accomplished, entirely out of the commander's sight. *He* never soiled his hands with violence! The second question was *would* he? There was much one might say about Donal Powers: that he was shrewd, aggressive, determined, unscrupulous, and cynical. But murderous? And Paul pictured him at home, carving the roast at the head of his table, flanked by the refined and gentle wife—whom he had chosen when he might certainly have sought a very different sort of person—and by the beloved and increasing family. Was that the picture of a man who could send a trusted companion to his death? Such were the secret thoughts that went with Paul on the ride to the cemetery.

It is the hole in the ground, Paul thought, that makes it all finally real. Prayers, music, and eulogy were all pageant, but when the coffin was lowered into the earth the fact was clear: He would never come back.

"Oh God! Oh God!" Leah wept.

They gave her a flower to toss into the grave, but she could only sob and bury her head in Dan's shoulder. So it was Emily who tossed the flower, while Alfie, awkward and looking as if he, too, were about to cry, kept patting Leah's back.

"Oh God! Oh, why?" Leah cried over and over, until at last she was gently led away.

Through it all Hank stood white and still, without tears. And Paul, as they walked back to the car and all the way home, held tightly to his hand.

Friends came. The house was filled with them, all with their flowers and baskets of food. Everyone crowded around Leah, who had by now composed herself. Donal Powers beckoned to Paul and drew him apart into the hall.

"I want you to know that I'm sending a package to Leah tomorrow. Some cash that rightly belongs to them. A hundred thousand."

If he had been waiting for a reaction from Paul, he must have been disappointed.

"The reason I'm telling you is that I know you've been handling her personal investments, so I wanted you to know she had it, in case she's too upset to do anything with it."

"I doubt that Leah would ever be too upset not to know what to do with money."

Donal looked at him queerly. "This is cash. I myself am liquidating all but some highly selected equities. The market's got to crash one of these days, you know."

"I'm well aware of that," Paul said.

"Well, just thought I'd mention it. My father-in-law is too stupid to listen to me. Last time I talked to him—we don't meet very often—I warned him, but he thinks he's infallible."

Paul was not in any mood to discuss anyone's business affairs. He suspected that Donal didn't give much of a rap about them either, that the whole conversation had only been an excuse, an attempt to mend fences. Donal wanted no overt enmity. Appearances were everything.

I despise this man, he thought, but remembering Meg, forced himself to be civil.

"Well, it's been a sad business today," Donal concluded. "We'll all just have to do what we can for Hank."

"Yes, of course."

So the two separated. Donal and Meg left for New Jersey, the visitors departed, and Hank was sent to bed. Hennie wanted to take Dan home after the strenuous day, while Emily pulled a reluctant Alfie away, still protesting, "Anything I can do, Leah, anything . . . you know where I am. I'll call you anyway, in the morning."

"Stay, Paul and Marian," Leah said.

Marian objected. "You must be worn out. Really, you ought to try to sleep."

It was Marian who was emotionally worn out and wanted to go to sleep, Paul knew.

But he said, "We'll stay as long as you feel like talking, Leah."

She was sitting on the sofa with her chin in her hands.

"He was a good man. Thank God it was fast. He didn't suffer. . . . You know, I've been thinking I'm partly to blame. I should have made him separate from Donal."

Paul's heart leapt. Was she saying that she thought—

"I always worried about his carrying so much cash."

No, she didn't think. Paul's heart subsided.

"And this whole liquor business with so many competing groups—maybe somebody felt they'd stolen the Rainbow's trade. Who knows?"

Obviously, she didn't know. Sophisticated as she was in so many other ways, she had little understanding of the way Ben's business ran.

"I must say Donal treated Ben well. Why, it got so that Donal was Ben's best client. Lately," Leah said ruefully, "perhaps his only client. He kept him so busy. Oh, but Ben was smart! Donal often said Ben was worth every penny he paid him."

Not smart enough. Instead of building a dependable practice right out in the open, he'd gotten himself mixed up in this underhanded business outside of the law. And Paul, in spite of all, felt a surge of anger toward the dead man.

The words kept pouring from Leah. "You've no idea of the scope of Donal's interests. I'm talking about legitimate investments. Steel mills in the Midwest, office buildings in Chicago and Buffalo, and they've even bought a distillery for when liquor becomes legal again. That's why Ben had to travel so much. A lot of all this came from his ideas, you know."

A little smile touched her. Good, Paul thought with compassion. Let her feel pride, rather than shame. Then he thought: Speaking of Ben's ideas, it must have been Ben who arranged Donal's buy-out of the company that provided Hank with a major part of his income. And Paul's anger almost choked him.

Marian ventured again, "I really do think you need your rest now, Leah."

Leah's little smile turned wistful. "I guess you're right. I'll need all my strength, won't I? I'm so worried about Hank. . . . He loved Ben so, and Ben was such a good father. He'll need a man to guide him, but Dan's too sick and too old to do much. Will you do it, Paul? Will you take him in hand? He needs someone he can trust to help him get over this."

"You know I will. As if he were my son."

Marian stood up. She opened her pocketbook and shut it with a nervous snap. The tragedy and tensions of the last few days had begun to overwhelm her. She identified with suffering; when reading, she would skip a page on which some grief or horror was too boldly described; at the movies she would close her eyes.

So Paul finished quickly. "You ought to take him out of town for a while. A little trip for a few days, with time to talk things over, would be a help."

"You're right, Paul. But do you think you could spare a few days to do it with him? You'd be better for him right now than I would."

"I think I can manage it."

Leah put out her hand. "You're always so kind to us, Paul. So kind and wise."

Yes, he thought, on his way downstairs, how wise I am! I can't even straighten out my own head.

As late summer turned to fall, before school started, Paul and Hank headed toward the Boston Post Road on their way to New England.

"Where are we going?" Hank asked.

"I don't know. Let's just keep pointing north and see what happens."

Paul looked very tall at the wheel, compared with Ben. Hank tried not to look at the wheel, so as not to see Ben's hands in their pigskin driving gloves, and he tried not to remember how carefully, with a chamois, Ben used to clean the shining hood of his beloved car.

He hadn't known, during the early days after Ben died, what to expect. He had feared that everything would change, that they would leave the house and he would go to a different school, losing all his friends, maybe even have to get rid of the dog. It had seemed as if everything must tumble.

But the first time they were alone together, when the mourning period was over, his mother had told him what they were going to do.

"I intend to work as I've always done, and you'll go to school as always. We'll stay in this house. Yes, you'll miss having your good father, but you'll still have your grandfather and Paul, especially Paul."

So it was good, and Hank had a feeling of safety, in the car now with Paul. They drove on back roads, wandering through Connecticut toward the Berkshires. Late in the afternoon they arrived at an overlook on the Massachusetts border, where they bought ice-cream cones and beaded Indian moccasins. Then they traveled a little farther and stopped at an inn for the night.

At dinner, Paul, who finished long before Hank did, sat back in his chair and watched Hank eat. "Two hollow legs," Paul said, as though there were something extraordinary about Hank's appetite.

And Hank was back at Tony's with Ben. . . . It came to him that he would never hear those words or eat spaghetti without remembering.

Paul was being very talkative, which was unusual for him,

making conversation about tennis and Grandpa Dan's angina and whether Hank ought to choose German or French as his modern language. He thought he was being helpful. Perhaps he had been reading one of those books on child psychology that Mom had. *Adolescence is a vulnerable time. So many changes are occurring.* Et cetera.

Hank had to smile at the foolishness in those books. Then he thought that maybe they were right about the changes; he did feel as if he had grown years older in this one summer.

Suddenly now, Paul said a surprising thing. "I suppose you're sometimes terribly angry at Ben."

Hank was shocked.

"Anger is natural, Hank. Even when people die quietly of sickness or old age, we feel angry at them for leaving us. In this case it's harder, since we don't really understand how this happened to Ben. What we do know is that in some way it was connected with the work he was doing, so we can't help but blame him a little. I blame him, too, sometimes."

Hank did not answer. "But don't let's judge. Remember the good that was in Ben, that's all I'm trying to say. And after a while the only things you'll remember at all are the good and the love."

There was a silence, then Paul changed the subject. "The farther north we go, the more we'll see of fall. New Hampshire will be turning red and gold."

Hank was thankful to change the subject to the scenery. For an idea was taking gradual shape in his mind, an idea that he was afraid to acknowledge.

On the fourth morning, they were close to the Canadian border. The hotel was an old-fashioned wooden pile with rocking chairs on a long porch, but there was no one in them and no one in the dining room when they came down to breakfast. It was past the season.

There was a fire on the hearth. An enormous maple had turned all gold at the window by the table. Hank ate slowly with his eyes on the window. The golden tree gave him a feeling, oddly mixed, of happiness and sadness.

"You're very quiet," Paul remarked. "I hope it's been some fun being here with me."

He couldn't say it was fun exactly, but it wasn't bad either. "It's nice," he said. "I'm glad we came."

"You're growing up fast, Hank, ever since—" Paul stopped.

Go on, Hank told himself. The longer you keep it in, the more it will swell up and fill you. He took another forkful of food, giving himself time to choose his words, but they came out abruptly anyway.

"I think Donal wanted to have Ben shot," he said.

"You do? What makes you say that?" Paul's voice was calm, but Hank could see that he was shocked.

"I was asleep in the back room at Tony's. I was half awake, I mean, when some men came in and they were talking about somebody being afraid that Ben would talk in court. I didn't see them, but I could tell by the way they spoke that they were real toughs, like the ones in the movies. One man said Ben's too smart for that, and the others said, yes, he was, but he might get scared all the same."

"That doesn't prove anything. The case never even came to court. Donal paid a fine and the government settled."

Now Hank replied, "That doesn't prove anything either, Paul. You haven't heard the rest." He felt worldly and clever, saying that.

Paul leaned forward as if to study Hank's face. "Tell me, then."

He would have liked, quite suddenly, to take back what he had already said. After all, he had promised Ben never to tell. And yet it was too hard to keep it all inside. "Ben and Donal had a terrible argument on the telephone. Ben said he was quitting."

Paul took a glass of water. Then he said carefully, "Did Ben say why?"

"Yes, he said he wanted to be a professional. He wanted a change. But he said he would see Donal through his trouble first before he left. Donal was really mad, though. I could hear him yelling."

"And then what?"

"Well, I think Ben calmed him down, and it ended when Ben told him what time he was going to be at the Rainbow Inn."

Paul was still studying Hank's face. "And then what?"

"Well, we got in the car. Ben was really upset. He pretended not to be, but I could see he was. And he made me promise never, never to tell anybody about what happened, about those men or the argument, as long as I live. Oh, and now I've broken the promise! Was it awful of me, Paul?"

Paul touched his hand. "No," he said. "Sometimes in every life there's something that you just can't handle all by yourself." He looked out of the window, where the maple glittered, and then turned back to Hank, saying solemnly, "And now that you've told me, you must never tell anyone else. And I do mean never."

"Oh, I won't, Paul. I feel better with your knowing it, so I won't."

"It could be very—"

"Dangerous?"

"Let's say unpleasant. That's quite an accusation, you know."

Hank nodded. "I understand. And hard to prove. Circumstantial evidence and all that."

"Been reading detective stories, have you?"

Hank didn't answer. He stared back at Paul. "Let me ask you something. The truth: Did you ever, even for a minute, think that Donal could have had anything to do with what happened?"

Paul took a deep breath. Stalling for time, Hank thought; he doesn't like the question.

At last Paul spoke. "For more than a minute, Hank. I've thought too much about it. . . . And yes, I do believe there's a connection. And the police believe it too."

"Then where's justice?" Hank cried furiously. "Why don't they do something about it?"

Paul sighed. "It must scare you to see how imperfectly grown-ups rule the world. How can I explain? There are wheels within wheels, powers behind powers—no pun intended—and as you yourself said, you need proof. Proof is more than knowledge. You can *know*, without being able to *prove*. Do you understand what I'm telling you?"

The pain in Hank's throat was a hot thing, like a piece of burning coal. He swallowed hard. "I'm never going back to his house! Never."

"Oh, but you'll have to. You'll be invited for the children's birthdays, and most likely for Thanksgiving, too, this year. You'll have to."

"I can say no. Why can't I?"

"And do that to Meg? And put an idea in your mother's head that would drive her crazy? Listen to me, put all this out of your own head and go forward. There's nothing you can do about it. You hear me, Hank?" Paul lowered his voice. "Besides, for your own sake, listen to me. Rage eats you up. Only remember Ben, remember that he loved you, and forget the rest."

"I guess you're right."

"Then will you take my advice?"

"Okay, Paul, you can trust me."

Again Paul touched his hand. "I see that I can. You've grown a whole lot older. . . . Tell me, would you like to go to temple with me on Saturday mornings? You might hear things there that will help you understand about people, about evil and good."

Hank considered. Mom never went, for Saturday was another busy day at the shop. Ben had been indifferent.

Grandpa Dan was a nonbeliever, a secular Jew, he called himself. But Ben was gone now and Grandpa had a way of lecturing that was growing hard to take. That left Paul, who could play tennis and make jokes; he could also be serious without giving a boring lecture. So if Paul recommended temple, Hank would go.

"That would be fine," he said. And he thought of something. "Mom says the war's changed the way people feel about evil. They aren't as shocked by—well, by people killing a man as they used to be once. Do you believe that, Paul?"

"I'm sorry to say, yes, I do." Paul looked thoughtful. Then he smiled. "Well, enough of that! Shall we stop at the antique store in the village and buy a little something for your mother? A vase or a bowl or something she'd like?"

They went outside into the bright, crisp morning. Bees buzzed in fallen apples on the grass. The sun burned, but in the shade you felt a promise of the coming winter.

"We'll buy some apples along the road on the way home," Paul said. He put his arm around Hank's shoulder.

Hank thought: I'll remember this. Paul will die; many, many years from now he'll be dead, and I'll still remember the things we said in the summer of 1929, and remember yellow maples and the apples in the grass and his arm around my shoulder.

Nine

Meg was walking in the general direction of Leah's place, still not sure that she really wanted to go there, not sure she wanted to see or talk to anyone. She had gone to New York that morning with similarly vague intentions, thinking perhaps of a visit to Hennie, merely to feel again the warmth remembered from childhood. But Hennie hadn't been in. She had walked over then toward the museum on Fifth Avenue, had hesitated at the foot of the steps and kept going. She had come to the city without the car; in the mood of that morning, the chauffeur's presence would have been a constraint.

She turned downtown. Bright towers blazed in the noon light. In every one, in hotels, offices, and stores, people were busy, buying and selling things, making things, and talking on the telephone. She felt disconnected, thinking of all those busy people. It was as if she were in a foreign country, listening to conversations that she couldn't understand. And she knew that she had been feeling this way too often, and that it was sick, and that she must do something about it.

Weakness swept over her. She sat down on a bench with her back against the wall that divided the park from Fifth Avenue. The weakness was in her mind, she knew that perfectly, for the last baby was already six months old and her body had already regained its strength.

The idea that had seeded itself when Ben had been killed, had rooted and grown. She had torn it out, but it had grown back. The idea was that Donal had known too much about Ben's death. What horror! The man who slept beside her, who fathered and guided her children. No, it was not possible. . . .

A wind came, scattering rusty leaves on the sidewalk. It was too cold to be sitting there. And conspicuous, too, just sitting alone on a bench, watching the buses roll downtown. Abruptly, she stood up, blindly collided with a woman who was walking in the opposite direction, and stammered her apology. Had the woman looked puzzled? Was there anything strange about her that people could notice?

The new nursemaid, the one who had come to take care of the baby, Agnes, had looked at her like that just this morning. She'd looked at her queerly, with reproach, when she had scurried in to take the baby away. The twins had been plucking at Meg's dress for attention while she was holding the baby, when all at once a terrible anger had risen in her, and she had pushed them off, shrieking—she was positive she had shrieked—*Get away! Get away! If you don't stop this minute, I don't know what I'll do.* And they had howled in fear. Then the baby had begun to cry, and she had been holding its face to her cheek, weeping into its neck, and that was when the nurse had come running . . . she was a disagreeable woman who would have to be gotten rid of.

Meg kept on walking and thought: I don't really want to go

to Leah's, but I don't want to go home either. Maybe I should go to Leah's. Maybe not.

There was a gold lamé dress in Leah's window. Its matching cape was bordered in sable. If Donal were to see it, he would make her buy it. It was a dress for what people called "making an entrance." An entrance was what Donal loved and she hated.

A saleswoman met her at the door with a coaxing smile. "You were admiring the lamé? It's a new length, midcalf. Patou has just introduced it in Paris."

Leah rescued her. "Meg! How nice!" And then, "Is anything the matter?"

Alarm sped through Meg. "Why? Do I look strange?"

"No, no. I thought . . . have you had lunch?"

"I've been busy. I've been walking."

"Come back here into this dressing room. I'll get you some tea and cookies. Not much of a lunch, but better than nothing."

Meg sat down while Leah went for the tea. Leah knew there was something wrong. The light, dispersed three ways by the triple mirrors, showed a pale, drawn face and a body hunched in the chair like an old woman's. She straightened herself.

"How's the baby?" Leah inquired.

"Fine. She's sitting up."

"My memory's usually pretty good," Leah said, "but I've forgotten her name."

"It's Agnes."

"Of course. I knew it began with an A, but I don't see them that often, and you have so many, one gets mixed up." Leah swung her legs. Her two-toned pumps were correct with her beige Chanel suit and the gold necklaces. "But now I promise I'll remember all your kids. Lucy, Loretta, Agnes, Tommy, and Timmy."

I screamed at Lucy and Loretta this morning. Poor little scared things! I screamed. Tears filled Meg's eyes.

Leah turned away. Through the blur of tears, Meg could see the smart foot, the handsome silk leg still swinging.

Leah said gently, "Quite a family. Five children in five years. God bless them and all that."

Meg dried her eyes. "I know," she whispered.

Leah spoke more firmly. "Meg, you don't want any more babies. You're wrecking yourself. Your nerves are shot to pieces."

Meg set the tea aside. "But I don't understand why. I've so much help, I hardly lift a finger. I'm ashamed. Poor women in cold-water flats, women who have nothing and no one, have enormous families. How can I dare complain?"

"What makes you think those poor women don't wreck themselves, too, and fall apart? Some can stand it and some can't. Some even want it. You don't want it and you can't stand it. Look at yourself," she said roughly now. "Look at yourself. How long are you going to go on like this? Will you have five more in the next five years?"

"I don't know. I just don't know."

"What's wrong with you? Why don't you have the strength to stand up to him?"

"I try. But you know Donal. People don't stand up to him." She heard the tiredness, the hopelessness, and at the same time the foolish sound of her words.

And Leah said, "That's too stupid. I'm sorry, Meg, but I have to say it. You're a grown woman and it's your body. Besides, it's not as if it were a matter of religion with Donal. You told me so once yourself, right here in this room, you told me."

"I know."

"What is it, then?"

"I guess you could call it a quirk of some sort."

"Some quirk! No, my dear, it's power. Making *you* do what

he wants, and all the more delightful because he knows you don't want it. Bending you to his will. I'm not saying he doesn't enjoy all the kids. He's got money enough to bring them up in style and show them off. Some people really do like having a houseful, especially when they don't have to bear them."

Meg was silent. She was thinking: I wish I were like Leah. How strong she is, with her husband only one year gone! I suppose you have to be born that way. All the clever fashionable women who work here look as though they could handle anything or anybody. They look superior. Perhaps they really are superior.

Leah asked curiously, "Tell me, Meg . . . you must resent him terribly. Don't you?"

That, too, a direct question like that, was something only a woman like Leah could ask without flinching, or could answer if she were asked it.

"Sometimes I think I do," she answered softly.

"But then, when you get into bed, I suppose—"

Meg blushed; it was as if the other woman had seen through the very bones of her forehead into the secret places of her brain.

"All right, never mind. I see I've embarrassed you. But you've given the answer anyway."

And Meg said, "Not altogether. There are other things. His business."

Now Leah's face tightened and shut, as if a door had been closed. Then it opened partway. "As to that, I can't say anything. It's very complicated. Beyond me."

What must be Leah's thoughts about Donal and Ben? What had they been, even before Ben died? But she would never tell. Because of the nature of the "business," which brought about its own secrecy.

"But I can advise you on one thing, Meg. I told you last

year. See a doctor and get a diaphragm. You're a fool if you don't. I can't tell you any more than that," she said severely.

"And he wouldn't find out? You're sure?"

"He wouldn't find out." Now Leah was patient. "You remember, I told you about that doctor who used to come here with his wife. It's so sad, she died last month. He came in with his two girls to cancel an order she had made for a coat. He'll give you an appointment this afternoon. He'd squeeze you in, if I asked him."

Alarm sped through Meg. "Specialists don't give you an appointment the same day."

"He would. He's awfully nice. I didn't charge him for the coat, although it had been finished. Funny thing, it was Marian Werner who finally bought it." Leah stood up. "Let me go in and call him now. Maybe you can go right over."

Leah moved so quickly! Meg sought more time. "Isn't it strange, I keep having babies and don't want any more, while poor Marian—"

Leah stopped at the door. "Well, you can say 'poor Marian' and I know what you mean, but you could look at it another way, too. She's got a man in a million, and I don't think she even knows it." Her eyes flashed. "Let me tell you, if he gave me the signal, I'd make a play for him in a minute, and I wouldn't mind telling him so."

"You would really tell him?"

"Of course not, silly. And I'll have your head if you ever mention it to anyone. But if he made one move toward me, married or not, I'd jump. That's what I meant. Well, I'll go make that call for you."

I shouldn't think Paul would jump, Meg said to herself. She was at the same time aware that she was being really too naive and very unfashionable for a young woman in 1929, when adultery was fashionable; you had only to read the novels and the news to know that it was.

"He says you can come over at three o'clock. I told him that you were feeling rather desperate. He's very kind. You can tell him everything. Don't be afraid, Meg. Here's the address." Leah's voice followed Meg right to the door. "You're looking brighter already, now that you've made a decision. That suit looks fine on you, but you should carry a different bag. One of those honey-colored alligators would be nice to spice it up."

It was late, after the commuter rush, when Meg got out of the local train. The short fall day was gone, the little station plaza was brightly lit, and the taxis had all been taken. As she stood waiting for the next one, she became conscious of a small, quiet change in herself, a sensation of settling. The smell of burning leaves, a comforting country smell, was in the air; she straightened taller to breathe it in. The afternoon's adventure had, after all, not been so bad. The doctor had been extraordinarily kind. His manner, in spite of his youth, had been almost fatherly. She had hardly needed to explain herself and had been so grateful for that; it would have added humiliation to have burst out crying. At one moment only had she come close to doing it, when he had asked her whether it might do any good for him to speak to her husband. She had flung up her hands in such alarm, that he had at once reassured her.

"Don't worry, Mrs. Powers, there'll never be anything in the mail, not even an annual reminder. I'll leave it to you to come in. That's how you want it, isn't it?"

She tried now to recall what else he had said. That a woman must guard her health or she would be of no use to anyone, let alone herself. That a person shouldn't be afraid to admit it when her endurance was gone.

"Every one of us knows what it is to be overwhelmed," he'd said. "Don't try to fight it alone. Reach out for help." And he had given her a look both merciful and acute.

He had known she was falling apart. She'd felt at once that

he liked women, by which she meant that he cared to understand them. Some men didn't really like women, except in
bed. . . .

A taxi drew up. Meg got in. The pleasant suburban streets
were empty, for families were already home at dinner, and as
she realized how late she was, the morning's panic began suddenly to rise again. Her unusual absence would be questioned.
Valiantly, she thrust the panic down, scolding herself: Act
your age, you're not a child who's been discovered at the
candy jar. And she clutched her purse, which now bulging
with the box that had been added to its previous contents,
would scarcely stay shut. The box held guilt, it held fear, and
it held relief. An odd mixture.

Donal reached the front hall before she had even closed the
door behind her.

"What in blazes happened to you? I thought you must have
been in an accident—I don't know what I thought. And dinner was ready an hour ago. You've got the whole house upset."

Well, this was a normal reaction: worry and anger and relief.

"I'm sorry. I had a hard time in the city getting a taxi to the
train and the same on this end."

"What were you doing on a train? What's wrong with the
car?"

"Nothing. I just didn't feel like taking it today."

"Didn't feel like—what kind of a queer idea was that?"

"Let me go upstairs and put my things away. Then we can
have dinner and talk."

"I've had dinner. I got tired of waiting. You can't treat servants like this. They want to get through with their day, not
stand in the kitchen till all hours."

"I'm not asking anyone to stand in the kitchen. I'll make a
sandwich for myself. I'm not hungry anyway."

He followed her up the stairs. Even on the carpet, his steps were heavy behind her.

"Now listen," he said as he closed the bedroom door, "this won't do. I want to know what's wrong in this house. You've got a car and chauffeur at your disposal, yet you run off to New York like—like I don't know what! Why? Where've you been?"

Meg breathed deeply. "Well, I went to see Hennie and stopped in at Leah's, did some shopping—"

"Why didn't you take the car, I asked?"

"I felt like being alone."

"That's crazy. What are you hiding? You were crying this morning."

"I was not. Who told you such a thing?"

"Timmy did."

"He didn't, Donal," she said steadily.

"All right, then, it was Helga."

Naturally. The help always preferred the man of the house to the mistress, especially when the man looked like Donal, and was Donal.

"When you were so late and I was so concerned she told me what happened this morning. Don't try to lie your way out of it, Meg. Are you sick? What are you hiding?"

They were standing almost toe-to-toe. She had not taken her coat off and still clutched her purse to her chest. Since he was not much taller than she, their eyes were almost on the same level. How was it possible that his—they were after all, only lenses—could convey through their dark glitter so much threat? Nevertheless, she made herself meet their stare.

"I don't know whether you'd say 'sick' exactly. I felt *beset,* that's all. As if I couldn't bear any more."

"Bear? Bear what? Your hard life?"

She cried out, "Why are you so fanatical about having all these children? Why does it mean all this to you? When—you admit it to yourself—you don't follow your faith. Why? Tell me. I try, I have tried to understand."

"You don't need to understand. It's the way I am . . . better women than you, from some of the most outstanding families in the nation, are willing to bear children."

"Good! Good for them, but I'm me."

Once more they stood almost toe-to-toe. With the back of her hand, she smeared her tears. *If you don't take care of yourself, you'll be no help to anyone else either,* the doctor had said.

Donal went to the door and tried the lock. "I don't want my children to come in here and see their mother looking like this."

"I don't want them to see me like this either. Don't you see, that's the point? If only I didn't have to worry about having another one every year!"

"You're hysterical," he said. "Look at yourself."

She turned to the mirror. Her face was blotched. She was supposed to be docile, charming, and calm, when she would have liked to be honest, but it was no use. There was no way through the stone wall. The only route lay in the box in her purse, so she would use it. What he didn't know wouldn't worry him. Besides, there was that other thing, dammed back, that wanted now to flow out.

"I'm sorry if I've been acting strangely," she began.

"You have."

"I've been troubled, Donal. Thoughts come to me like a fog that lifts for a while and then creeps back. I try to push them away—"

"Thoughts! Fog! What are you talking about?"

"Sometimes I think—I think about the way Ben was killed, and—"

He grasped her shoulders. "What do you mean, the way Ben was killed?"

"You know there was all that business in the papers about

how it might have had something to do with his going to court. I know it died down, but still it makes you think."

"So my wife has been lying in her husband's bed with her secret thoughts in her head about how her husband had a man shot? God damn if I ever heard anything like this!" His fingers dug into her shoulders.

"Donal, I didn't say you! Only I couldn't help thinking, some of the men who come here look capable of doing terrible things. They're hard people. Couldn't you have sensed what might happen? Didn't you care enough to pay attention? I can't help having uneasy feelings. I didn't say you!" And she began to sob.

"Who put this idea into your head? Who was it? Leah, that smart little bag of tricks? Or your cousin, pious Paul, the high priest of morals? Who?"

"No one, no one, I swear it—"

"This," he said, "is the most outrageous thing I've heard yet. A wife accusing her husband . . . Why, Ben and I never had a cross word between us. We were a team, we'd have gone on together for the next fifty years, and you—you have the temerity to suggest that—"

"Donal, I didn't mean, truly I didn't—"

"Or that anyone connected with me—"

"Donal, I didn't mean—"

Strength, like a pool as it oozes away into dry earth, ran out through her arms and legs and was lost. She sat down on the edge of the bed.

His voice was low now, quivering with emotion. "That my own wife has no more regard for me—" He stopped and stared, not so much as if he were regarding her, but rather as if he were seeing something in the air between them. "Well, I'll not forget this in a hurry," he said.

She wondered whether he was feeling more sorrow or more anger. Then he went out, closing the door with a sharp smack.

She had said too much. Perhaps her accusation, that he had

not done enough to protect Ben, had been unfair. . . . She was bewildered. One problem, though, the most pressing one, had been solved. A little rubber gadget had freed her. And she got up to hide it.

Then she sat again for a while, stunned and numb. She was not quite certain whether she had lost or won.

Weeks passed with minimal contact and in cold civility. Meg's timid attempts at reconciliation met no success. She studied her husband's face for a sign and could read no forgiveness in it.

It was clear that he wanted no further confrontation, yet she always felt as if they were on the verge of another one. She walked around the house with a placating air. Her voice was an octave higher than was natural to her.

Once she said, "Donal, how long can you be like this?"

"Why? What am I doing?"

"Donal, please. Your face is like cold stone."

He put on a caricature of a grin. "There, is this better? Is this what you want?"

She hung her head, sighing. "Never mind. I don't want anything."

He was such a complicated man! Maybe a simple man could have suited her better, a quiet man, perhaps a teacher.

And yet she loved him . . .

During the nights she lay beside him, listening to his untroubled breathing. Nothing shook him. No, that wasn't true. With her suspicions she had hurt him. But the last thing she wanted was to hurt him. Tenderness for him was sore within her.

Once as she moved tentatively closer her arm brushed his back, and he drew away. Even though he was asleep, or seemed to be, he had rebuffed her. How long would he stay like this, remote and cold? And if he should, how was she to bear it? His punishment was out of proportion to her crime.

Was it so dreadful, what she had said? He ought not to have been so wounded by it. It was just something that had been bothering her, the thought that in some way he could have protected Ben, and he could easily straighten it out. Maybe it had been a stupid thought. Yes, it had been, since he had explained it all. Stupid, but not mean. He ought to forgive her for it. Perhaps he never would. Well she knew how inflexible he could be, so it was possible. And yet she loved him. . . .

Her eyes stayed wide open, fixed on the gray ceiling. The clock on the landing would chime the half hour, then the hour, while she waited for the nights to pass. And one morning, after many weeks, she woke up to a decision that had made itself during her brief doze. She was going to leave. She was going to show him that she would not be treated this way and stay with him.

She heard Leah's voice: *Don't be a fool. You can't live like this.*

You're right, Leah, whether I love him or not, and no matter how it hurts.

A plan took shape in Meg's bewildered head. There would be ample room at her parents' house in Laurel Hill, at least for a while. Then: clothes, carriage, crib, bicycles, toys, a school, a new dentist and doctor . . . Donal would simply come back and find they were all gone. She would show him. He would be sorry. . . .

It would take a week or two to put all this in motion. Carefully she studied the calendar on her desk. Yes, by the middle of November, surely before Thanksgiving, it would be done.

Something was happening in America. All through the golden days of fall, while others sewed costumes for Halloween and shops were thronged with buyers, examining the new long skirts just in from Paris, and boys played football on high school fields and turkeys were fattening for Thanksgiving and towers were rising on Manhattan's avenues, something was happening.

Not many were aware of it. Paul Werner was one of the few. Donal Powers was another. There were some financial writers who gave warning, but their warnings were dismissed as the ravings of unqualified alarmists. When in September the stock indicators, which had been soaring, took a dip, it was said that there was no need to panic. So it was stoutly, cheerfully spoken by those who had invested all they owned in stocks. There were a few more rises and a few more dips. Brokers who had lent their money out, began to want it back. When the money wasn't available, there was nothing to do but to sell out.

Pure disaster was in the making.

Doom and the bottom were reached on the twenty-ninth of October. Wall Street collapsed in shock, and some jumped out of a window on the thirtieth floor, and some went home to sit in stunned despair, and others went running around to everyone they knew to borrow or to plead.

Such were the golden days of fall in 1929.

A wood fire burned in Paul Werner's office. It was a pleasant, fragrant anachronism on this street of steel towers. He gazed across to an unfinished structure. With so many brokers having gone under, he wondered how much of its space could be rented when it was completed. Already, during these first weeks after the disaster, which he mentally compared with the eruption of a volcano, prices had plummeted. His own cooperative apartment, for which he had paid fifty thousand dollars, wouldn't fetch more than half that today, were he to put it on the market. Fortunately, he didn't need to. It had been bought and paid for in full. "No mortgages," his father had taught him; he could hear the old man's grating voice even now, telling how he had weathered the panic of '93 while much bigger men had gone under. He was thankful for the advice, for having been taught to be cautious. So he had protected himself and those, most particularly Hank Roth, whose affairs were in his care.

As distress deepened and business came almost to a halt, the city, except for a thin layer of dazzle on top, became a gray shambles. Once Paul had passed a man in an English tweed overcoat, someone he recognized from the country club, selling apples from a tray on the corner of Broad and Wall streets; wanting not to embarrass him, Paul crossed the street. Everywhere were signs: FOR RENT, GOING OUT OF BUSINESS, BANKRUPT STOCK. Hundreds of builders had gone under and as many more would do so before this business was over. *Had Anna's husband been one of them?*

Deeper and deeper, Paul dug into his pocket. He gave to Hennie for the settlement house downtown; he gave to his wife for her adoption agency, and to the blind in the clinic that his father had founded. And the more he gave, the more he worried about Anna and Iris. But there was nothing he could do. He had given his word.

These thoughts went through his head while he made believe to be studying some papers, until, reluctantly, he had to return and face the agony in Alfie's face.

"You see," Alfie said, "I had it all figured to the dollar. With the market rising, I planned by Christmas to sell out and use the cash to meet my mortgage payments. I would have gotten rid of my mortgages, or most of them. You always advised against heavy mortgaging, I know." His voice trailed off.

All the lines of his face turned downward; the eyebrows over the large sunken eyeballs were inverted *U*'s. The mouth was a convex semicircle; from the nostrils to the corners of the mouth ran two folds of exhausted flesh, deep enough to conceal the tip of a fingernail. The entire face was in the process of collapse.

"People trying to get their hands on your money as fast as you get hold of it yourself," he mumbled. "Can't wait half an hour after a payment's due. After all these years, with my reputation, you'd think my credit could be extended till I straightened things out. It's not as if the values weren't in the properties. First class, every one of them, you know that, Paul. I never bought junk." He wiped his damp forehead. "My God, it's a jungle out there! A jungle!"

Yes, of course it was. And always had been. People wanted their money and yours, too, if they could get it. And Paul saw wolf eyes in the last faint dusk before total dark; electric bright, yellow and unblinking, they waited in a circle between your fire and the towering dark trees, waiting for your last embers to blink out into total night, panting in expectation of the rush to destroy you. He saw the picture that Alfie must be seeing.

And he said, very, very kindly, "I'm not that rich a man, Alfie. I've already advanced a hundred thousand. I can't do any more. I just can't." He hesitated. "Have you thought of going to your son-in-law?"

Alfie groaned. "It would kill me. Like sticking my head in the gas stove."

Neither spoke. Paul was thinking how brutal it was to have come as far as Alfie had, without help from anyone, and now —also without help from anyone, for he had been warned, Paul himself had advised him that stock values were false—to be hurled back where he had begun. Yet one couldn't blame him too much for not listening. Hardly anyone had been listening.

He watched the man get up. All the familiar jaunty cheer had gone out of him. He wiped his hat with the back of his hand and moved toward the door.

"Well, Paul, it's tough, but I see your position. I understand. It was a good try, anyway."

Paul went to the door with him. "Alfie, if I can think of some way, talk to anybody, buy some time for you, I'll do what I can."

Empty words.

Alfie put two fingers to the hat brim, giving his old salute. "Thanks, Paul. I know you will. Regards at home."

The weather was mild enough for them to be sitting on the veranda steps. They had probably been waiting for her all morning. They had that patient look, Meg thought, as she stopped her little Nash. She hadn't brought the big car with the chauffeur, hadn't used it at all since the trouble with Donal. Anyway, in these circumstances it would have been flaunting wealth before them.

"Come inside. There's lunch on the table," Emily said.

She had thought perhaps her mother would be crying, or show signs of tears. But on second thought, she ought to have known better, for Emily, like Marie Antoinette, would meet disaster with dignity. Her father looked like death.

They helped themselves from salads on the sideboard. Emily poured tea and the three sat down at the table. The day was dark gray. Emily lit candles. If it hadn't been for the expression on her father's face, there would have been no difference; the linen mats and napkins, beautifully ironed, the Waterford goblets, the heavy silver candlesticks, were the same as always.

Halfway through the meal, Alfie put his fork down. "It looks as if Laurel Hill will have to go," he said abruptly.

"Oh," Meg said, "no, Dad." And impulsively, "I've so much jewelry I don't even like. I'll sell it for you." She had planned to leave the diamond necklace, the emerald bracelet, all the rings, in Donal's dresser drawer with a contemptuous letter.

Her father was very moved. "Meg dear, thank you, but it wouldn't be nearly enough. You've no idea of the extent of the ruin." He shrank down in the chair.

Emily said, "You upset yourself talking that way. You need to eat something. You can't let yourself go."

He wants to cry, Meg thought, but you won't let him. I think you should let him.

Emily had always been like that. Cheerfulness, the denial of grief, were her particular ways of giving comfort. Meg could remember how, while tenderly binding up a cut knee, her mother would be murmuring, "There, there now, it doesn't hurt!" She meant well. But it had hurt, all the same.

Meg finished her lunch. It was a good one and, in spite of everything, or rather, she corrected herself, because of everything, she was hungry. So she took another helping and listened to Emily's local gossip that so carefully and absurdly avoided the subject on their minds.

All the while, she was conscious of her father's silence at the other end of the table. So cheerful and talkative he had been, master of this house, so pleased with himself and with the world! She could still see him coming up the driveway after his day in the city, wearing the morning's blue cornflower in his buttonhole. He picked one every day before leaving the house. And often, too, there had been a package under his arm, chocolates or a book for his "little bookworm." She could still see him.

When lunch was over, they went into the living room. The dogs, who had been lying in the corner of the dining room, took their usual places on either side of Alfie's chair; their eyes looked up at him as though they sensed his trouble. Emily got out her needlepoint. All those needlepoint pillows, the work of most of a lifetime, Meg thought, those innumerable bellpulls and footstool covers! She was so earnest about them, too, holding them to the light, with her forehead puckered, as though there were some great purpose in the work. And Meg felt a sudden sympathy with the honorable, tidy, narrow-minded woman who, all her life, had been protected according to a standard, the only one she had known or could perhaps even conceive of. She had never tended a house by herself—any more than I have, Meg reflected, and no credit to me! If it was as bad as they had been led to believe and Emily had to lose all this, how would she manage? She was probably too old to learn how. It wasn't much of a tragedy, when you thought of all the world's forlorn and outcast souls, but things were relative and for the two who were sitting here, this was a tragedy.

Just yesterday, Donal had addressed one of his rare remarks to her.

"I suppose your father is weathering the storm all right."

And she had answered, with what she hoped was dignity, that she didn't know, that he hadn't discussed it with her. She had thought, as she replied, that the plans which she had so thoroughly worked out, from the return of the jewelry to the hiring of the small van that was to take her and the children away, must now be revised. She could surely not now descend upon Laurel Hill, assuming that there would even be a Laurel Hill. Where, then? she had asked herself, standing in the front hall before Donal, who wore his sardonic look. Where, then? she was thinking now.

Her mother was still talking and talking. "The Warriners are going to stay the winter here this year. They've rented the New York apartment to cut expenses. Very sensible of them, I think." She spoke complacently, belying her nervous fingers that moved as they always did: quick, quick, quick. Meg started. Had her father not told her the true extent of his losses? Quite possibly he had not. It would be like him to shy away from a truth so formidable, to evade and postpone.

"Look at all those leaves on the terrace," Emily complained. "We've let Jim go and no one else seems to care about sweeping. I suppose I'll have to do it myself. I hate the bleak look of dead leaves."

Meg looked out through the French doors. Dry leaves were skittering before the wind. After one good rain, they would be a rotting dark brown mat. The wrought-iron chairs and tables had not yet been taken indoors. She had a vision of summers, of iced tea in a pitcher on the table, of women in Sunday afternoon dresses, sitting on the chairs, and the dogs lying asleep in the shade. A safe world.

How Alfie loved it all! At five o'clock on a winter morning in the city he would rise to drive out here to "the place," to walk around and see how his trees, the locusts and birches he had planted with his own hands, were weathering the cold. With what innocence he boasted about his strawberries, the largest, and his Jersey cows whose milk was the richest! But then, everything that belonged to him was the best, his daughter, his grandchildren, everything. Imagine him losing it all! Driving out through these gates for the last time! It would kill him, or kill his spirit, which was the same thing.

"I guess I'll go upstairs for my nap," Emily said, folding the needlepoint back into its bag. "You won't mind?"

Neither of them minded. Alfie said, "I'll just let the dogs out. Be back in a minute, Meg. I have to wait outside with the young one. She's taken lately to running down the road."

He stood with his back to her, almost ankle-deep in leaves. She saw that his head was sunk on his chest.

"It's really bad, Meg," Paul had told her when she had called to ask. "He's got four more mortgage payments due next month. He did too much pyramiding. I've been trying to use what connections I have to get extensions for him, but even if I can get them, and I probably can't, what would be the use? Taxes are due and the next quarterly payments will be coming up—"

Pyramided. Yes, he would have done so. And it hadn't been greed, Meg thought now. It was only because he was careless with money, never knowing how much he had. It went out as fast as it came in, and that had been all right as long as it had kept coming in through all the boom years during the war and after. His simple love of luxury was so different from Donal's, who kept on wanting more and more than anybody could possibly need, because of the power it gave him. Alfie, poor

Alfie, like a child in a toy store, just wanted his few pleasures, chiefly the pleasure of being what he called a "country gentleman," which really didn't cost all that much when compared with what some others spent.

He came back in and sat down. One of the dogs jumped into his lap, almost pushing him off the chair.

"There's something I wanted to ask you, Meg," he said almost shyly, not looking at her, just stroking the dog's ears.

"Yes, Dad?"

"It's something not easy for me to ask. It's never easy for a parent to ask a favor of a child. It should be the other way around."

He was going to ask her to speak to Donal about a loan. A cold shiver shook her. The man from whom she had expected shelter and comfort now waited, hoping for rescue from her.

"Go ahead, Dad," she said.

"Well, I thought, Paul thought maybe—would you ask Donal whether he might maybe tide me over?"

Tide him over. It's all gone, Paul had said. He's up to his ears in debt.

"I have security, good properties. This place, and the Lexington Avenue piece and the two West End Avenue houses, all the best locations."

Meg swallowed hard. "Why don't you ask him, Dad? It would be better if you did it."

"You can't?" His eyes pleaded.

There was just so much any one human being might call upon himself to do. She felt the tension, the muscles tight in her forehead.

"Really, I think you should do it, Dad."

"You see, he and I—we've never been close. I don't have to tell you." Alfie gave a little dry laugh. "And after all, you're his wife."

Oh, my God! Meg thought. She said evenly, "I can't describe properties, can I? I don't know anything about them.

You'd have to talk to him yourself in the end anyway, so you might as well do it yourself from the beginning."

There was a long pause. Then, "I suppose you're right," Alfie admitted. "Yes, of course you're right, but you can't know how I hate to do this, Meg. What it costs me."

"I do know, Dad. Believe me, I do. And I'm just so terribly sorry, I can't tell you."

Indeed, I can't tell you. If *you* only knew! I hope Donal won't be too cold when he refuses. Oh, he'll be courteous, one can be sure of that, but his courtesy can be hard and cold as ice.

"Is there any particular time I should call? I don't want to intrude."

He's terrified, poor man, poor Dad. Poor cocky Alfie is terrified.

"You won't intrude. The phones ring anytime. He won't mind."

"Then if it's all right with you, I'll just pull myself together and make that call."

Alfie's face brightened. He had somehow retrieved a portion of his old optimism. Mr. Micawber. Probably he already saw himself with the big check in his pocket, saw everything solved just like that, with the bright sun shining again.

Until Donal lets him down.

Meg's heart ached for him when she left. It ached for herself. She felt a small, bitter smile on her mouth. Mrs. Micawber. My father's daughter.

She was upstairs, feeding the baby, when she heard Alfie calling to her. He was coming up.

"In here," she answered. "In the baby's room."

He had been downstairs for over an hour with Donal, and she dreaded seeing him.

"Well, Meg," he said, pausing in the doorway. The greeting came out like a chuckle, like joy gurgling in his throat.

"Well, Meg." He bent to kiss first her and then the baby, who continued undisturbed to slurp mashed banana. "He's a prince, your husband. So easy, he made it. Considerate, didn't press me for a thousand details, just took my word as a gentleman in the old-fashioned way. We shook hands on everything only a minute ago."

She was bewildered and incredulous. "You mean that he lent you enough to cover everything?"

"No loan. He bought everything. Seven properties. Not Laurel Hill. I'm keeping Laurel Hill. It's going to be our all-year home. You know, that was the thing that would have killed me, Meg. I swear I can stand a lot of loss, but Laurel Hill is in my blood. It's like a living thing." His eyes filled. "God, I don't know how I could ever have walked away from the place."

Donal had paid for the New York properties exactly what Alfie had paid for them, so that Alfie had broken even, and now had a small amount of cash, not much, because there had been little equity in any of the properties. In addition, Donal agreed to pay Alfie a modest salary to manage the properties. So, by being careful about expenditures and living very quietly in the country, he and Emily had come out of a debacle and were safe, thanks to the unbelievable generosity of Donal Powers.

"I can't believe it! I hardly hoped—" Alfie paused for breath. He put on a shamefaced expression. "He was the last man in the world we wanted you to marry. I'm sorry to say I wasn't nice to him in the beginning. When you think about it, he's a pretty large-minded man to overlook that now." He sighed. "However, I suppose it was understandable. I know it was. We all thought his business was scandalous. But after all, when you think about it, some of the fanciest families in this country got their start a hundred years ago in the slave trade, or bringing opium to China. That's true, isn't it?" Alfie's tone was almost hopeful.

She was thinking that she was now forever in Donal's debt. . . .

"Oh, I know you worry about what he does, Meg; you never say, you have pride, and I'm proud that you have, but I know all the same. Let me tell you, though"—and here Alfie leaned forward as if he were implanting a secret—"listen to me, that fellow Hoover is finished. The Democrats will be in with the next election, Prohibition will go, and Donal will be aboveboard. He can either stay in the liquor business or take his cash and go into any other thing he's a mind to. An enviable position." Alfie looked dreamy for a moment. "So you needn't worry, Meg, it won't be long."

She didn't answer, just removed the mashed banana and began on the cereal.

"Donal told me—you don't mind if I speak openly to you, Meg? After all, who cares more about you than I do? Donal told me you and he hadn't been getting along together too well lately. He didn't tell me why, and I—"

And you want me to tell you, Meg thought fiercely.

Receiving no comment from her, Alfie continued, "I guess it's none of my business, but it seems to me it can't be anything too bad. People have their little spats. Your mother and I haven't gone through all these years without a few words now and then, but gosh"—and here he waved his arm toward the white crib, the lace curtains, and the pink walls— "gosh, what woman could ask for more than all this?" He put out a finger and the baby curled her hand around it, while staring back at her grandfather. "And a family like this! Five of them, one more beautiful than the other. Your mother and I always wanted more, but it never happened. Say, may I use your phone a minute? I want to call your mother. Poor soul, she's been trying not to let me see it, but she's been dying inside. She won't believe this." He stood up. "I can hardly believe it myself. Oh, Meg, I feel like a man who's been rescued from drowning."

It was, of course, necessary for her to say something to Donal. After her father had left, she went into the room, known as the office, where he was sitting at his desk. She stood in the doorway.

"I came to tell you that what you did for my father was extraordinary. It was a kind of miracle for him. I came to thank you."

He swung about in his chair. His eyes twinkled. "I made a good deal. I was glad to do it. He's not a bad sort, kind of foolish at times, but still he did pull himself up by his own bootstraps. Like me. I'd have hated to see him thrown back where he started."

"I know," she said stiffly, "and I appreciate that. I do. More than I can say."

Donal hadn't looked as friendly in many weeks.

"So! Truce, Meg?" he asked now.

"I'm a peaceable woman, you must know that about me."

"Yes, I know. Why don't you come in all the way and sit down?"

He drew up a chair. When she sat their knees almost touched, and a little tremble went through her. She thought, there was a time, such a short while ago, when he would have leaned over to kiss her or he would have pulled her to him.

"I'm over my anger," he said now. "I've thought it all out. Somebody—Leah or Paul, probably Paul—filled you up with a lot of hokum."

"No," Meg said. "Neither one."

"Well, what difference who? I shouldn't have let it get to me. You weren't feeling like yourself, and you're an innocent anyway. That's what I liked about you in the first place. Loved about you. I do love you, you know."

She pouted. It was a kind of flirtation. "You haven't shown it recently."

"I was hurt. Really hurt. Really deeply hurt."

Two tears stood in Meg's eyes. "I was, too, Donal."

"So we're even. Come here and kiss me." He stood up and drew her to him tightly. "There. That's better. Isn't it better, Meg?"

It was good to be taken into his arms again. It was like coming home. And she wondered, while his mouth was on hers, whether when the moment actually arrived, she would really have been able to leave him. For he still held her, had always held her, even when she was beset and frightened. Even then.

He said, when he let her go, "If it weren't broad daylight and the house full, I'd take you upstairs. You're ready for it again, aren't you?"

The two tears fell. She wiped them away and smiled. "I guess I am."

"You always are. That's another thing I love about you. Say, shall we take the kids out for Chinese dinner tonight? It's been a long time since we did."

The news of Donal's amazing rescue went around the family.

"He'll do fine, Donal will. Someday this panic, this depression will be over" was Paul's comment.

"Not for years," Leah replied, "in spite of the songs." And she began to sing sardonically, 'Mr. Herbert Hoover says that now's the time to buy.' "

"Exactly. Now *is* the time to buy if you've got anything to buy with."

"Not for years," Leah repeated.

"No matter. One day it will end, and when it does, Donal will be sitting with a fortune in real estate. Never underestimate him."

Ten

It had long been Paul's custom, inherited from his father, as a philanthropist and community leader, to talk things over from time to time with his rabbi.

The old man was tired. He was old when he married us, Paul thought irrelevantly, as the conversation rested for a moment.

"And how are things with you? Marian well and happy, I hope?"

He gave the expected smile. "Everything's fine, thank you."

He wondered whether the benign old man would be at all dismayed to know the truth; most likely not, for he had lived long enough to know that much was not what it appeared to be.

"Yes," the rabbi said. "In times like these, we must guard more dearly than ever the love and peace of the home. It's the only place to shelter a little bit from the storms." He lit a pipe, blew out the match, and continued from where they had left

off. "That scoundrel in Germany is filling the camps with in-
nocents. It's insanity."

"Organized insanity. I stopped in at the movies to watch
the news yesterday and saw a Nazi torchlight parade. Thousands marching and hundreds of thousands cheering as if they
were drugged with some substance that turns rational human
beings into savages."

"You have German relatives. What do you hear? Anything?"

"My cousin, God bless him, is an educated fool. He'd been
writing for years that Hitler would never get anywhere. And
now that Hitler has gotten somewhere, he writes that the reports are exaggerated, that the arrests have mostly been of
Communists and troublemakers who deserve to be put out of
the way."

"Is it possible that he doesn't mean what he says? That his
remarks are deliberate?"

"I don't understand."

"Look here. This is a copy of a cablegram from the Berlin
Jewish community. They protest, they urge all Jewish organi-
zations here to stop slandering the German government with
these untrue reports and to stop the boycott of German goods.
It seems we are doing undeserved injury to Germany and to
German citizens who—who happen to be Jews."

"I don't make any sense out of that, do you?"

"Yes. Obviously they've been told they had better call us all
off if they know what's good for them."

"It makes you wonder what's really best for us to do."

"I sometimes think that it won't matter what we do. The
future is black, and the sooner they all get out, the better."

"Where are they all going to go? Who will take them in?"

Silence answered. A sound truck went by in the street below, blaring the usual enthusiastic election slogans. It flashed
across Paul's mind that no matter who won, this fellow or

that one, there'd be nobody battering the doors down at night to haul people away.

He said after a minute, "If one were really there on the scene, one could get more of a feel in an hour than through all this correspondence."

The rabbi stared at him. "Are you thinking what I think you are?"

"Maybe. I'm not sure."

"You had a dreadful experience there before."

"All the more reason."

"I don't know, Paul. Prominent as you are in Jewish affairs, I wouldn't be surprised if they had a whole dossier on you. I don't think that going to Germany is the safest thing."

Paul was back on the street with Joachim. The band was playing, and people were running to keep up with it; hard-faced men they were, and the delirious women were more frightening even than the men. He seemed to remember that they were carrying flowers. Then there were the guns, and he and Joachim caught in the narrow street. . . .

"Perhaps not," he said. "Anyway, I'm in the middle of the hospital drive. These are hard days. People aren't able to fulfill their pledges and the new wing's waiting to be completed. No, I've got my hands full right now."

But he was restless that night. For a long time he watched the shadows on the ceiling, his mind roving from the day he had met Iris back to the morning on which she had been conceived; his mind roamed like a vagrant, picking up papers in odd corners of the path. He went as far back as Alfie's house, where he had spent so many sunny summer hours with Marian, who, in her helpless innocence, now lay in the other bed. He could see every corner of Alfie's place, the tennis court and the pool and the walk through the cedar woods where he had first kissed Marian and sealed the bargain.

Then, falling asleep, he flitted through wretched dreams.

He was in the dentist's chair and told that all his teeth had to come out. But teeth were indestructible. How can that be? he cried in his dream. And then he was at Leah's house, and Hank was crying because the dog had been run over and lain suffering in the street. He woke with relief.

Without raising his head, he could see the bedside clock. It was only six, and although he was ready to rise, he lay awhile, not wishing to awaken Marian. And while he lay watching the ceiling turn from gray through pearl to white, a thought took shape; surprising him at first, it grew solid and firm, until after an hour or so it emerged as a decision. It was quite clear and simple: He would buy a country house.

No doubt the idea had developed from the night's detailed recall of Alfie's place. But that makes no difference, he thought. I must have something for myself, an adult toy, if you want to call it that. It would be a place on Long Island at the shore. He'd have a sailboat and teach Hank to sail. He'd get Dan and Hennie out of their stuffy flat in the heat.

Yes, he must have something for himself, trivial as that something might seem to be. The making of money, community service, friends—all these were not enough.

I must have something for myself, he repeated.

By the time the city woke, when the sounds of the knife-grinder and the old-clothes man were heard in the street below, he had laid his plans.

Far out on the Island, he found an old house. It was a little place, a Cape Cod cottage, in need of much repair. Five acres of windblown scrub pine, sedge grass, and bluff and dune went with it. The nearest neighbor on this promontory, reached by the sandy road that paralleled the shore, was a lighthouse, a Victorian structure with gingerbread carving on the eaves below the tower. Its light would be a comfort on some pitch-black night during a summer storm.

The real estate broker, obviously overjoyed at Paul's quick

decision and afraid to upset it, went outdoors, leaving him alone to walk through the little rooms and climb the stairs, as steep as a ladder, to the pair of tiny bedrooms under the eaves. Plain whitewashed walls, he was thinking. A rag rug, so your feet won't get cold when you step out of bed. Bare windows, so you can look straight down to the bright little beach, or in the other direction to the solitary oak, now rosy red as a Bordeaux in an old bottle. No decorations, except a few pictures like that primitive he'd seen last week, a stiff early-American patriarch with his hand on a globe. Maybe he'd find a child somewhere, a dark-haired little girl holding a cat.

When he came home and told her about the place, Marian made comment. "It's an awfully long drive and terribly lonesome, the way you describe it." And when he had refuted neither of these objections, she had said, "Well, it's your decision. You've been generous to me with the Florida place, so it's only fair for you to take your turn."

Hennie, frugal as always, was cautious. "Hadn't you better ask Alfie about it? After all, he does know real estate."

"No. Maybe it's a bad investment, but I don't care. I want it."

Right after the closing, on a brilliant windy day in November, he suggested a picnic to celebrate.

"It will be freezing at the shore," protested Marian.

He had expected her not to want to go. But he persisted, as he knew he was expected to persist. "Don't you even want to see the place?"

"But it's not as if I hadn't seen it once."

They had taken a ride there some weeks before and, although she had obviously not been enchanted as he had been, she had been kind enough to pronounce the house "very sweet." It was clear that she had no intention of spending much time in it.

"Well, all right. Then I'll take Hennie and Dan and maybe Hank. They'll enjoy the day."

"As long as you're back in time for dinner."

He made an early start. He had a new car, a Renault which, according to Hank anyway, looked as if someone had flattened its nose. But there was always a gala feeling about a new car and Paul, looking up at the encouraging sky, a bright dry blue, was in high spirits. Leah—it occurred to him that, for some odd reason, he hadn't mentioned that she was coming too—brought a picnic basket, along with the dachshund, Strudel the Second; at the age of twelve, he was still in good condition and went everywhere with her. They all climbed in and rolled off to Long Island. Leah and Hank sang part-songs. Hennie and Dan just sat back to enjoy the rare pleasure of a ride into the country. And nobody complained about anything.

The only remark that came anywhere close to a complaint was from Dan.

Paul had pointed out a great mansion surrounded with lawns and greenhouses. "It belongs to a client of mine. It's a middle-sized Versailles."

"Greenhouses?" Dan almost spluttered. "What for?"

Paul, explaining that the main house would require fresh flowers every day, expected Dan's reaction. "Revolting display! Immoral!"

A socialist to the end! Paul had to chuckle to himself.

"We're almost there," he said as they bumped down the lane that led from the main road. "I warned you all, it's not a fashionable neighborhood. No greenhouse, Dan."

"Good," Hennie said.

He drew the car up behind the house. They all got out and following him to the beach, stood in silence before the immense sparkle of the Sound. There were no waves; it was absolutely quiet, nothing moved except for a solitary sail far out on the horizon.

Paul broke the silence. "There's nothing to do here. Just a little clamming and fishing. It hasn't changed in two hundred years. Let me show you the house. And after that, how about some food?"

He had expected Hennie and Dan to approve of the house for no other reason than its simplicity. He was surprised, though, when Leah made comment.

"I don't know what your plans are, Paul. But if this were my place, I wouldn't do anything more than clean it up. I wouldn't even curtain the upstairs windows. Nobody can look in, and I'd want to look at the world that's out there."

"I do want to build a little dock and a boathouse," he observed, when they had spread their blankets on the shaggy grass. "I'd like to teach you to sail, Hank. It beats a motorboat all hollow. With sail, you're really one with the sea."

Leah unpacked the basket, which was expensively fitted with proper napkins and cloth, glasses and utensils.

"Here's pâté—I was feeling French today—and French bread. Feel, it's still warm. Three different cheeses, take your pick. There's soup in the thermos."

Neatly and deftly, she spread the meal, roast chicken, little sausages, fruit, and cake. "Oh, if we were in France—how I loved France—we'd have wine; even you would, Hank, you'd have yours watered. But as long as we're here, we'll have coffee instead and fruit punch for you."

It was a pleasure to watch her, Paul thought; she wasn't tired, she didn't have a headache, and she ate with appetite, chewing the chicken down to the bone, sucking the last juice from the orange.

When they had finished, Hennie wanted to help clean up, but Leah would have none of it.

"No, no. Hank and Dan want to take a walk toward the lighthouse. Go along. It'll do you good."

She put a cigarette into her long, black lacquered holder and leaned back, sighing, "Oh, that was delicious." She had wrapped herself warmly in a wine-colored wool cloak, simple and perfect for the time and the place, over her brown woolen skirt. She looked like herself again, recovered from grief and horror.

"I want to thank you for being so good to Hank," Leah said. "Spending time with him. It's meant so much to him and to me."

"It's not been difficult."

"You've gone to a lot of trouble, taking him to science museums and working on his chemistry set, which I know nothing about."

"I assure you I know very little myself. Hank knows more than I do; he tells me about prehistoric brain development and I listen. I have a hunch he'll be a doctor. Anyway, things are finally returning to normal for you both," Paul finished.

"Yes," she said. "It was that or go mad. I've had to look at the truth." She seemed to be making a confession. "Ben was guilty, as guilty as Donal, the politicians and all the bluebloods who are making their fortunes out of the same pot. So his end could have been predicted. His end was written in his beginning."

"Donal's end, too, you're saying."

"Who can tell?" She was silent a moment, watching the trail of smoke from the cigarette. "But in the meantime, it's Meg I care about."

"I don't see her much, I'm sorry to say, except at duty affairs like Alfie and Emily's anniversary."

"I don't see her that much either, although they keep inviting us to use the pool or to spend Sunday with them. But Hank absolutely hates to go. I can't understand why he makes such a fuss. Can you?"

"No," Paul said.

"Look, Paul, they were in a rotten, risky business, but I can't blame Donal because some thugs tried to rob my husband and shot him. Right?"

"Right," Paul said.

"Personally, I enjoy myself whenever we go. It's lively, Meg's in much better spirits than she used to be, and the kids are adorable."

Paul, wanting to leave the subject of Donal, remarked, "She hasn't had a baby lately. Isn't it time for another?"

Leah made a face. "There isn't going to be another. That's why she's in good spirits. I made her get a diaphragm."

"*You* did? You?"

"Yes, I. She was falling apart. And he wanted nine children or more. Imagine forcing a woman like that, against her will! So I sent her to a doctor, with Donal none the wiser." And Leah grinned her satisfaction.

Paul thought irrelevantly, Imagine Marian talking to a man about diaphragms! But plenty of women today were as free in their speech as only men would have been before the war. Now everybody talked about sex. Women drank; women used lipstick and rouge; only prostitutes had done that before the war. And he glanced at Leah's nails, which were the same bright rose as her lips, and very becoming, too.

The walkers returned. "It was a bit far for Dan," Hennie reported. "Perhaps he shouldn't have gone walking on the sand, although Hank helped him."

"It's time to go home anyway," Leah said.

"Who'll race me to the end of the lane and back to the car?" asked Hank.

His mother made the offer. Hennie and Dan climbed into the car, Paul turned it about, and they all watched the race between the boy and the woman, with the old dog lagging behind. The wind raised Leah's short skirt, exposing her strong thighs. Hard flesh, Paul thought; she would be hard, and soft in the right places.

What was the matter with him? You'd think it was spring, the time when a man was expected to have aberrant thoughts, when the earth was rich, sap rising, and the air so soft on the skin after the long, dry winter. Now here was the long, dry winter about to begin, he having springtime reactions and in the presence of Leah. Of all people, Leah!

They had turned and were running toward the car, with the boy only a little ahead of his mother, who was running fast, with her cloak flying and her sumptuous hair bouncing. Nearing the car, she dropped her purse and as she stooped to pick it up, he saw a thin gold chain between her breasts. It held a plump gold locket. The sight of it puzzled him, staying with him even as he put the car in gear and rolled away.

After a while it came to him: Anna had had a locket like that. Not that there was anything unusual about it, but yes, Anna had worn one under her blouse, under the ruffles. It was all so confusing, enough to make the mind reel, that anything, even a common object worn by a woman he didn't care about, could return him to Anna. . . .

As usual, the desk was piled with mail when some months later, Paul walked into his office. Miss Briggs put his personal mail on the blotter. Although Joachim's letters with the foreign stamp were never marked "Personal," she knew that they were.

> Joachim was still an ostrich. I would say that things, at least for me, are rather better than they have been in a long time. True, the anti-Jewish propaganda continues, but economically there has been a real upsurge. Business is booming so much that I believe the Jewish problem will die a natural death. When money jingles in their pockets, people are happy, and they don't have the wish to hate.

At the bottom of the letter, surely written without Joachim's knowledge, Elisabeth had added a tiny postscript.

> I want us to leave. I am terribly frightened, even though Joachim isn't.

The postscript was a faint whisper. He could hear Elisabeth's voice as clearly as if she had been standing there, pulling at his sleeve.

He got up again and walked to the window. A thin rain was falling; the tops of cars crawling beneath him shone like beetles. Scraps of tinsel from discarded Christmas trees, the remnant of the year's last office parties, blew on the sidewalks. It was a good day to be indoors out of the wind, and because there was no inducement to go out, a good day to accomplish a lot of work. But he was still restless. He had been working steadily, he realized, since the summer, without a break. He was always so busy . . . and why? Surely it was not to lay aside a fortune for a family. He wasn't even free to buy a chocolate bar for the one child he had.

He went back to the desk and turned over some papers, a proposition for a buy-out of a machine tool factory in Illinois. It seemed to be a profitable venture, a rarity in these years that were still lean in spite of the New Deal. If Alfie had money to invest, it might be a good thing for him. Hank's funds, he thought sourly, were doing well in Hitler's Germany, thanks to Donal Powers's manipulation.

The restlessness grew. It grew into a tremendous desire, pulling at him as it had done only once before, in the time of the stillborn baby and all the trauma that came after, when he had gotten on the ship and sailed away.

And then he remembered the talk he had had with the rabbi some months before. He picked up the telephone.

"I'm going to Europe, Rabbi," he said. "To Germany. Is there anything you want me to do, anyone you want me to see?"

The old voice crackled. "You're not going inside Germany?"

"Yes, I'll be safe enough."

"I don't know." The voice was doubtful.

"I've made up my mind."

"Well, then, I'll get some letters and notes together for you. When are you planning to leave?"

He hadn't planned. It was all coming together while he spoke.

"As soon as I can get passage. It shouldn't be hard this time of year. I'll be going to England first. Do you remember what you were telling me about the Palestine situation? I've got clients in England too. Important political people. Money talks, Rabbi. Even though they don't give a damn about getting refugees to Palestine, money talks."

"Unfortunately yes. Well, come in and talk to me. Any morning this week. I'm at your service."

"I want to get all your thoughts about the Balfour Declaration. I know the theory, of course, a homeland for the Jews, but I'll want to know facts and figures. What arguments to present, and a pile of information that I know you must have at the tips of your fingers."

"I'll give you the best I can . . . Paul?"

"Yes, Rabbi?"

"God bless you."

He rang for Miss Briggs. "Will you find out now when the *Normandie* sails again? I want passage for England."

"For one, Mr. Werner?"

"For one. I have to see the Morehouse brothers in London." And he added, feeling at the same time foolish for making any explanation, "Mrs. Werner will be going to Florida."

"If there's an earlier sailing instead of the *Normandie,* shall I book that?"

"No, I'll wait for the *Normandie.* "

She was only a year old, a fabulous ship, he had heard. There was nothing else like it on the high seas. He might as well have some excitement while he was at it.

When he called her later in the day, Marian complained, "Why do you always have to go to Europe in the middle of winter?"

"Not always. This is only the second time."

Her sigh almost blew across the telephone wire. "Well, if you have to. Business is business, I suppose."

"It surely is, my dear. Besides, you're leaving for Florida next week, so what difference does it make?"

"That's true. While you're in London, perhaps you can get a few pieces of our Royal Crown Derby. That clumsy girl just broke another cup last week."

"I'll do that."

"Also, while you're there, you might get yourself some sweaters. Yours are too worn. They all have pills on the sleeves."

Pills on the sleeves? For a moment he didn't understand what she was talking about. "Yes, yes. Anything else?"

"Oh, I'll have to think. I'll make you a list."

Yes, and it would be a mile long. He didn't care. He didn't care about anything except that he was going.

The sense of adventure remained with him and he was filled with the joyous expectation that he would have said, only a few days earlier, he would probably never feel again. He had not realized how "down" he had been.

When the taxi deposited him and his bags at the pier, the ship loomed like a mountain alongside. He strode into the cavernous, echoing building and got in line with his ticket and passport. It was foggy, damp and cold; horns honked out on the street, men shouted each other out of the way as they trundled trunks, a brassy woman, probably a movie star, carried a yelping poodle under her arm and fought her way to the front of the line ahead of Paul, who didn't mind. He was loving it, loving every hectic second of it.

There was no great crowd, with mountains of luggage, as there would have been in a clement vacation season. There were obvious business travelers like himself, for whom weather could be no impediment. But the others, bound on a stormy crossing toward Europe's frozen winter, set his imagination to work. He fancied that they were people running toward new loves on the other side of the ocean, or away from lost loves, or maybe they were fleeing from embezzlement or some other crime. Romantic fancies! So he amused himself.

Then he went up the gangplank and stepped on board. Had he been on a Cunard ship, an officer would have been there to greet him by name, but he liked the feeling of newness now, of being alone in a new place.

He decided to tour the ship. It was surely different from the others that he had known so well. It had vast spaces, vistas and sweeping stairs: a palace plan. The dining room glittered like Versailles; the ceiling was glass and the glass columns, he saw now in the wintry afternoon, were illuminated. The chandeliers blazed. He recognized an abundance of Lalique crystal.

There were no tables for one, so he reserved a small table for two, for he had no wish to take chances with a table full of strangers. This time he would simply relax and observe the scene.

Continuing his inspection, he saw the gymnasium, the blue mosaic swimming pool and the winter garden, a splendor of foliage, a tropical enclave of blooming flowers, with twittering budgerigars in enormous cages. Bemused by this superfluous luxury, he shook his head. Admittedly, though, he would enjoy it!

Then he went to seek the deck steward to reserve a chair on the promenade deck on the starboard side, which would be sunny, if by some chance there should be any sun. When he came downstairs, the chimes were ringing the last call for going ashore. The ship blasted its long, mournful warning note of departure. The sound was always thrilling, sending a shiver down the spine. And if I should go a hundred times, he thought, it would still send a shiver down my spine.

He went back up on deck. The cold was savage. The wind

cut through his heavy coat, but he wanted to see the departure and to watch the little tugs push the great ship out into the middle of the river, where it would move on its own power downstream, past the Statue of Liberty and out. Lights were on around the foot of the statue, and he gave it a salute. Lights were coming on in office buildings all the way down to the Battery. The ship gathered speed. The engines throbbed like a beating heart. He could barely see the gulls that had been following them, and would stay with them through the Narrows, into the channel. By the time they reached the Ambrose Lightship, it would be entirely dark. The pilot would go down the ladder and they would be finally at sea.

He was reluctant to go inside. There was no one else at the stern except a man with two teenage boys to whom he was showing the sights. This was probably the boys' first crossing, and Paul was reminded of his own first time, and how it had seemed to him that he was going to the moon.

But he turned about at last. Hurrying against the wind, he almost collided with a woman who was coming toward the door; stepping aside to let her pass, he excused himself, and saw that the woman was Leah.

She burst out laughing. "I didn't say a word when you told me you'd be on board. I thought a surprise would be fun. Oh, but don't"—she touched his arm—"don't feel obligated, please. This is pure coincidence, and if you had planned to be solitary, don't worry about me. I can find companions."

"I'm sure you can," Paul said.

Then they both laughed. He thought: She knows I know she's fibbing. She did this on purpose.

"Well, you do look stunning," he said.

She was wearing a black Persian lamb coat with a silver fox collar and a peacock-blue velvet hat. It was the silly little hat, the Eugénie, that the women were all wearing.

"No, I'm ridiculously dressed up, all wrong. But some friends gave me a bon voyage luncheon at the Waldorf and I didn't have time to go home and change. I've got a proper steamer coat and all the right things in my stateroom."

Assuredly, she would have the right things. "Let's get out of this wind and warm up with a drink," he said.

He followed her down into the warm depths of the ship, reflecting that only a few minutes ago he had rejoiced in the prospect of a long, quiet voyage in which he would be only an interested observer of others' sociability; he would have been exasperated to be told that a companion was to be forced upon him. And now suddenly he was feeling a small leap of pleasure in the prospect of a companion at his dinner table. But first a drink.

"Let's call this a get-acquainted drink," he said, when they were seated in a friendly nook. "I have just picked you up and we are introducing ourselves."

"It was the other way round, wouldn't you say?"

Leah settled back with a sigh of pleasure. She was wearing, with her very plain black woolen dress, a sumptuous necklace of carved turquoise, with a pair of bracelets to match. Estimating the cost of these, Paul decided that Ben must have left her with even more than he had thought. In a flash, his mind went back to the girl whom his mother had called, not unkindly, "Hennie's little waif." But she never had looked like a waif or behaved like one either.

"What shall it be?" he inquired when the bar steward approached. "A lady's daiquiri or are you game for a martini?"

"Neither. I'd like an aperitif. A Campari and soda."

Paul raised his eyebrows. "Gone European, have you?"

"Why not? This is a European ship and I'm on my way there."

"What takes you over at this time of year?"

"Buying. I don't go to the big showings in season. I have little couturieres who make things to order for my special customers. My business is very personal, you see. My women don't want Seventh Avenue copies of the big designers, so I keep everything individual and it pays. I couldn't be busier."

"Even with the Depression."

"Well, there are always people so rich that depressions don't touch them. You should know." Leah grinned. "And those who aren't all that rich still buy good clothes, because it's an advertisement for their husbands. After all, the best way to put yourself in a position to make money is to appear to have it. Hank thinks I'm disgustingly frivolous when I talk like this. He thinks it's terrible, when there are people who don't have a warm overcoat, to care about things like lowered hemlines and raised waistlines."

"He sounds like Hennie and Dan."

"He always has, hasn't he? He's a contradiction, my son. His friends and his politics are way-out liberal, but his morals are strictly middle class, almost puritanical."

"He's growing into a life of his own," Paul said, "which is as it should be. But still I miss the years when he needed me."

"He adores you, Paul."

In those first anguished days after Ben's death, the boy had been a mass of conflicts. And then gradually he had resolved them by condemning everything, chiefly money, that was involved with the memory of Ben. It troubled him that he need have no thought of money, that he had been able to stay in the private school when so many others had had to drop out, that he could go to Yale without applying for a scholarship or needing to wait on tables. He would have taken the sufferings of the world upon himself if he could, Paul reflected.

"He'll make a fine doctor," Paul said. "You'll be proud of him."

"For the first time, though, I'm sorry I didn't have one more child. It might have been a daughter. A girl must be such a comfort."

"I suppose so," Paul said. He turned his glass, staring into the rosy liquid.

"You look thoughtful. I suppose I sound pretty light-headed to you, too, going abroad to buy what Hennie calls 'doodads.' Are you like Hennie and Hank, or are you like me?" She leaned toward him with chin in hand and fixed him with a bright impertinent gaze.

"I should say I'm somewhere in between. I think you must do what you can for others, but there's no harm in taking some pleasure for yourself along the way."

Her eyes went serious. "Hennie told me why you're going. What this trip's for."

Automatically he felt in his breast pocket for the envelope containing the bank draft to be used at his discretion in England or Germany or both. He dared not trust it even to his locked luggage.

"I'm going to try," he said. "God knows how much I'll be able to accomplish."

"Is it really as awful as I've heard?"

"I daresay it's worse."

They were both silent. Voices at the surrounding tables came sharply into their silence. A young couple was speaking French and four Americans were discussing their plans.

"I can get all my Paris shopping over with in a few days. We're in such a hurry to get to Germany. Bruce says it's simply wonderful now, so clean and orderly and the people are really friendly—"

Paul and Leah looked at each other. What comment could one make? So they made none, finished their drinks, and stared out of the window into total darkness.

They were now unmistakably in the open sea. The ship creaked and lurched. "They say the *Normandie* vibrates too much," Paul remarked. "Not good for seasickness, I'm afraid. Does it ever bother you?"

"Not yet. But this is only my third crossing."

"Well, I've got Mothersill's seasick remedy. I haven't had to use it either, so I don't know how much good it does. Maybe no more than the standard remedies, chicken sandwiches or oysters. Some recommend champagne."

"You're making me feel starved." And of a passing steward, Leah asked, *"A quelle heure le dîner, s'il vous plaît?"* When he had replied, she turned with a little air of triumph to Paul. "How's that? I've been taking French at Berlitz."

"You have a good ear. Your accent's perfect." And he remembered how, from her first employer, who had been Irish, she had acquired for the length of her stay there a delightful lilt. Clever monkey!

"I tell people I learned it from my governess. Aren't I a riot?"

"That you are," he said. "Come, let's get dressed for dinner."

They'd have an excellent dinner. He planned to get pleasantly drunk on champagne.

"Oh, I'm stuffed," Leah said happily.

They had eaten their way through pineapple Pompadour—a concoction of caviar, sour cream, and pineapple chunks—salad, and roast veal. Now, after the fruit and cheeses, came the *friandises*, a plate of spun-sugar sweets and candied fruits.

"Can't eat another mouthful," she said, tasting a sugared strawberry. She giggled. "Isn't it marvelous?"

"I'm thinking it's marvelous that you keep your waistline."

"You don't think I eat this way all the time, do you? Oh, but look around, Paul. How gorgeous it is! Don't you love it? And nobody's even dressed for it. Wait until second night out, with the men in white tie and tails. The dresses will be something to see, I'll bet."

Paul looked around at the glitter, the flicker, the gleam of all the mirrors and flowers. He motioned toward the grand staircase.

"The French know how to do it. Every woman making her entrance at the top of that staircase will feel like a queen."

"She'd better be dressed like one, too, with all these eyes on her. Oh, but it's marvelous. I love to dress up."

He had to smile at her pleasure. "You don't change," he said. "You still keep your enthusiasm. You don't even look any different."

"I change. I'm thirty-seven."

"You don't look it."

"We go back a long time, Paul, don't we? I remember the first time Hennie and Dan took me to your house. It was a Sunday dinner, and Aunt Hennie had bought me a new dress. For goodness' sake, she had to buy a whole wardrobe for me, I had nothing! I was so impressed and scared, too. I knew nothing about table manners and there were so many different forks on the table."

"My mother was a fanatic about silver. I hope I was nice to you."

"You've always been nice to me." She raised the coffee cup and gazed out over the rim. "Yes . . . when you think of all the things that have happened to us since then . . . the loves and the marriages."

He had no wish, just then, to think about them.

"Tell me more about your business," he prompted.

At once she was eager. "The wholesalers tell me I ought to open a Florida place, put in a manager and maybe go down for a month or so myself every winter, but I'm not sure I want to. I wouldn't even know where to open, Palm Beach or Miami." She laughed. "Depends on whether I want to cater to the Jewish trade or the others. It's a total divide down there."

"Where isn't it?"

"Nowhere. New York's divided: Jews on the West Side, except for a handful of fancy ones like us." She gave him a shrewd grin. "And the Jews are divided themselves. People who live on the Grand Concourse are on another planet from the ones who live on West End Avenue. And the country clubs! The name-calling: this one's stodgy, that one's nouveau

—though I notice that people who condemn the stodgy would give their eyeteeth to get in. But then, you know all about that, don't you?"

"Oh, I know."

"I hear that sort of stuff all the time. Women gossip when they shop, the way they do at the hairdresser's. It's all such rot, especially when you consider the state of things, as Hank would say." She frowned and asked abruptly, "Tell me, where do *you* think we're heading?"

"Maybe toward a war."

"God, no! Not another. The damn Germans again. Of course, they're the whole problem."

"Not the whole problem. I'm concerned about France, too. I think they're in deep trouble. People have lost confidence in their government."

"When I was there two years ago, everybody was complaining about taxes."

"The rich don't pay any. They send their capital abroad instead. I've got plenty of French investors in my office right now."

"But that's blackmailing their own government, isn't it? It's like saying, raise taxes again and we'll send all our money out of the country."

"Right. If you ever get tired of the dress business, maybe we can find a job for you in banking," Paul teased. "Come on, this talk is getting too serious. How would a little night air suit you?"

"Fine. I'll run and get my coat."

"By the way, where are you?"

"On A deck."

"So am I. Meet you back at the elevator in two minutes."

She came back wearing a huge plaid steamer coat with a plaid scarf wrapped around her head.

"I'll take you up to the boat deck. You'll think you're halfway to the sky."

The ocean heaved and the bow tilted upward. Here and there, through moving clouds, a strip of silver, thin as a scimitar, appeared; for an instant the strip of silver was reflected in the water, and covered up again as the waves engulfed it. They stood at the railing, watching the turbulence.

"It makes you feel as if you're on some dangerous adventure," Leah said. "All those miles of fierce ocean underneath us."

"Ship's sound as a rock," Paul assured her while he remembered, but did not mention, the *Lusitania*. "What's up there?" inquired Leah.

"The kennels. We can go up in the morning and have a look if you'd like."

"Freddy told me how you brought Strudel home that summer when you and he went to Europe together."

She never mentioned Freddy. No one ever mentioned Freddy. Surprised, Paul answered quietly, "Yes, he was so worried about the little thing. He visited the kennels half a dozen times every day."

"Freddy was a tender soul."

"Yes. I loved him. You don't mind talking about him?"

"Of course not. What's past is past. Ben's past now, seven years already, and I don't think very much about him anymore. And Freddy's longer past, as if I'd known him in another life. The only reminder of him is Hank, and he's so different from Freddy that he isn't much of a reminder." A flash of light, as two clouds parted again, illumined Leah's face. Her eyes were soft. "Paul . . . I always wonder whether I thank you enough for being so fatherly to him."

"You thank me all the time and you don't have to."

"You've been so good to him and for him. Excuse me for getting sentimental. I'm a little drunk, I think."

"That's all right, I am too. How about going downstairs for a nightcap while we're about it?"

"I have champagne in my room. Why pay for more?"

"Practical soul! Fine, we'll drink some of yours."

In Leah's cabin, which, except for the color scheme, was the mirror image of Paul's own, the bed had already been turned down. A nightdress, robe, and slippers were laid out. On a table under the porthole stood a tall vase with American Beauty roses and a box of chocolates in the familiar lavender tin from Saks Fifth Avenue.

Leah followed his glance. "Five pounds of chocolates and two dozen roses. Pretty nice, don't you think?"

"Indeed! Who's the admirer?"

"Bill Sherman. He's a lawyer. Such a sweet man. The champagne is from Meg."

"Thoughtful Meg. Have you seen her lately?"

"Oh, yes, she buys clothes like mad. It's not that she wants them, but Donal does. He calls me with a list of what she needs, mostly evening things, the most expensive. I swear, the man's got to be made of money. He's collecting more real estate, must own a quarter of New York, Chicago, and heaven only knows where else, by now."

Paul, recalling the confrontation over the German affair, would have liked to speak his mind, but was afraid that she might accidentally let something slip to Dan. And then, suddenly, some basic need for fairness compelled him to say, "We owe him a good deal, though, don't we, for the time he rescued Dan and then Alfie? No small favors, either one of them."

"True enough." And Leah reflected, "I daresay Meg feels pretty grateful. That, plus the diaphragm, mostly the diaphragm, have kept things going rather well between them."

Passion. You left that out, Paul thought. Once Leah had spoken of Meg's "infatuation," but that was a passing thing, and not the same. A passionate attachment could last a lifetime. . . . He didn't think Leah would understand, except to give sympathetic lip service. He didn't think she would ever be as wildly swept away as Meg had been, or as he himself had been, and was. . . .

Leah crossed the room. "Have some of my admirer's chocolates. They don't go too badly with champagne."

"Yes, they do. Tell me about your admirer."

"I told you. He's very special, very smart, with a top practice, and he would like to marry me. Or he would, if I gave him any encouragement."

"Why don't you encourage him, then?"

"A third marriage? Doesn't that make me seem like an awfully fast woman, and you know I'm not . . . will you have another glass? I won't, I'm dizzy already, and blazing hot in this wool dress. Do you mind if I take it off?"

"Not at all, I'll simply turn my back."

"You needn't. My slip's perfectly decent. In fact, it's nice enough to be an evening dress if it were longer. All handmade and real lace. There's nothing like French underwear. Take a look."

He looked. She was all curves; her breasts rose in two white hemispheres above the lace; her hips arched from her small waist. She stood still, watching his eyes travel up and down and back, to stop at her own bright, half-mocking eyes.

She wasn't a beautiful woman, but she was strong, bursting with life, and would be warm. He wondered what she had been doing since Ben's death. Probably nothing. Women didn't travel every few weeks to other cities and find a man expecting them. Quite possibly she had simply been waiting and wanting.

He crossed the room and put his hands on her shoulders. The ship rocked and they swayed with it. Leah, laughing, steadied herself with her arms about his neck; her hands almost burned the back of his neck.

Then the laugh died, and she pulled his face toward her own, toward her full ready mouth, and he caught her closer, while everything went whirling: the certainty of what was about to happen and the astonishment that it should be with Leah, here and now. Why should it be Leah? Why should it have been Ilse? he thought in the flash of a second; that, too, had been an unexpected storm. . . . He had not thought about her in months, even years.

Now, though, he was answering Leah's need, matching her need, with all the while this whirl of astonishment in his head as he saw himself, saw themselves hurrying, until they were together on the bed, and the light went out, and the ship rocked and the fire mounted, racing, and would not be put out.

The crossing was a rough one. The ship pitched and ropes went up in the corridors. Several times, the dining room was almost half empty. But Paul and Leah never missed a meal, not tea and cake at five in the lounge, nor bouillon at eleven in the morning. Side by side, they sat on the promenade deck, wrapped in their rugs, reading or simply gazing out at the gray-green heaving sea.

Out of the corner of his eye, he watched her as she gazed. Blaming himself as always for being too analytical, for never being able simply to take his pleasures, to accept a gift without looking for motives or pondering where it might lead in the future, he nevertheless proceeded to analyze his feelings. Chiefly, there was gratitude for these few nights that had given him more pleasure than he had had in far too long. He had had no idea . . . they'd known each other—for how many years? And now this, out of the blue. He chuckled inwardly and felt a surge of tenderness.

She was a brave, good-natured soul. She'd give you the shirt off her back. He wondered what her expectations might be. She couldn't possibly be expecting these few nights in her bed to mean anything permanent . . . still, one couldn't be sure.

"What are you thinking?" she asked.

He started and lied. "Nothing special. Just looking out at where the sky and the water ought to meet, and can't find the place with all these clouds."

"No, you aren't. You were looking at me."

"Well, so I have, some. You're very nice to look at. Did I tell you I like that plaid suit? I like all your clothes, as a matter of fact."

"Do you like me better without clothes?"

"Need I tell you?"

She threw the blanket aside and sat up straight on the side of the steamer chair. "I could easily fall in love with you, Paul."

He laid his hand over hers, not knowing how to answer.

She caught his hesitation. "You don't have to answer. And I'm not asking for anything. Only tell me this much, is it wonderful for you, too, being here like this?"

"I'm very happy, Leah dear, can't you tell that I am?"

She nodded. "Yes, you've done more laughing than I remember seeing you do in ages."

"That's true, I have."

"Of course, you know I planned this."

He grinned. "I suspected as much. But have you—" He didn't want to say "been in love," so he said instead, "—had ideas like this for a long time?"

"It's hard to say. They've been creeping up for a while, I guess. I've been with you more these past few years, with you being so close to Hank, and I've been seeing other things—" She stopped.

"Such as?"

"Well, frankly, that you and Marian aren't the most blissful pair. I suppose—no, I'm sure, that if I thought you were, nothing like this would have entered my mind."

He felt his lips tighten. Some deep inhibition, owing either to pride or loyalty and probably to a combination of both, would not permit him to talk about Marian.

Leah asked quickly, "Are you offended? I'm sorry. I respect Marian. Everyone does. You're a respected couple, but I can't help seeing things, little things. I've known you too long not to see."

"Let's put it this way," he said dryly, "you're very acute."

She searched his face. "Yes, and acute enough to know when to stop. I hope you're not angry at me now."

She looked so appealing that he relented. After all, she had only seen the truth and said it. He got up and pulled her to her feet.

"Come on, five times around the deck is only a mile. Are you game for two miles?"

It was so good to be with a healthy woman. No dampness bothered her sinuses, no wind—and the wind was enough to blast you off an open deck—took her breath or disturbed her hairdo; she wasn't seasick and didn't tire. They played shuffleboard on the top deck and went swimming in the turquoise pool. They combed through every shop on board. At the movies, they still marveled at pictures that talked.

And always Paul was aware that attention was being paid to them. People looked when Leah made the grand entrance at the top of those spectacular stairs. He liked to catch their dual reflection on the mirrored walls: himself tall in his tailcoat, and she striking in cream-colored satin or in her black velvet with ermine bands. She still wore a broad diamond wedding ring, as well as the eight-carat solitaire on the other hand. Surely, then, it was assumed that they were married. Because they stayed conspicuously to themselves, it was probably also assumed that they were on their honeymoon. And with good fortune, there was no one on the voyage who recognized either one of them.

To think that he had looked forward to a restful, solitary six days at sea! This was the liveliest time he had ever had, as she transferred to him her own delight in everything. He couldn't remember when he had had such pleasure in dancing, sliding with the roll of the ship, with the sweetness of Leah's Shalimar under his nose.

Only sometimes . . . sometimes when they were dancing, a sudden pang like a stitch in the side or a shooting dart through the temple, would come as he thought of Anna. Leah, were she in Anna's place, would not let *conscience* restrain her; she would come to me, if only for a day or a night; she would find a way. She would let me know our child. Fear would never hold Leah back.

Then he would scold himself, repeating his own sensible admonition: What's past is past. Go forward.

The time went too quickly. When the paper hats and the noisemakers appeared at the Captain's Dinner on the next to last night, the mood changed. One prepared to rearrange one's luggage and to be early in line at the purser's window in the morning to change money. Paul was to debark at Southampton, while Leah would continue across the Channel to Le Havre.

She sighed. "I wish we could go on for another week, don't you?"

"I do. But if I were to keep on feeling younger every day, I'd probably be back in grade school after another week."

"You've made me very happy, Paul."

Hearing the little quiver in her throat, he kept his own tone light. "We've made each other happy and that's a big part of what life's about." This is no time to sort out one's feelings; indeed, must they always be sorted out? "It's been an unexpected gift from the gods. So let's simply say thank you to the gods and take what comes one day at a time. Does that make sense to you?"

She said at once, "Perfect sense. Absolutely perfect."

"When you get to the Crillon, change my room reservation to the same floor as yours. I'll be there on the first. And have a time for yourself till I get there."

"I will. Who can help having a time for himself in Paris?

But Paul, do be careful in Germany. You're very much needed.
Hank needs you."

Clever girl. Not "I need you," but "Hank needs you."
Clever girl.

"I'll be careful," he said.

Eleven

Down from the fairy-tale world of the ship, Paul descended into reality. In handsome Belgravia drawing rooms and once in a grand half-timbered country house, he sat among grim-faced gentlemen, the leaders of the Jewish community in England. They were a varied group, the same as at home, except that in this country a few bore titles. Others were the sons of immigrants. All were fearful as they gave reports of bad news.

Almost a quarter of the Jews in Germany, deprived of their means of livelihood, were now reduced to eating in charity kitchens, the charity being largely given by America's Joint Distribution Committee and by the Central Jewish Fund in England. Even as Paul handed over the large check which he had been empowered to bring, he was aware that in the face of fresh disaster, it was not large enough. How much would ever be enough? he wondered.

The British government, Balfour Report or no, was tightly

limiting the numbers of Jews allowed to go to Palestine. Powerful industrial interests, fearful of offending the Arabs, were holding firm control. The attitude of the British upper classes toward the persecutions in Germany ranged from indifference to—and this, to Paul who had so loved England, was most shockingly painful—approval. Lloyd George himself, upon returning from Germany, had actually praised Hitler as a bold achiever who had taken hold of a foundering economy, set it afloat, and brought order out of chaos.

He was given a list of people to see when he went to Germany: heads of a Kultusgemeinde, rabbis, and business leaders. He prepared to set forth. The few personal business appointments he had to keep in the City were suddenly of diminished importance, as the fact of Germany loomed closer. As he boarded the boat train, and looked out at the wintry sunlight glistening on suburban rooftops, he felt that, disappointing as England had been, he was leaving a flowering meadow to enter into the moldy cellar that was Germany.

On the train to Berlin, he would have liked to plug his ears and shut out the sound of American and British voices. They were the animated voices of tourists who were coming here for pleasure. He recognized the feeling that one has on the way to the funeral of somebody one has known all one's life. There was the same dragging at the stomach, the same tightness in the throat. So he sat buried in his thoughts.

At the great central railroad station, he took a taxi and gave Joachim's address. It was late afternoon. The streets were jammed with shoppers and homebound traffic. The taxi's crawl gave Paul a chance to observe and read signs. In spite of all he had heard, the reality seemed not quite plausible. Signs in windows and on hoardings: DON'T BUY FROM JEWS. And everywhere the Brownshirts, singly and in groups, all swaggering and inordinately tall. Then he thought, that's absurd, they're no taller than I am. It's just my fear.

And he felt for the American passport in his breast pocket,

where it lay along with the checks and lists. He felt as though he were carrying a gun to protect himself. And yet there had been tales of foreigners who, in spite of orders that foreigners were not to be harmed, had mysteriously been run over or fallen out of windows.

The taxi turned into a residential quarter. Wide streets, old trees, and the even facades of the apartment buildings declared that it was an expensive quarter. So it was true that Joachim was doing well. The courtyard into which they drove was much like the one he had had in Munich, with tall wrought-iron gates and flourishing evergreens in stone pots. Paul paid the taxi and was directed to the floor above.

The door was opened at once when he rang, and Joachim's arms went around him.

"Thirteen years!" he cried. "Thirteen years!" His eyes were wet. "Elisabeth, where are you? Our American is back."

She came running from an inner room. "Oh, how bad you are! You promised to come with Marian and spend a summer vacation with us. You waited all this time and now you come again without her. Well, never mind, we mustn't scold you. Come in. So much has happened, we have so much to talk about."

She was still voluble, still blond and pretty, except that, like most German women, she had grown too plump.

"And here's our Gina. You remember Regina?"

She was an athletic wiry girl, about fifteen years old, with long curly hair and a strong-featured face. Around her neck, over a plain gray sweater, hung a small Star of David on a gold chain.

"You were two years old when I met you," he told her.

"And this is Klaus, Klaus Wilhelm. You never met."

"How are you, Klaus? You weren't born yet when I was here . . . you look like your father."

The boy smiled. Good, Paul thought. At his age, I would have resented a dumb remark like that, but no one ever made it because I didn't look like my father. He winked at Klaus, who returned the wink.

"We've got dinner all ready," Elisabeth said. "You must be starved. I hope you are."

"I'm sorry I'm later than I said I would be. The train was late and the traffic coming from the station was unbelievable."

"Yes, there's plenty of traffic. Everyone's busy working and buying." Joachim's voice boomed with enthusiasm. "Here, let me take your bags. Wash up and join us when you're ready."

On the way to the guest room, Paul took in a quick impression of the home, recognizing the Biedermeier desk, the Empire chairs, the Bechstein piano, the gloomy library, the ferns and the marble mantels. All was the same as before, except perhaps larger, more lofty and ornate.

Joachim took his place at the end of the same long refectory table. "Come sit next to me, Paul. Elisabeth has a feast prepared. It's not like the last time. Remember the inflation, when we had to measure the sugar and the butter? We were so afraid we wouldn't have enough for you. No, it's not like that anymore." He unfolded his napkin and waited for his wife and daughter to bring dishes in from the kitchen. "We have no maids, you see. Our two helpers had to leave us after fifteen years. Irma we had longer than we've had Gina. Imagine! But Aryan women may not work for us. The government is afraid I will seduce them. Imagine me and Irma, that beefy, good-hearted creature! Do you know, she cried, she didn't want to leave us? Poor soul."

An enormous roast was placed in front of Joachim. He sharpened the carving knife and began to make expert slices. "Ah, that smells delicious. Just the right flavoring. Let me have your plate, Paul. Gina, give Cousin Paul the gravy boat. Yes, they do all right, my two girls. The apartment is really too large for them to handle without help, it's too bad. Still I feel it's beautiful here and it's home, so we manage. There's no point in trying to find someplace else."

"Especially," Gina said clearly, "when we're going to leave Germany anyway."

"Well, of course, unless there should be a military coup first and Hitler thrown out," her father replied. "And that will happen sooner rather than later, I'll wager. The old Prussian army people are all against him. They despise him, you know." He tucked his napkin in. "Potato pancakes, Paul? You see, as long as one can eat well, things can't be all that bad."

Paul said quietly, "We hear there's great need. The local Jewish communities don't have the income they used to have and can't meet the need. That's true, isn't it?"

"It's true that many Jews have been bankrupted. But those were the smaller, weaker firms in the first place. The people who do a big import-export trade, you see, those people bring foreign exchange into Germany and that's what the country needs, so nobody molests them. There are thousands, maybe fifty thousand Jewish firms still operating, like ours. We're doing splendidly, all this will pass like a bad dream. It will pass and be forgotten. I know my family thinks I'm stupid. Stupid but lovable, eh, *Liebchen?*" He touched his wife's hand. "But believe me, I know what I'm doing."

No one disputed him, and Joachim continued. "Of course, I'm aware that there's never enough money to help everyone who needs it. When was there ever enough? We do what we can. I know I do. Elisabeth will bear me out. She knows what I give."

"No one ever said you were not generous, Joachim," Elisabeth said. "But that's not what I think Paul means."

"I've brought a considerable sum," Paul said, "raised in the New York area. And there will be more coming from other parts of the United States and from England also. I can speak freely here, I feel. This is cash for clandestine use, for anyone who may need to get out in a hurry. To speak frankly, for bribes, to get to Palestine or anywhere."

A silence fell over the table. The candle flames jumped,

making eerie hollows in the still faces, and by contrast, darkening the farther ends of the room, so that it became a cave, and one had a sensation of something hovering behind one's back.

Elisabeth was the first to speak again. "How long will you be here, Paul?"

"Only a few days. I've come on Jewish affairs only, nothing private. After that, I go to Paris on private banking business." He turned to Joachim, saying seriously, "I have lists, names of people I should see. Forgive me for interrupting the dinner, but I feel such urgency. Will you take a look at this, please, Joachim? Are any of these men people you know?"

Joachim scanned the paper. "This one is my rabbi. I can take you to see him anytime. He lives right near here."

"I shouldn't want to disturb him in his home."

"He's used to that these days. We hold big meetings, community affairs, in private homes instead of public halls. You never know who'll be there when you announce a public meeting."

"Yes, you know very well," Elisabeth said. "The Gestapo will be there. They're at temple services, everywhere. That's how we live, in fear and trembling. The whole world ought to know how we live."

Joachim interrupted her. "The whole world knows too much, that's the trouble. And talks too much. Please, Paul, take no offense, but I have to tell you if your people in America and all the rest of Europe would stop your publicity and your agitation, we here would be better off. You're only fanning the flames. Left alone, they would no doubt gradually die down and we would survive in peace."

Elisabeth gave a long, audible sigh. Klaus rolled his eyes toward the ceiling. Only the young girl answered back.

"Papa, with all due respect to you, how can you talk like that when, even in school, they are preparing us to leave?"

"Gina is studying modern Hebrew to be ready for Palestine," her mother explained. "She knows how to do laundry, she's learning dressmaking and practical nursing. She'll be able to support herself, which is more than I can do."

"Palestine!" Joachim cried. "For how many centuries have we been here in Germany? Ever since the expulsion from Spain in 1492, and for some of us, centuries before that, a thousand years or more under the Roman Empire. How much more German can one be? To talk of emigration, of leaving it all," he said emotionally, "is fantastic. For God's sake, I belong to the Federal Union of Jewish War Veterans, I have the Iron Cross! Leave Germany? Desert our homeland now just because she's going through a bitter time? Ach, what's the use! And here you've come to dinner to listen to all this heavy argument. *Liebchen,* get the dessert, please. What have you made for us?"

"Pflaumetorte." Elisabeth rose at once.

Gina stood up, and the two who were female cleared the table. Young Klaus, being male, sat with his elders to be waited on. A German atmosphere indeed, Paul thought.

Joachim lit a lamp on the buffet. It had grown darker outside. "Heavy clouds," he said. "It's snowing." He lit another lamp, enlivening the dark hangings and the heavy furniture. When he returned to the table, he spoke with obvious intent to clear the atmosphere.

"She's a darling, my wife, but she talks nonsense sometimes. Palestine! What, shall we pick olives or herd sheep? It's all rocks and sand, from what one hears. Well, they're all upset and understandably. But one must be calm. Without calmness we shall fall apart. I'll take you to meet the rabbi tomorrow. Ah, what a handsome torte! And after dinner, we shall have some music. Elisabeth shall play for us. It's a good night for Chopin. He makes one think of spring and Majorca and the blue sea. Yes, after you have served the coffee, Elisabeth, you will play Chopin," repeated Joachim, thus bringing the discussion to an end and showing who was master in the house.

The rabbi's house, though as darkly and richly furnished as Joachim's, was smaller and much more crowded with books. The four walls of the study were covered with them from top to bottom; the rabbi's white head appeared from Paul's side of the desk, above another pile of books and documents. He looked like a rabbi, Paul thought, like one of the ancients, a Maimonides with a hawklike profile and luminous eyes.

"We are all of us very moved by your generosity, Herr Werner, that of the American community and your personal gift."

Seven men were present, in addition to Joachim and Paul. From their manner and dress Paul, who had a "nose" for such things, identified them: with the exception of one professor, they were men in authority, used to leadership, owners of factories and large establishments.

He told them, "The American community is still not doing enough. Too many of us still don't realize what's really happening. In fact, I think that there are some right here in this country who don't realize it either."

The rabbi nodded. "That's all too true, Herr Werner. It's very complicated. There were some who committed suicide when the Nazis came to power and there were others who stiffened themselves. Well, of course, that has happened throughout our history whenever persecutions break out. So it is."

Paul's eyes traveled over inanimate things so as to avoid the circle of troubled faces, and came to rest at a small landscape that stood on an easel near a window. The rabbi followed his gaze.

"Charming, isn't it? A gift from my congregation after thirty-five years. It's forbidden to show his work in the galleries today. It's forbidden to play the music of Mendelssohn, too. Yes, they think it will be just Jews who suffer. But already hundreds of Protestant pastors have been arrested.

These criminals have no regard for Christianity either. Did not Nietzsche call it a curse and a perversion? The only truth was war: women to give birth to fighters and men to fight."

"I am sixty-five years old," said the professor, "and when I was a student at the University of Berlin, I heard that kind of teaching even then."

"I had a letter last week," the rabbi said. "You used to live in Munich, Joachim, you knew Dr. Ilse Hirschfeld. They've taken her son away."

"Is that so? Yes, she was Elisabeth's doctor. Paul, you remember her." And Joachim explained, "We had some trouble, an accident, one day when Paul was there."

An accident! Paul thought. And he asked, "What happened, Rabbi?"

"She writes that he was passing out antiwar pamphlets when he was arrested. An exceptionally bright young man, I recall. She doesn't know where he is. She's desperate."

"He's a young, misguided socialist," Joachim said. "Always was." He spoke irritably. "My daughter, Gina, too. I only hope she stays out of trouble."

The rabbi continued as if he hadn't heard. "Mario. They named him after a relative on his father's side who went to Italy after the Russian Revolution and took an Italian name. As a matter of fact, Ilse had been preparing to go to Italy to join those relatives. But she wanted to keep earning some money here while she learned enough Italian to pass the licensing examinations. A great upheaval, a new language, a new start . . . Terribly difficult. And now this. Ah, well." He looked at his watch. "I'm sorry, but I have another appointment. It's very hard these days to keep everything in one's memory, all the lists and appointments. We don't put anything on paper," he explained to Paul, "not even the minutes of our meetings. Everything must be committed to memory, and at my age that's not easy," he added with a rueful smile. "Anyway, I want to thank you again on behalf of all of us.

God take you safely back to America, and please pray for us here. Pray that the storm will pass."

"He doesn't believe it will pass, though," Paul said as he walked out with Joachim.

"Perhaps not."

Their feet crunched on the previous night's fallen snow. Ice crystals glittered on posts and railings. The air was clean and keen in the nostrils; the world looked optimistic in the winter sunlight, making the inner burden all the heavier.

"That's a terrible thing about Dr. Hirschfeld," Paul said presently.

"I know. She probably doesn't know where to turn. No connections, being an immigrant and a woman besides." Paul hardly remembered what she looked like, only that they had warmed each other at a time when both needed warmth. And he wondered whether she had found a man who was right for her. A man would be fortunate to have her; kind, sensible and wonderful in bed . . .

"Is there no way you can help her?" he asked.

"No. I used to have connections. But these days you can't be sure who wants to remember you and who would rather not be reminded that you were once friends. I can't take a chance." Joachim seemed to be arguing with himself. "Can't risk my own neck." He glanced over at Paul, who was staring straight ahead, and then changed the subject. "I'm sorry I can't offer you entertainment, a concert or something. But it's not advisable to appear in public places, one isn't—" he gulped as though there were something in his throat.

Paul stopped in the middle of the sidewalk. "Dear Joachim," he said very gently, "I don't wish to revive last night's argument, but tell me honestly: You do know in your most secret heart, you do know, don't you, that you'll have to leave here eventually?"

The other man looked away from Paul and blinked against

the glitter of snow. "Perhaps. Unless things change for the better. If they don't, yes, then we shall have to go."

"As long as you don't wait too long."

By the end of the week, Paul was ready to say good-bye. Having done all he could do in Germany, at least for the present, he felt a rush of desire to free himself from German air. Once in Paris, he would breathe lightly again.

Yet it was painful to part from the Nathansohns.

He feared to think of what might become of them, forced out of this world into which they had been born, and through which his taxi, on the way to the station, was now taking him. It was a world of comfortable homes, of museums, parks, and shops full of fine things; a world of concerts, libraries, and schools. But it was crumbling. . . . One afternoon, while he accompanied Elisabeth on a brief household errand, they'd had to stop at a curb to let a short procession go by, some two dozen middle-aged men, each wearing a placard reading I AM A JEWISH PIG. The effect of this sight on an otherwise normal, workaday street was surreal. Every pulse in Paul's body had been jumping. The most remarkable thing, he had thought, was that the passersby on the street had paid so little attention to the utter horror of it.

After a moment, as though she had read Paul's mind, Elisabeth had said, "It happens all the time. We're used to it by now."

He had asked her what was to happen to the men they had just seen.

"It depends. They'll be taken to the police station where they'll be beaten up. Sometimes tortured. It's a question of who's in charge, what mood they're in. But before anyone's release, if he is released, he has to sign a statement saying that no one has harmed him."

"If he refuses to sign?"

"That would be very foolish, or maybe very noble and

brave, according to how you want to look at it, because the next stop is one of the camps."

Then she'd said, "I suppose that's what happened to Mario Hirschfeld. He wouldn't sign a statement like that. He'd die first. He's the kind of man who can believe in something enough to die for it. Do you understand, Cousin Paul?"

Ah, yes . . . how always willing they are, the best of our youth, to die for something!

"I understand," he'd answered gently.

"If there were more people like Mario, there wouldn't be" —she'd stopped for a moment and gone on— "if I only knew somebody important! There are people in the Nazi party, among the authorities, who can get people out of the camps. Not always, but if you have money and know whom to go to, sometimes."

That had been one of the most painful episodes in Paul's whole week of sharp impressions. The recollection of it rode with him now and was with him while he paid the driver, carried his bags into the terminal, and stood in line to buy his ticket to Paris.

The line was long. He stood with his bags at his feet and inched forward. Surrounded by the usual rush and commotion of the railroad station, he was yet seeing a different picture, or rather a collage of pictures: the men with the PIG signs, blood streaming from Joachim's head, Ilse Hirschfeld in her white coat, and Elisabeth telling him that "Mario would never sign . . . Mario would die first."

Something happened. Herr von Mädler, Paul thought. He had been a Werner client since before the last war, after all. Because his wife was an American, the family assets in the United States had not been frozen as enemy alien property, and because the Werner firm had managed them with skill, the assets had grown and handsomely supported the von Mädlers during the German inflation. He owes me something, Paul thought. At the same time, he remembered with disgust that meeting at which the man had predicted the last war and denounced all pacifists as degenerates, Communists, women, or Jews. "Not like you, of course, Herr Werner. A different type of Jew."

But such a man would have important contacts in the government. He owes me something, Paul thought again as he progressed toward the ticket window.

What a crazy impulse! To extend himself for a woman he hadn't seen for thirteen years, or for her son whom he had never seen!

And yet . . . "Mario would die first." Dan would, too, if he were here. The world moved forward inch by inch, like this line, because of such people. So if he could save one life . . . that's what he had come for. . . .

He had reached the ticket window. He took out his wallet.

"First-class ticket to Munich," he said.

There were a few gray threads in her dark hair, which was still drawn simply into a knot at the nape of her neck. Her eyes lay in the shadows that form and deepen, as nights without sleep follow one after the other. Except for these, Ilse Hirschfeld had not aged. She stood now in the authority of her white doctor's coat, with her forehead calm and her words direct.

"But why, Paul? Because we slept together?"

He looked around the room, as if to find some explanation that would not be grandiose, making her too pitiable. But the room, being merely the consulting room with its desk, its few straight chairs, diplomas, and shelves of books, offered no help.

"Why you?" she repeated. "Because I took care of Joachim Nathansohn that day? He hasn't come forth, important as he is."

"People are afraid, you know that. They have their own families to think of. But I'm an American. I can afford to try.

If you ask me why I want to—" He shrugged. "I don't know. I have a need, that's all."

Mud-colored clouds hung in the sky beyond the window. Ilse lit a lamp, and suddenly out of the gloom a face emerged, the face of a young man framed in leather, on a table in the corner. Paul, leaning closer, saw large melancholy eyes and a full tender mouth, a beauty both masculine and Eastern.

She followed Paul's gaze. "Yes, that's Mario."

"Let's get down to business," he said. "Tell me what happened."

"Mario is a peace activist. I warned him over and over. This isn't the time for pamphleteering, I said. The country has gone mad, you won't do any good, you're risking yourself for nothing. Of course, he wouldn't listen. So they came for him one night. They pounded on the door. It's terrifying. You can't imagine, at two o'clock in the morning, those angry men coming into the house. They took him away." She put her fingers to her lips. In a moment she resumed. "I went to the police station in the morning. They wouldn't tell me anything. I kept going back and back, until they threatened me, too, and so I don't go anymore and I still don't know anything."

A human being disappears, evaporates into space. How had the German people allowed this to happen? At home, when that man Palmer overstepped the bounds of decency and law, he was pulled down from his high place; Americans wouldn't have him.

Paul controlled himself. "I have a contact, I think, an influential man. I don't say I'll be able to help. I only say I can try."

"It will cost money. I know how those things work." Ilse's hands twisted in her lap. "And I have none. My practice has fallen way off. Aryans are not allowed to come to me. I had a good necklace and a pair of bracelets, but I sold them and now there's nothing."

"You needn't worry about that. I'll have whatever is needed."

She was silent a moment, looking out at the darkening sky. Then she said as she turned back to Paul, "If I try to thank you with all that's in my heart, I'll cry, and that will embarrass you, I think."

"You're right. It wouldn't do either one of us any good," he said. "Is that coffee, there in that thermos jug? A hot cup will be all the thanks I want."

"Of course. Let me get a coffee cake to go with it."

When she returned from the kitchen, she looked more troubled.

"I've been thinking, perhaps I shouldn't let you do this. There have been cases of foreigners being arrested, accused of aiding the Communist underground."

"If they were that stupid, the American consul would get me out."

"You might not recognize yourself after the couple of days it would take to get you out."

"I'll take that chance."

She studied him. "I'm curious. What brings you to Germany in these times, anyway?"

When he told her what he had been doing in England and here, she warned him again.

"They must know you. They know who's active in every country, who's on all the committees raising funds. They read the Jewish press in every language. You don't know how thorough they are. There's a special branch of the security service, and it's right here in Munich. No, it's too dangerous, I can't let you."

"But I want to. Don't try to change my mind."

"My son is probably dead already. One day they'll ring the bell and bring in a coffin, sealed, which I shan't be allowed to open, and they'll tell me he died of a heart attack. That's how it will be."

Never had Paul seen such anguish in human eyes.

"Then all the more reason to act quickly."

"How good you are," she murmured. "It's the only hope, that there are still good people in the world. My grocer whispered to me—he's not supposed to sell to Jews, but he saves some milk and eggs for me—he whispered, *'What can I do? I would like to do something, but I'm afraid.'*"

Paul stood up, feeling, above and beyond tremendous sorrow, a surge of energy. Was there a kind of vanity in his wish to endanger himself? Yet there was also the ancient admonition: To save one life is to save the whole world. He was charged with excitement.

"We must waste no time. I want to get back to the hotel, make that call and, if I'm lucky, arrange for a car."

The von Mädler villa stood near the river, where Paul had once walked so many years before.

He had had no trouble getting the appointment. Von Mädler had been quite willing, thinking no doubt that the American banker had something agreeable to report concerning his, or rather his wife's, investments. Yet some of yesterday's certitude had died in Paul; now almost at von Mädler's front door, he was still not quite sure how he ought to proceed.

A dumpy, rusty-haired woman, strikingly like a little red hen, answered his ring. She wore no uniform so, although she did not introduce herself, he assumed her to be the lady of the house.

"Herr von Mädler is expecting you," she told him. "This way."

She left him at the door of a sunny room, with flowering plants and a wall of windows overlooking a lawn. In a chair near the windows, evidently enjoying the heat that poured in through the glass, sat the man Paul remembered. He did not rise, nor offer his hand, but merely called, "Good day, Herr Werner, it's been a long time. Sit down."

Paul sought a chair. Since no one had taken his hat and coat, he laid them on another chair.

"You're looking well, Herr von Mädler," he began.

An overstatement, if ever there was one! The man had grown fatter, but also smaller. He was now completely bald; three gold teeth matched the gleam of the watch chain that scalloped across the potbelly.

"Thank you, I keep well. And you—of course, you're a young man yet."

Paul, smiling acknowledgment, was still searching for the right way to present his request.

"And how do you find our new Germany?" came the question.

Glaucous eyes, unblinking as those of a fish, met Paul's. The two pairs of eyes held one another for only the space of several seconds, yet long enough to solve Paul's problem. Frontal honesty was the way to take. Humble or subtle indirection—"By the way, *mein Herr,* I happen to know of, etc."— that sort of thing would only amuse this man, who would delight in Paul's discomfiture.

And so he replied with a question. "How can you ask me, a Jew, a thing like that, Herr von Mädler? You must know I can only despise your new Germany."

If a mouth could twinkle, Paul thought, one could say that the other man's fleshy wet lips twinkled.

"In that case, what brings you here?"

"Many things. For one, I have relatives to see."

"Ah! And one of them is in trouble with the authorities."

"No, no relative of mine. But there is someone, a young man, the son of a friend. I want to ask for your advice, your help."

"You know, when you telephoned, I thought at first you wanted to discuss my account with you. But on second thought, I knew it must be something like this." Herr von

Mädler lit a cigar. His fingers played over it, enjoying its texture. "I get too many of these requests," he said.

"That says something about what's going on here, then."

"Yes, it says that we are at last cleaning house, scrubbing from cellar to attic, emptying the garbage."

Paul's neck muscles were taut. His face burned and he wondered whether it was as red as it felt. But he kept his voice level and bold.

"I'm an American. Your government is your business. You'll live with it or you'll die with it. I haven't come to you to talk about your government. Will you allow me to talk about what I have come for? I'll not be long."

"I'm a very busy man, Herr Werner. And as I told you, I'm tired of these requests. They're all the same. Besides, I'm not a politician."

"One doesn't have to be a politician to have influence. Politicians are the servants of the powerful and you're a powerful man."

The German puffed the cigar, removed it and grimaced. "You flatter me."

"Not at all. I speak the practical truth. Will you hear my story or not?"

"Yes, go ahead with it."

The tale was short enough, a matter of a dozen sentences. Von Mädler had closed his eyes and laid his head against the back of the chair. Needlepoint, Paul observed, even as he spoke; against a background of faded green, a pair of knights jostled on horseback over the side of the chair. The Lohengrin touch. Handiwork, perhaps, of the little red hen who had opened the front door.

"The boy is harmless," he concluded. "Foolish, perhaps, but harmless." Adding for whatever good it might do, and just in case there might exist a remnant of human pity behind that grim, cunning forehead, "The only son of a widow, as I told you. Dr. Ilse Hirschfeld."

Von Mädler opened his eyes. "I venture to guess that the widow is charming, perhaps? A rather special, an extremely special, little friend of yours? Yes?"

"Herr von Mädler, I hadn't seen the woman in thirteen years until yesterday."

"So you're taking this trouble only to help another Jew."

"To remedy a criminal wrong. There are thousands more in your country whom I would help if I could, and not all of them are Jews, either."

"But if I don't look upon these cases as criminal wrongs, why should I help? Can you tell me that?"

The man was beginning to enjoy himself. His interest and his perception of his own power had been aroused. Life and death lay in his hands, to be given or withheld at whim; the feeling was pleasurable to him.

Paul sat up straighter. "I'll tell you why. Simply because you owe me a favor. My father and I protected your investments in America during the last war and through the Depression. We served you well."

"So now you want repayment."

"Not repayment. We've had our commissions, we've been paid. This is a favor. There's a difference."

Von Mädler waved the cigar, dropping ashes on his belly. "Twaddle! Hairsplitting! Repayment is what it is. Jews always demand a price."

"And you don't, Herr von Mädler?"

There was a pause. Then: "As a matter of fact, I shall demand a price. What you ask, you will have to pay for. My contacts will want their share."

Paul's heart beat faster. "I'm ready and willing."

"It won't be cheap. I promise you. But then you won't care, you're a rich man."

"I'm not a poor one."

"You will pay in dollars. The Fatherland needs foreign exchange."

Paul's muscles relaxed. "That can easily be arranged."

"It will be somewhere—this is only an estimate—between ten and fifteen thousand dollars. And you will hear from me with instructions at your hotel tomorrow. Or the day after, but no later."

"I shall be waiting, Herr von Mädler."

On the second morning, a car came to the hotel. The driver was a neutral type, somewhere between the laboring and the lower middle classes, dressed not in chauffeur's garb but in a cheap suit and cap.

Paul inquired where they were going.

"Out of the city" was the reply.

"Where, out of the city?"

"It's a three-hour drive."

The man's face was reflected in the rearview mirror. It was a closed, tight face, forbidding questions, and Paul asked no more. He had a few seconds of panic: was it possible that he was being mysteriously spirited away to be beaten up, as punishment for his remarks to von Mädler? He recalled having said that he detested the new Germany. But no, this was a simple business transaction. A product was being delivered and paid for, that was all; the fifteen thousand dollars now in Paul's pocket were to be handed to someone who would, at the proper time, identify himself as "Dietrich O."

At any rate, Mario must be alive. They wouldn't ask payment for a corpse, would they? Would they?

The countryside, picturesque even in the dun colors of winter, unrolled itself. Ponds, cottages, grazing sheep, and village streets all passed. Late in the morning, when the car stopped in front of a restaurant, the driver offered to go in and get lunch for Paul.

"I'm not hungry," Paul said, "but you go in if you want. I'll take a walk and stretch my legs."

He set out down the chief street. It was a pretty town with windowboxes, now filled with greens, that would in summer be filled with geraniums. On a side street there was an inn, one of those old inviting places that call to mind an open fire, hot soup, and a featherbed in a low-ceilinged room under the eaves. He stopped to look at it.

Beside the door, beneath the swinging wrought-iron letters of the inn sign, a hand-lettered placard had been put up: JEWS STRICTLY FORBIDDEN ON THESE PREMISES. He read it again. He understood then the driver's offer to bring his lunch, and hastened back to the car.

People walked by on their various errands. A painter carried his pail and brushes. Housewives carried their market baskets. They all looked like normal people. . . . he closed his eyes and pretended to be asleep when the driver returned; he felt the car move and kept his eyes closed until, perhaps an hour later, he felt it slow up.

They were passing through gates in a high stone wall topped with barbed wire. Identification, permission, and salutes were exchanged. Paul had a quick impression of ghastly cold, of barracks, bare concrete and vacant spaces stretching into an unknown distance. The car halted before a little building guarded by soldiers who came to attention.

The driver said only, "They are expecting you inside."

In a large room, divided at one end into cubicles, typewriters clacked, telephones rang, and papers were piled on desks. It could have been the office of a busy insurance agency. A slim, youthful man, wearing a black uniform, passed Paul on to another slim, youthful man in black uniform. This one was sitting behind a desk. There was no expression on his face, and this absence of any identifiable attitude brought fear, catching in Paul's throat; open hostility, even, would have been more human.

"Dietrich O.," the man said.

"Paul Werner."

"Have you brought what is required?"

"I have it here." Paul touched his breast pocket.

The man extended his hand. Paul hesitated. "Mario Hirschfeld?"

"Quite well. He will be released when you hand that over."

"Then I'm to take him back with me?"

"Not at all. There are formalities. He will be sent home tomorrow."

Paul wet dry lips. It could be a trick, total deception. He had no way of knowing.

"May I ask how he will get there?"

"You needn't concern yourself with his transportation."

The hand was still held out. Reluctantly, Paul drew the packet of bank notes from his pocket, watched them slip into a pocket of the uniform, and understood that he was being dismissed.

He made one more try. "I should like to see Mario."

"That's impossible."

"I don't mean a long conversation. Only for a minute, to let him know—"

"Didn't you hear what I said? I said impossible."

Dietrich O. picked up the telephone, leaving Paul in limbo. There was nothing to do but turn around and go back to the car.

On the way to the main gate, the car was halted to let a file of prisoners cross the road. Paul looked, looked away and then back again as they shuffled past. They wore striped suits of thin cotton cloth, while Paul could feel the arctic cold even through his heavy coat. Their heads were shaved, so that at quick glance, they might all have been one age, an old age, with their cadaverous, ugly naked skulls. Silent and bowed, they moved between captors in the vanguard and at the rear, as in some ancient, monumental frieze of beaten men. Horror seized Paul. He, the free man in the warm coat, shrank down in the car.

As if he had been drugged, he slept all the way back to the hotel. From there, he telephoned to Ilse, being careful, for fear that something might yet go wrong, not to sound too positive. Then, remembering that he had not eaten since breakfast, he ordered a supper of toast and eggs and fell again into the heavy sleep of escape, the mercy that sometimes is given when reality becomes unbearable.

When on the following day the call came from Ilse, he rushed to the apartment. She opened the door and threw her arms around him. She had been crying.

"Happy tears, I hope?"

"Yes. But what they did to him . . . do you want to see him? He won't wake up for hours. I wanted to give him some forgetfulness."

On tiptoe, they entered a bedroom, a young man's room with photographs, many books, tennis racquets, and a record player. Dull light from the window fell over the bed where Mario lay. And Paul, looking down, had to stifle a cry.

The dark head, which he recalled from the photograph, had been shaved. A long cut, lined with dried blood, curved over the naked skull. The lips were puffed; one swollen cheek was turning livid blue, purple, and green. The hand that lay beside the cheek was bandaged from palm to fingertips; the fingers had been crushed.

The two of them stood without speaking. When finally they looked at each other, it was through mutual tears.

"His teeth, too," whispered Ilse. "All his front teeth are gone. Shall I ever restore him?"

Paul put his arms around her. And so they stood, she with her head on his shoulder.

At last she drew away, and Paul found a few words.

"Tomorrow you'll be safe in Italy. Get him to the right doctor and dentist. Rest in the sun, in the quiet, peacefully—" They were the expected words, strung together to encourage and soothe; he only half believed them.

"We should have gone to Palestine. He'd been wanting to go since he was a child. Do you remember, I told you then?"

"You did what you thought was best. Don't blame yourself. Besides, the British have made Palestine illegal and dangerous. You have no idea what we're up against, trying to negotiate in London. They signed the Balfour Declaration in 1917, but now, if they could, they'd withdraw the promise of a Jewish homeland. That would really look too bad though, so instead they just sink the old tubs that carry refugees and intern them in Cyprus."

Ilse sighed. "I know. Don't stir up the Arabs; we need oil. Are you a Zionist?" she asked.

"Do you mean, do I want to live in a Jewish state? No, I'm an American. I belong in America. But as to whether there ought to be someplace where Jews can save themselves from what's happening here, yes, with all my heart I hope for a Jewish state." Then he saw that she was very weary. "I'm staying too long. You need some sleep."

"I won't be able to sleep. I wish you would stay. Can you, Paul?"

"Of course, if you want me."

Apologizing, as if for weakness, Ilse said, "I've never really minded being alone before."

"Tonight is rather different, I should say."

They sat down in the little parlor on opposite sides of the room. He remembered the spot in front of the bookcase where their dance had turned into an embrace, and wondered how often, during the intervening years, she might have remembered it too. It had meant even more to her, by her own admission, than it had to him.

"Do you feel like talking, Ilse, or not?"

"I really want to talk, but my mind's in such a muddle that I can't think of a way to begin."

"All right, tell me what's been happening to you all these years. You're not married. . . ."

She smiled slightly. "That's the first thing a man would ask a woman, isn't it? Not whether I've taken my degree in endocrinology."

"Well, have you?"

"Yes. And I also have had two chances to be married. I lived with a very fine man for a while, to make sure of us, and was very happy until he emigrated to Australia."

"Why didn't you go too?"

"Money. You have to have enough or they won't admit you. And he didn't have enough for the three of us. So that was that." She threw out her hands. "And you? You're still married?"

"Yes. I've no reason not to be." Paul stared down at his nails.

"And the other? The one you told me about?"

"The same."

"You never see her?"

"No. I promised. Her husband is good to her. . . ."

An expression of great kindness passed across Ilse's face. Paul looked back at her in wonder: At the nadir of her own sorrow, she could yet give thought to his.

"I've thought of you very, very often, Paul."

To respond in kind would insult her integrity as well as his own, because it would be untrue. He had thought of her only on fleeting occasion, recalling a beautiful and valuable experience; in the same way, he would remember the week at sea with Leah and the days yet to be spent in Paris, as a passing happiness; neither woman had yet touched that deepest place where Anna remained and lived.

"I hoped you would find someone to take her place," Ilse said.

Abruptly, he was overwhelmed with a sensation of nakedness. The experience of these last few days had stripped away the soft, concealing layers of convention; what did one's privacy or personal dignity matter in the face of raw brutality and anguish? Feeling overflowed.

"You see, there is a child," he said. "I didn't tell you before."

"Ah."

"A daughter, almost grown. Sixteen." He paused to estimate. "Yes, sixteen last December."

"You don't see her, either?"

"No. Only once, a long time ago."

Ilse frowned and shook her head. "That must be a terrible pain for you."

"Yes." An unknown individual was alive in New York this very instant because of him. She walked and read a book and laughed—he hoped she laughed—because of him. And he couldn't make himself known, couldn't give her things, things of which he possessed such an abundance. But more importantly, he couldn't give her his thoughts, her inheritance of ideas and—and all that was his.

"I've never told anyone about her until just now," he said. "You're the only person who knows."

"There is nothing to be done?"

"Nothing."

Now too much feeling had overflowed. The little room was heavy with it.

"I'm sorry," he said quickly. "Your burden is already too much to carry. I had no right to add mine, which is so small."

"Not small. Just different." And again she gave him that look of extraordinary kindness. The look touched him, and caused him shame over his lapse toward pity for himself. He got up and touched her shoulder.

"Now I really want you to rest. I'm going back to the hotel. You can reach me there if, God forbid, and I don't expect it, anything should go wrong."

She caught his wrist. "Can you sleep here instead? Can you?"

Surely on such a night she couldn't be thinking of—

She read his mind. "Nothing, nothing like that, Paul. Only comfort." And she smiled.

"Yes," he said. "Yes, of course."

So he lay down beside her. For a long time she held his hand. In the ominous dark of the last night before final escape, they listened for sounds from the room where the victim slept his drugged sleep, and counted the hours lurching past on the alarm clock. Late into the night, close to morning, her hand fell away from Paul's, and they, too, slept.

He left her at the door before Mario awoke.

"Here are the addresses on my card. My office in New York and the Crillon in Paris for the next ten days. Will you write to me at once so I'll know you're safe in Italy?"

Her eyes, raised to his, were almost reverent.

"What thanks, what's the price of a life, what am I to say to you, Paul?"

He had to stop the rush of her gratitude. "Don't. Don't make it harder for me." He kissed her cheeks. "God bless you both." And he ran out.

In the hotel room, the timetable lay on the dresser. His ticket to Paris was for the next day, but the thought of sleeping one more night in this country appalled him. With luck, he might be able to catch a train today; he began to throw things into suitcases.

And quite suddenly he broke down. He was overwhelmed. The boy with the broken body . . . Ilse . . . God only knew what lay in the future for them both. . . . And farther back, those beaten men shuffling and freezing in the camp. And still farther back, the troubled, skeptical face of Elisabeth . . . He dropped a pair of shoes and put his head down on the desk. His ears were filled with the sound of ancient wails, old as the earth and the sea.

"Oh, my God," he murmured.

After a while he got up, finished packing, paid his bill, and went to the station, where he found that it was possible to leave within the hour. Too impatient to sit in the waiting room, he went to the platform and stood there until, with a great hissing of brakes, the dark blue cars of the Compagnie Internationale des Wagons-Lits drew to a stop.

Once in his place, he ordered a double brandy. Maybe it would put him to sleep, at least until they crossed the border and he was out of the country. It came to his mind, as he touched the American passport in his pocket, that there were sure to be others on this train who, for one reason or another, were even more anxious than he to get out, and for whom the customs officer's tap on the compartment door would be a heart-stopping ordeal until it was safely past. He could have taken the passport out and kissed it.

The train began to move forward. And now, perhaps owing to some benevolent effect of the brandy, he was able to turn his thoughts forward with it. Paris and Leah. They would be medicine, and how he needed it! Leah's laughter, wine, food, picture galleries, walks in the Bois and love in bed . . . and freedom! Most of all, freedom!

The train raced on into the dusky afternoon.

Twelve

"How did you manage this?" inquired Paul, "since we're not traveling together?" His room was next door to hers and the door between them had been unlocked.

"Easy. Tipped the chambermaid before we went down to dinner." Wearing a black nightgown as transparent as moonlight, Leah was brushing her hair at the dressing table. Through the glass, she gave him a smile of pure happiness. "Honestly, you gave me the surprise of my life when you walked in today. But I've nothing planned till next week: concert tickets, the ballet, and I've arranged a car for one day. I thought we might drive out for a country lunch. The rest of this week is blank, though."

"That will suit me perfectly. Come on, that's enough, your hair is beautiful."

"It's a mess. It needs a cut."

"It's a satin hat," he said, stroking it with his cheek. He

turned her around on the bench. "Come on, put the light out."

"Just take one look outside. Imagine, we're on the Place de la Concorde!"

"It's gorgeous, but don't tease me."

Her eyes went suddenly somber. "I'd never tease you, Paul. I'm not like that. It's just that everything's so wonderful that I'd like to prolong it. I don't quite believe it."

"Believe it," he said. "Here, do you want me to drag you?"

He picked her up and laid her on the bed. Gently, careful not to tear it, he rolled the black silk cloud back over her ankles, over her strong thighs and narrow waist, over the breasts whose size always astounded him by their contrast to her narrow waist, past the plump, sloping shoulders—Edwardian shoulders, he thought—and over her head.

He stood for a moment looking down at her.

"What are you thinking just now, Paul?"

"You want to know exactly?"

"Exactly."

"I'm thinking: how luscious, how ripe and luscious. Like fruit, you are."

She smiled. "Then take it. Take whatever you want."

It was not until the third day that his heart was really freed. And that was when a postcard came from Ilse.

Safe here with friends. Mario beginning to come to himself. Will keep you in touch. Blessings on you.

At dinner he showed the card to Leah. He had told her the story, omitting anything personal about Ilse and himself; he had a feeling that she would resent it, although if the situation were reversed, he did not think Ilse would mind. Now he exclaimed, "This calls for a celebration! Dom Pérignon and plenty of it."

Her fingers, tipped with oval, scarlet shells, circled the goblet. She sipped thoughtfully.

"It was hell, wasn't it?"

"What, Germany? Yes. Unbearable pain to watch it sliding down into that hell and not be able to stop it."

"Paul, you've carried the weight of other people's troubles on your shoulders as long as I've known you. As far back as when I married Freddy. Dan, who's twice your age and now with this Ilse, and my son—we all come to you. You can't take Europe on too. There'll be nothing left for yourself."

"I don't see it that way at all."

"Perhaps not. But listen, I want you to think of nothing except pleasing yourself while we're here. I want you to loosen up."

He laughed. "You don't think I've been loose enough these last three nights?"

"I'm not joking. Sex is a need, a release. It has nothing to do with being happy inside or free of care."

"Very well," he said cheerfully, "I shall do nothing but free myself of care starting now. I've got a couple of good clients to see, Americans who live in Paris, but that will be pleasant business and the rest of the time, when you're not looking at dresses, shall be yours."

La ville lumière! The city smiled. Even the police were polite here. Sometimes, waking early, they went out for coffee when the cafés were just opening. The flower vendors, under the awnings, were just setting out bouquets of curly roses and lilies of the valley. After the brioches or the croissants, they walked to the Luxembourg Gardens to sit on the green iron chairs and watch children, too young for school, playing around the Medici Fountain. Through a light dust of snow one afternoon, they studied the ancient hotels on the Place des Vosges and walked back to the Île de la Cité to look again at the great rose window of Notre-Dame. They dined at La Tour d'Argent, saw the ballet at the Opéra, went to cabarets on Montmartre, and strolled at midnight.

Now Paul allowed himself to be introduced to the fashion

world. It had always seemed silly to him for people to make such a serious business out of draping some cloth over the human shape, but the curiosity that had led him all his life into learning the function of the carburetor or of the flute, led him now to follow Leah, and he had to concede that some of the cloth draping really could be art. In a smoky salon he sat on a little gold chair and watched as Chanel, in sweater and skirt, gold chains and hair bow, watched her models perform on a little gold stage.

"I'd like to treat you to an original," he told Leah afterward at lunch. "The yellow Chanel suit, perhaps?"

Leah shook her head. "No, no."

"Why not? You practically fell off your chair when you saw it."

"Really not. I don't want anything," she said, looking rather grave.

He considered for a moment, and decided to speak bluntly. "You think it has something to do with us. A man's repayment, or something nasty like that."

She didn't answer.

"Do you know how wrong you are? If that were so, for all you've given me, I'd have to pay with something a lot more substantial than a suit."

"Really, no, Paul. I want *things* to have nothing to do with *us,* in spite of what you just said. You do understand?"

He understood that possibly he was going in deeper than he had meant to go. Perhaps even deeper than she had meant to go. . . . A slight disturbance moved through the air, and he concentrated on buttering a roll.

"But it was dear of you, all the same." For an instant Leah's forehead puckered, then straightened as though a hand had grazed it. "Oh, it's a show, it's theater, isn't it, all this fashion business? Lanvin serves champagne, and at the Maggy Rouff opening there's an orchestra and guests come in evening clothes." So, with bright and easy skill, she moved away from the personal.

The situation, as they entered the second week, grew more troubling. What was to happen once they were back in New York? There were so many ramifications in the whole context of the family, first her son and then all the relatives, should the affair be discovered, to say nothing of Marian . . .

On the final afternoon, Leah rushed around to do last-minute shopping. She had innumerable friends and loved being generous.

"I'll beg off and meet you for dinner," Paul told her. "I haven't once been in the Bois and this is the day for it."

It was one of those February afternoons when shreds of breaking fog float through the tops of the trees, the lower branches drip and the damp air melts into the deceptive feel of spring. The path around the lake was deserted. It was so still that Paul's slow footsteps crackled. There was something mournful in the stillness; yet the very mournfulness was pleasurable. It was like listening to a requiem, he thought, and a mood stirred in him; something pricked at his memory, disturbed him in some remotest corner of the brain, something that wanted to be remembered. What was it? He stopped, trying to summon the struggling recollection, and stared out over the murky black surface of the lake, on which three ducks were floating in perfect V formation.

It came abruptly . . . the Hudson River, black and murky on a winter day. Large flakes of snow sank slowly to the water and clung to Anna's eyelashes. They walked back up the hill. In a house near the top, a string quartet was playing, sending to the passersby, even through closed windows, a grave and lovely music. "Schubert," he said, and they stood there listening until the end, and walked on hand in hand, in a peaceful silence.

A long time past. The way had been open then, but he hadn't taken it. And he stood now, solitary, on another continent, while the duck flotilla circled the lake and returned, thinking, *Anna*, thinking, *Iris*.

A blast of sudden northern wind roared through the pines at his back. It was melancholy winter, after all, and light was ebbing. He shouldn't have come here alone like this. He should find Leah, cheerful, reassuring Leah.

And he turned his steps, running, hurrying to find a taxi, and directed the driver back to the hotel.

The lounge was a cordial space designed to dispel just such a mood. Pink lamplight and a deep fauteuil welcomed Paul to a corner, from which he could watch a lively promenade of luxurious women, either hideous or charming, men of affairs both French and foreign, and patient, intelligent poodles wearing rhinestone collars. He ordered an aperitif and, cupping the glass, sipped slowly, allowing the delicious fire to slide and glide to his very toes.

He consulted his watch. An hour more until dinner. He ordered another drink and was contemplating a thin blonde, whose enormous emerald pendant—six carats at least, he estimated—had caught his eye, and wondering whether she knew how discontent was spoiling her face, when over her shoulder he saw Donal Powers in the doorway. A second later Donal saw him. The meeting was then unavoidable. Donal, accompanied by another man, pushed his way across the room.

"Well! Small world! Here on business or pleasure?"

"Business." Paul stood, offering his hand.

"Mr. Werner, Monsieur Corot. No relation of the painter's."

The Frenchman bowed. "Unfortunately."

Hesitation followed. A fraction of a second's worth. If the other man had not been there, would Paul have said: Let's not go through false motions, we don't have to sit together, we despise each other? It bothered him not to know whether he would have said it.

"Mr. Werner is a cousin of my wife's."

The Frenchman raised polite eyebrows. "A delightful coincidence for you both, then." He was waiting to be invited to one of the vacant chairs.

"Do sit down," Paul said.

"We don't see many Americans in the winter, Mr. Werner."

"Paris is beautiful any time for me," Paul replied.

Donal, having ordered drinks, turned his attention to Paul. "Been here long?"

"Week before last. I came from Germany."

"Oh? So did I. What did you think of it?"

"I'm still trying to shake off the horror. It's like having a monkey on my back."

"As an American, you naturally have a different perspective. Europeans, of course, being so much closer, can see more clearly," Corot said.

The remark on its face seemed critical, but the manner was soothing. Paul was not sure he understood and said so.

Corot explained. "What I mean is, quite simply, that strong leadership is effective. You Americans haven't come to see that yet. You have only to look at Germany and Italy, too, to see their order and prosperity. In my country, all we do is argue, never get anything done. A new government every time we turn around. It gets to be sickening."

"So you want to kill the Third Republic?" Paul said.

Corot shrugged. "I? I'm not killing anything. Let's just say I won't cry if it should die."

Paul didn't answer. His eyes were lowered to the vacant chair on which lay a crocodile attaché case and a pair of fur-lined gloves. In some queer roundabout way, these objects infuriated him, although he possessed rather similar ones himself. And he raised his eyes, looking from one man to the other.

"Monsieur Corot is a man of experience," Donal said. "He

owns one of the largest machine tool plants in the country. Founded by his grandfather," he added respectfully.

Corot addressed Paul. "I believe you said you also were in business?"

"I didn't say. I'm a banker."

"Ah, then surely you're a practical man. It's men like us who keep the world's wheels turning. We mustn't let the Léon Blums throw sand in them. If the republic falls, it will be because of men like him." Faint red rose into Corot's cheeks, and he set his glass down hard on the table. "Crooks and corrupters, the lot of them."

"Surely you aren't calling Blum a crook," Paul said.

He thought he saw Donal's knee give the other man's a nudge. Of course, Blum was a Jew. Never mind that he was a democrat, a scholar, or anything else.

"Well, perhaps not," Corot conceded. He must have received the nudge and interpreted it correctly. "But the people don't want him anyway," he added.

Why am I arguing here with this stranger? Paul asked himself. It was absurd. Two strangers who had met ten minutes before and would never meet again, were feeding their controlled and civilized anger, while a fan of red and white gladioli spread itself at their backs and somewhere in another room a piano tinkled. It was surreal. Nevertheless, he resumed the argument.

"I've been reading in your papers about the Action Française. They're the same young toughs they have in Germany and Italy and began the same way, with riots and beatings on the streets."

Corot took a handful of nuts and crunched them. "They're only kids. They don't worry me, nor the German boys either."

Paul persisted. "The German boys will worry you when they come marching into France."

"Nonsense. There'll be no war. We have the Maginot Line, the strongest defense on the planet."

"It's in the wrong place, my friend. The Germans will come at you through Belgium, the same as they did in 1914."

The dialogue was a ball, batted back and forth, while Donal, like a spectator at a tennis match, turned his head to keep up with it.

"I've been in Germany many, many times, Mr. Werner, and I can tell you the Germans don't want war any more than we do. I have connections in high places in government and industry. Mr. Powers knows. He's been there with me. Ask him." Corot finished his drink and stood up. "I shall be late for my appointment. Donal, see you in the morning? Happy to have met you," he said with a formal bow to Paul, and, gathering his possessions, departed.

"Nasty sort, your friend," Paul said.

"Not a friend, a contact. Helpful to my mission." Donal paused, waiting to be asked what his mission was. When Paul didn't ask, he continued. "You knew, or maybe you didn't, that I'm on a semi-official, part governmental commission on housing? Because of my real estate investments, I'm becoming something of an authority on public housing. So I've come over at my own expense to get an idea of how they do things in Europe, especially in Germany. And you know what? Even in housing, they're way ahead of either England or France. Way ahead."

"According to your Monsieur Corot, at any rate. You nudged him, didn't you?"

"It could have become embarrassing if I hadn't."

"He reminded me of a vulture, feeding on a corpse. He and the Germans will fatten on France's corpse together."

Donal contradicted him. "The French and the Germans are getting along very well these days, investing across the frontier. Frenchmen invest in German machinery and Germans buy French publishing houses. Why, you can hardly dine out at an important house in Paris without meeting Germans, industrialists, writers, or intellectuals. Big names."

Intellectual. Important houses. A picture flashed before Paul's eyes: Ben's funeral, the crowd of sharp-faced men and the FBI observing them all. He'd come a far way, Donal had. By the looks of things, he would be going a good deal farther, too.

"I'll be glad to get home," he was saying. "I miss my kids."

And he handed over a wallet-size photograph. Five children, with a Labrador retriever, stood on a lawn in front of a flowering rhododendron.

"You haven't seen them in a while. Would you believe Timmy's as tall as I am and only just past twelve? Tom's on the way, too, built like a football player." Donal, taking the photo back, held it up to his own view. "I would have liked more sons. Not that the girls are disappointing. Look at this one, Lucy. She'll be the family beauty with that head of curls. I never could figure out where they came from." The fond chuckle and soft gaze did not belong to the man Paul knew. "I tell my kids, all of them, but especially the boys, you can be whatever you want to be. You can do whatever you want to do. Life's a contest from start to finish and don't let anybody get ahead of you. You be the best."

This now was the man Paul knew. And he thought, If I had sons, what would I tell them? He was quite sure it would not be that. Donal spoke with some satisfaction while replacing his wallet, after which he went on talking as though Paul and he were amiable friends. "I had some personal affairs over here, too, Hank's company among them. Have you seen the figures lately?"

"Of course I've seen the figures."

"Well. Going great guns, aren't they?"

Paul nodded grimly.

"Business is really booming in Germany, let me tell you." Donal glanced around, lowering his voice. "It's amazing that I should run into you here like this, because I planned to see you as soon as I got home."

Paul was immediately wary. "Yes? What about?"

"Of course you can guess it's about Finn Weber, or I should say, Finn Weber's parent company, HW Elektrische Gesellschaft. There's a big merger in the making—one of the largest electrochemical combines in Germany—and naturally, a new stock offering goes with it. It'll be a tremendous thing, a chance to make millions, literally millions, for anybody who can get in on the ground floor." Donal hesitated. "There's only one hitch. There's a floor under possible bids. You have to have a solid unit of twenty-five thousand shares."

There was a silence, but by no means an empty one. Paul's mind, racing, had anticipated Donal's request from almost the first word, and he was already making an effort to restrain his anger. Aware that Donal was trying to read his expression, he kept his eyes deliberately turned toward the middle distance, where the light glinted on a silver coffeepot.

"The problem is that I don't own twenty-five thousand shares. Not that I couldn't easily buy them, but the thing's retroactive. You have to have owned them since last January first. You understand?"

Paul brought his eyes back to Donal. "I understand that it lets you out."

"Well, not really. There's a way of getting around it. We can combine Hank's shares with mine in a single ownership, one unit. We can form a corporation solely to cover this investment—a holding corporation. As far as the people in Germany know, it already exists. They aren't going to check back to New York for the date. What the hell, I've already told them about it, and they're perfectly satisfied. All they need are a couple of papers."

Paul's silence lasted for a full minute, during which time, resting his gaze back again on the coffeepot, he enjoyed the other man's discomfiture. At last he said, "Of course you know that I'm not going to do it."

Donal sat upright. "Of course I know nothing of the sort."

"I gave you my answer the last time you made a similar request, didn't I?"

"Listen, Paul. Put on your banker's hat and be reasonable. I can understand that maybe you were doubtful then, but by now you've seen the profits for yourself, and you should have confidence in my business acumen."

"I have perfect confidence in your business acumen."

"Well, then?"

Paul stared at him. "Can you really ask?"

"You mean you're still singing Uncle Dan's old song?"

Paul nodded. "I am. As loud as I can sing it."

A flush mounted Donal's cheeks. "You're a banker, third generation. Don't tell me you've gotten where you are by being so holy."

"We've been honest."

"I'm not asking you to do anything dishonest."

"You're asking me, asking Hank through me, to go into business with international criminals."

Donal laughed. "Excuse me, but you sound like a Bible Belt preacher with that talk."

There was so much, in the face of this man's scorn, that Paul would say. What words he could explode before that insolent, amused face! Pictures exploded in his own vision: men huddled, scheming in locked back rooms, Ben shattered with twenty bullets in his chest. But he had sworn to Hank and to himself never to speak.

"I'm sorry. I didn't mean to insult you by laughing," Donal said, recovering himself. "It just struck me funny for a moment. Nobody would believe that a man would actually turn down millions of dollars. Actually, I don't believe it myself."

"I think you should," Paul said.

"No. Wait. You're fearful of war, aiding the enemy. Okay, I'll go along with that. But this stuff that these people are working on is stuff that'll be useful too in peace, in industry.

I'm certainly no scientist, but I understand enough to know that Germany produces brains, some of the greatest scientists in the world—"

Paul interrupted. "I will not help Nazis in peace or in war," he said. The words came out stiffly and primly. Why did this man always manage to tie his tongue this way?

The pink turned red on Donal's cheeks. "Just like that, you're throwing Hank's profits. What kind of a trustee are you?"

"An honorable one, I hope. I shouldn't want Hank to have that kind of money. It's bad enough that he's already getting some of it from Finn Weber."

Donal shoved his chair back, as if to avoid even accidental contact with Paul's knees. "Personally, I want money for my children. They'll never have to fight their way up as I did."

More pictures slid through Paul's mind like takes on a film strip: a grandiose house, the rows of European cars in the garage, the lavish pastel gardens, lanterns in the trees and music on the lawn, a rope of diamonds around Meg's innocent neck . . . "How much do you want, for God's sake?"

"As much as I can get. There's never too much. If you and your wife had a child, you'd know what I'm talking about. Or maybe you wouldn't. There's no getting through to you. I've done business with hundreds of men in my time, but I'll be damned if I've ever—" He broke off.

Paul turned to see what Donal was staring at. There in the doorway stood Leah with her arms full of packages. She was scanning the room, looking for him.

"Oh, here you are. I called the room just now," she said clearly, and then, seeing Donal, stopped short.

"Well, this is an unexpected pleasure!" Donal cried as he and Paul stood up. His voice was high and excited. "I had no idea you were both in Paris together."

"We are not together. It was a last-minute decision of mine. Paul didn't know I was to be here." Leah's cool tone contradicted her startled expression. "You'll excuse me," she said swiftly, "I'm going upstairs with these packages."

The two men were still standing, and Donal remarked, "She's not exactly a beauty, but she's a dish, that Leah."

Paul didn't answer.

"I admire your taste."

Paul said evenly, "Do you know what you're talking about? Because I surely don't."

"Come on! I wasn't born yesterday. She didn't fool me, nor do you. What difference does it make? Why should I care?" Donal looked at his watch. "Well, I'm off to dinner. I'm at the Georges Cinq, in case you change your mind, and want to get in touch with me."

"I shan't change my mind, and I'm leaving for home tomorrow," Paul answered.

"Oh. Enjoy the voyage, you and Leah together," he flung out as he left the room.

"You're all upset because of that man," Leah said later. "You really don't think he's going to pick up the phone and call Marian the minute he gets back, do you?"

"No, no. It's the things he's saying, he and that Frenchman." From where he sat on the chaise longue, Paul could see the reflection of his dejected posture, and he straightened his shoulders. "I'd just been starting to revive, too, thanks to you."

"There must be fortunes to be made if Donal's here," reflected Leah. "Wouldn't you think he had enough? Between him and the rest, Bergman and Roselli and the lot, they must have split fifty million over the years before Repeal."

"I don't think it's just money that he wants anymore. Prestige and power are more like it. I've a hunch he may try something big in politics."

"For a man as polished as he can be, he can also be so crude . . . Meg almost left him once, did you know?"

"No. Why didn't she?"

"Because of Alfie's trouble. She used to come into the shop and talk to me, but not anymore." Carefully, Leah outlined her lips with a brush, then filled in the outline. "It really would have shaken him up if she had moved out with the children. If I couldn't see Hank, I don't know what I'd do. Not to see your own child—it must be awful."

"Yes," Paul said.

Leah stared at him. "You really do look done in! Oh, to hell with Donal and everybody else! Let's go eat. And afterward, there's a Charlie Chaplin playing, dubbed in French. It should be fun for our last night. What do you say? Okay?"

The westbound voyage was a rough one. The ship was battered; spray washed the decks and the foghorn sounded its bleak warning all the way across.

On the last night, they found a centerpiece of roses on their table and the steward informed them that for dessert a Grand Marnier soufflé had been ordered. It was a soufflé for ten, since apparently the donor had expected Mrs. Marcus to be seated at a large table.

"Oh, that's all right," Leah said, "we'll eat what we can and you can do what you want with what's left." She opened the envelope and read the card aloud. " 'Welcome home. Fond regards from Bill.' He's such an awfully nice man."

"Obviously."

"He's only a good friend, Paul. Really. And I need friends."

"You can't mean that," Paul said, feeling a touch of resentment.

"I do mean it." Leah put her fork down and leaned across the table, speaking intensely. "My son is about to leave me. He'll undoubtedly be going to medical school. You know how he loved riding the ambulance with the first aid crew last summer. He'll be making his own life, as he should, and I'm happy because I've done the best I could for him—with your help, Paul—and he's a wonderful person, a better person than I am. So all right, I'm happy about that, but I'm already lonesome and I shall be more so. I need all the friends I can find. Sex I can always get—" Leah's eyes were fixed on Paul's. "But sex alone can leave you as lonesome as ever, and lonesomeness is—well, I can't even try to describe it."

"Don't try."

The moment broke apart with the uncorking of the wine. Paul tasted the offered glass and approved it. They drank to each other's health, admired the soufflé, went dancing, slept together, and were careful not to approach any delicate subjects.

The next morning, though, while waiting in the lounge with passport in hand for the immigration officer, Paul considered a delicate subject. What was Leah expecting? It was clear that his marriage was drying up, with Marian in Florida for three months every winter. Yet it wasn't completely dried up. After all, they had their home together and went as a couple wherever they were invited. So maybe Leah only hoped that he and she might continue this unexpected new relationship? If so, they would have to be very discreet indeed; the one thing he would not do was humiliate Marian. Still, discretion would not be all that difficult, he reasoned, and Leah was delightful. . . .

"Back to the real world," she said, startling him out of his thoughts. "Just look! The ship's practically got its nose on the street. You can almost hear the taxis honking. New York! It's a crazy place, but I love it."

A cold rain beat down on the pier. Leah was prepared with a smart British raincoat. Her Leica was slung over her shoulder and she carried a pigskin jewel case.

"You look like a transatlantic commuter," he said with a smile.

"Not I, you're the one. I hope you're staying on this side awhile."

"Awhile. I'm trying"—he lowered his voice— "I'm trying to raise more money to get the young out of Germany, to any place that'll take them. If I'm successful, I may have to go back again soon. Would you go with me?" he asked directly.

"You know I would. Anywhere. Anytime, Paul."

Thirteen

"We must keep out of European affairs," Dan would declare positively, whenever he and Paul were together, "or we'll find ourselves drawn into another of their bloody messes. I said so the last time and I'm saying it again now."

"Even after the things Paul's seen?" asked Hennie, who had heard with horror Paul's account of the Ilse Hirschfeld affair.

"They're unspeakably awful," Dan replied. "But there are other ways of stopping them and war is worse."

Of course, he was quite right about there being other ways. But no one was taking them.

It had seemed impossible for Paul during this past year or more to convey to people here at home what he had seen and what he knew. He felt impatient and exasperated with their resistance. Yet those who ought to have known better, those at the helm of governments, were just as obtuse. In England, Winston Churchill cried his warnings into the wind, France was still in disarray, while out of Italy there sounded the bombastic threats of a strutting, bloated second-rater. Here at home, one heard Father Coughlin's ugly ranting, followed by the more moderate voice of Lindbergh, assuring the American people that Hitler didn't want war and that he was invincible anyway.

And it boggled the mind when opposite voices from the liberal left reached the same conclusions. The intellectual young were all taking the Oxford Pledge: "This House will not die for King or Country—" in any war, for any reason, ever.

To Hank, who had proudly taken the pledge, Paul said, "Don't suppose I'm one who wants to see another war. I saw enough of its wreckage."

"You don't act as if you had," Hank had accused him. "You act as if you think it's inevitable."

"The way things are going, I'm sorry to say I do think it's inevitable. And I think your Oxford Pledge and all the rest of the pacifist talk are giving encouragement to the enemy."

"What we need is a Gandhi. Passive resistance," Hank declared. "Let all the young men fill the jails to overflowing. Just sit down and refuse to budge."

"Gandhi," Paul persisted, "is not opposing himself to Hitler. Whatever you may think of the British Raj, it isn't fascist Germany." And he had added, "Even Einstein, a life-long pacifist, has changed his mind because of what's happening."

"Let Einstein fight, then!"

Paul was tired of arguments. They got nowhere. Sometimes he caught Hank looking at him as if he were trying to fathom an offensive stranger. We are growing apart, Paul thought, and was touched with sadness. The boy who had once revered his every opinion had grown into a man, stuffed with a sense of his own dignity.

But it was, after all, only natural. . . .

In the outer office a cessation of typewriter clack announced the day's end. He reached for the telephone to call home. Marian had been asleep when he left that morning, so he had not asked whether they were to have dinner together. Sometimes on Tuesdays she went to visit a widowed cousin in Rye. She had made a life, a feminine existence, in which women visited each other, dressed for one another's approbation and kept fine houses for the same reason. The older women were often widowed; some of the younger might as well be, he thought now, while the phone rang at the other end, and wondered how many couples lived as they did in a sibling amity, bestowing dry kisses on each other's cheeks as they came and went their independent ways.

"Hello?" said Marian in her pleasant voice.

"I'm at the office. How was your day?"

"Wonderful. We raised two thousand dollars at the rummage sale. I'm exhausted, but it was worth it."

"I thought this was to be your evening at Cousin Nelly's."

"I can't because of the sale. I hope you won't be annoyed if I skip dinner. Somebody's got to box the unsold stuff and I've said I'd go back to help."

"Fine. I've a deskful of work myself. I'll eat downtown."

"You needn't do that. I told Emma to grill a steak and make the potato pudding that you always love."

She still hovered, she still fussed over her wifely duties. And he said gently, "Tell Emma not to bother. That way I won't have to rush home. Will you be late?"

"It may be close to midnight."

"That's too late to be out alone. You'll have trouble finding a cab. I'll come for you."

"No need. Rena Marshall's car is dropping us all home, don't worry."

"Fine. See you later, then."

He hung up. Her image moved in his mind's eye: she'd have a cup of tea and a biscuit, then tidy her hair, powder her cheeks to cover the freckles, which she detested and which he had once, long ago—so long ago—found rather girlishly appealing, take fresh white gloves from the drawer, and hasten out on her mission. A good woman. But I'm a good man, too, he thought. Foolish to put on modest airs in the privacy of one's own head. So, yes, we are two good people and yes, together we add up to nothing. Or very little.

It was just after five o'clock when he came out into the damp spring air. The sky, still light, was streaked low in the west with a tender pink that shaded into lavender, then rose abruptly overhead into a darkening blue-green. An extraordinary sky! He stood a moment, oblivious to the going-home bustle on the street, to marvel at the colors. One wanted to hold them, to keep them as they were. Great painters could do that. Turner with his vaporous sunsets, or El Greco with his violent storm-split clouds. But I am only a banker, he thought, and laughed at himself.

He felt suddenly in good spirits again, no doubt because he had just decided what he was going to do with his unexpectedly free evening. He usually did know what to do with one unless, of course, Leah had another engagement, which wasn't often. They'd have supper together. A hearty one, for Leah, unlike Marian, loved to eat well; a little while later, they'd go up to her room, shut off the telephone and lock the door.

The room was a bower. He would have felt claustrophobic if he had had to live in it every night, but it was a perfect setting for the brief hours that he spent there. In the lamplight, against cream-colored walls, the furniture glowed like jewels. There were two Louis XVI chests of rosewood with satinwood marqueterie and marble tops; there was a chaise longue, upholstered to match the hazy blue carpet and covered with pillows of old lace. Between the windows hung a Degas ballet scene, which Paul had prodded Ben into buying for Leah's birthday years before. The bed had a canopy and curtains; it was a room within a room, with walls and ceiling of millefleur silk. There they would stay until some plausible hour, usually eleven, had struck, at which he would get up, get dressed, and go home. A felicitous arrangement for them both, he thought now. Certainly it was for him and hoped it was for her. She had never said otherwise nor, since those few brief words on the ship, complained of loneliness.

Nor had there been any mention of Bill Sherman except in reference to his daughters, who, now coming into an age that entitled them to grown-up dresses, went shopping at Léa's with their father.

"Really darling girls," Leah would repeat. "Not spoiled at all, even though he's so generous with them."

Paul was curious. "No more roses for you?"

"The next time I sail, I'm sure there will be. It's his way. He's lavish and he can afford to be."

Paul knew she was being vague on purpose, wanting to say enough to let him know that another man found her desirable, and wanting also to let him know that he came first. A woman's privilege, he thought, and asked no more.

A maid admitted him and, familiarly, he went upstairs to the library where Leah liked to read before dinner, to surprise her. But the surprise this night was his: Hank was sitting there with his mother. On seeing Paul, he stood up; the prompt motion, straight posture, and extended hand gave Paul immediate recollection of the times he had taught the little boy how to behave like a gentleman.

Hank gave an honest handshake. "Nice to see you. Mother didn't say you were coming."

"I thought I'd let Paul surprise you," Leah said.

"Where's Cousin Marian?"

"She had a job to do, a thrift shop sale, and your mother very kindly offered me some dinner so I wouldn't have to eat alone. And you—why aren't you in Philadelphia probing a cadaver or whatever it is you fellows do?"

Hank said briefly, "I came in last night to see my own dentist."

"He just got the first cavity he's ever had and it's made him mad. He wants to be a model of physical perfection," Leah said fondly.

"I'd say he comes close to it," Paul replied.

"I wish you'd have dinner with us at least," Leah complained. "You run in and you run out."

"Next time, Mother. I promised to meet a guy downtown near Penn Station, so we can catch the train back to Philly together."

"All right, darling, go ahead. Call me during the week. Don't forget."

"I never do."

"I know. You're very good about it."

"He really is good about it, too," Leah said when Hank had gone. "I'm very lucky." A bottle of sherry and a cluster of crystal goblets stood on a tray near her chair. She got up and poured drinks. "Lucky tonight, too. Unexpected pleasures are the best."

Paul smiled. "Your health."

"You know, Dan will be sixty-nine in November. I was thinking I'd like to give a party, a real party at my house. We'll dress up and have music and make it a gala."

"Do you think he'd enjoy that kind of thing?" Paul asked.

"I don't see why not. He loves good food and wine, at any rate."

"But the crowd, and having to dress. You know Dan."

"He's never had a bang-up celebration. I think it's time he tried one after sixty-nine years."

"Why not make it seventy, next year? A milestone."

"Because," Leah said, "he just might not be here then."

"Oh, his heart's been bad for the last fifteen years."

"Even so, I feel I want to do it now. It'll be the end of the month, around Thanksgiving. I'll talk to Hennie."

She was bright with enthusiasm. She liked to use the house, to display the silver, the Baccarat, and the embroidered linens that, through her own labor, she had acquired. The candelabra would be entwined with striped lilies; pinecones in every fireplace would put a tang in the air; violins would sing in the upstairs hall. Paul saw it all.

Alert as always to every change in his expression, she asked him, "What are you thinking now?"

"Nothing much. Just a phrase that came into my head. 'A garden of many delights.' Your house," he said, and knew he pleased her.

But in truth, he was thinking of something. November was a long time away, yet he was already considering the prospect of sitting at table with Donal Powers. He hadn't seen him since that furious encounter in Paris; since then Donal's rage must have burgeoned, along with the growth of HW Elektrische Gesellschaft as it earned the millions that Paul's stubbornness had denied to him.

He wondered how much Meg knew of what had happened. Undoubtedly Donal had had some tale to tell. Now and then he saw Meg at Hennie's house on Sunday afternoons when she brought the children to visit; she was as affectionate as ever, but she never said anything about another meeting, which was just as well.

He put his glass down to stare for a moment across Leah's familiar room where, now quite clearly, he could see young Meg standing at the curve of the piano. *Her startled eyes are turned to Donal Powers's skeptical, handsome face. There is between them the unmistakable tidal pull of sexual allure, as palpable as a sudden gust of tropical air.*

It was absurd that he should feel guilt—or if not guilt exactly, then a certain regret that he hadn't done more to stop that marriage up in Boston that time, when Alfie had asked him to talk to her. He knew his own powers of persuasion. He could win his point for a million-dollar account, he could raise more millions for refugees and charities, he could talk Ilse's son out of a concentration camp. Why hadn't he been able to dissuade a young girl from a totally unsuitable marriage?

He had been a romantic, that was why: Meg had been euphoric, and he had gone all soft at the sight.

Yet the marriage seemed to be thriving. A pink-and-white mother surrounded by healthy children—why should he not rejoice for her? Except for what he knew about Donal . . . It was strange to think that Hank was the only other person who knew it, and he wondered whether the knowledge haunted Hank as it did him. By tacit agreement, they never brought up the subject. Of what use would it be to do so?

Leah struck a match, making a sound as smart as a slap. Her long nails clustered on the small white cylinder of the cigarette. Her eyes were half shut in sensuous pleasure as she inhaled. "By the way, would you mind if I invited Bill Sherman to the party? I know it's to be a family affair, but Bill almost feels like family. He even had me at his daughter's graduation party. You won't mind?"

"Not at all."

She pursued the subject. "The older girl's specializing in child psychology, so she'll probably talk to Meg's kids. So it's really all right to have the Shermans?" she repeated.

"Of course, of course," he answered, feeling amused and touched by this rather unusual effort to make him jealous.

It had grown quite dark. Leah turned the lamps on. Well chosen and well placed, they comforted the darkness as warmly as firelight might have done, turning the old Oriental rug into a field of gold. Paul felt at home in the fine room and said so.

"This is a wonderful room. A wonderful house."

"All except the bedroom. My room. You don't approve," Leah said mischievously.

"It's—it's a very feminine room," he fumbled.

Leah laughed. "You don't have to be tactful. I know it's overdone. It doesn't go with the rest of the house."

"Well, you are usually more restrained. I've generally admired your taste."

"I know. I broke my own rules in the bedroom. It was an impulse. Throwing your cap over the windmill; isn't there some saying like that?"

"Don't remember." He looked at her with pleasure. She wanted to be "literary," chiefly to improve herself, which was laudable; she had done a remarkable job of self-education. Also, he knew, she was trying to please him and that was unnecessary, because she was highly satisfactory without any improvements. She sat now, settled back in the leather wing chair; a bright white pleated collar circled her neck, and the dark blue skirt of her soft dress flowed. He liked the clothes of recent years. The flat-chested, flapper mode of the twenties had never suited Leah anyway. It had been far more suited to Marian. . . .

"Come to dinner," Leah said, "and then we'll go up to my overdone bedroom."

They lay together in the flowered silk room-within-a-room and he let himself relax into the contentment that comes when desire has been satisfied. He lit a cigarette and inhaled the fragrance. Leah never minded tobacco smells. Marian never objected vociferously, since that was not her way, but with pathetic appeal, making him feel guilty.

Leah, naked, slid out of bed, put on a blue satin nightgown to match the room's blue, and slid back under the covers. Her pert fingers tapped Paul's cheek, rousing him.

"What are you thinking about?"

"Nothing much."

"Come on, you were frowning." Her fingers smoothed out the double lines between his eyebrows. "Come on, Paul!"

"All right. I was remembering that Marian never let me smoke."

"She's on your mind all the time—a lot of the time anyway —isn't she?"

"Well, naturally."

Leah was silent so long that he turned, raising himself on his elbow, to regard her. Her round dark eyes were troubled.

"Is it that you feel so terribly guilty about us?" she asked.

He needed time to examine himself. What answer could he give? *Guilt* was an overburdened, heavy word, depressing and somber. This marvelous conjunction of two bodies, this glow that pulsed through his blood like wine or sun's heat—whom did it harm? No one. And yet . . .

"I don't like lies," he replied at last.

"Nor do I."

He knew that was so. Leah was not one of those women who are stimulated by their own power or who triumph by luring away another woman's man.

"I feel . . . sometimes, Paul, I feel awful when I'm with Marian. At your seder, or when she comes into the shop. She thinks I'm her friend."

Yes. Marian was the archetypical friend. Yes, even to him she was still a steadfast friend, as loyal to him should he ever be in need, as he was to her.

"She seems so innocent and I feel nasty. Nasty, Paul. Yet I don't stop what I'm doing and I don't want to stop."

He wished she would let the subject go. It was destroying the very mood that she herself had created for him.

"You know I've never mentioned it, but I was really afraid that Donal might say something about Paris."

Paul shook his head. "I never gave it a thought. He'd have gained nothing by stirring up a hornet's nest. There'd have been nothing in it for him. Donal's got bigger things on his mind."

Leah giggled. "A hornet's nest it would be, too!" Then she

grew sober. "And Hennie would lose all her regard for me. She'd try to be open-minded, modern and all that, but I'd know what she was feeling inside no matter what she said."

"True, Hennie's a puritan."

"People who grew up before the war see things very differently, don't you agree?"

"Not always. How do you think Hank would take it?"

"I don't know. He's very straightlaced, yet sometimes I don't think he's shocked at all. He's of the new generation, such insight, such compassion. Let me tell you what happened last night. I'd had a question about the furnace, and the man who takes care of all the furnaces on the block came by with his little boy. So after they'd been in the cellar they came upstairs, and we talked in the front hall. I didn't notice anything, but Hank got really upset on account of the little boy— this was after they'd left, of course—and wanted to know why I hadn't seen that the child was shivering in his thin coat, and what I paid the father. I told him I paid what the man asked for. I can't take all the world's troubles on my shoulders and Hank can't either, I told him. And he said he knew that, but that something went through him when he saw them go out into the wet night with the box of tools, and he thought of the room upstairs in this house that he had had when he was that child's age. You should have seen his face! He was truly deeply moved. He meant every word."

"He comes by it rightly, doesn't he?"

"Yes, yes. Hennie and Dan. And my own mother. Well, I'm not like them. Heaven knows I give, I give plenty, but I can't agonize. I can't wear myself out—good God, what's that?"

The outer door, two floors below, had closed with a heavy thud. Now someone was whistling on the stairs.

"Oh, no! It's Hank," and Leah jumped out of the bed and pulled on her robe. "What on earth—why didn't he go back to school? Oh, my God, quick, get dressed. Oh, what'll I say?" She tossed Paul's clothes to him.

"Mother?" Hank knocked on the door. "You awake? I saw your light."

"Oh, I'm just getting out of the shower!"

"I'll wait. I met my friend Mac and we talked so late that I figured I'd do better to come back, sleep here, and take the first train in the morning. I'll be leaving before you get up, so I want to tell you something funny Mac told me. His mother met you once and . . ."

The voice dwindled away. Leah had pulled Paul into the closet at the far end of the room.

"Stay in here while I talk to him," she whispered.

"Leah, that's ridiculous. I can't skulk and hide in a closet."

"Please. I can't have him find you here."

"I thought you said he wouldn't think anything of it."

"In general, in general, I meant. One's mother is different."

Paul felt a suffusion of shame. To be caught with one's pants down! he thought, even as he was pulling them on, buttoning his shirt and knotting his tie. He stepped out of the closet to retrieve his jacket from the back of the chair.

Leah pulled at him. "Go back in there. It'll be only a minute, then you can tiptoe downstairs and out. Just don't let the door thump when you close it."

In all his imaginings, he had never seen himself trapped in such a degrading, nasty situation. Yet suddenly, in a way, it seemed funny too.

"Are you all right, Mother?" Hank called.

"Yes, wait a minute—just stay in the closet, he won't know. Where are you going?"

"Out into the hall, like a man."

She had begun to cry; she, the worldly independent, the new woman, implored and clung. "Don't do this to me. How can you do this to me?"

Gently he pulled free of her. "Come, Leah. He'll have more respect for honesty. We are, after all, a pair of adults, and he's an adult too."

So saying, Paul unlocked the door in Hank's astonished face. He mustered a brisk, friendly manner.

"I was just going, Hank. I'll leave you two together."

Hank looked over Paul's shoulder to the chaise longue on which his mother had huddled into her blue silk wrap.

There were then a few seconds during which no one spoke. Hank was the first.

"Am I supposed to say 'I don't understand'? Isn't that how the dialogue goes?"

"I'm sorry this has happened, Hank," Paul said; that, too, was the way the dialogue went.

"You should be."

Paul drew in a long breath. *You should be.* So much for free thought! He exhaled a long sigh.

"Your mother's awfully upset. I think you should go to her and talk."

"I'd rather talk to you first."

"As you like. Then come downstairs."

They stood together under the chandelier in the front hall. Hank's eyes, black with anger, lay in dark rings like an owl mask. He looked menacing, almost as though he intended to use his fists.

"How long have you been coming here like this?" he demanded of Paul.

Paul answered severely, "If your mother wants to tell you, she will. As to my life and habits—I don't report to you."

He heard the defensive anger in his reply. To be judged and interrogated by someone half his age!

"You've robbed me," Hank said. "You've both robbed me of something you can't ever give back."

"Robbed you of what?" Paul's heart was pounding.

"Of my respect, of my illusions."

"I don't know what kind of illusions you had."

That was a lie, because he knew quite well. One didn't have to be a psychologist to know that a mother was to be "untouched." And as for the father image that he had so carefully cultivated, that, very likely, had been exploded into a thousand pieces. A thousand pieces in a single moment.

"You're a married man!"

"Don't be childish, Hank. Where've you been keeping yourself?"

"You think I'm childish?"

"Right now. But I think you'll be more reasonable when you've given this a little more thought."

"It's fine for you to talk. She's my mother."

"Yes, and she's been a widow for almost ten years. Must she live like a nun as well?"

"Let her find someone to marry, then, not this."

" 'This,' as you put it, has harmed nobody, has it?"

"How can I tell? What if my grandparents knew?"

"They don't need to know."

"And your—and Cousin Marian?" The black eyes reproached him. "You—you always stood for so much in my mind."

He was really only a boy after all, Paul thought, in spite of medical school and the surface sophistication of New York. He laid his hand on Hank's arm.

"People, good people," he began, "can be led into doing things that are less than ideal. Things that, if they could, they would choose not to do. You should know that."

Hank's mouth twisted. "Are you reminding me of Ben? You don't have to. I remember him well. Both halves of him."

"It's a painful thing when idols break. Our mistake is to make idols of them in the first place."

"But you! You stood for everything that was good. Except this last year, when you changed. All your talk of preparedness, your politics. We haven't been able to talk to each other . . . and now this."

"This . . . tell me, is it bad to be happy now and then, just tell me, is it bad?"

Hank didn't answer at once. "I don't want my mother to be hurt," he said at last.

"I haven't hurt her and I never will."

"I think you should marry her."

"There are complications, as you know."

"Then you should work them out."

Youth and the direct attack! "We'll see" was all Paul could answer.

"Don't you two ever talk about it?"

"No, we don't."

"That's crazy! Why don't you?"

"Marriage isn't always what everybody wants. It's not always the right solution."

"How can you know what anyone wants if you don't talk about it?"

"Perhaps we shall. And I know you should run up to your mother now. And don't allow her to apologize. She has nothing to apologize for."

About to put out his hand, Paul read Hank's face and withdrew. Hank wasn't ready. "I'm going," he said. "I'll let myself out."

The spring night had turned raw, reminding him that Manhattan was an island between the winds of two rivers, and he walked fast through the swirl.

He had told Hank that they were harming no one, and it was true. They had simply drifted into a relationship that worked. It worked for him, anyway, and Leah had never said that it didn't work for her. So it was a working relationship, just as in another way his relationship with Marian was working. Of course, if Marian were to know the truth . . . He had no idea what Marian might suspect about him. She never questioned him; the last thing she would want would be a session of that sort. She would think of it as a "scene" and she abhorred the vulgarity of scenes. Perhaps, too, she feared the truth that would emerge; as long as you didn't put a thing into words, it didn't exist.

For that matter, it was possible that Leah, in her very different way, was also avoiding the truth. And he thought, I suppose one really shouldn't just go on like this, getting nowhere. Yet must one always be getting somewhere? Why not just stay where one is and enjoy the moment? On the other hand, one really ought to have direction. He had always made careful plans: in business, certainly, and on his charitable boards, where you had to have goals, and in his work for peace there surely was purpose.

It was axiomatic, too, that a woman craved security, wanting to know whether she was loved and for how long. The indignant son had come directly to the point: *You ought to marry her.*

Joyous Leah! She knew something about joy, she did. There would be a lot of laughter in a home that she made. Love? Well, but—where there was peace and laughter, was that not a kind of love or even love itself? And he tried to remember the time when he had known beyond the least doubt what love was. But it irked him, it tantalized him, because he could not bring the feeling back, because it was so engulfed in bitter, painful anger.

I have resolved to put you out of my mind, Anna. You and our Iris too. Out. You won't take me in, so I put you out.

Maybe then, a life with Leah was the direction he ought to take. He really owed it to her. It was all the more credit to her that she had made no demands. It might be the best thing that had ever happened to him and to Leah too. Surely he could do better for her than either of her husbands had done, poor troubled Freddy and misguided Ben.

Arriving at the apartment house, he counted the windows up to the fifth floor. The light was on in the bedroom. She would be reading in her solitary bed. He foresaw the events of the next few minutes.

"You're home, Paul? Did you have a good supper?" And without waiting for an answer, "I'm absolutely fagged out. It was a big success, but I think I'll try to sleep late in the morning. Good night. Sleep well."

He began to plan how he would go about talking to her about divorce. Maybe it wouldn't be as hard as he had once thought. Divorce was no longer quite the scandal it had been in the years before the last war. Oh, Marian would weep and care and cling! But she didn't care so much that she wouldn't go off to Florida without him. . . .

He'd stay her friend and adviser all her life. He'd never abandon her. He'd buy her a better house in Florida, do anything to make her happy. And she would get over the divorce. It would be hard, but she would get over it.

There's no hurry, though, he told himself, rising up in the elevator. Next winter, when she was in Florida, having a fine time with her numerous relatives and friends, he would go down there and convince her that it was quite possible for them to remain kind and loyal to each other, while making official what was already a separation. Yes, that's what he would do. There was no use talking about it to Leah until it was over and done with.

A clear voice rang out at once from across the hall.

"Is that you, Paul? Did you have a good supper?"

Fourteen

The summer passed agreeably enough in the usual way. Paul and Marian went with three other couples to the same inn on a lake in Maine, where for the past ten summers they had spent three hearty weeks sailing, fishing, and swimming. He'd had a few queer twinges when he imagined himself informing the tight little group that this was the last time he would be with them. Home again in September, he spent a couple of balmy, gilded Saturdays at the Long Island cottage with Leah. Conveniently, Marian preferred the golf course at their Westchester club. He would have liked to take Hank along sometime, to reclaim his old affection and—yes, admit it—his respectful admiration. But Hank had spent the summer working in a Philadelphia hospital, obviously taking good care, whenever he came back to see his mother, not to encounter Paul.

"Hank's getting over it. We've had some nice talks, he and I," Leah assured him.

The assurance was too pat. Paul wanted to ask more about their "nice little talks," but it was clear she didn't want to tell him, so he didn't ask.

No doubt she had admonished her son to be patient, had told him that he, Paul, must be gently and peacefully led; that he, Paul, if not nudged or needled, would of himself come round. And how right she was! By the end of the winter, he thought, it would be all over. How he longed for quiet at the heart of things! He had never really had it. Maybe now, at last, he would find that peace and purpose at the center which makes it easier to live through the disorder of the outer world.

His thoughts were rudely jerked back to that disorder by another letter from Ilse. Now, after two years of peace, during which Mario had gradually recovered as much of himself as he ever would, after two years in which she had mastered the language and supported herself on the staff of a small hospital, the persecutions had caught up with them. Italy, pressured by Hitler, had started down the same path: Jewish doctors were forbidden to treat non-Jewish patients. Where was she to go? Palestine was practically closed and her wait on the Polish quota for the United States would take years. For a moment she came alive before his eyes; he met her clear, honest gaze and heard her bright laugh, and felt her despair.

The world was lurching toward some unfathomable darkness.

A strange thing happened one night at Madison Square Garden, where Paul had gone to hear Jabotinsky, the militant Zionist from Palestine. Friends who were emphatically anti-Zionist had invited Marian and him to hear the speaker "out of curiosity." Unwillingly, and at Paul's urging, Marian had accepted the invitation.

"I don't see why you want to go," she protested. "You don't agree with the militants."

"All the more reason why I ought to hear his argument."

Thousands crowded the Garden. Paul scanned them so-berly. In the difference between conservative Zionists like Justice Brandeis, who believed in using political persuasion and reasoned arguments to sway the British toward fair play in Palestine, and this militant group who believed that a Jew-ish army in Palestine was the only solution, lay the possibili-ties of terrible confrontation. Paul was silent and thoughtful, while Marian made conversation with the other couple.

Suddenly his attention was caught by a girl who was sitting in the row ahead, just in front of him. He looked and looked again. Could it be? He felt his heart accelerate.

No, it was absurd, here among these thousands! Yet why not? And he strained to listen. The girl was talking to her companion, a girl of her own age. She had a mellow, attractive voice.

"Well, I don't think violence is ever the answer. It may accomplish something immediate, but in the end there'll be more trouble. More ill will," she finished.

Then, as if she had felt Paul's eyes boring at the back of her head, she turned with a look of surprise and turned back again to the other girl.

Yes, he thought, the long nose, the long chin. He could see her face now in three-quarter profile. Yes, it may be. Should I ask on some pretext? No, it's idiotic.

"Well, Iris, you may be right," the other girl said.

Later, he did not remember having made any decision to do what he did. He simply leaned forward and tapped her on the shoulder.

"Miss, excuse me," he said.

She turned about in the seat, opening astonished eyes. His mother's eyes, like the rest of her face.

"You know," he said, with his heart racing faster and faster, "I think we've met before. It's been years, but I think we met a long time ago when you were a schoolgirl. Paul Werner is my name. I met you and your mother accidentally in a restaurant and we had lunch."

Recognition shone in the great eyes. "Oh, yes, I do remember. How odd that we should meet by accident again!" She turned all the way around in her seat. "This is my friend, Milly Kohn."

"My wife. And Mr. and Mrs. Berg," Paul said properly.

Neither of the Bergs nor Marian seemed to want anything more than an acknowledgment of the introduction. They returned to their conversation, leaving Paul to make something out of the occasion.

He spoke quickly, before Iris could return to her companion and dismiss him. "Are you a follower of Jabotinsky's?"

"I? Oh, heavens, no. He's far too extreme. At least, I think so. At home we are all admirers of Weizmann. I only came out of curiosity."

"I, too. It will be too bad for him if all these people also came only out of curiosity."

Milly giggled, while Iris said, "He's an interesting man. My father says he read that, growing up in Italy, Jabotinsky got a lot of his ideas from the Italian independence fighters."

"So I read, too," Paul answered.

Milly, having something to say, then gave him a minute or two, while pretending interest, to watch Iris. Yes, she had a fine intelligent expression, with a small frown of concentration. On second and third look, she wasn't entirely like his mother, either. His mother had been regal; her eyes had made calm survey, while Iris with the same eyes, heavy-lidded and heavy-lashed, *appealed*. It was unmistakable. And so earnest, to be only nineteen! He understood what Anna had meant. The dress, of a color neither tan nor gray, was prim; the white collar was almost clerical. She certainly had not inherited her mother's taste, for even when Anna had had no means at all, she had had style, a way of tying a belt around her waist or a flowery scarf around her throat.

He was perplexed. The situation was so bizarre, not unique, for surely this business of concealed paternity had been happening since the beginning of time! But bizarre for me, he thought in painful mockery of self, for me, paragon of respectability that I am supposed to be. He imagined himself opening his mouth, right now, this very minute, and saying to Marian: Do you see this young woman? She's my daughter.

He felt a wave of dizzying weakness. The overhead lights were painfully, unbearably brilliant. He wanted to get out, to go home and lie down in a dark room. What did he care about Jabotinsky, about Palestine, England, Germany, or the world? And at the same time he wanted to prolong the moment, to keep the girl talking, to fill his eyes and his ears with the look and the sound of her.

"Of course he wants to seize Palestine from the British," Iris was saying, "and who can disagree? It's such blatant cruelty, not letting those desperate, tortured people get in. My mother lost a brother and his whole family when Hitler took Austria."

"I have relatives in Germany, too," Paul said. "Not as close as a brother, only distant cousins, but I'm very fond of them and worried about them."

"How can you explain a world like this to children?" Iris cried. "I teach fourth grade. Some of them read the newspapers and they all listen to the radio. It's very hard . . . well, I do the best I can."

Yes, I'm sure you do and always will; it's written all over you, Paul thought.

There came a hush then. Jabotinsky walked out to the podium and the crowd stood roaring and cheering until he opened his mouth to speak.

Later, Paul could not have repeated a word the man said. He was only aware of the dark head in front of him. She had a thin gold chain around her neck. When she raised a hand, he saw that she wore a class ring. She was concentrating. He could see, when she turned to the side, the rise and fall of her breathing. His flesh, breathing.

When the speech ended and the cheers rang, Marian was in a hurry to leave, urging, "Let's get out before the rush."

Iris looked back. "Well, good-bye," she said politely.

Paul took his time putting on his coat. "What did you think about it?" he asked.

She was doubtful. "Most people here seem to be thrilled. It is kind of thrilling, though, isn't it? A Jewish brigade? And yet Weizmann and Brandeis are against it, so I'll stay with them. They surely know more than I do."

"I think you're right."

Marian and the Bergs were already pushing out toward the aisle. "Do come, Paul, will you? We'll be caught in the downstairs crush."

"It was nice talking to you," Iris said as Paul lingered. He thought she looked faintly puzzled by his attention, although perhaps he only imagined it. At any rate, she would surely mention the encounter at home. He had an instant's image of her telling Anna . . .

"Nice talking to you too," he said.

And he followed Marian downstairs, moving slowly through the crush, thinking they would never reach the street and the fresh air, thinking that the pressure in his head would shatter him.

When they had parted from the Bergs, who lived downtown near Washington Square, Marian said seriously, "I thought you'd never get through talking to that girl. Who was she, anyway?"

Despising his lie, he answered, "I met her a couple of years ago with her parents."

"And who are they?"

"Just some clients." Then he couldn't resist a question, a useless question. "What did you think of her?"

"Oh, I don't know. There was nothing remarkable about her. I'm surprised you remembered her that well."

"You know I seldom forget a face. It's one of my accomplishments, my dear."

The following day, the telephone rang on Paul's private line in his office.

"Something happened this afternoon," Leah began.

Since he was not in the calmest mood, alarm sprang instantly. "What's wrong?"

"Nothing bad. It's just that I need to talk to you. I really do."

Relieved, he forced himself to sound almost jovial. "I don't think that'll be too hard to arrange."

"Can you come over this evening?"

"Oh, golly, Marian and I have a dinner invitation at eight. People I hardly know, darn it. So will tomorrow do?"

"You could stop in on your way home from the office, couldn't you? It won't take long."

On his way uptown, he tried to guess what she might want. Obviously, it was no disaster, so why the haste?

She was sitting in the library in front of the fireplace when he came upstairs. A small pile of cigarette stubs lay in the ashtray; evidently she had been sitting there for some time, not reading or listening to music, both of which she liked to do at the end of the day. One leg was curled under her; one hand gripped the arm of the chair; even the puffed smoke rising from the cigarette was agitated.

"Bill Sherman wants to marry me," she said abruptly. "He's been waiting long enough, he says. Too long."

An emotional crisis now loomed: crisis on top of crisis.

"He wants an answer."

"Well, I surely can't blame him," Paul said, and thought: I'm dodging; I don't know how to meet this.

"He wants the answer tonight."

"Tonight?" Paul repeated.

Leah ground out the cigarette and regarded him. He found himself looking directly into her eyes; it would have been impossible for him, without shaming himself, to look away.

"I can understand all right, but still, tonight," he faltered.

"Listen, Paul, I'm not about to throw down my glove. This is no ultimatum, at least not in the way you might expect." Her tense low voice went husky, and she spoke so rapidly, without a second's pause to search for words, that he supposed she must have rehearsed what she was going to say. "And yet, in a sense, perhaps it is. You do what you have to do, and then I'll know what I have to do. I'm not about to cry on your shoulder. That's never been my way. You know that. You know me almost as long and surely as well as anyone does."

"That's true," he said, not knowing what else to say.

"I've had two big holes drilled right through my chest, here"—and she put her hand, on which Ben's great diamond lay glittering, to her heart— "first there was Freddy, and then Ben, a bigger hole, a cannonball. One more, and I'll look like a sieve." She gave a queer little laugh. "I had bad luck, didn't I? You always said I did. You always admired me, you said, for not whining about it. Oh, Freddy couldn't help not liking women, poor boy. But how could I have known? He was so sweet, so easy to be with and such a gentleman. I was very much impressed by gentlemen in those days. Still am, I guess."

Wounded now, she was sitting where Freddy had sat, with his Scotch plaid blanket hiding his more terrible wounds, covering the space where his legs should have been.

"Then I had Ben, who was manly and loved me, but weak, too, in his own way, when he chose bad companions and couldn't resist the money. Well, you know it all, so I don't have to tell you."

"No, you don't have to tell me," he said bleakly.

"I don't have to tell you how I feel about you, either."

He had turned to watch the fire while she spoke; little gold flames scurried and hurried, so that one wished one could turn one's mind off too, and just keep staring into them, thinking of nothing at all except the light and the warmth. But he was forced by the demand in her voice to look back at her. What to reply, how did one answer that brave honesty?

He found some words. "You're one of the most wonderful people I've ever known." They were his total truth and they were entirely inadequate. He knew it as he spoke them.

And she ignored them, which was what they deserved. "I need someone steady and someone just plain good. An all-around good man, someone free of encumbrances, whom I can depend on now and when I'm old, or if I should be sick and lose my looks—"

Leah sick? Leah old? She would be stunning at eighty, a slender woman with magnificent white hair and a diamond choker around her throat.

"—someone who'll give me, all the way, what I'm prepared to give. Heart and soul, don't they say? Isn't that what they say, Paul?"

His misery mounted. "Yes," he replied.

"Have you given them to me, Paul? Your heart and soul?"

He couldn't answer.

"It's been a happy time, at least for me it has."

"And for me," he said quickly.

"Well, then, Paul?" And again the eyes, those round bright eyes, held him fast. Monkey face, Hennie always called her, and he felt a physical pain in his chest.

"You see, Leah, you just said 'free of encumbrances,' but I'm encumbered."

"Not really, Paul. You could get a divorce. You could."

"It's not so easy . . ."

And Leah continued, very quietly now, "Are you afraid it would hurt Marian too much? I don't think it would. Not from what you've told me and what I've seen myself. I truly don't think so."

He cried out silently: This is impossible! Why am I tongue-tied, why can't I speak?

"Listen to me, Paul. I've been feeling something for a long time. I've never told you. I think it was there from that first time when we were on the *Normandie,* and it was all so wonderful. Yet I felt even then that something was missing. It was almost as if *you* weren't there, not all of you. As if it wasn't *me* whom you were needing."

"You were, you are, the most desirable—" he began.

"No, no, I'm not finished. I have a question. If there were someone you cared about terribly, someone you had to be with, *had to,* do you understand—could you, would you do something not to lose her? Settle things with Marian, I mean?"

He was thinking, as he watched the struggle, as he watched blue cords in her neck and heard the tears in her voice: I was going to do it this winter, dear Leah. But yesterday I saw Iris. . . . And he wished he could tell her, he wanted to tell her, yet didn't know how to begin.

She was waiting for an answer. When it didn't come, she repeated, "Would you then ask Marian for a divorce?"

He braced himself. Fundamental decency demanded the truth. "Yes," he said, so low that she had to strain to hear him. "Yes."

"Ah! Then there either isn't anyone whom you need all that much, meaning me, or else"—the bright eyes judged him keenly— "or else there is someone, but it's hopeless and you can't have her. Which is it, Paul?"

His own eyes were wet. Absurd for a grown man!

And Leah said quickly, "Your pause is the answer. There *is* someone else. The truth, please, Paul. I must have it. Don't do this to me."

He looked up, not caring now to hide his brimming eyes. "Yes, Leah."

She got up and drew the curtain aside, admitting the night. Her shoulders were hunched. Her fingers clutched the silk. When she turned around, she said quietly, "I've often thought there might be. She's a lucky woman, whoever she is."

"No, I don't bring much luck to any woman."

"Don't say that, Paul. It's of our own making. You didn't force me. I daresay you don't force her."

"No, that I don't. And I didn't," he said bitterly, thinking, *although I should have.*

Leah still stood outlined against the night beyond the window. With visible effort, as though a terrible ax had severed something inside, she straightened herself. And they looked at each other, she with unspoken questions, and he half pitying her, half pleading for himself.

He knew that he owed her an explanation, total and true. So he began to speak.

"The woman . . . she . . . we fell in love while I was engaged to Marian. It's a long story. Any love story is, I suppose, once you begin to tell all of the conflict in conscience and searching of soul. But I'll make it short. Each of us married someone else. Just after the war, when I came back, we met once and had a child. She's nineteen now. Iris. Iris Friedman," he said, casting the words from his mouth. "No, not Iris Werner. Never that. Yesterday I saw her for the second time in our lives." He passed his hand over his forehead, which was moist. "I had been thinking, I truly thought, that you and I— that I was ready, and it would be so good for us both. But suddenly last night I knew I wasn't ready. I'm confused. I'm numb."

And, as Leah still did not speak, he finished, "Well, that's the story. That's it."

"Surely not all of it?"

"Yes. Except that of course nobody knows about Iris, my daughter. And nobody must, ever."

"Thank you for trusting me."

"If I couldn't trust you, Leah, it would be the end of the world."

"Tell me, does she—the mother—"

"Anna."

"Does she—Anna—still love you?"

His answer came quickly. "Yes." It had been years since that day in the restaurant; yet he knew she had not changed and would not, any more than he would.

"But you never thought of leaving Marian for her?"

"She won't—can't—leave her husband. A matter of conscience, which I mentioned before."

Leah sat down, laid her head against the back of the chair, and closed her eyes. Paul could hardly bear to look at her. The carriage clock on the desk chimed the hour; its little music left a faint reverberation before the steady tick resumed. Somewhere in France, a hundred years ago, it had begun to chime and tick; the ears that had heard it were now long deaf; the human sorrows that must surely have burdened the air in the rooms where it had stood, were long over and buried with those who had suffered them; why, then, should they matter so much? He didn't know, he only knew that they did.

And suddenly Leah cried out, "It's all so sad! So unspeakably sad! You don't deserve it, Paul."

For a second he was unsure of her meaning, until he saw in the look she gave that she was thinking not of herself, but of him. Wounded herself, she could yet feel his wound, and he was moved almost beyond words.

"Oh, God! I'm sorry, Leah. Sorry. Am I as cruel as I feel I am?"

She got up and came to him. "There isn't a drop of cruelty in you. I've had too much happiness with you not to know that." She gave him a small, wan smile.

"How I wish," he answered, "that the happiness could have gone on!"

He thought, Just yesterday I knew where I wanted to go. But today, it's all too complex. I can't see my direction. I know I only want to be left alone.

Leah sighed. "I suppose this will pass in time. Everything seems to. And at least Bill Sherman has his answer. He'll have it tonight."

Paul groaned. "Do you love him at all, Leah?"

She thought a moment. "Not in the way that you must love Anna. Not enough to give up what's at hand. No. But I'm very, very fond of him. He's the good man whom I said I'd be needing, and he loves me very much, enough to have waited as long as he has, and perhaps as foolishly."

"He won't regret it."

"Oh, I agree to that. I'll see that he never does. I'll make him a wonderful wife and I'll be good to his daughters. Actually, I've done a bit of mothering for them all this time, anyway, and they think the world of me."

"I suppose Hank will be glad."

"Yes. I shall be respectable again, shan't I? But seriously, he likes Bill. People always do like Bill."

Paul pulled himself together. Best to get back to mundane, practical things before the heart broke. "When will it be, and where will you live?"

"He wants it as soon as possible. And we shall live here. Bill has a beautiful apartment, but he likes this house, too, and I want to stay in it."

"I'm glad. I want to think of you in this house always, because you've loved it so." He took her hand and raised it to his lips.

She looked at her watch. "It's seven. You'll just have time to go home and change and get to your party."

"God knows I don't feel like going. I don't know what I feel like doing. I feel emptied out."

"It hasn't been easy for either one of us tonight, has it? But I at least shall be somewhat happy, Paul. I really shall be. Because I know where I'm going and I'm grateful for that. I wish I could say the same for you."

"Thank you, dear Leah, thank you," he said simply.

He stood up, prepared to go, and yet reluctant, unable to walk out of her life.

"You don't want to tell me, do you, anything more?"

To confide! To talk about Anna and Iris, about all the years and the longing! He saw the pity and kindness in Leah's face, but he also saw curiosity, and it repelled him. It was the curiosity that brought him to his senses.

"No," he said quickly, "there's no point in it."

She nodded. "One thing, before you go: Don't worry about me. And have no guilt, either, for heaven's sake. I want you to smile at my wedding. You'll come, of course? Do you promise?"

He pressed a swift kiss on her forehead. "I promise. I'll be there, and I'll smile."

Another chapter closed, he thought as he walked homeward. A full, majestic moon hung in the gray silk sky. Turn, turn; half-moon and crescent, the sliver of a fingernail; then back again, round and silver, taking the tides along and, so it is said, the moods of man. Possibly so.

Leah was married one afternoon in the same upstairs library. The mantelpiece was banked with crimson roses and baby's breath. The curtains were pulled back and the slanting rain that slid on the windowpanes made the room all the more warm and tight. A rose-colored chuppah stood between the windows, the chuppah being a concession to the groom, whose family belonged to a Conservative synagogue. The guests, who were chiefly from Reform congregations, found it rather charming.

Leah wore a crimson satin jacket and skirt; the jacket was

embroidered in silver thread. *Chinoiserie,* murmured a woman who stood near Paul. *She really knows how to do it, doesn't she?* On Leah's right hand, Ben's diamond shone. Black pearls and diamonds gleamed softly on her left hand and in her ears. The bridegroom had been very generous. When Hank gave his mother away, Paul asked silently: A penny for your thoughts; we two are the only ones here beside your mother who know the truth. Hank had still not spoken to Paul and, still silently, Paul told him: You'll grow up in time. You'll find to your sorrow that things are never either black or white.

And he thought also: We two are the only ones here who share another secret. . . .

The glass was broken under the bridegroom's heel. He embraced the bride, and there was a little round of applause. Bill was a calm man, Paul saw, of a quiet nature, earnest and kindly. A woman could well feel secure with him. He would manage whatever life might bring. He was nice-looking, too, very nice-looking, well-groomed and even-featured. Paul felt a twinge, the merest twinge, of jealousy.

Waiters appeared with trays of champagne. There was a buzz of conversation, sounds of kissing, clink of glasses and toasts. Hank looked actually pleased. So did the Sherman girls, kissing their father and kissing Leah. Good-natured and practical as she was, she would be good for the girls; she'd steer them through the world with sensible advice.

"A nice family, aren't they?" remarked Dan, who, with Hennie, had come over to Paul. "It's just too bad she didn't do something like this sooner."

"Yes, too bad," Paul agreed.

"A pity Marian isn't here," Hennie observed. "It's such a pretty wedding, intimate, not too big."

"Well, it came so suddenly and Marian had already made all her plans to see her aunt in California. If you cancel your train reservation, you may not get another," Paul explained, not adding what a relief her absence was at this particular intimate wedding.

Now Alfie joined them. "Up, up in the world! That's our Leah!" He was feeling jovial, like the old Alfie. Wonderful how a bit of returning prosperity can lift a man's spirits, Paul reflected.

"How's Meg?" he asked.

"Fine, fine. Sorry she couldn't get here for the wedding, but there was hardly any notice, and they'd already planned the boat trip to Nova Scotia with the kids."

"Sounds like fun," Paul said. The absence of Donal was another source of relief, although he would have liked to see Meg.

Presently the sound of music came up the stairs and the party trooped into the drawing room, where the little orchestra sat around the piano and the rugs had been pulled back. There were more roses everywhere. Between the long windows at the front of the house, a painting had been removed, Paul saw, and in its place, his wedding gift had been hung.

It was a treasure. He had bought it from a gallery on Fifty-seventh Street, where it had been on display in the window. He went over now to get a better look at it. He had meant it as a parting message to Leah, a reminder of something happy that had not been intended to last. It was a view of a Paris street, glistening under a shower of silver snow.

Leah came up behind him and tapped his shoulder. "Admiring your present? You shouldn't have done it, Paul, but it's marvelous and I—we both love it. Bill knows a little about art, too."

The bridegroom came over and caught the remark. "Bill knows almost nothing about art, he regrets to say, but anyone can see how beautiful this is, and we certainly thank you, Paul."

"I hope you enjoy it for a hundred years."

Bill put his arm around Leah. "A hundred years won't be

too many." And he added, "I've heard a great deal about you, Paul, not only from Leah but from Hennie and Dan. I hope I can get to know you better." He extended a frank hand.

"I hope so too." Paul, shaking the hand, had to struggle inwardly with contradictory emotions. And, liking the man, he wished he had nothing to conceal.

"Uncle Dan's another one I'm hoping to know better," Bill said. "I've spent a couple of evenings with him already and I like him immensely, even though . . ." He smiled. "I don't agree with everything he says."

"I don't always, either," Paul told him, "but I'm awfully fond of him, all the same."

"Leah tells me we're to have a birthday party for him. It'll be a nice way to warm our home. You'll be here, I hope, and your wife will be back by then?"

"Yes, neither of us would miss it."

"Wonderful! Now I think I'll have to circulate for a while—I see some relatives I've neglected."

Leah's eyes followed Bill. She was glowing; the glow was unmistakable. Then suddenly she thought of something.

"Paul, I want you to talk to Hank. Hank, come over here. Now listen, you two, I want to tell you both something important. I am really happy today."

She waited while they both looked at her. Yes, she would transfer as healthily and as happily to this other man as she would have been if she had remained with Paul.

"I want you both to believe me," she said, "and I want you to love each other again. You owe it to me."

"I never stopped," Paul said.

Hank accepted Paul's hand. But his eyes looked away and there was no smile on his mouth.

"There, that's better!" cried Leah, not seeing. "Now come dance." And she bustled away to dance with her new husband.

Paul stood a moment, watching the dancers turn and whirl.

The orchestra was playing something plaintively familiar, a melody with a sweetness that touched some memory. *They asked me how I knew my true love was true . . . I in turn replied, something here inside cannot be denied . . .*

A wave of utmost loneliness swept over him. "This won't do," he said, standing there at the edge of the vivid whirl and swirl. "This won't do at all."

And catching the hand of a woman standing next to him, a pleasant lady with gray curls, he led her, pleased and surprised, into the dance.

Fifteen

Early in the evening of November 10, Paul went to the library after dinner and turned on the radio to hear the news. What he heard, he could scarcely believe.

Now at last, the beast of Germany, which had been threatening and snarling and rattling his cage, had broken free. With bared teeth and bloody claws he had raced through the towns and cities, all up and down the darkened streets, slashing and breaking and filling the night—the night of November 9, while here we were asleep in our beds, Paul thought, filling the night with terror and despair. Spontaneous demonstrations, the newsman said, "had broken out all over Germany."

"Spontaneous!" Paul cried. His cry was so loud that Marian came hurrying in.

"What is it? What's happened?"

"Listen."

"It is reported that thousands of Jewish shops and homes

have been destroyed. The fires of burning homes and synagogues lit the sky. All over the country, from the great cities
to the small towns of Bavaria. Looters, with arms piled high,
rampaged through the streets, which are still awash in broken
glass. Thousands of Jews have been arrested. It is not yet
known how many have been killed."

See them coming, wave after surging wave, as you saw
them even before they were in power.

"In Berlin alone, along the Kurfürstendamm—"

Static faded and crackled; for static substitute the crash of
broken windows; in place of this lamplit room high over the
broad reach of Central Park, see the cobbled courtyard of
Joachim's house; boots are pounding up the stairs, fists are
hammering on the door . . .

"I wonder what can be happening to your cousins," Marian
remarked.

"I don't know. I'll cable in the morning."

"But as you say, they're prominent people. They must have
influence."

"I don't know."

"He's been doing business, you said, doing well. Surely he
must know people who can protect him."

"Maybe."

"A man wouldn't be so foolish as to stay if there was any
real danger."

The radio rose above the crackle of static. "It is reported
that some of the most prominent Jewish industrialists have
been imprisoned. There are unconfirmed rumors of orders to
seek and arrest all wealthy Jews."

Paul clapped his fist into his palm. "God almighty! I warned
him. I begged him to get out."

He stood up. The curtains were pulled back; he could see
the evening glitter of the city and the lights of cars moving
downtown toward the restaurants and theaters. In Germany,
too, there were restaurants and theaters, filled now, this very

night no doubt, with people laughing and drinking, not caring about or even perhaps applauding the savagery on the streets outside.

"I suppose you won't sleep tonight," said Marian.

"I'm going to set my alarm for five and get downtown early to cable. It will be afternoon over there."

"It may not be as bad as it sounds, you know."

She meant to comfort, of course. He thought, No, it's not as bad as it sounds, it's worse. When the whole truth is known, and it may not be known for years, it will be much, much worse.

There was no answer to either of his cables, one to the house and one to Joachim's business address. On the second day, Paul cabled again, and still there was no answer. Then he called one of his senators in Washington to ask whether cables were getting through. Yes, certainly, transmission was normal. Then would the senator please call the embassy in Berlin and find out what he possibly could?

Two more days passed. On the third afternoon, Paul learned that the embassy had received too many requests from frantic relatives to be able to fill them. German authorities were refusing to answer questions anyway.

He set the telephone back into its cradle and sat for a while staring out at nothing. Suddenly, floating toward the ceiling, appeared the face of Ilse's Mario, that damaged face out of a nightmare. Then, in the instant, the image dissolved into the face of Joachim's girl, Gina. This face was strong and stubborn under its corona of curly hair; the eyes were filled with appeal. Seventeen now, he calculated.

What would they not do, those savages, once they got their hands on her?

After a while an idea came: He would telephone to Herr von Mädler. There might still be capital enough to draw on for another favor. When he had put through the transatlantic call, he sat quite still, waiting, until the telephone rang.

"I have your call to Germany," the operator said.

Von Mädler had a voice like a bark. "Herr Werner! You're in New York?"

"Yes. I'll get right to the point, since you're a busy man, I know. I wonder whether I can ask you for a favor."

"You can ask, but I doubt I'll be able to do it."

"You haven't heard what it is, Herr von Mädler."

"What I meant is, if it's what I think it is, then in that case, I won't be able to do it."

Disappointment drained through Paul, like weariness after labor. "You were so helpful that other time," he said cautiously.

"That was a couple of years back. Things are very different now. Very different."

"You're quite sure you couldn't? This time it's personal, someone quite close."

"I'm sorry, Herr Werner."

"You couldn't even just inquire? I'm quite at sea. There's been no reply to any communication."

"Then I should think the answer would be plain."

"But if you could just inquire—no more than that."

The bark softened. "Herr Werner, I can't extend myself. Do you understand me?"

That he, too, was afraid? Even he, the "von," the man of influence? Or of erstwhile influence.

"I'm sorry, Herr Werner."

"I'm sorry too. Then you have nothing to suggest? No one?"

"Nothing and no one."

Joachim, the starched gentleman with the Iron Cross, beaten to his knees . . .

"Keep well, Herr Werner. *Auf wiedersehen.*"

Auf wiedersehen? Till we meet again? We are never going to meet again, Herr von Mädler.

"Good-bye," Paul said.

His heart was still drumming when he hung up. Joachim, you fool, you didn't see the truth when it was staring you in the face! Joachim, if you're dead, if they've killed you and poor Elisabeth and your children, I hope it was quick. I hope you didn't suffer too long.

His desk was piled with papers. He read a few pages of a letter setting forth the stipulation for a bond issue and understood none of it, although he himself had dictated it. Finally he thrust the whole pile of papers back into their baskets and called Miss Briggs.

"I think I'll call it quits for the day. It's almost time anyway."

At home, Marian's Thursday bridge game had just ended. Lamps were lit against the iron-gray autumn afternoon, making the room shine faintly pink. The air smelled of flowers, chocolates, and perfumed furs as the ladies put on their coats.

Paul's appearance off schedule alarmed Marian.

"So early? Don't you feel well?"

"Just didn't feel like working."

Apparently Marian felt compelled to explain such an aberration. *Men worked.* "Paul hasn't been himself since the dreadful news came from Germany. You do take everything so hard, Paul."

"Not *everything*," he said, controlling his irritation over the banality.

One of the women spoke up. "Of course, it's awful for any government to allow such things and hoodlums to run amok like that."

"The German government didn't *allow* them to, it *ordered* them to," Paul answered.

"But are we really sure of that?" The second woman, some third or fourth cousin of Marian's, had an authoritative manner. "George says we must weigh these reports very carefully. Newspapers exaggerate. After all, they want to sell papers."

Paul said only, "Photographs don't exaggerate. The rabbis who report to us here don't exaggerate!"

"But"—doubtfully— "even so, George says that we, as Jews in this country, should be careful not to make too much noise about it. If it's true, we can't stop it, and we'll only draw attention to ourselves and arouse the American public against us. That's what George says, and I agree."

Paul turned his back. He hung up his coat in the empty closet and walked off down the hall. He wasn't going to wear himself out in futile arguments with asses.

"Asses!" he repeated as Marian came into the library.

"You weren't very polite, walking off like that," she said.

"I know I wasn't."

"It wasn't like you, Paul."

"I don't feel like myself."

"You care so much about Joachim?" she asked, rather gently.

"Not just Joachim." Not just Ilse, either, he thought.

How to explain? A huge globe stood between the two windows. Europe was green, a soft, misted green. Europe, that lovely little spur on the Asian continent, was sinking. Like a ship, like the *Titanic,* it was going down. Paul's hand spun the globe. His parents had had friends who died on the *Titanic,* like the Strauses whose story had become a legend: *I lived all my life with my husband and now I will die with him.* Or something like that. His parents had also known a survivor. He could remember listening in horror to her description of the lifeboat, of watching the great ship go down with its lights still blazing and the far sound of music carried across the black water. She had told the story well and he had been awestruck. Now the black water was rising again . . . the little villages, the geraniums in the windowboxes, the Opéra in Paris, the hillside vineyards, the stone lace cathedrals and the precious ancient synagogues, the children playing in the flowery parks, all, all would sink. . . .

Sixteen

The party was a wonderful idea and Dan was touched by the attention. It had been wise of Leah, Paul reflected soberly, not to have postponed it, for Dan, in spite of his cheerful animation, was decidedly blue about the mouth. He had the complexion of heart disease. Everyone saw it and all were glad to be here tonight, all with the possible exception of Donal Powers, who was no doubt bored by this outpouring of affection for a man in whom he had no interest.

Leah had outdone herself. The dining room walls had been repapered in a Chinese pattern of silver and peach; trailing blossoms on fine stems reached to the ceiling. Coral-colored roses in small silver bowls marched in a file down the middle of the table. At the center, in a large épergne, the same roses were interspersed with pale brown baby orchids.

Old houses like this one were made for grand occasions. They were also made for large old-fashioned families, with room for widowed grandmothers or even an unmarried cousin who was there ostensibly to help oversee the household, but was actually there because she had no other place to go. Such responsibilities were once taken for granted and were now done for, done for by the Great War, like so much else. A dinner like this, in a setting like this, was a holdover, a reminder of what had once been. And in a curious way it pleased Paul that Leah, who had no personal tradition of this kind, should be the one to continue it with so much charm. It warmed his heart now to see her presiding here, supported by the very evident affection and pride of her husband.

There had been so many ritual dinners like this in Paul's own life! So many pivotal events had occurred in his parents' overstuffed Victorian dining room! And he thought again— would he ever live down the memory?—of the night when his father had announced the engagement, while Anna served at the table. He could still see the platter trembling under her hand, still smell the stifling flowers, still see the quiet, modest pride of Marian. She had worn summer blue and pearl earrings. It was all as clear as yesterday. . . .

A dinner table was a perfect vantage point for observation. For a period of time no one moved from his place, so people were forced to look at one another. And he looked now toward his wife, whom Leah, tactfully, had seated in a place of honor at Dan's end, as far as possible from herself. There Marian sat, all unsuspecting, talking now to Alfie and Emily. He could barely hear them. Alfie was talking about diets; he was always dieting to lose weight, but one never saw any results. Marian was always on a health diet of some sort, cracked wheat or cranberry juice or something, either to cure this or to prevent that. But she looked well; she had kept her figure, and tonight it was accentuated by the simple Grecian cut of autumn-red silk.

"It is rather nice, isn't it," she had admitted when he had complimented her. "I couldn't very well go to Leah's party without wearing one of her dresses, but really she is too frightfully expensive. I never feel I can afford her prices."

Not afford her prices! He had to smile at that; Marian's frugal streak amused him. And yet, in a way, he had to commend it, for her donations were correspondingly lavish.

Meg, too, was beautifully dressed by Leah, but her splendid adornments were Donal's, and they were not frugal. A chain of cabachon emeralds, set in diamond loops, hung to the V of her neckline; she wore a pair of matching bracelets. It was a regal display, and she wore the glitter very well, yet to Paul there was something puzzling, something incongruous, about what he was seeing and what he was remembering of the earnest girl in sweater and skirt.

Her children were lined up in a row, with their father at the other end, which put him far down the table, away from Paul. With obvious pride, Donal was showing off his boys. Vigorous and handsome blonds that they were, sturdy all-American types, they deserved to be shown off. The subject was football, and Hank had joined in. Paul, who had played tackle in his time and still followed the games, would have liked to join too, but Hank had avoided him all evening and so he turned back toward Meg, who was conversing with the host about their daughters.

"They do get more discipline at a good private school," Bill Sherman was saying.

Meg spoke. "Lucy and Loretta are in separate classes. The modern thinking is to keep twins apart."

The twins, dark, handsome girls, giggled. They resembled their father. Curious that girls of just eleven could already have a sardonic expression, yet unmistakably they did. Meg would have a time managing those two when they were a few years older.

Five children. Automatically, Paul counted. He had almost overlooked the fifth, who had been sitting directly across from him all the time. Agnes, that was her name. She was the youngest, the quiet one, different from the others, it was said.

He addressed her now. "Hello, Agnes."

She raised polite eyes and turned away. Plainly she did not want to talk. Then he became aware that, like him, she was listening. While the others were busy listening to themselves, she was taking them all in. Some might think because she was so quiet that she was merely listless; but her moving eyes and the small smile that twisted now and then about her mouth revealed that she was not. She looked poetic, Paul thought, searching for a word and coming up with nothing better. She touched him. There was something lonesome about her, an air of being *outside*, looking in, that brought Iris to mind, and it appealed to the part of himself that also wanted to be outside looking in.

He was still absorbed in these reflections when he heard Leah's voice cut through the general murmur.

"I grew up hearing the story so often I almost felt I had lived it, although I was born in New York. After the pogrom, when my grandfather was shot, my parents came here. It cost thirty-five dollars to make the crossing, which was almost all they had in the world."

Now what on earth had started that conversation?

"Of course, they were beastly sick all the way over. Oh, well, it's the usual steerage story. You've all heard it."

"I really haven't," said Emily, "unless you mind talking about it."

"You wouldn't want to hear the rest."

"Oh, but the rest must be much happier! After they landed in America, I mean."

Dear, cheerful Emily, Paul thought. She has really forgotten about the tenements and tuberculosis and Leah's parents, or she wouldn't have said that.

Leah gave a small shrug, ignoring the remark. "Well, there's no more to be said, is there? Except that it seems we're about to see the same sort of thing all over again on a hundred times larger scale."

Germany again. That must have been what started the topic. But it was inevitable these days, a topic that wouldn't go away. Paul wished they would let it lie just for tonight.

"Oh, dear," exclaimed Emily, "you don't suppose, I mean, they can't just murder a whole population after all, can they?"

Bill Sherman answered, "My rabbi thinks they can."

And your rabbi happens to be right, Paul said to himself.

"Oh, but," Emily went on, "you remember—you're too young, of course—all the propaganda we heard during the war about the atrocities the German soldiers were supposed to have committed in Belgium and it turned out to be all lies. All lies."

And where have I heard that before? Paul thought.

Emily persisted. "Isn't that so, Alfie? And Dan, I remember when you said the same thing about the Hearst papers during the Spanish-American War."

To his credit, Alfie murmured, "This is different."

"Not really." Donal's firm tone caught everyone's attention. "The papers are full of distortions. Left-wing writers, Communists, most of them. Look at France! They put Blum in office and almost wrecked the country."

"What?" Dan cried. "Communists? Blum? Because he gave them the forty-hour week and two weeks vacation with pay? And made schooling compulsory up to the age of fourteen? You call that communism?"

"You can't deny that the labor movement in France is loaded with Communists," Donal said.

Against his will, Paul had to speak up. "There wouldn't have been so many embittered workers if they'd had some social security and if the rich had been willing to pay some taxes."

Donal looked over at Paul. "I suppose you like to pay taxes, do you?" His eyes were cold.

Paul didn't answer the taunt. How the hell had they strayed into this subject anyway? He cut into a slice of avocado. He only wanted to eat and be left alone.

But Donal went on playing with him. "You will never convince me that Blum isn't a warmonger too."

Heads were turned in Paul's direction, so he had no choice but answer. "He foresees the danger. It's a pity no one else does, or did when Hitler reoccupied the Rhineland and thumbed his nose at the world."

"They had to let him do it. Do you realize that France has fewer than half as many men of military age as Germany has? The situation is hopeless."

Now Hank joined what seemed to be turning into an attack on Paul. "War is always hopeless, although people who should know better may not agree."

"You agree, of course," Donal said. "And I don't blame you. You'll have to fight if it comes."

And Dan joined in. "Well, I may be too old to go, but I'm dead set against all the preparations that are being talked about in this country by certain elements."

Me, Paul thought.

"All our lives, Hennie and I have been fighting pacifists, if that's not a contradiction."

"Then you'd better keep on fighting," Donal said. "Let Germany alone. Let's let Hitler get rid of the Russians for us. After that, we can learn to live with him."

Paul put down the fork. Never mind the gentlemanly control. Gloves off.

"Live with him? And with what's been done in Germany this week, and what's happening in their streets this minute while we sit here?"

"Highly exaggerated, just as Emily said. I've spent a lot of time there, and let me tell you, the streets are orderly. There's less crime on them than on ours."

"I've been there, too, and that's not what I saw."

All conversation had ceased except for the passage of words between the two men. Meg looked nervous; she was trying to catch Donal's eye and not succeeding. Leah and Bill had caught each other's eyes and had evidently passed some signal, because Leah, loudly and deliberately, called for attention.

"Are we ready, everybody? The cake's coming in. Bill, will you turn off the lights?"

Poor old Dan, Paul thought. All this anger on your birthday.

The cake was now carried into the candle-lit room. Just as if nothing had happened to jar the mood, everyone stood and sang "Happy Birthday." Dan made a wish. What did one wish for when one was almost seventy? Probably for some more years.

The lights were turned back on, revealing the cake as a spun-sugar marvel, and champagne was poured. Leah raised the first glass.

"To Dan, who's been father to us all."

Then Dan stood. "To everyone here, my thanks and love. And to the world around us, the great gift, the only gift, peace."

Paul couldn't resist an amendment. "To a just peace and to the destruction of the tyrants in Germany."

"So we are all to go to war now. Is that it?" asked Donal.

"Certainly not." Dan said at once.

"Well, then you had better pay attention to what's happening in Washington." Donal spoke with vehemence. "It's still undercover, but I can tell you they're readying big aid for nothing. Hitler will crush England overnight whenever he decides to."

"I believe you're right," Hank said.

Paul shook his head. "I sit here and listen to you, Dan, and to you, Hank"—he nodded toward Donal without speaking his name— "all so staunch for peace and no preparedness, but for entirely opposite reasons. Don't you see what strange bedfellows you are? You, Dan and Hank, you at least are men of goodwill. Don't you see that sometimes, terrible as it is, wars have to be fought or at least prepared for in order to survive?"

"I'm surprised to hear you say that," Donal said, giving slight emphasis to the "you."

"Why me?"

"I should think you'd be standing pat with Dan and Hank. It's known that Jews don't like to fight, isn't it?" He looked about. "No insult intended, I assure you. It's merely a given. You might even take it as a compliment."

From a surprising quarter there sounded a thin little voice, as Agnes spoke. "You sound like Father Coughlin, Dad. You ought to stop listening to him."

There was an audible intake of breath around the table. Faces, all except Donal's, on which a high flush spread, looked disbelieving.

Meg's voice quavered between reprimand and apology. "Agnes! Your father never listens to Coughlin!"

"Oh, yes," the child said calmly, "he does all the time. He just doesn't want you to know."

Paul felt a flash of comprehension. The odd little girl had never met her father's expectations, and knowing it, she was now throwing down the gauntlet. With comprehension came sympathy, and Paul gave her a look of kindness before he returned to his attacker.

"I'm sure I don't know about *liking* to fight," Paul said carefully. "I don't suppose many men really like it, but when we have to, we do it, like everyone else." He thrust his napkin into a ball and put it on the table beside his plate. "I did my share in the trenches in 1917, and so did Bill. Hennie and Dan lost their son, as you very well know. . . . Oh, I understand what else is in your mind, Donal Powers! You think this war that's coming in Europe is a Jewish issue. Well, think again.

True, we are the first to suffer and we'll know extraordinary suffering, but do you think all would be peace if the Jews had never existed? No, Christians' values, too, your morals and families and homes, will be destroyed. Millions will die because of those maniacs and the world will be altered—"

Paul's anger was choking him, but he had to finish. "So to hell with everybody. To hell with helping England. Just let's go on trading with Germany. It's so profitable, isn't it?"

"I don't agree at all with Paul's politics," Hank said unexpectedly, "but he's right about that. What we should do is declare an embargo on Germany. Starve her to her knees and her senses. That's the real alternative to war."

"Embargo? Germany?" Donal's expression was quizzical. "That's an odd remark from someone who's been making a fortune out of Germany."

"I don't understand," Hank said.

"A fortune. Your money's quadrupled. You didn't know? Paul never told you?"

"What can you be talking about?" demanded Hank, looking from Donal to Paul.

"I'm talking about your stock."

"What stock?"

"Why, the original company that first bought your grandfather's patents! Didn't you know it was taken over by a German conglomerate? It's been selling in Germany for years! I put the deal together myself. I'm really surprised you weren't ever told." And Donal shot Paul a look of triumph.

"What are you saying?" Dan cried. "My patents, my inventions? What is this? Paul, you knew about this?"

Paul opened his mouth, closed it, and opened it again. "Yes, I knew. But there was nothing I could do. I'm only a trustee, remember? Empowered to invest the income but not the principal." He turned to Hank. "That's how it was left in your father's will."

"You could have told us," Dan said furiously. He was almost hysterical.

"I didn't want to be responsible for your heart attack, Dan. There was nothing at all that anyone could do about it, except Hank, and he had to be twenty-one."

"Why didn't you tell me? I've been twenty-one for more than a year." Hank was equally furious.

"Perhaps I should have," Paul admitted. "Frankly, I didn't think of it. We haven't been seeing each other much lately." He was trembling. "This is no place for such talk. This is an outrageous imposition on Leah and Bill. I have an office. You can see me there anytime, any and all of you."

He knew he should stop, but he couldn't help himself. "And you, Donal, what you did here today, when you knew how it would hurt Dan, hurt that good man—" He stammered. "But what should I expect from a man who can see good people slaughtered, such injustice—"

"Unfortunately, injustice is the way of the world," Donal replied. "It's life. Sometimes the good have to suffer with the bad. I'm sorry if I've made Dan suffer. It wasn't by intention."

Donal's face was still painfully red. Meg's hands were making rapid little movements with her necklace, her fork, and her glass. Marian, with an appalled expression, turned in her chair toward Paul. His heart pounded so that he could scarcely catch his breath. He stood up straight. It was the first time in his life, a life bound by good manners, that he had done what he was about to do. But there was always a first time.

He bowed to Leah and then to Bill. "I beg your pardon, but I must stop this discussion. It will be better if I leave the room."

"He was spoiling for it," Bill Sherman said.

Paul admitted, "Well, I was too." Having cooled off during the last hour, he had begun to feel contrite about his outburst.

"A long-standing enmity, I suspect."

"Leah's told you?"

"As a matter of fact, she hasn't. But it's not hard to deduce from the evidence."

Paul smiled. Sherman hadn't risen as high as he was in the legal profession without being observant.

"I should have buttoned up my mouth. . . . I'm sick over the way Dan had to find out about the stock, though. I truly had every intention of straightening the matter out with Hank and never letting Dan know." He sighed heavily. "Now the damage is done for good."

"No, Dan's reasonable. Emotional, but amenable to reason. Give him a few days to get over the shock and then talk to him. He'll understand. I'm sure he will, Paul."

Fortunately, the house had so many rooms and halls that Donal and Paul had not even seen each other since they left the dining table. The women had all rallied to lighten the atmosphere; through the open double doors Paul could see and hear Meg at the piano; Hennie and Meg's twins were singing, while Marian appeared to be having a chat with Emily. Maybe it wasn't as bad as it seemed, he tried to tell himself. All's well that ends well.

In the usual flurry of departure, with thanks and good nights and coats, Paul and Marian found themselves with Donal and Meg and their family at the closet in the downstairs hall. While her husband held out her sable coat for her to put on, Meg's eyes appealed to Paul. In deep distress, she spoke to the air.

"Why do things have to happen like this? We came here to celebrate. . . . It was going to be lovely."

Neither man answered.

She pleaded then, "Won't one of you say something?"

It was Paul who responded. "I'm sorry, Meg. Things just got out of hand."

"You overreacted," Donal said sharply. "You take that political stuff too seriously. You always did."

This effrontery rearoused Paul's anger. But he kept his manner quiet.

"It wasn't necessary to let Dan know about the stock. I can forgive that least of all."

"So now it's forgiveness! Holy forgiveness!" And Donal glared.

Never on your part, Paul thought. You'll go to your grave still hating me because of the millions you missed when I wouldn't agree with you that time in Paris. But he did not reply.

It was as if Donal had hold of a rope and was unable to let go. "Holiness goes with your do-gooder image, of course."

Meg pulled at his sleeve. "Donal, please . . . Timmy, Tom, girls, go out and get in the car."

Donal shook her off. "You've always thought that you were better than anybody else," he said to Paul. "It's written all over you."

He wants to fight. He wants this to escalate, Paul thought with some astonishment. And he made retort.

"Better than you, at any rate."

"Oh, for God's sake," Marian whispered. After her nervous habit, she was snapping her purse open and shut, open and shut. "Paul, I want to go home."

"Of course," Paul said, aware at once of her fright. He moved toward the door, which the children had left ajar.

Donal stopped him. "Just a minute. What did you mean by 'better than you'?"

"What do you think I meant?"

"Suppose you tell me, you superior gentleman."

"Very well. I meant that you're a fascist—which fits with the rest of your way of life."

"My way of life? Do I sit at a dinner table with my wife at

one end and my mistress—or pardon me, former mistress—at the other end? And you dare talk of my way of life?"

Over the drumming in his head, Paul heard his wife's gasp.

"Why, you're the lowest—" he began.

Donal interrupted him. "The upper classes! Sneak away to Paris in high style with your lady, leaving your wife at home, then when you're tired of the lady, marry her off and take your unsuspecting wife to dine with the newlyweds. The upper classes!"

Marian began to cry. Paul heard her; he couldn't look at her. Meg sat down with her face in her hands. The two men, standing beneath the crystal chandelier, were squared off. It came to Paul that if there were weapons at hand, a murder would surely result; this was the way it happened, even to people who thought themselves civilized. Rage took over, so that he no longer cared what he said.

"Maybe it's just as well that we bring everything out into the open. I may not always have done what I should, but at least I have no man's death on my conscience."

"Oh," Meg said.

Rage mounted and mounted. "There's been too much hidden . . . ugly suspicions." Paul put a finger in front of Donal's face. "You had a violent quarrel the day Ben was killed."

"You're out of your goddamned mind!"

"Oh, no, I'm not! Ben told you he was going to leave you, to resign. It's none of your business how I know, but I know. That quarrel was never mentioned in the investigation, was it?"

Meg jumped up from her seat. "Please, Paul. I can't stand this. Look at Marian. Stop it, both of you."

Donal repeated, "Out of your goddamned mind!"

"I'm sane enough to see that you knew a lot more about Ben's death than you admitted."

Meg put her hands to her temples. "Oh, God, I can't believe

the things I've heard!" She whirled on Paul. "Look at Marian, I said. Don't you see you have to take her home? Look at her!" Meg screamed.

Marian was standing still in the glare of the light, still as if frozen, while tears slid down her cheeks out of staring eyes. Terrified, Paul grasped her arm.

"Are you all right? Wait at the door, I'll get a cab, get home—"

Something exploded in Marian. Pushing him violently out of her way, she ran to the door and out into the street. Paul ran after her.

"Wait! Marian!" Coming abreast of her, he tried to take her hand, but she flung him off.

"Get away from me, don't touch me!"

The cry rang out through the empty street. It was a cry of anguish, a witness to some awful and unexpected death; it struck a sickening fear in Paul. What was she going to do? Throw herself in front of a speeding car? And he stayed close at her back as she ran in her delicate slippers, her heels tapping like hammers on the pavement.

At the last intersection before their street, she paused. Paul held his breath, as she seemed to be considering where to go; for a few moments he thought she was about to enter the nighttime wilderness of the park, there to do—what? What, then, would he do? He had a panicky vision of police cars and ambulances, of questions and answers: *Yes sir, it's a total collapse because I—*

But she turned into their street. They entered the building and rode up in the elevator together. Relief at having reached home without disaster now cleared Paul's head enough for him to start thinking about how he was going to handle the situation. He had not long to think.

"You come in here! I want to talk to you." Marian's face, never colorful, was green-white, death-white, but her eyes were dry.

He followed her into the library. She closed the doors—so that the maids would not hear, he understood—and slapped his face so hard that his eyes teared.

"You bastard! You filthy bastard!"

It was the first time he had heard her use the word. And he stood quite still, allowing her to slap his other cheek. She was entitled to her fury.

"Have you nothing to say to me?"

"Yes. I want to say I would do anything if I could undo the hurt you had tonight."

"What he said, of course, must be true."

"The facts are true, but not the interpretation he put on them."

"Interpretation! Calling mud by another name doesn't turn it into chocolate. A whore is a whore, even when her name is Leah."

He didn't answer. Let her spew it all out first. After that he would try to explain. Yet how did you begin to explain the indescribable? Laughter, lonesomeness, sexual delight, moods, attractions, passing needs . . .

She demanded an answer. "Do you realize how you've shamed me, and cheapened our marriage, allowing me to sit at that woman's table, sitting there in my innocence while she, that dirty thing, was laughing at me? You and she, laughing at me?"

"No, no. She—we— No one ever laughed at you, Marian. Listen, listen. It was just a thing that happened accidentally. You're not all that innocent, you know these things happen and are then over and done with. I don't say it's right, but a lot of things in this world aren't right."

"I am never going into that house again, do you hear me?"

"You don't have to," Paul said quietly.

"How did it happen? Did you travel on the same ship?"

"You don't really want to know all the details, Marian. It's over with. She's married, you and I are married—"

"Don't count on being married to me much longer, Paul. I asked you, were you on the same ship?"

He sighed. "Yes. The *Normandie.* I didn't know she was going to be on it."

"What difference does that make? So the affair began on the ship? In your cabin or hers?"

"Marian . . . There's no purpose in this. You're only tormenting yourself. It's finished, I tell you."

"In your cabin or hers, I asked."

"All right. Hers."

"And you slept together in Paris? Yes, naturally, why am I even asking such a ridiculous question? And then afterward here . . . How long did it go on?"

The wronged spouse always wants to know the details and also dreads to know. Paul understood.

"Not long. She's married now. Happily married, as you can see."

"Who broke it up? You or she?"

"I—it was mutual. Mutual."

"You're lying."

"No."

"She was better in bed than I am. She looks the type. I suppose she did things—"

"Marian, please. You're only hurting yourself."

"I want to know. If you don't tell me, I'm going to go to the phone and call her. I'll talk to her husband."

She moved toward the telephone. Paul grabbed her.

"You'll make yourself ridiculous. You'll accomplish nothing," he said, and, feeling desperate, added an appeal to his wife's sense of propriety. "You'll only lower yourself."

"How I hate you!" she cried out. "Hate you!"

Tears dripped on her red silk dress, scattering small stains. She ripped the sleeve. "This dress—it comes from her. She touched it. I'm getting rid of everything she touched." The silk screeched as it tore from neck to wrist. "Getting rid of you, too. Oh, how I hate you!" she cried again. And, clutching the flapping pieces of her dress, she stumbled out, down the hall to her room.

Paul heard the door slam. There was a poignancy in the sound, something frightening and final, as in the Ibsen play. The door slams and echoes. What next? it says. He went to the window. In a time of stress one went to the window and looked out. What else was there to look at or where else to go? Surely not to sleep.

He stared at the lonely night. There were not more than two or three lighted windows on the block. His skin crawled with cold. His head ached. He should never have said what he had about Ben; he had promised Hank not to, and all these years had kept the promise. In losing his temper—how the man had goaded him tonight!—he had assuaged his anger, but it had accomplished nothing. The whole business had been a disaster. Disaster. And what was he to do now about Marian?

Alarm shot through him. Suddenly he was aware of the silence. He thought of the medicine cabinet; who knew what she might—and he tore down the hall to the bedroom.

She was lying on the bed, still wearing the ruined dress. In a heap on the floor near the wastebasket lay a pile of clothing, a wool suit trimmed in mink, a black velvet dress, a white summer coat, and others, all things purchased from Leah. There was something pathetic about the way they lay, these beautiful garments crumpled and blameless, as though they could know they had been discarded. He picked them up and laid them smoothly on a chair.

Then he went over to the bed and stood looking down at his wife. She, too, was crumpled; her knees were drawn up, her hair had fallen over her face, and one hand clutched a wet, balled-up handkerchief. She sobbed; long, gulping, stifled sobs shook her weak shoulders.

He stood there for a long time. He knew he was expected to feel remorse, and yet he did not, for it was impossible to link remorse to the natural joy that he had known with Leah; it was far more possible to apply it to his rejection of Leah. What he did feel was pity, much more now for Marian than for Leah, who knew how to cope and survive. He put out his hand and touched her head.

She looked up. "Why did you? Why did you, Paul? You must hate me, that's why."

Hate her! She had no comprehension, none at all.

"Oh, my dear," he said, "it had nothing to do with you or what I feel for you. It was only the time and the opportunity. The flesh, if you want to call it that. Never the heart."

And that, he thought as he spoke, was more of a truth than a lie, for if what he meant was the whole, pure heart and the whole, pure spirit, why then—these had always and only belonged to Anna.

Marian was whispering. "The anger's gone now. I could have killed her and you. . . . And suddenly it's all gone, just drained away. I'm only crushed. I'm nothing."

"Oh, Marian," he said. He understood that her self-esteem, under the proper and proud facade, was shaky. A childless, neurasthenic, frigid woman, she lived on the surface of life, and perhaps in some unconscious way, she knew it. Not her fault, not her fault, he said to himself, while still stroking her head.

"I'm nothing," she repeated. "Nothing."

He felt a lump in his throat, a helpless ache. No human being should feel like this.

"How can you say that about yourself? You are a kind, good, valuable human being. Think of how many friends you have. People admire you." And he added, "You're a pretty woman, besides . . ."

She wiped her eyes. "I don't know. Do you really think I am?"

"Of course." He tried a touch of joviality. "You know my

weakness for art. Do you think I would have married you if you hadn't pleased my taste?"

A small smile touched her mouth. "But then I don't understand. Why Leah? She's no beauty." And while he was preparing an answer, she gave it herself. "Just sex, I suppose. It's the animal nature of man."

"Ah, yes."

"It's sometimes hard for me as a woman to remember that you're different. It means so much more to you than to a woman."

She really believed that, still.

"I'm glad you can look at it so," he said gently. "Do you think you can keep reminding yourself of it, so that we can put this behind us some day?"

"I'll try." Sitting up, she saw her reflection in the mirror opposite. "I look a mess. I've ruined this dress, and it was new."

"Never mind. Buy another tomorrow."

"Not at Leah's. I swear I will never see her or talk to her again."

"I understand. Just as well for all of us."

"What about you?"

"Finished, I told you."

She grasped his hand. "Paul . . . if anything like this ever happens again . . . will you leave me?"

"No, no. Nothing's going to happen again."

"But it might. You're a man. Oh, if you ever left me, I couldn't bear it, Paul! We've been together so long. . . . All my life, since I stopped being a child."

You're still a child, he thought. And his throat was filled again with aching.

"Even when I'm in Florida, I know you're here. I wouldn't have gone, I still wouldn't go, if you didn't want me to."

"It's all right, it's fine. I want you to enjoy yourself."

"What would I do without you? Don't leave me, Paul.

Promise me you won't. Say it." Her swollen eyes, her blotched and mottled cheeks, were piteous.

"I won't leave you," he said.

"Never? No matter what happens?"

"No matter what. But nothing's going to happen, I told you. Now go bathe your face, get comfortable, and let's go to sleep. We both need it badly."

On her way to the bathroom, Marian remembered something. "Is that true about Donal and Ben? They'd had a terrible quarrel that day?"

"Quite true."

"Can you tell me how you know?"

"No. I shouldn't have said what I did. It served no purpose, and I'd given my word besides."

"Then you really think that Donal—"

Paul countered grimly, "What do you think?"

"I think the answer's yes. It happens all the time, according to the papers."

"You had better forget it, Marian, as if you'd never heard it."

"Of course. But how awful for Meg! What do you suppose she'll do?"

"I have no idea. . . ."

Tumultuous thoughts kept Paul long awake. Ben, Donal, Leah, Marian, and Meg, all went whirling through his brain. Then among the confusions of the past week and the events of this painful night, there appeared of a sudden a queer fantasy: that Anna's husband had died, she was free and had come to him. What then would he do about Marian? A fantasy, to be sure, only an imagined complication on top of the existing one. Nonetheless, he was wrung out.

Meg had been silent all the way home, aware that Donal was stifling speech only because the children were in the car. She was so shaken that she had actually felt a sharp pain dart in her chest. Disaster! Again and again she had gone over it all, beginning with the dreadful instant when Paul had left the dining room.

After the stricken silence, suddenly all the civilized and proper people around the table had begun to talk. Lightly their voices had rung in slightly hysterical chatter about Fred Astaire and *Flying Down to Rio* or the coming Picasso retrospective at the Museum of Modern Art. But Meg, with stinging-hot face, had been silent, careful to meet no one's eyes for fear of what they might read in her own.

Then that explosion at the coat closet. Never had she seen such hatred in Donal! Pure, naked, terrifying hatred of Paul, it had been. And why? Because of what Paul knew. . . .

Harsh white lights in the Lincoln Tunnel had revealed her desperate hands knotted in her lap. Beside her on the limousine's rear seat, Donal had stared straight ahead; his mouth had a downward curve; he was still angry, probably at Agnes, too, who had revealed what Meg had not been supposed to know. So even in the total union of marriage, the nightly honey-sweet connection, things were hidden. . . . Had she not been doing the same?

And as the car had rumbled through the tunnel, she'd had a sudden flash of recollection, of sitting on a bench near the museum on Fifth Avenue, filled with panic and despair; then of making her way to Leah's place. It was Leah who had sent her to the doctor and saved her sanity, who had made it possible for her to be happy again with Donal. And if it was true about Leah and Paul, it was no business of hers, because they were people she loved, kind people.

Home now in their bedroom, Donal spoke. "What a ridiculous display from your fancy cousin!"

Not answering, Meg went on methodically undressing, hanging up her clothes and replacing the heavy necklace in the locked box.

"You always thought he was so holy, didn't you? I could

have told you about him long ago if I weren't the gentleman I am."

"I wouldn't have listened and I won't now."

"Not interested in Leah either?"

"No. She's my friend."

"Defiant tonight, aren't you?"

"I just don't want to talk about people I like or someone that I love like Paul."

"Well, love him or not, that's your privilege, but he made a fool of himself tonight. That moral lecture at dinner—"

"Well, somebody had to answer you! You were actually defending Hitler! Don't you realize how outrageous you were!" Her voice was intense. "It was shocking, when people are being tortured! And your remarks about the good having to suffer for the bad! Who are the good? The Jewish millionaires or the Jewish socialists? Perhaps the fish peddlers or the operatic sopranos? The Jewish Nobel prize winners who fill up the universities? Oh, you should have heard yourself! And then, what Agnes said about you listening to Father Coughlin—"

"Have you ever listened to him? You don't know anything about him. You just mouth the things you think you're supposed to mouth. He makes a whole lot of sense, let me tell you."

Meg stared at her husband. He looked the same as he did every night getting ready for bed. How was it possible?

Indignation rose, choking and hot. "He'd do well to remember, he and all the rest, that it doesn't stop with the Jews. As Paul said, they go first and most, but others go too."

"What makes you so Jewish all of a sudden?"

"I'm not, I'm nothing. But it's a matter of human decency."

"After all the years your father spent trying to forget he's Jewish."

That she could not deny. Poor Dad. Poor Alfie. And she thought of the country club that still refused him as a member, although he had given them liberty to ride their horses over his land. Other memories came: the dancing class that had refused to take her, the child who had let the real reason slip, and Alfie's insistence that it was not so, that it was only because the class was already filled.

"And your mother," Donal persisted. "Believe me, she's felt the handicap plain as the nose on your face, as your father would say."

That, too, was true. With a child's eyes and ears she had known that, in spite of her mother's protestations of total tolerance, it was her mother's one regret that the husband whom she so loved had had the misfortune to be a Jew. Yes, yes, he was right, Donal was. He saw everything. Well, to be sure, he had not gotten where he was by being stupid.

She could only say stiffly, "I don't want to talk about my parents, either."

"You don't want to talk about anything, do you?"

"That's right, I don't."

It wasn't quite true. She wanted to talk about Ben, but she was also afraid to talk about Ben. The subject was in the room between them, the spectre risen again from the grave, jolted out of it by what Paul had said this night. And she knew that before the night was over, they would have met it head-on. Now each of them was only waiting for the other to start first.

Donal drew a cigarette from the pocket of his robe, lit it, threw his head back and inhaled.

"But if your parents don't want to be mixed up in Jewish affairs, I can't really blame them. Why look for trouble? It's funny, I really like them both, even though they didn't exactly welcome me at first. But they're harmless people, and they've treated me decently all these years since. Goodness knows, I've treated them more than decently too."

What did he want? She couldn't take her eyes away from him. Dark and nonchalant and graceful, he waited. And she stood as if she were hypnotized, as if she were still the girl who had gone to her marriage on that spring day so long ago, the girl in the gentian-blue suit who had gone with him so willingly.

"Well, haven't I?" he asked.

She started. "Haven't you what?"

"Treated them well. Your parents."

"Yes, of course. You've been wonderfully generous. I've thanked you many times, haven't I?"

"I've treated you pretty well too." He looked around. In the window bay on a shelf stood an array of plants, rich greenery overflowing onto the rosy carpet. Porcelain lamps stood on the bedside tables, which were piled with books. On the chest of drawers the children's photographs stood in silver frames. Meg had decorated this room in her own taste; now it looked like a room in old Virginia with an eighteenth-century dignity.

"Yes, there's good living in this house. Nothing to worry about anymore."

The look on his face alarmed her. There was something too deliberate about it. "What do you mean?" she asked. "I don't understand."

"I mean that I'm respectable now. No more liquor business. So when people ask you what your husband does, you don't need to evade the way you once did. You can say straight out that he manages his investments."

She had the impression that he was mocking her—as if respectability were not what he himself had wanted from the very beginning.

"And pleasant it is, I admit, not to feel the government breathing down your neck."

"Why are you saying these things, Donal?"

He had moved so close that she could smell his cologne. He grasped her arms. "I'm saying them so you'll put your crazy ideas out of your head and keep them out." His nails dug into her.

"I haven't got any crazy ideas."

"Don't play cat and mouse, Meg. I know you too well. You're all worked up over the Ben affair again."

"Yes," she said quietly, "I would like to know the final truth about it."

"We had this talk a long time back, Meg. We almost split up over it, if you remember, until you came to your senses. Don't try it again, I warn you."

"I didn't know then what I learned tonight."

"From Paul Werner?"

"He wouldn't lie."

"But I would?"

"You would conceal. You are concealing. Playing cat and mouse, as you put it."

"Damn you, Meg, you think your husband's a killer, do you?"

"I know you know more than you've told." As her fear grew, so, paradoxically, grew her daring. "You closed your eyes to Ben's death, you close them now to the sufferers of Europe, you don't care about anybody or anything but growing richer—"

He flung her away so hard that if the bedpost had not been within reach, she would have fallen. The locked box on her dressing table was still open. He dug his hands into it and came to the bed with his palms full.

"Look here at what I've given to you, I who don't care about anybody! Look! Diamond earrings, ruby bracelets, Greek gold, Burmese pearls—"

A little rubber object fell out among the glitter and lay on the quilt. Meg's hand reached to cover it, but Donal was quicker.

"What the hell do you call this?"

She raised her eyes to meet the astonishment in his. There was nothing to say.

"Then you've been using this? And that's why there've been none since Agnes? You did this?"

She nodded. Her heart seemed to be slowing down, whereas one would expect it to be racing. Queer, she thought, in that long instant.

"Why, damn you to hell and back. . . . Who put up to this? That smart piece of work, that Leah, ten to one. So, you put something over on me, did you? Take your clothes off. Take that thing off."

"No," she whispered, pulling the sash around her robe.

"Take it off, I said."

Suddenly she was terrified, as if she were in a room with a stranger. "What are you going to do?"

He laughed. His mouth made the sound of laughter without the shape of it, for the lips were grim. "Beat you, do you think? No, but I'm going to show you. I'm going to show you who runs things here and will run them. My way from now on. Do you understand that, Meg?"

Forcing her hands away from her robe, he slid it to the floor.

"Donal, stop this. You're acting a role. You don't mean it. You only want to—"

"Are you telling me what I want?"

He threw her back onto the bed. His contorted face, his furious strength, and the pain in her wrenched back all terrified her. "No, Donal, don't do this to me. Don't."

"Now. Come willingly or else I'll force you. We're having it my way, I said."

She struggled, pounding him with her fists. He caught them, pinned her down, and ripped the nightdress. She heard the silk part, and heard her own strangled cries. Otherwise the struggle was soundless. It had to be; the hall just outside the door was surrounded by the rooms where the children slept. So she was bound to lose in the struggle. Cold tears trailed down her temples. Her knuckles stopped up her mouth.

The shame of it! How ugly it was! An act of contempt. And for the first time in all the hundreds of times that this man had entered her, she felt nothing, nothing at all but horror.

When at last he got up, she turned her face into the pillow and sobbed.

"I'll let you sleep alone tonight," he said. "I'm going to Washington tomorrow for a couple of days, but when I come back you'll throw that thing away and we'll live the way we used to. You'll get to like it." He patted her shoulder. "Cry it out. You'll feel better," and softly he closed the door.

Self-loathing like this was not to be borne. When the sobbing stopped, Meg turned over and lay staring at the ceiling. Once in a while, a car passed through the street; she heard the swish of tires and the rustle of dead leaves in the wind that the car made. . . . Lights passed over the ceiling and darkness surged back. She fell asleep, woke trembling, and relived her disgrace. Her fury rose and choked her, fury at him and at herself for being so helpless, even for being a woman. No, it was not to be borne.

The room grew lighter. She lay without moving, fearful of making a sound: he might hear her and come back. Then, remembering that he had said he was leaving early for Washington, she felt relief. She raised herself on one elbow and looked at the bedside clock. It was almost eight, long past her time to get up and have breakfast with the children. She went to the mirror and was dismayed at what she saw: the bloated cheeks and the swollen eyes with shining red rims like wounds. If she could get some ice downstairs—but then the maids would see her. She heard the front door close and children's voices on their way to school. They must have been told to let their mother sleep. There was a light tap at the door.

"Mrs. Powers? Are you all right?"

"Jenny, I'm all right, thank you. I've been fighting a bad cold all night, an infection or something. My nose and my eyes are all swollen."

"Can I get you anything? Coffee?"

"No, thank you. I'm going to get up in a minute. I might go out and get a little air. Maybe that's what I need."

In the shower, she splashed her face with cold water, making some improvement. With makeup and a hat pulled down to shadow her face, she might be presentable. She had to get out of the house. The walls were contracting. She flung out her arms to thrust the walls apart.

Once in the open air, she breathed more easily. A wave of cold was coming from the north; one felt it in the bones. The birds knew it. Sparrows and one lone cardinal were huddled in fluffed feathers on the front lawn. Frost had browned the tips of the yellow chrysanthemums on people's doorsteps. She raised her eyes to the second stories of each house as she passed, wondering what really went on behind other bedroom windows.

It was two miles to the village center, a small center with a post office, a card shop, and a tearoom facing the railroad station. She went into the card shop and after buying some Christmas cards, stood outside not knowing what to do next. A train passed through without stopping. For a moment she thought how wonderful it must be just to get on a train with a couple of books and sit there alone, watching the land roll by. Just going, with nothing and nobody to think about. Such luxury, such peace! After a while one would go into the dining car . . . they always had delicious food . . . a good thick soup, a hot roll.

Then, feeling hungry, she walked down the short block to the tearoom. It was eleven-thirty, a reasonable enough time to eat. The place was empty except for one woman who sat at a table with a suitcase beside her; she was probably a stranger waiting for the next train. She sat down and ordered a salad and tea. From Donal, she had acquired the tea habit. What had she not acquired from Donal? Five children and a safe-deposit box full of jewelry that she seldom wore.

She sat there eating slowly and thinking about her children.

The two boys needed their father. Virile and active, they were already beyond her. The twin girls were Donal's girls, quick and smart. Somehow they reminded Meg of Leah; like her, they would get along. Already they knew what to wear, what to say, and what they wanted. They, too, in a certain way were beyond their mother. Only Agnes, the young one, was different. Small and weak, she clung to her mother, perhaps more out of need than affection. Poorly coordinated in a family of athletes, pallid and uncompetitive, she would always be scorned by the robust, the joyous, and the fleet. How well Meg knew! Such children take refuge in writing melancholy poems about the stars or the suffering poor.

She sighed. She had finished the salad, but still didn't want to go home, so she ordered another cup of tea with a dessert, and prolonged the eating of it. It bothered her that there was nothing to look at, and she wished she had bought a magazine so that she might linger. Every time she glanced up from her plate, she looked into the face of the woman with the suitcase. The woman, having for some reason changed her chair, now sat opposite. She was having a conversation with the waitress, talking with her mouth full, eating the way squirrels eat nuts, munching with their front teeth. It was irritating to watch, yet Meg was drawn back to look and suffer disgust; as soon as the woman had chewed enough, she stowed the mouthful in the pocket of her cheek and took another mouthful, talking, talking all the while. The bulge of her cheek grew larger. When would she swallow what she had already chewed? Meg wondered and couldn't bring herself to look away.

She felt a cry rising in her throat: "It's disgusting the way you eat!" was what she wanted to say, and knew at the same time that she was running out of control. She stood up, paid her bill, and walked rapidly home, almost running. Rounding the hedge, she saw that there was a car in the driveway, a bright little car with its top down, Paul's car.

He was in the library reading the *Times.*

"But what are you doing here?" she asked.

He read the meaning behind her intonation. "Why have I risked another meeting with your husband? Because I'm not at all afraid of one. However," he smiled, "I wasn't disappointed to hear that he's away."

She sat down and ran her hand through her windblown hair. "I look a mess. I can't believe you came just when I needed you. How did you know?"

"I didn't exactly know, but I rather thought you might. Last night was a shocker for all of us."

The light was cruel on her face but, having no pride in her face just then, she turned it up toward Paul and asked him directly, "How was it in your house after the revelation?"

With equal directness, he replied, "Painful and sad. I shall have to be very careful of poor Marian."

His voice was so gentle. Gentle and yet positive. In him one saw how a man could be positive and soft at the same time. Feeling a rush of tears, she got up and walked to the other end of the room. When the spasm was over, she apologized.

"I shouldn't be so weak."

"Is that how you see yourself? Weak?"

"I honestly don't know. Sometimes I think that courage is being able to go forth and fight and change things. Then sometimes I think courage is the fortitude that hangs on, and bears whatever has to be borne for some greater reason than oneself. Which is it?"

"Funny," Paul said, "that's what I sometimes wondered about you. I've often thought you must have had conflicts. Unanswered questions. Being you, you must have had them."

Meg was astonished. "But I've been very happy, too."

"Nothing's ever pure black or pure white, is it?" He sighed. "But I still think I should have fought harder that time I came to Boston."

"I'm afraid it wouldn't have done any good."

"That's what Leah said. Perhaps I should make up for it now."

"In what way?"

"By giving you any help you may need. Unless I'm all wrong and you don't need any."

She thought of last night's demeaning horror. *We'll do it my way.* More childbearing. And she was only thirty-four.

"I need it," she whispered.

"Do you want to tell me about it?"

"Not now. I can't." She raised her voice. "I can't bear it."

"Can't bear talking about it?"

"Or living it."

"Then it's time to change . . ."

"Do you really think I can leave here, or should?"

Paul looked down at her. "Dear Meg, I think you should finally do whatever is best for Meg. It's time. You've always done things to please everyone else. The only exception was your marriage, and that was the one time when you should have listened to your parents. But one owes something to oneself."

"There's so much to consider. The children's school—"

"Children change schools. They'll manage."

"And they love their father, they really do. All except Agnes."

"They can still see him. Hank lost his father, the only one he knew, and he's survived."

The unspoken loomed: Ben's death. And Meg, shuddering, met Paul's gaze.

"I think you really do want to end it here," he said.

"Yes . . . yes, I do. But where would I go?"

Paul considered. "For the moment, back to the farm, I should think, to Laurel Hill. They've got enough room, that's for sure."

"Isn't it childish to run home to my parents?"

"Meg, listen to me. There's nothing wrong in needing some

moral support. We all have our times, every one of us, even the strongest on whom others lean, when we would like to lean on somebody else."

And again he looked out of the window. She followed his glance.

"The world looks so large and threatening out there."

He turned quickly to her. "It is large and threatening. But you have to walk out into it and make a place. Listen, Meg, you can do it. Stay for a while at Laurel Hill, just temporarily, until you can see what comes next. I think you ought to be thinking of a job or training for one."

"With five children, Paul?"

"Why not? You'll still be young when they're grown and gone, and then what? Yes, you must consider something to do with your life."

"Donal will be stunned. I'm sure he doesn't believe I have it in me."

"Well, you have, haven't you?"

She looked around the room, her thoughts flitting with her eyes. In a corner stood the radio, the fancy-carved console that brought the violence of Father Coughlin into the house. On the desk lay the telephone, perhaps the very instrument that had sent forth or received—no matter which—the violent word of a good man's death.

"Yes," she said softly, "I think maybe I have got it in me after all."

Paul was glad he had gone to Meg, glad of the powerful instinct that had led him to her that morning. Quite obviously there had been a fearful crisis of some sort. He wasn't sure, he could only hope, that she would be able to surmount it.

"Revelations," she had called the previous night's horrendous disclosures. And guiding his car through traffic, hurrying home to take Marian to dinner and a cheerful comedy at the theater, he reflected on the curious contrast: A revelation had removed whatever possibility there had ever been of ending his own marriage, while another revelation had done just the opposite for Meg.

A few days later, Hank came in from Philadelphia on the early train.

"Ever since I heard Donal Powers I haven't been able to sleep," he began. "I've got to separate myself from this dirty business and I want to do it now."

Paul rang for Miss Briggs. "Please bring the file for Mr. Henry Roth."

He would be as formal and stiff as Hank, who, for the second time, refused to sit down.

"I shan't be here long enough to sit."

How young he still is! Paul thought. And he said quietly, "It will be longer than you think. There are things to explain."

"There's nothing to explain. I want to sell out, that's all."

"But that's not all. There's the question of how to invest the proceeds."

"The proceeds? Give them to charity. I'll select the charities. The peace movement, for one thing."

Paul raised his eyebrows. "You surely don't mean to give away all you own?"

"That's exactly what I do mean."

"You're a fairly wealthy young man, Hank. Do you want to know what you're worth?"

"I'm worth nothing unless I get rid of that stuff. Gun money. I want no part of it."

In back of the angry young man, Paul saw the stricken, disillusioned boy at Ben's funeral and in back of him, the freckled child wearing his first baseball cap.

"You'd better talk to Dan. He wouldn't approve of this, I can tell you."

"How can you know what my grandfather would think? You two live on different planets."

"But it happens that I talked to Dan myself just yesterday. We're not as different as you think we are."

Hank raised sullen eyes and Paul continued.

"I was caught in the same sort of moral conflict that Dan knew when his first patent was sold to the War Department, just before the last war. It's true he didn't keep anything for himself, but he did keep it for his son, your father, and that was the seed money on which you've been living ever since."

"All right. I don't have a son or anyone to give it to except the unknown poor. I can do the same as he did and live the same as he does."

"You've never lived in a walk-up flat. You buy books, you ride a horse. All your pleasures cost money. Even the money you give away now is a form of pleasure to you, whether you admit it or not. It would be harder than you can have any idea of for you to be poor."

"Hennie and Dan have lived in a walk-up flat and they've seemed satisfied."

"They're very special people, Hank."

"And I'm not?"

"I don't know whether you will ever be special in their way. It's too soon to tell."

"I can tell. If I don't know myself, who does?"

"To know yourself is the hardest thing of all."

Hank didn't answer.

"You'll need money for medical school. Where is it to come from?"

"Poor boys go to medical school. They earn their way."

"It's damned hard. You should know that by now. Permit me to tell you that you're talking like a child." Paul's impatience was growing. "You haven't talked to your mother about this either, have you?"

Hank flushed. "My mother and I don't agree on everything, as you should know," he added.

Paul ignored the jibe. "Your mother's a very practical

woman. She's made her way in the world as few women have."

"If that's the kind of way she wants."

"Are you still that angry, Hank?"

"I happen to love my mother, but we're different. *Things* mean so much to her and nothing to me."

"You just might have a child someday to whom they would mean something."

"I can't guide my behavior today because of a child I might or might not have someday."

Was I that determined? Paul wondered, so sure of where I stood when I was twenty-one? And knowing that he had not been, he could not help but feel a wistful admiration, in spite of his impatience with the young man who stood before him.

"It's curious," he began, "the way this fortune has been handed about like a hot potato. Your grandfather giving it to your father, your father leaving it to your mother, your mother turning it over to you—"

"That never worried her. As you just said, she can take care of herself."

"She's young yet. Suppose Bill were to get sick or have an accident? And that she would then be sick, unable to work? A widow, with an only son—wouldn't you be the one she'd have to turn to?"

Hank's lips tightened. His resentment was almost palpable. He despises me, Paul thought. Nevertheless, he continued.

"I sometimes find that the most world-minded people can neglect the needs on their own doorsteps."

"What are you trying to say? I like people to be direct."

"So do I. So here it is. I propose that you divide the market value of the trust. Give ten percent away to your good causes and split the rest in half. Give one-half of that to your mother and keep the other to educate yourself and have a nest egg. You can always give money away later on if you still feel the way you do now."

Hank was silent. A stubborn hothead! The kind who jumps feetfirst into a pool without seeing whether there's any water in it. And Paul waited for him to speak.

"She does love the house," he said at last.

"And you don't."

"It's not my kind of place."

Again, Paul waited.

"She even offered to buy it from me."

"That should tell you something, shouldn't it?"

And when Hank didn't answer, but sat staring out of the window, Paul repeated, "You can always give away what you have. There'll always be need for it, rest assured."

Hank looked up quickly. "I rest assured. Especially after the war that's coming. I can count on you people to wreck whatever's left of the world."

If he dared strike me with his fists, Paul thought, he would.

"All right. Draw the papers," Hank said. "My mother can have the house and whatever you think she ought to have."

"I don't draw papers. Lawyers do that. I'll get in touch with Mr. Pierce about it."

"So that's all for today?"

"That's all for today."

It was good to get out of that office where money was king, Hank thought as he walked down the street toward the subway.

Clever! Leave it to Paul. I could read his mind: Stubborn, hotheaded fellow, he was thinking. Thinking he tricked me, the way you trick a child into taking his medicine.

But I have to admit, he was right about the house. The way she walks around on a Sunday morning, watering the flowers, the way she fusses with the bric-a-brac on the shelves . . .

He must have cared about her to protect her interests like that. But why the hell didn't he marry her instead of letting another man have her? He can't give much of a damn about his wife. What's the matter, isn't my mother good enough for him?

The subway rumbled uptown. He needed to divert his thoughts from Paul. Things that can't be changed mustn't be allowed to rankle. Look ahead to your own life. Concentrate on becoming a doctor.

See that young girl sitting there in the corner with her eyes closed? She's about nineteen, much too thin, with dark rings under her eyes. She'll have tension headaches when she's older. I've seen the type before. She'll imagine she has heart disease.

And in his mind, Hank continued to examine the unconscious stranger as if she were a specimen in a text. She probably works in a department store, a low-priced store in the basement. She isn't fashionable enough to work upstairs. She couldn't work for my mother.

I wish I weren't so easily saddened by people like her, or by the streets I have to pass through. I think of my street, so quiet, with its fanlights and green, potted shrubs. And then of the mean, cluttered streets I saw those summers when I rode the ambulance. I remember a flat over a bar on Tenth Avenue . . . that's where Donal Powers came from . . . Ben told me years ago, and Donal used to be proud of telling how far he'd risen, that incarnation of evil . . . But after a while he stopped talking about it . . .

When he got out on Lexington Avenue, the girl was still asleep. At the subway exit sat a legless beggar. Everybody rushed by him; they were accustomed to him and his kind. Hank fumbled in his pocket for a coin and dropped it to the man, avoiding the touch of his unclean hand. Then, ashamed, he wanted to go back and say something, forcing himself to look at the man in a human way. But he didn't know what to say, and anyway, he was barely in time for the train back to Philadelphia.

I can feel so sorry for people, he thought, and when I do, I know, I really know, what's meant by the brotherhood of man. But at other times I'm a self-centered bastard, thinking about myself and where I'm going. Top of the class. Nobel prize for medicine. All that stuff.

Seventeen

"You're a damn fool," Donal said. "What chance do you think you stand in a divorce court? You left our home. Took my children and left our home."

They were in Alfie's office at the back of the house. It was a small room, part of the original farmhouse, with a low ceiling and a single diamond-paned window. Donal, although he was quiet in his chair and spoke softly, seemed to fill the whole room. Meg had to turn away from him, toward the window and the orchard where a thin snow was blowing, to get her breath.

"I had a reason," she said, still not looking at him. "What you did to me . . ." The recollection of that night, the humiliation and the feeling of being helpless, of being worth nothing, robbed of the freedom, the privacy of her own body—the recollection suffocated her.

"Reason. Who would listen to that? You're my wife. I had every right. Reason! It's laughable."

"The time will come when it won't be. When a marriage license won't entitle a man to rape."

"Rape! The time will come! Yes, and I suppose the time will come when we'll go walking on the moon, too! No, give up, Meg, you don't stand a chance in a divorce. You haven't a single valid complaint against me. Anything you ever wanted, you got."

"I never wanted ninety percent of the things you gave me."

"That's neither here nor there. You left my bed and board. That's the sum total and that's what counts."

"I'm not going back." They were approaching the third hour of argument and she was tired. Perhaps it was her awareness of her own fragility, in contrast to his vigor, that roused her strength. "I'm not going back. There's nothing, there's no one in the world to make me."

Donal got up and stood over her, regarding her with a new curiosity, as if she were some puzzling creature he had never seen before. "Why, if you hate me so much—"

"I don't hate you, Donal."

She thought, hatred is wishing someone were dead. She merely wished him away. Let him prosper, as he was doing and would do. He was a foreigner. Everything about him had suddenly become foreign; his rumored crimes, his politics, and his appetite for money.

"You've always been odd . . . different," he mused.

"That's why you chose me in the first place. Because I was different from the women you knew."

He walked to the window. A group of boys was in the orchard, having a snowball war. He watched them for a moment.

"Who are those kids with our boys?"

"They go to school together."

"I would have guessed that. Who are they? What sort of boys are they?"

She understood what he wanted. "One of them is a minister's son, the others come from the village. Jimmy's father mows lawns in the summer and does odd jobs in the winter. Angelo's family just came from Italy. The father's a barber."

She saw Donal's anger coming on with a twitch of his cheeks.

"You took them out of a first-class private school and dumped them in no-man's land to associate with barbers!"

"You went to school in Hell's Kitchen, for heaven's sake. What are you talking about?"

Donal slapped his fist into his palm. "And do you think I want them to go back and start scrounging all over again where I began? No! I want them to start where I left off! Not that I've left off yet, not by a long shot. I want my sons to compete with the best and to come out on top of the best. It's all caste and class, don't you even know that much? The best schools, the contacts—it goes all through the business world and up into government. No, they can't stay here. That's final."

The snobbery disgusted her. And yet, there was something to what he said. She herself had been given the best education.

"Listen, Meg, while I go over it once more. There are two ways we can handle this. We can have a quiet, decent divorce. I don't want one and you do, so you'll start it in spite of me. I know that. But if you ask for too much, I'll fight. In that case it will be a dirty divorce and I'll win anyway. So which is it to be? That, or a quiet compromise?"

"What kind of a compromise do you want?"

"I want to keep a father's authority over my children. Timmy and Tom to go away to a fine prep school. They're twelve and thirteen, so it's time. The girls are young enough to stay as they are for the present. I'll support you adequately." Donal's mouth twisted in a semblance of amusement. "There'll be no ermine wrap and no chauffeur, though, as there used to be."

"I never asked for either one. Remember? The ermine wrap was against my principles. I don't believe in torturing some poor creature in a trap so I can wrap myself with its fur."

"A good thing I saved this place for your father," Donal said, ignoring the answer. "Lord knows it's big enough for the lot of you. Unless you'd rather move back to our house with the girls—with me moved out, of course. I'm already looking at an apartment for myself in New York. On Fifth Avenue."

"We'll stay here," she said. "I grew up here." An echo sounded in her head. There was something elegiac in the words *I grew up here,* something far and sad and also peaceful.

"You're sure you don't want the house?"

Meg shook her head. That ornate suburban house, *his house, his choice*—no. Besides, he would feel free to come into it whenever he wished, up the stairs and into the bedroom. She had no faith in any law that would forbid him to. He would do what he wanted to do. He always had.

"The apartment will be large enough for all the children. We will share them. I will be fair."

She thought: They will be more his than mine anyway, the older they grow. It's clearly to be seen. Even strangers have remarked on it. All except Agnes. He knows that too. He's disappointed in Agnes already, although he would never admit it. He sees too much of me in her.

Someone knocked at the door. "Oh, excuse me," Emily said, entering into the silence. "Excuse me, I thought you would be finished by now, ready for a little something to eat. An early supper, Donal, before you ride back."

"Thank you, Mother, that's very kind, but I'm not hungry."

"Mother," he says so pointedly, and Emily is so humbly cordial. Of course, with her only income being Dad's salary from managing Donal's properties! The Depression is far from over. How many millions unemployed? And it won't be over, Paul says, until the war comes.

Donal took his overcoat, which he had thrown across a

chair. "Are we pretty much agreed, then, Meg? If so, I'll be going."

"Yes indeed."

Emily looked from one to the other, questioning.

"We're getting a divorce, Mother," Donal told her, "what they call an 'amicable' divorce. But you and Dad have nothing to worry about. He'll keep his job."

"Thank you, Donal. You've always been very kind."

"I'll just see the kids before I go."

"They're playing outside." Emily hurried after him. "I'm so sorry things have turned out this way, Donal."

"Roll of the dice. You can't win everything. So long, Meg. I'll be in touch."

The two women watched through the half windows on either side of the door as the little girls, who had been pulling each other up and down the driveway on a sled, came running to their father. Whooping and screaming, they climbed all over him.

"Look, they don't want to let him go," Emily said.

The remark was an oblique accusation: A woman belongs with her husband, keeping the family together. Don't tell me about your personal problems, they're between the two of you. A clever woman puts up with things, solves things. No one could be more generous than he has been.

"Of course, you're welcome, dear, all of you," she had told Meg. "We'll manage somehow." She had cried and put her arms around Meg in pity and sympathy. But she had also been doubtful and confused. "It's really rather embarrassing, though, isn't it? I mean, your leaving so suddenly, just walking out like that? People will wonder."

I wonder myself, Meg thought now. Such a long, long path from the instant I saw him leaning against the mantelpiece in Leah's house and wanted him more than anything in the world, wanted him to love me . . . such a long path up till now. Is it possible that he, too, sees how sad it is?

"Look at them!" Emily cried again.

They were trying to pull him on the sled. And Meg turned away, saying, "I'll go help Elsie in the kitchen."

Elsie was old, the last of the servants; it wasn't fair to bring six more people into the house and expect her to do all the work herself.

After the supper had been eaten and cleared, after the children had gone upstairs to do their homework and go to bed, came the hard times. Now questions lurked in the four corners of the room, sometimes unasked, but visible in the set of Emily's lips while she worked her needlepoint. Questions lay in Alfie's troubled glances which, mistakenly, he thought were hidden behind the newspaper.

The hall clock, one of Emily's antique finds, rattled as if it were clearing its throat, then resonantly bonged nine times. It was a signal to fold and put away the needlepoint. A few minutes later, the rush of water in the old pipes would be heard downstairs as Emily ran her bath.

Alfie lowered the paper. "Your mother's pretty upset. Worried about you. What's going to become of you."

"She thinks I should go back to Donal."

Alfie didn't deny that. "Well, you haven't explained things very much, Meg, have you? But then, between husband and wife—" he fumbled. "I don't suppose that ugly business at Leah's party is the whole reason, is it?"

"Of course not. But it certainly told a lot about the man, didn't it?"

The dogs, who had been asleep at Alfie's feet, jumped suddenly and raced to the back of the house. He got up to collar and quiet them.

"Raccoons. There's a family in the orchard. I put scraps out every night." He looked at his watch. "Half past. They're early this evening. They don't usually come before ten."

Over his head, where he stood holding the dogs, hung a deer head; it was a young buck, with graceful antlers. Undoubtedly, he had bought it; he, who fed raccoons, could no more handle a gun than a Stradivarius. He wanted it to appear that he had taken up the sport of a country gentleman. It was spurious, a deception like his halfhearted attendance at church with Emily.

The dogs had broken the thread of his thoughts. He came over and stroked his daughter's head.

"I'm glad you're here, Meggie. I mean, I'm sorry you're having so much trouble, but I'm glad you came here. The house has been lonely. It's good to have it filled up with children, five little ones and now my big one again." He kissed her forehead. "This is your home, remember that."

When he left her, she roamed the room in search of something to do. An enormous photo album lay open on a table. She guessed that her father was the one who had been looking at it, for Emily was not given to nostalgia or soft sentiment. But I am, Meg thought, and she took the album on her lap.

They were old, old pictures, twenty-five years ago and longer. Here they are on the front porch, sitting in wicker chairs under the scrolls and curlicues of the roof: Carpenter Gothic. The women are wearing what looks like white; the colors are very pale and the fabric is lawn or handkerchief linen; the buttons are tiny crocheted knobs that elude the buttonholes. The men are wearing knickerbockers, knitted socks with argyle cuffs and, in all that heat, their jackets are double-breasted wool. But it is Sunday, and Alfie likes to make a proper tradition out of Sunday.

They've had their dinner. There is an afternoon torpor in the picture. The dinner was heavy with starch and sugar; butter dripped from the corn and gravy from the yams; ice cream, churned that morning on the kitchen steps, stood like a dome or derby on every slice of pie.

Meg flipped the pages. Here is her first pony. Here is Dottie the Jersey, who took second prize at the county fair. Here are

Paul and Marian before their marriage; Paul looks the same now, but how she has changed! Here is the cat who had twelve kittens, of whom the extras were given to Meg to feed with a dropper; every one of them lived.

The photos are fading, yet still there rises from them the feel of summer, the trembling heat of August, of beloved summer.

The clock struck ten and Meg closed the album. She put on a coat and went out. Moonshine glimmered on the whitened earth. Packed snow on the path toward the barns squeaked underfoot as she stepped through her father's footsteps.

After the first greeting to Donal that afternoon, her father had stayed discreetly away and gone out to the barns. He made a daily check there anyway, as if overnight the roof could have developed leaks or the floors begun to rot. She knew why he went. It was to remember the fine herd of Jerseys in their stanchions, munching grain, and the riding horses, now long gone, in the stalls. It was to remember these things and to tell himself that one day he would have them all back again. The foolishness of all this made her tender.

And she climbed on up the slope through neglected fields now turning back to scrub growth, into the woodlot. Through the bare trees, the pond, barely visible, was an oval of dark glass; through those same trees, in the extraordinary ignorance of her fifteen years, she had had her first realization of human desire when she had caught Leah and Ben in a passionate embrace.

All past and over. Ben dead and Leah married now to a man as different from him as night is from day. Who could have foretold that then?

Change and flux. A flowing river, a rapid river that you can't hold back.

Alfie would like to hold it back. He'd like to live everything over. He wants me to stay here as a child again, the eldest child among my own children, belonging to him, as in an entirely other and terrible way, I was supposed to belong to Donal. My father's would be a loving ownership and I would be safe here, like the little girl on the front steps that Sunday long ago. That would be the only difference.

So Meg stood, leaning her back against a birch trunk. For a long time she stood there thinking, searching for an answer. Then clouds came up to darken the moon and, still with no answer, she made her way over the downhill path back to the house.

Eighteen

Nineteen thirty-nine sped by. Only a few months ago Paul had sat at the Pathé News Theater in Grand Central Station and watched Mr. Chamberlain—black stork with black furled umbrella—return from Germany with "Peace for our time." He had read Churchill's speech to the House of Commons: "We have sustained a total unmitigated defeat . . . all the countries of Mittel Europa . . . one after another, will be drawn in the vast system of Nazi politics. . . . And do not suppose that this is the end. It is only the beginning."

And there was no peace. The beginning was here, and Paul was feeling a tremendous sense of urgency. These were the last days, the last chances of escape from the boiling cauldron that Europe was soon to become. It was too late for his cousins, and the only other people he personally knew were also beyond his help. A letter from Ilse had given another brutal shock to his shaken sense of human decency: Mario and she had become citizens of Italy last year, but now their citizenship had been nullified and they had been ordered to leave the country. They were going into hiding until they could find a country that would take them. This would be her last letter, therefore, until—until when?

Hiding, whispering, running from danger to danger . . . proud, strong woman in her doctor's garb . . . bright, laughing woman swinging the car along the mountain roads . . . Surely, surely something could be done for her!

But there was nothing to be done. "It's the Polish quota, it's filled for years," Hennie told him. She had gone to work as a volunteer in aid of refugees, as so many concerned and charitable women, including Marian, were doing.

In the spring the Nazis destroyed the brave republic of Czechoslovakia; Chamberlain had to admit that Hitler had lied and that the Munich agreement had been a fraud. In the spring, too, the Russians kicked out their foreign minister, Litvinov, because he was a defender of the peace and a Jew besides. And in August, to an astounded and disbelieving world, Stalin and Hitler, archenemies, announced their alliance.

Hitler invaded Poland on the first of September. This is the first step, Paul thought, before he double-crosses Russia and leapfrogs across the Polish border. Two days later, France and Britain entered the war and the *Athenia* was sunk off the coast of Ireland, not far from the spot where the *Lusitania* had gone down so many years before. And even though Paul had long predicted what had now come true, he felt a sense of unreality.

It was all this, beginning with the Nazi-Russian pact, that killed Dan Roth. Hennie, at least, was ever afterward to declare that it had. Certainly, Dan had never been a Communist but, like too many misguided liberals of his era, had merely argued that the Russian experiment ought to be given a fair chance. When the news of the alliance was confirmed, he was struck numb and dumb. And when the war broke out, the war that he had said would never, could never, happen, he retired into himself.

For several years he had been working in his laboratory on an idea for an electronic scanning device that he hoped would facilitate the diagnosis of hidden disease. He had had an exhilarated notion that he was approaching something valuable. Now he sat still at the workbench, sometimes with his head in his hands. How could they have done such a thing? So then their word meant nothing; all the high-sounding phrases about humanity and equality meant nothing. . . .

Later, Paul wondered what mysterious configuration of the stars had led him to Dan's lab on that particular autumn night. Driving along the Hudson, he saw great liners that had been caught in midocean when war was declared, now tied up at the piers, awaiting instructions from their owners. There lay a familiar Cunarder, his favorite, *Queen Mary;* close to it lay the *Normandie.*

He had a quick recollection of departure, the long, mournful, heart-lifting call of the horn, a dark winter afternoon, and Leah's mischievous face in the frame of a silver fox collar and a silly peacock-blue hat.

Only three years had passed since then, but they might have been a century for all that had happened. The war now menaced everything that made the world a home; the anticipation of summer, even the sweetness of art, and most of all the kindness of man to man. In his private world at home, the crisis had subsided; a graph would show a return to the previous even level. Except for an occasional wistful, worried glance from Marian, to which Paul responded by some sort of reassuring smile or word or gesture, all was outwardly as it had been before. Inwardly, he felt the pressure of her frightened need: *Don't leave me, Paul . . .*

This evening he was feeling the stress of loneliness, a bonedeep ache, a need for someone who was close to him. Leah, of course, was out of bounds, Hank still avoided him, and Meg was hidden away in the country trying to put her life together. Then he thought of Hennie and Dan, that it would be nice to take them to dinner. Dan was no doubt still at work in his lab.

The lab was stuffy. Even with the windows open, the air that blew in was unseasonably hot.

"This heat's not good for you," Paul remonstrated. "Listen, I'll give you the key to my cottage on the Island and I'll get a car to drive you out. Why don't you and Hennie use it for a couple of weeks?"

Dan shook his head. "I don't want to leave this while the idea's still fresh."

"The idea will be there two weeks from now. You can take your thoughts with you."

"I can't give up two weeks at my stage of life, Paul."

"Well, then," Paul insisted, "at least take a weekend. I happen to know that Alfie's been inviting you."

"Let's talk it over later. I'll have dinner with you, that I'll do."

"You're only stalling," Paul said, "but come on."

With effort, Dan got up. He took his jacket, closed the outer door, and was turning the key in the lock when he fell over.

For three days, he lay at the hospital in a coma. For three days and part of the nights, Paul and Hennie sat watching and waiting. They spoke little, each with his and her thoughts, and many of them, Paul felt sure, must have been the same thoughts.

"Simple, kind, gentle," he heard her murmur to herself.

Overnight, two furrows had cut her cheeks, but her eyes were dry and she hardly took them away from Dan.

"Yes, he is all those things," Paul might have said, and added to them many more: proud, brave, unselfish, impractical, hot-tempered—all of these were the sum of the man who lay now inert in the bed.

And, as if Hennie were taking up his thought, she said also, "We'll never know what else was revolving in his brain. Now it will never come to light."

For they knew, as they waited, what the end was to be.

She stroked Dan's hands. *The work of the hands.* She must be thinking those words, Paul thought, and of the ways in which the hands had known her. Once she laid her head, ever so softly, on her husband's shoulder. How many nights must they have lain like that!

They brought food, but she could not eat. Tearless and still she sat, watching Dan's weak breath go in and out.

She looked up at Paul, who wanted her to take a rest.

"I'm memorizing everything," she said fiercely. "Don't you understand? I shall never see him again. Don't you understand?"

Hank came to see his grandfather. For some minutes he stood looking down at the figure on the bed. Dan had suddenly grown smaller, curled like a fetus.

"Dammit! Damn them all! They've taken all the skills of your mind to use them again for wars and the killing that you hated," Hank cried.

Dan all over again! Paul thought, as always. And he knew what the young man was remembering. He could see the small boy sitting on the piano bench while Dan placed his fingers on the keys. He could see all the birthday celebrations as the boy grew older in the house that Dan had given. And he would have liked to embrace Hank now, but the rift had not healed; Hank's glance was cold.

Then his own memories crowded: the kitchen in the downtown flat where, as a schoolboy, he had talked with Dan about world affairs, subjects that were seldom talked about at home, and Dan had listened to him as though he were a person with opinions worth hearing. He helped me grow up, Paul thought.

So they all watched and waited. On the evening of the third

day, the doctor insisted that Hennie go home to rest. So it was Paul who was alone with Dan when he died.

How different was death from the fictional portrayal, in which the dying man lies in dignity and speaks some simple words, some heartbreaking good-bye, and in full consciousness takes his last breath! The reality was a slipping away, a slipping so imperceptible that there seemed to be no change from one moment to the next, so that only the measurement of the pulse could tell the difference between being *here* and being *there*. Gone, with no word and no smile, gone with nothing. How small! one thinks. But only a few days ago, he was large! And where is all his knowledge gone? Vanished. And Paul thought, I wish I could have the certainty that some have, that there is a beautiful life after death, in which nothing perishes that is dear, and all will survive in some vast blue eternity.

People came flocking to Hennie's little home: the Orthodox in black coats and side curls, the nonbelievers, labor organizers, workmen, teachers, and former pupils, now middle-aged.

Even Donal Powers came. Fortunately for me, Paul thought, it was during an hour when I wasn't there. He was reminded again of the time when Dan had been freed from his prison cell, and that Donal Powers was the one who had freed him. Even as he knew that his feeling was a narrow and petty one, he knew also that he would never get over it.

It was during the week of mourning for Dan that Meg Powers reached a decision. A fleeting idea from long ago, one never seriously taken, had returned one day. She had dismissed it as foolish. But it had come back again. After a while, as the months moved by, it had begun to possess her.

Why should she not go back to school and become a veterinarian?

She talked to herself. That's laughable.

Don't laugh. There's nothing funny about it.

It's ridiculous. You're thirty-five years old, with two sons and three daughters.

What's that got to do with it? You know you come rightfully by the idea.

That's true, I do.

And she remembered long-forgotten sick or wounded creatures, rabbits, stray cats, and broken-winged birds that she, in her lonely childhood, had cared for. A moment later she thought: Pure sentimental folly! How do I know I have the aptitude or the persistence to follow it through?

Yet she could see herself doing it. Was she to stifle, while her children grew up and away, waiting for Donal's monthly check?

She went to see him. It was the first time she had been in his office—in the old days, he hadn't even had a real office— and she was more than uneasy. From behind three telephones on a sleek desk, he frowned.

"I thought we had reached a financial agreement."

"We did. But there's something I want to add. I've been doing some thinking about myself and I—"

"If you don't take too long. I've just come back from paying a condolence call at your aunt's, and I'm late for an appointment."

"I can say it in a very few words. I'd like you to give—to lend—me some extra money for a couple of years. I'll pay you back."

"Extra money for what?"

"I want to go back to school, and the tuition's expensive."

Donal raised his eyebrows. "You went to college. You graduated."

"I know. This is different. A profession."

She hesitated. He was ready to scoff; the lifted eyebrows and the one-sided twitch of the mouth were all too familiar. Nevertheless, she continued.

"I would like to be a veterinarian. It will take four years."

"What!" The word was a hoot of astonishment, followed by laughter. "If that isn't the craziest—whatever put that in your head?"

She faced the laughter. "It was always a thought, because of the way I feel about animals. A vague thought, something I'd have liked to do, but knew was impossible, so I stopped thinking about it. Now it's occurred to me that it's not impossible."

"It's absurd. What do your parents have to say?"

"Naturally, my mother says it's outlandish for a woman and Dad just wants me at home," she answered truthfully.

"Right they are. I couldn't agree more."

"You never thought my parents' opinions were worth very much before."

"There's always a first time."

"I've had an interview at the University of Pennsylvania. They were very encouraging and I think they may accept me."

"You haven't wasted any time, have you?"

"No. I wrote to Wellesley for my transcript. I was an A student."

"Why don't you put this nonsense out of your head? You've got enough to do being a mother."

"I can do both. The boys will be away at school and the girls are at school all day. I can do it. Look at Leah! She seems to have raised Hank all right."

"That woman! Is she the best example you can find? No, I don't want to look at her, nor at anybody else, for that matter."

Meg stared at him. Nothing could move him if he didn't want it to. Taking a memorandum pad from a drawer, he began to write. When he was finished, he looked up.

"I've a dozen things to do this morning. Can we bring this to a close?"

"Then you won't advance the money? Let's say my idea is stupid; all right, that's my misfortune, isn't it? But once I start, I'll go through to the end, and I'll repay the loan with interest. A business proposition, Donal, nothing more. That's all I'm asking."

"The answer is no, Meg, and now please go away and don't bother me with this. If you want to talk about something sensible, I'll be glad to listen."

It would mean nothing to him, less than the price of one of the bracelets he had brought home during their smiling years. He stood up as if to escort her to the door, but she brushed past him, quivering with anger.

"Thank you for nothing. I'll ask my cousin Paul."

"You do that," Donal said.

That afternoon Meg sat for a while with Paul on the front stoop of Hennie's house. Perhaps they lingered because sunshine had warmed the stone and brought a cheerful life to the modest street: gossiping women, children on roller skates and an ice-cream vendor ringing a bell on the corner. It was a different world from that which either of them knew, it was Dan's world, and perhaps that is why they lingered.

Presently, after a peaceful silence, Paul said, "So Meg, dear, don't worry about the money. Let me know what you need for tuition and a little apartment in Philadelphia. Hank's down there. I'm sure he'll help you find one."

"Paul, I'm going to straighten out my life this time, I really am."

"Of course you are. You're on the way. And sooner or later on the way you'll meet another man, too, the right one."

"Man! Who'd want a woman with five children?"

"Why not? You're still a very lovely woman, Meg."

She was thinking that if he weren't her cousin, she could love him. . . . And she wondered about Leah and him. Somehow she couldn't quite see them together. But for that matter, she had never thought that he really belonged with

Marian, either. It was too mysterious, this business of coupling! No one had thought that she and Donal belonged, and yet they had been happy for a long time, and probably would be still if the truth hadn't come out. All very strange.

And following this train of thought, she said, "They were an amazing couple, Dan and Hennie. You almost thought of them as one person, they were so alike."

"That they were."

"A once-in-a-lifetime love, I suppose."

"Once in a lifetime," Paul repeated.

Something in his tone, a vibration in his voice, made her turn to look at him. He was gazing out over the street; yet she had a feeling that he wasn't seeing the street at all.

I wonder—she thought, and stopped herself. No sense wandering into useless speculations. Besides, it was growing late.

"Paul, how do I begin to thank you?"

"By doing well, that's all I want," he said quickly.

"I'm going to pay you back the minute I begin to earn. With interest."

"Oh, of course. Prime rate plus one percent," he said, and kissed her.

Meg was accepted by the veterinary school. Together with the three girls, she moved into a small, neat apartment near the university, furnishing it with a few simple pieces that she bought, plus all her books and a few odds and ends of furniture contributed by Alfie and Emily, who were aghast at the whole business. The result was cheerful, but so modest that Lucy and Loretta were quite dismayed. Agnes, who had been given a little north bedroom, once a maid's room, where she could place an easel at the window, had no complaint.

Timmy and Tom left for Choate, where they immediately made the football team and wrote enthusiastic letters home, which surprised no one, enthusiasm having always been the salient quality of the brothers.

Donal bought the Fifth Avenue apartment he had talked about, a handsome spread not far from the Plaza Hotel. Meg never saw it, but the children gave her detailed descriptions, more detailed than she wanted to hear. Lucy and Loretta were enormously impressed. Twelve years old now, they were better informed about trends and styles and prices than their mother had ever been, and far more interested in them, surely, than she was now.

"You should see my bedroom," Loretta reported. "It looks right out onto the park. Daddy's decorator brought in an artist who painted a mural on one wall, a garden walk, going downhill toward a pond with two swans floating on it. Absolutely gorgeous."

After their week in New York, the twins returned to Philadelphia wearing new white fur coats. Donal had taken them to two Broadway shows and to dinner at the Waldorf. They couldn't wait to go back.

Agnes, who hadn't gone because she had a cold, was due to go the next time. "But I don't want a fur coat," Meg overheard her say. "I think it very cruel. Mother thinks so, too, and so does Hank."

"Hank is a jerk," Loretta said.

Hank, now in his third year, had taken it upon himself to look out for Meg. On her behalf, he complained to the janitor and finally got some small repairs made. He counseled her before a test and complimented her when she did well—and she did surprisingly well for someone who had so long ago gotten away from the habit of study. Apparently he had plenty of time to give, for unlike most of his friends, he had not yet fallen in love and his dates were casual.

His mother, on the other hand, having made up her mind to do so, had fallen very much in love, this time with her new husband, who was obviously very much in love with her. Their life was busy. Sherman had one of the largest and wealthiest law practices in the city, while Leah had expanded the shop, which now encompassed three floors and catered to the most fashionable trade in New York. Well known, then, in their respective circles, the Shermans were invited everywhere. Openhanded and open-hearted, they gave generously, and were seen at all the charity balls.

Hennie reported with awe on the size of Leah's personal benefactions to the refugee committee. The awe was not unmixed with irony, too, as one reflected on the previous generation of Jews descended from German immigrants who had helped, deplored, and condescended to the poor Russians. Here, now, were the despised poor Russians like Leah, no longer poor, opening their purses to a new wave of Germans fleeing persecution in their turn.

Paul felt a quiet satisfaction, for this life was what Leah had wanted. She had worked hard for it and she deserved it. Often he wondered what a different turn her life and his would have taken had his meeting with Iris that night not thrown him into some sort of emotional chaos. Would he have stood fast against Marian's pleading and gone ahead with the divorce? Having since come to a full understanding of his wife's pitiable fragility, he thought not.

Leah did not apparently question why she never heard from Marian. Very likely she was too busy in her new life to notice or care. To be sure, she rarely heard from Paul, either. When he appeared alone at the engagement party for Bill's daughter, she accepted his casual excuse for Marian without comment. Very likely she was even relieved at Marian's absence. She would have been even more relieved if she had been aware of what Marian now knew.

As to Paul, he wasn't sure whose presence made him more uncomfortable, Leah's or her husband's. He was well aware that there were plenty of men who wouldn't be disconcerted in the slightest degree, and who would have found his sensitivity amusing, but he couldn't help the way he was.

Nineteen

A quiet winter passed. People called it the time of the phony war, since no shots were fired and nothing happened. The French and the Germans faced each other across the Rhine, so close that the opposing armies were in sight of each other's daily unremarkable routines.

On this side of the ocean, extensive military preparations were being made, and they were good for business. The Depression at last was lifting and, as it had during that other war, the stock market prospered. "Disgusting war profits," Dan would have said; he would have had plenty to say. At the end of the year, Paul cashed in his stock profits, gave the sum total away, and felt that he had cleansed himself. In passing, it occurred to him that Donal Powers must be making another fortune, and he felt doubly cleansed.

Then abruptly, in the month when chestnuts bloom in Paris, the Germans struck. Their tanks and bombers came pouring over the frontiers that they had pledged not to violate. Belgium and Holland were overrun in hours, the British fled home from Dunkirk and pictures of refugee hordes appeared again in the newsreel theaters of New York.

Paul sat in his office reading *The New York Times.* "All markets brake severely on possible end of the war soon," ran the black headlines, ". . . a wave of speculative selling . . . if the current 'Blitzkrieg' settles down into a stationary war again . . . commodities may just as easily reflect this in a complete rebound."

He put the paper down angrily. After a moment, he picked it up again and read on. "Moreover, it is by no means certain that, even in the event of a complete revision of previous ideas regarding the war outlook, American business prospects would seriously be affected . . ."

Anger gave way to a profound sadness, as again he laid the paper aside. Business prospects! And all the dead. Business prospects!

The summer passed. It was a lovely summer, if one could stay away from the desperate nightly news on the radio. London was losing as many as six hundred lives a day as its homes were bombed into smoking rubble. Even the Houses of Parliament were struck. German submarines, like killer whales, were threatening the Atlantic sea-lanes. Germany invaded Russia. President Roosevelt proclaimed a state of national emergency.

In Washington everyone knew that sooner more probably than later the country would be at war. Business and government began to stir with joint plans for tanks, planes, steel, coal, trucks, and railroad cars. This was all too familiar to Paul; two dozen years of peace had flown past and now those years were simply being rolled back. So he did not hesitate when he was asked to go to Washington as a semiweekly volunteer to help draft methods for the financing of the enormous effort.

On a Sunday afternoon in December, on the way back from the capital, he stopped off in Philadelphia to visit Meg. The little apartment seemed more crowded and cramped than it had in the beginning. Possessions had accumulated: more books, bicycles, and skis for the winter vacations that the children had been having with Donal in Colorado. And there was another addition to the family, an old English sheepdog. A huge, broad, friendly animal, she lay with seven newborn puppies on a bed between the stove and the refrigerator. If one had wanted to be charitable, one could have said that the apartment was in disarray; if one, on the other hand, wanted to be totally honest, one would have called it a mess.

However, Paul thought as he surveyed the place with affectionate amusement, it was unmistakably a happy mess. The twins were out, as they usually were, while Agnes was painting in her room and Meg was cleaning the kitchen floor.

She looked up, smiling. "You're thinking how sloppy I am. Well, Donal's not around anymore to inspect, so I can be myself."

"How are you doing? I needn't ask, you look wonderful."

"I'm doing fine. I'm making good grades and loving it. I haven't made a mistake, Paul, in case you're wondering."

"I'm glad. You're never lonesome?" he asked, meaning: a woman as young as you, without a man . . .

She understood. "I might be—yes, I would be—if I weren't so darn busy. I honestly don't have a second to think about myself."

"You'll be coming down the homestretch before you know it."

"Yes, and I can't wait to finish, to get back into the country somewhere and start earning money." She laughed. "I hope you're not in too much hurry to be repaid."

"Right now, the only repayment I want is some lunch. Whatever you've got. I'm not particular."

"Chicken sandwiches. Pull that card table over by the window. That's where we eat."

Arranging the thick plates and tin cutlery, Paul was humorously reminded of Donal's ornate Danish silver. A burly tomcat, jumping from a shelf, just missed his shoulder and landed on the table among the dishes. Agnes came, wearing a streaked smock and a blob of green paint on her chin. He was to remember it all quite clearly, even the way the child said to him, "Oh, it's you, Cousin Paul! I didn't hear you come in," and then saying, "I'll just go help Mom with the sandwiches."

Everything's changed, he thought. Meg has surely, and now Agnes has too.

He reached up to the shelf and turned on the little portable radio. His other hand held a coffee mug, which he almost dropped because of what he heard.

The Japanese had bombed Pearl Harbor. The damage was almost total, the disaster almost complete. The loud voice was agitated, almost hysterical, as the words tumbled, and Meg came running in from the kitchen with Agnes following.

In the little room the three stood for a minute quite still, staring into each other's faces. Meg spoke first.

"Tim's only sixteen, thank God for that."

"So this is it" was all Paul could think to say.

The moment was different, the feeling different, from the way he had imagined they might be when war finally came. And he saw himself, years hence, standing among people who were all talking about where they had been when the news arrived, the news that once again would alter each individual in ways then unforeseen.

"I was setting the table," he would say, "and my cousin came running in with a puppy in one hand and a head of lettuce in the other."

Late that winter, Hank Roth joined the service as a first lieutenant. The farewell was at Leah's house. With her customary fortitude, she affected a business-is-business approach; the country's business right now was to get it all over as fast as possible, and one had to be sensible about it. But Paul understood her feelings about Hank's father, who had gone off so heroically the last time, and now about Hank, who was going so soberly.

The single remotely cheerful person in the gathering was Alfie. He had begun work on a housing project for an aircraft factory, and was in good spirits.

"My partner doesn't know a thing about building, but he's got cash. So he's putting up the cash, I'm doing the work, and we split fifty-fifty. Not bad, eh? I had to tell Donal I'm resigning."

Strangely enough, it felt good to hear Alfie boasting in the old way.

Hennie worried. "Do you think he'll be going overseas soon? One hears so much about U-boat warfare."

"It's ironic," Paul answered, "that Dan's invention, his original work, will make the voyage safer. They've got radar now. All the detection instruments are based on his work."

He wished he could feel as sure as he had made himself sound. With an ache in his heart, he watched Hank, looking older and larger in uniform, go around the room making his individual farewells.

"Well, Paul," Hank said, "you always told us America would have to get into this." The boy—Paul supposed he would always think of Hank as a boy—looked almost accusing.

And Paul could hardly speak. "Just take care of yourself," he said.

They shook hands, and Hank turned away. They heard him hurrying down the stairs and heard the door make a thud in the silence.

Faster than anyone might have thought possible, life was transformed. Meat, gasoline, shoes, and sugar were rationed. Women learned to wear cotton lisle stockings. Marian rolled bandages for the Red Cross. Leah presided at fashion shows in which movie stars modeled for the benefit of War Bonds. Hank went overseas and arrived safely in England. And Paul grew restless. As the months went by, he tired of merely shuttling back and forth between New York and Washington to sit on a committee and juggle figures. This was all important to the war effort, but still it was too far away from the real thing and not what he wanted.

Then the president appointed a civilian commission to go along into action with the troops as soon as the invasion of the continent should take place. They were to observe and report on the effectiveness of air support. The prospect was appealing. It meant being in the heart of things. It was not difficult for Paul to get himself appointed to the commission.

Marian was aghast. They went through a week of lamentation. "I should think you'd have had enough of risking your life in one war!"

"I won't be in the trenches this time. Nothing's going to happen to me."

"You can't know that. Anything can happen." Her lips quivered.

"I have to go," he said gently.

"Why? Because of your cousins, I suppose."

He thought, yes, and Ilse, and Mario . . .

"You always feel obligated, even though they're almost surely dead."

"All the more reason."

"You go too far. You always do."

"It's the way I am, then. You should be used to me by now."

"Oh," she said, "the only thing I'm used to is knowing I can't change your mind when it's made up."

"Sometimes you do, Marian. More than you know. But not this time."

He couldn't really explain why he had to go, because explanation would have sounded childish, as if he had some misplaced conception of heroism or else a desire born out of boredom. The truth was far deeper: It was a wish to do something real, not to be a bystander in this cataclysm.

He was in high excitement, getting his gear together: foulweather clothing, a new camera, writing materials and binoculars.

Walking up Madison Avenue, he realized he wasn't far from Leah's place. He had intended to telephone, but then thought better of it and went there instead. In her private office, she showed him a letter from Hank, a cheerful report written with obvious intent to keep his mother's spirits up. They spoke a few words about Hennie, who was still occupied with refugees, and after that Leah arrived at the personal.

"I suppose everyone asks you why you're doing this, so I won't ask."

"Thanks." Paul grinned. "I appreciate that."

"No, I'll not ask. I'll tell you." She pointed a pencil at him from across her little desk. "You're running away, Paul Werner. No, don't look as if you'd like to shoot me. I know there's real good, real purpose in what you're doing. I understand that you're going *toward* something. But you're also going *away* from something, or rather somebody. Do you want to talk about it?"

She had put her finger directly on the sore place that he hadn't wanted to think of in this connection. Now, suddenly, it felt very sore.

"No, you don't. You're thinking it's none of my damn business, and it probably isn't, except that I've known you pretty well, Paul, and maybe that makes me think I can take liberties." She got up and laid her hand on his shoulder.

"You want your privacy. Okay, I won't say any more. Except one thing, and that'll be the end of it. I know you're thinking of your daughter and of—of her. How long are you going to go on like this?"

He didn't answer.

"Look at yourself! You could have the world at your feet. When are you going to find somebody to love?"

"How do you find somebody?" He heard mockery in his voice. "Do you turn love on like a faucet?"

"Well, you found me, didn't you? You just didn't keep me."

He stood up and put his arms around her. He could hear her muffled against his chest, "Don't misunderstand, I'm Bill's wife and it's Bill I love. Don't misunderstand."

"I won't." He dropped a kiss on top of her head. Strange, he thought, remembering the canopied bed and the room in Paris, where the very sight of Leah had so inflamed him; all that was gone and only this tenderness remained.

"I'm sorry, Paul. I shouldn't talk this way. I suppose it's because I'm so afraid you won't come back."

"I'll be back," he said. "I'll fool you, I'll be back."

The *Queen Elizabeth* lay in total darkness with its portholes blacked out. He walked through the cavernous pier on the way to the gangplank, pausing to let a long column of infantry, young men, baby boys, shuffle past under the weight of their packs, leaving their country. Then he went up the gangplank after them.

The engines vibrated, no whistles blew, and in silence the great ship, with its young human freight, moved slowly down the river. Like a great shadow on the water, it gathered speed and slid out to sea.

Twenty
June 2, 1944

Why am I, Hank Roth, keeping a diary? I'm putting down things that I probably won't want anyone else to read when I get home. So maybe it will end up being thrown away. I know Paul always said he didn't want to remember his war, and probably I won't want to remember this one either. Maybe I'm writing because I need something to do with my hands in the times we spend waiting. There's so much waiting, as we're doing right now. The invasion has got to be coming soon. We all feel it.

I try to imagine what it will be like across the Channel. Times here have been awful enough, especially when I've been up in London. I'll never be able to describe what it was like the night I met that girl, when we had the thousand-plane raid. We ran to the shelter in her garden, what we call a yard, and sat there for hours holding our ears against the roar. It sounded like a freight train going through your living room. We held hands, not talking, too terrified to talk. She was a nice girl. I'd just gotten to know her. When the all-clear sounded, we crawled out. They'd missed her house, but the ones on either side were crushed and they were pulling bodies out onto the sidewalk.

Can it be much worse in France?

June 10, 1944

We're here. The sixth was the day, a day that will go down in history like Appomattox, that my great-grand-mother used to tell about.

So many were seasick on the crossing that they couldn't save themselves, if saving had been possible, against the gunfire from the hills above the beach. They didn't even get as far as the beach, just died in the water as they waded in.

But I got through. I'm in a little village now, where we've set up a tent. Pure luck. So far.

June 16, 1944

We're on the way to Cherbourg, still a long way from Paris. I met my first Germans, very young, some only fifteen years old and scared to death. Pitiable. Poor kids.

The public should see this. It should know how tanks are blown up and bodies are smashed. It should smell the stench, and see blasted trees and houses and dead farm horses on the roads.

Oh, I thank God I'm a doctor and don't have to kill! Paul said once that you think you couldn't possibly kill, and are astonished to find that when you have to, you can. Maybe that's true. I'm glad I don't have to find that out about myself.

July 2, 1944

I haven't had a chance to write a word for the last two weeks. We've been moving forward, inch by inch, every day. We set up a hospital for three or four hundred beds and as the troops gain ground, set up another behind them, so we're building a string of hospitals as we move. Heaven help us, we need them all.

Whenever a man is sent back to the rear for amputation, I try to imagine what thoughts are going through those poor young heads as they lie on the litter, knowing what's ahead. Surely they must know. And I think about my father.

We're supposed to work twelve-hour shifts, which is a mighty long shift when you think of what we're doing through all those hours. It's not like a twelve-hour shift in a civilian hospital back home. Actually, there have been so many wounded that I've often kept going for twenty-four hours without sleep. It's incredible that you can still keep on your feet and think clearly, but you can. I guess it's like what Paul said about killing: If you have to, you can.

We're getting a lot of prisoners now, some top ranking Nazi officers, S.S. and others. They're entirely different from the poor kids in the ranks. They're still incredibly arrogant, still talking about how they are going to win, even though they see our continual advance. I must say I hate them. Hate them, as I never knew I could hate. We treat them well, of course; they get antibiotics and blood and all the rest, but Americans do get first call and that's as it should be.

July 10, 1944

I seem to be thinking a lot about Paul. Last night I dreamed about him. We were in a car, riding to New Hampshire after Ben was killed, and he was so kind to me, he knew just what to say, and not too much. When I woke up, I lay for a long time thinking about what had happened between us, after all those years when we swam together and played tennis and bought my first real suit.

I was so damned angry at him, especially about my mother. Still, maybe it wasn't any of my business. He said it wasn't. And it's true that neither he nor she ever questioned me about what I was doing. Being overseas and seeing so much has sort of eased my thinking. Maybe I was even beginning, before I left home, to look at things a little differently. We'd argued so about war and Paul's despising the Oxford Pledge. I guess I really knew after a while that he was right, though.

I'm sorry I didn't tell him when he came to say good-bye. But when you've been feeling cold for so long, it's hard to reach out your hands. It's like an unanswered letter. You put off answering, and then after a while it's really too late to answer, so you throw the letter away.

July 29, 1944

Slogging ahead. We see very few German planes anymore. The rumor is that they've run out of fuel. I wonder whether it's true. Anyway, we're getting closer and closer to Paris.

The *Queen Elizabeth,* traveling too fast for a convoy, zigged and zagged across the Atlantic. The crossing was rather different from Paul's prior ones; there were fifteen thousand men on board this time. He had expected to feel tense all the way in momentary expectation of a torpedo attack; instead, he was remarkably relaxed, reading, walking, and occasionally playing checkers.

London was almost unrecognizable, sandbagged, bomb-pitted, and filled with foreign uniforms. At dinner with English friends, in a blacked-out dining room, he learned for the first time of a new kind of threat from the air: planes without pilots, he was told, and filled with explosives. This, then, was the harbinger of the future, just as the lone biplane of the old war had been the harbinger of this war's sky fleets. The prospect was too sobering, and he did not voice it.

Several times he made an attempt to find Hank, whose outfit was somewhere in the south, no doubt in readiness for the assault on the Continent. Unable to make contact, he stood one evening on Shakespeare Cliff, near Dover, and watched wave after wave of American bombers coming back from Germany, while wave after wave of British bombers set out toward Germany. And he knew that the big day was coming, sooner than soon.

He had not long to wait. One week after the Allies, under the command of Eisenhower, landed on the Normandy coast, Paul and his group of observers crossed the Channel. He did not know it then, but he was following Hank's tracks through St.-Lô and Cherbourg, heading toward Paris.

There could be no question about the importance of air power. He made voluminous notes, asked questions, and prepared himself for the detailed observations he would be making as he followed the invading army across the Continent. To his technically detailed and accurate reports, written in a small, rapid hand, he often added his own personal, more emotional observations, which would be deleted when the report was officially handed in.

He wrote about things he knew he would want to remember, moods, atmospheres, and incidents. He wrote about the French 2nd Armored Division, pounding its way back home again, with weeping, cheering crowds in the villages and on the roadsides. He wrote about the undulating fields of Normandy, the ripening grain and the reddening apples. And he wrote about his fears for Paris, as he remembered Rotterdam and Warsaw lying in ashes.

One morning past the middle of August, in an orchard where they had camped for the night, he woke to a small commotion. A man from the Resistance had somehow gotten through the German lines with a message for Eisenhower. He had come to plead for Paris. The Allies, persuaded by Patton, had intended to rush past the city on the way to Germany. This desperate messenger reported now that an insurrection had already broken out; the French police were firing at German ranks and barricades were going up in the streets. The entire city, that masterpiece of art in stone, was rife for destruction.

All that day the decision waited. Patton wanted to save gasoline for his tanks, but Paul was thinking of Paris, and in silence prayed for it. Toward afternoon of the following day, word finally came down from Eisenhower's quarters; he had decided in favor of the most beautiful city in the world. So the troops turned northward, and on the second day, after crushing the last German defenses, they entered the city's gates.

Paul walked. He could have hopped onto any military vehicle, but he wanted to walk. He had learned where to find Hank's outfit and was on his way there.

The city lay under a cool blue silk sky. A slight wind rustled the thick shade along the boulevards, and already there were signs of normalcy: children sailing boats on the pond in the Tuileries and men fishing in the Seine. German signs were being torn down and barricades dismantled.

He was not yet over the miracle of the previous day, and probably never would be, probably never would forget the people's delirium at their first sight of American troops. Flowers, flags, cheers, tears, and church bells—it had been a magnificent wild revel.

He had been present at the commotion in front of the hotel where General von Choltitz was captured while at lunch. Paul had watched him come out with his hands up and seen lines of German officers being led away. And he remembered the goose-stepping youths in the brown shirts he had first seen so long ago, von Mädler talking of war's ennoblement, Donal's smile and shrug, and the fallen silence among the listeners at Leah's table. He had to clench his fists in his pockets, remembering all these, as he stood there on that sidewalk in Paris.

It was not yet all wine and roses. There had been a good deal of savage fighting, and Germans were still holed up all over the city. They still had grenades and armor-piercing shells. He had seen a dead German lying on the street, a common soldier, very young. For a moment he had stopped and looked into the face. It told nothing. Perhaps the fellow had even hated the regime for which he was forced to fight. But if he had not, should one not feel a certain pity for him anyway? To be so young and so misled! How easy it is to mislead the young if you get them early enough! Paul shivered and walked on.

It was just past noon when, arrived at the command post, he almost collided with Hank, who was on the way out. Hank had to look twice to believe what he was seeing.

"I've been thinking about you, Paul, ever since they wrote me from home that you were on your way over. What a miracle that we should meet!"

"Not such a miracle. I found out where you were. I've been following, always a couple of days behind you. In safety," Paul added ruefully. "There's nothing heroic about me."

"You had your heroics the last time," Hank said. They waited uncertainly in the sunshine. Then he said, "I guess I've been pretty hard on you. I'm sorry."

Standing here in uniform, on this foreign street, after so long, Paul felt the swelling of too much emotion. He answered lightly, "Oh, not too hard. You were always mannerly, anyway."

"I'm not even sure of that. And in my thoughts I was even harder on you."

"Well—" Paul began.

"No, hear me out. I owe it to us both to say you were right about a lot of things . . . including my mother," he finished.

Paul looked away from the flushed, embarrassed young face. And suddenly the emotion spilled over and he put his arms around Hank. "It's okay, it's okay."

The moment passed, and they both laughed. "God damn!" Hank said. "You're looking great! How are you? How's everybody at home?"

"All well, the last I saw or heard. They spend their time waiting for your letters. Your mother's busy, Meg graduated, and Hennie's the same as ever."

"What's next on your agenda?"

"I'm supposed to keep going on into Germany, following you. I wish you had a little time off, though, so we could sit and talk somewhere for an hour."

"As a matter of fact, my C.O. gave me the rest of the day off."

"Great! We can have dinner. Here's where I'm staying. I'll write it out. It's a hotel not far from here."

"Wow! Only the best."

"Why not? It's at my own expense. I've a report to file or I'd stay with you now. But can you come at six?"

"Sure can. I could use some real food. See you then."

People were pressing gifts on anyone in an American uniform, and a woman gave Hank a little bag of peaches. He stood on the sidewalk eating one, bent over to let the sweet juice drip onto the street. In the other hand he held a letter from his mother, which he had picked up in the mail after seeing Paul. He read it now for the third time, feeling a surge of happiness, then took another peach, and stood there in the sun, just feeling the happiness.

A girl passed on a bicycle. "Hey," she called to him, "Hey, that's like eating gold. Are you going to eat them all?"

"No, of course, not. Have one. Have the rest of them."

"Oh, you speak French? You're the first American I've talked to who speaks French."

"I learned it in school," he said. In the fancy private school that Dan had objected to. "Where are you going?" he asked, for lack of anything else to say.

"Home. Want to come?"

She wore a clean flowered cotton dress, and had long, thick, kinky dark blond hair.

"All right," he said, "all right, I will."

"Then hop on in back. I can't believe it," she said, "the war's almost over."

"Not for me. I'm on my way to Berlin and it's a long way."

"Stupid of me! I'm sorry. What's your name?"

"Henry. Henri. They call me Hank."

"Hank. That's funny. I'm Antoinette. They call me Toni."

"Are you tired? Shall I pedal?"

"No, I'm used to it. I suppose you wonder why I asked for the peach. It's because we haven't had anything like that, unless we pedaled miles out to the country and picked some. When I saw you eating, I was dying to have one."

They were riding through a quiet section of wide streets, trees, and elegant houses that looked old. They were rich-old, with tall windows and flowerboxes.

"This is Neuilly. It's near the Bois. It's beautiful to walk there. We get off here."

He followed the girl up the front steps and into a cool hall with a wide, carpeted staircase. He followed her up past mirrored rooms, marble fireplaces, and damask-covered walls, up and up until, on the fifth floor, she unlocked the door into a little room under the eaves. It was clean and plain. There was a neat bed, a table, some chairs, a food cupboard, and an electric grill.

"My home," she said. "You look puzzled."

"Well, no, I—" he began.

"You thought the whole house belonged to me."

"I didn't know, I—"

She laughed. "Neuilly is one of the richest parts of Paris and let me tell you, it's more full of Germans and French traitors than any other part. The only reason I'm here is that the lady who owns this house has a husband who's been in London with de Gaulle and she needed money, so she had to rent out rooms. This used to be a maid's room."

"It's a very nice room."

"And you're a very nice man. Would you like some wine?"

"Yes, thank you."

"I've bread and cheese too."

He remembered that he had an orange in his pocket and gave it to her.

She sniffed it. "Such fragrance! I haven't had one in four years."

He watched her peel it. She had pretty fingers and no ring, so she wasn't married.

"Are you looking at that photo? That's my fiancé. He's a prisoner in Germany."

He didn't know what to say.

"God, how I hate them!" she cried. "How can I know what they're doing to him? And it's been bad enough here. If you were caught out after midnight, here in your own city, you could be shot. We had almost no gas or electricity. We burned newspapers to keep warm. We were so hungry . . . we kept chickens on our rooftops to get some eggs, but collaborators ate in the best restaurants. I hate them too."

She had a husky voice. He listened, only half hearing her words, but held by her voice and the afternoon warmth and the strangeness of being here in this country, this city, this room.

"—you could hear screams from the Gestapo. Seventy-four Avenue Foch, I had to pass it on my way to work. It was awful. Awful. Those poor people . . . they used to deport them to Germany from the Pantin freight station near the stockyards. You could hear people shrieking inside the cars. In the beginning it was the Jews, and after that anybody, for any reason."

"I'm a Jew," Hank said.

"I'm a Catholic. Well, we all pray to God." She nodded toward the photo. "I pray for him every day. Do you know if it weren't for that picture, I would have forgotten what he looks like. I haven't seen him in five years."

"Five years," Hank repeated.

"Yes, and I've been faithful, too, but that's a long, long time."

She was young, perhaps twenty-three, he guessed. She had sat down on her bed and leaned back against the pillows, which were fresh and white. In her eyes, he saw a mixture of purity and frank desire. It had been a long time for him, too, ever since London. In between there had been week after week of bloody death. . . .

He smiled and moved to the bed. Her dress had loops and buttons down the front; four hands slipped the buttons out of the loops; two brief scraps of silk fell to the floor, while a pair of wooden clogs dropped off with a clatter. He thought, as he lay down and covered her, that he caught the scent of peaches and sweet grass and summer . . . it was all quite simple and very quickly over.

Afterward, when he got up, he watched her retie the ribbons in her hair.

"Do you have a girl at home?" she asked.

"No."

"If you had, would you mind if she did what I've just done?"

An odd question! And he thought of his mother and Paul.

"No," he said. "It was natural and good."

"You're right . . . Because I love André, and this had nothing to do with him. . . . You're looking at your watch. You have to go."

"Yes, there's someone I have to meet at six."

"Do you remember the way we came?"

"Oh, I'm good at directions."

"Well, go then."

The city was almost quiet. At the western edges, the sky was as pink as the inside of a shell, while a dusky blue haze lay overhead. Here and there, as he walked back toward the inner city, he passed a burned tank or an overturned German staff car with a torn swastika flag draped in mockery over its hood.

He felt a dreamy glow, a sense of wholeness seeping gradually back within him, as he moved among normal people, without guns, on a normal street; he was filled with the joy that the girl had given, and the joy of seeing Paul again. He heard himself singing softly under his breath. And so, bemused, he only looked up with a feeling of mild surprise when he heard the shot.

The second one caught him in the chest with so violent a blow that he clutched himself there with both his hands, as if to keep himself from falling.

Oh, no! he thought. *It can't be . . . just when I . . . when everything was so good . . . I . . . Henry . . .* The red letters of his name were dancing in front of his eyes. *Not I . . . I . . . have so much to . . .* And fell.

And Paul, who had been standing outside of the sandbagged lobby of the hotel, waiting for him, glanced up and saw the sniper behind the parapet. He saw Hank coming unaware, called out, and not caring about himself, ran to warn.

He felt a hot pain in his shoulder, and feeling it kept running, running to where Hank lay, and seeing what he saw, seeing death, could only kneel and cry his heart out.

On August 29, the Free French, with de Gaulle at their head, having had their grand triumphal parade, it was the turn of the Americans to march down the Champs-Elysées. Without regard to the snipers who still lurked in the city, the 28th Infantry Division stepped smartly, proud among flags and flowers under a sparkling sun.

Among the cheering thousands at the curb, Paul stood and watched. The ache in his bandaged shoulder was nothing compared with the ache in his heart. There they went, on their way to Germany, and Hank Roth not with them.

"But I'm staying with them," Paul said aloud to himself.

The doctor had spoken of sending him home, but he wasn't ready to go home. He didn't know when he ever would be ready. He was going to stay here and see it through, to the end and beyond.

The news arrived when the Shermans were at dinner. Hennie, who was often alone these days, had been invited, and the three had just sat down when the bell rang. The maid came back from the door looking anxious.

"It's a telegram. Somebody in the family has to sign."

Bill Sherman rose at once. The women said afterward that they had known at that instant what it was; they hadn't needed to hear Bill's slow, hesitant return on the stairs, or to see his gray face.

A few times he opened his mouth to speak and stopped, while Leah, Hennie, and the young maid stared at him.

"Perhaps we'd better go inside somewhere and sit down," he finally said.

Leah jumped up and seized the telegram. Her husband

caught her as her knees gave way. She fought him. She screamed.

"It's not true, I don't believe it, oh, my God, God wouldn't let it happen, why did God let it happen, it's not true—"

"Hank?" Hennie whispered.

"No!" Leah cried. "Don't you believe it, Hennie, it's a lie, a lie, a lie—"

"It's true," Hennie said. "Yes, it's true. I expected it. The same as his father. The wars take our men. Yes, yes." She covered her face with her hands.

Nora, the young maid, was terrified, and she began to wail. "Oh, Mr. Sherman, what'll we do?"

Leah's screams brought the cook from the kitchen, and she, too, began to sob. "Mr. Hank . . . I gave him cookies after school. Mr. Hank."

"We'll need the doctor," Bill said quickly. "My wife needs help. And Hennie, too." For Hennie was still sitting with her hands over her face, not making a sound. "Will one of you call him, please?"

Leah's terrible primitive cries were loud enough to be heard on the street. "I want to die! Let me die, do you hear me? Leave me alone!" as Bill swept her up and carried her, kicking and struggling, to bed.

When the doctor had given her heavy sedation, he and Bill came back downstairs where Hennie was sitting quietly with Nora. Bill came over and took her hand.

"I didn't mean to neglect you, but I had to take care of the emergency. Dear Hennie," he said. "Life hasn't treated you very well these last few years."

"There are a few million others it hasn't treated very well, either."

"Do you never cry?" he asked her gently.

"I don't seem to. I don't know why I can't."

"I'll give you some medicine to help you sleep," the doctor said.

"And you'll sleep here," Bill told her. "Across the hall if you need me."

On the way out the doctor said, "It's curious how differently people react. Unspeakable as it is, Leah will come out of this better than Hennie will."

"She's so much younger."

"It's not that. She lets go. Things don't get corked up."

The two men stood for a moment looking out to the street, where an old couple walked a huge white poodle and two little girls in plaid dresses went skipping. It was absolutely crazy that human beings were being killed on the other side of the ocean.

"Not even a funeral, for whatever comfort that is," Bill murmured. His wet eyes shone in the dusk.

The doctor answered, "It is a comfort. The prayers, the music, the friends . . . We'll go to services with her Friday evening or Saturday morning, of course."

"Of course."

"She'll be able to go. She'll be under control when she wakes up tomorrow morning."

Bill took his hand. "Thanks for everything. I'll take good care of her. And of the old lady, too," he added. "Poor soul."

"Knowing you, you'll take good care of everybody. Good night, Bill."

Twenty-one

The war had been over for more than a year when Paul finally came home, having spent the intervening months as a relief volunteer in the devastated areas of northern France. His last sight of Europe was the wreckage of the harbor at Le Havre, where the Germans in the rage of defeat had blown up the railway and the docks. Yet in the midst of ruin lay hope and a good deal of pride, too, in an America that had given such massive aid to the war and was now giving it again to the peace.

America itself, he saw, was booming. People seemed to be in need of everything, of cars, houses, and shoes; money was beginning to circulate as fast as blood in the arteries of a long-distance runner.

Marian had exchanged her Palm Beach house for a larger one, lavish with fountains, Spanish tile, and royal palms. The season had been growing longer, she explained, and more of their friends had acquired the Florida habit during these years when the Riviera was closed to them.

Although she had obviously prepared for his homecoming with new clothes, and was making an attempt at gaiety with festive menus and flowers in every room, he sensed her anxiety. She looked much older. There were few lines in her face, but there were signs of suffering in her questioning eyes. *Are you going to leave me again?* they asked. *Can I depend on you?*

He replied obliquely to her unspoken questions. "It's good to be back." And looking around the room, he felt the welcome, even of inanimate things: Joachim's crystal horse, books, and the photographs of his parents in carved walnut frames. "You've had them reframed!"

"Oh, do you like them?"

"Beautiful, Marian. You've kept everything beautiful. You always do."

"So you're really glad to be home?"

"Of course I am. Glad to be here and to stay here."

A small, pleased smile quivered at her lips, and after a moment she said softly, "You had a terrible time. About Hank, I mean."

"Yes."

"I wrote a note to Leah when I heard."

"That was good of you."

"Not that I've changed my mind about seeing her. But I did feel sad. He was such a nice boy."

"Yes. Yes, he was."

"Almost a son to you, the nearest you ever had to a child of your own."

Melancholy seeped over the red flowers on the table.

"I guess I'll start making the rounds tomorrow," he said briskly. "Let people know I'm back."

Leah was the person he dreaded to see. The letter in which he had told her about Hank's death was the most painful piece of writing he had ever had to do. He supposed that she would want him to tell it to her all over again, which would revive his anguish. The scene had blackened his wakeful nights and fired his dreams for too long, and he was still trying to get free of it. And so he was relieved to postpone the meeting by stopping off first at Alfie's.

There, it seemed like old times. Alfie's new office, although a good deal smaller than the one he had occupied in the heyday of the twenties, was at a good address, well situated on the nineteenth floor, with a view to both the rivers.

Alfie's clothes and his posture also bespoke the return of prosperity, and Paul told him he looked well.

"I feel well," he answered. "Keeping busy, that's the ticket. Keeps you young . . . terrible thing about young Hank, wasn't it?"

"Yes," Paul said.

"It was pretty awful here when we got the news. I don't know who was worse, Leah or Hennie. It was Freddy and 1917 all over again." Alfie regarded Paul carefully. "Is that why you stayed longer over there?"

"In a way, maybe that had something to do with it. I should see Leah today, I know, and I'm not looking forward to it."

"Don't worry. She'll be all right. It took her about six months to get going again, but she's back in shape, right as rain. Took another floor for the business and bought the building. Putting out her own line of perfume with a big ad campaign. Never could keep Leah down, could you?"

Paul acknowledged that you couldn't.

"And you can't have heard about Meg, either. She's going to be married."

"No! She never wrote anything."

"It happened suddenly. Last week while you were sailing home. If you wait a few minutes, you'll see her and Larry. Lawrence Bates. They're in the city today to buy a ring." Alfie beamed. "A real nice guy. Everybody likes him, even Meg's kids. He's a vet. I've given them a piece of land at Laurel Hill for an office."

Paul's immediate reaction when they walked in was a warm spread of pleasure. By the end of the hour, his pleasure had firmed into satisfaction.

Larry Bates had a strong handclasp, a ruddy, open English face, and a simple manner. In short, he was the masculine complement to Meg, who, now in sweater and skirt, with her pretty windblown hair, seemed suddenly to have become again the girl Paul remembered. It was as if, after all these years, she had stepped out of a disguise and once more revealed her *self*.

There was irony: Here at last was the husband who would be able to get Meg into the club to which Alfie had so long aspired, but Larry Bates would almost certainly not be interested in any club. He came from a midwestern farm, and the farm, even though he had become a doctor, was still part of him.

"You're going to be very happy," Paul said when the time came to leave. "I see it ahead of you."

And Meg answered, "It wouldn't have happened, we wouldn't even have met, without you."

Her words glowed in Paul as he made his way downstairs. But after a few steps out into the street, the glow subsided; he began to feel a stirring, not exactly of pain, but rather a small suggestion of pain, something that had begun that morning and been renewed in the atmosphere of Meg's happiness. He had been walking rapidly, encouraged by the fresh April air, which was still cold, and by the general rhythm of the city in which everyone seemed to be bent on going someplace in a hurry. It came to him now that once he had gotten past seeing Leah, there was nothing else he had to do for the rest of the day. He hadn't planned to take up work at the office until Monday next. And if he were never to go back to the office, what difference would it make? His partners had managed very well without him these last years. Who needed him? What was there to look forward to? Unlike Meg, who could now look ahead again, down years that he hoped, that he believed, would be good ones, he had no one. . . .

Envy, he thought as he stopped before the window of a bookshop and stared in; the truth is that I'm envious and empty.

So he would go back to the office, to his charitable causes and occasional women. A dreary prospect.

He resumed his walk to Leah's shop. Best to get that over with, anyway. Perhaps, as Alfie had said, it wouldn't be too terribly hard.

When he announced himself, he was directed to her office at the rear. He passed through a series of salons, all very hushed in dove gray and dusty rose, in which at proper intervals stood life-size models wearing taffeta or brocade or Irish tweed. He found her busy at a Chinese lacquered desk in a pretty flower-papered cubicle.

With a cry like a war whoop, she jumped up and threw her arms around him. "I don't believe what I'm seeing! It's been a century! How's your shoulder? You never told us about it! We had to hear it from your friends."

"It's nothing." The better to see her, he held her at a little distance. Except for a fine ray of wrinkles at the corners of her eyes, she was no different. "But you, I worried terribly about you."

Her eyes filled. "I'm as all right as I'll ever be . . . Bill pulled me through. And he was wonderful to Hennie too. He's a prince, Paul." She sat down again at the desk, clasping her hands under her chin. "You know," she said softly, "marrying Bill is the best thing that's ever happened to me."

Again there came that faint stir of envy, which shamed him, so that he made himself respond with grace.

"I'm so glad. And glad for Meg, too. I've just come from seeing her."

"Yes, it's wonderful, isn't it? What a change after Donal!"

"What's been happening to him? Do you know?"

"Flourishing, naturally. He pulled his money out of Germany just in time."

"If I remember correctly, he always said Hitler was unbeatable."

"It's Donal who's unbeatable. God knows, they may be making him an ambassador yet. Still, as Hennie says, we mustn't forget what he did for Dan."

"She's a good soul, Hennie is, better than I am. I still resent that he was able to do it when I wasn't."

"Nobody's better than you. Don't you ever realize what you do for other people?"

The praise embarrassed him. "Oh," he said, "one tries. We all try to do what we can."

"We had a letter . . ." Leah's voice was almost a whisper. She began again. "We had a letter from a captain, someone who saw what you did when Hank—when Hank was killed. He said you ran out, you tried to cover him, to take the shots yourself."

She seemed to expect a response. There was only one thing he could think of to say.

"I loved him."

"Marian wrote me a letter, but I never see her. She found out something, I suppose."

"Perhaps."

"Meg hinted something once, I thought. Then she wouldn't say any more. . . . You don't want to say anything either, I see."

"There's nothing to be gained," Paul said.

Then there was a silence. We people have been away from each other too long, he reflected. We don't want to go back through the calendar of lost time. At least, I don't.

So he said, "I see you've a deskful of papers. I mustn't keep you."

"No need to rush away. I've been waiting for you anyway, to tell you something." A troubled frown drew lines across Leah's forehead. "Something I ought to tell you."

"Nothing bad, I hope?"

"To me it doesn't seem so. But perhaps it will be sad for you. I don't know."

"Well?"

"All right, this is it from the beginning. I'd been dressing a bride, doing a whole trousseau. The girl's marrying a refugee, a doctor from Vienna. And one day we happened to be talking about what's happened in Europe, and I happened to mention you, my cousin Paul Werner, who'd rescued people in Germany. Your name just slipped out, and it seems that the girl knows you."

Something leapt in Paul. But he put it down and waited.

"Why don't you ask who she is?"

"Fine, I'll ask. Who is she?"

"She's Iris Friedman."

He knew that his face had on the instant gone bright red, with the heat running up his neck. And he stammered words without meaning. "A—coincidence."

"Not really. This is the most fashionable establishment in the city for bridal gowns. Any bride who can afford to, comes here."

The pulses were hammering now. She was twenty-seven. It had taken her a long time. She wouldn't have appealed to most men. Sober and shy . . . He remembered the eyes, the beautiful, soft, intelligent eyes.

"Is she—is she happy?"

"Oh, yes, she's thrilled. Very much in love, I think. And her father's outfitting her in grand, grand style." Leah's curious, frank gaze rested on Paul. "I saw the mother, too. A striking woman. Very distinguished."

"You spoke about me?"

"Not to her. That conversation was with Iris."

"What did she tell you?"

"Not much. Only that she'd met you a couple of times, that you knew the family, or had known them." Leah put her hand over Paul's. "I didn't mean to hurt you, to bring this back. I just thought you might want to know. She's lovely, Paul, not pretty, but very fine, different from what I usually see coming in here."

"Yes, different. I remember." And he stared down at the cherry-red nails that were lying on his hand.

"Paul . . . I still have my bad habit of putting my foot in my mouth. Are you still chasing a fantasy? A ghost that can never come to life?"

"I don't know what you mean," he lied.

"I'm the last person in the world to hurt you, after what you've done and been, but I told you once before that you're wasting yourself and I'm telling you now again. Do you hear me?"

"I hear you."

"Well, then. Oh, my dear, I truly wanted you! But you didn't take me, so I took Bill instead, and it's been wonderful. Meg hung on with that bastard long after she should have quit, but now she's got someone really perfect for her. So what I'm asking is: When are you going to start living?"

"I'm living."

"You're not. You and Marian—"

Paul cried sharply, "I can't abandon her, Leah."

"Who's asking you to? There are other ways. . . . You're annoyed with me."

Paul swallowed hard. "It's all right. I'm not annoyed."

"Forgive me."

"It's all right, I said."

"Do you want me to tell you any more about Iris?"

He both did, and did not.

"The wedding's to be June twelfth at half past four, at Temple Israel."

"Well," he said, "I can only hope life will go better for her than for—" He did not finish.

"Than for her mother, or for you."

A sudden awareness brought Paul up short. "And you? You're not complaining, and you've had enough cause."

"What good would it do? Listen, you were on your way to Hennie's. She phoned. She's expecting you."

Paul stood up. "I'm going. Don't let's be strangers, Leah. We'll have to see each other once in a while."

"Of course. Give Hennie my love."

Hennie had grown thinner and grayer but, as vigorous in her enthusiasms as she had ever been, was still working with the world's refugees who, in the aftermath of the war, had multiplied a hundredfold.

"Damned old men who start the wars!" she cried. Her gaze moved across the room and came to rest at a photograph of Hank. His ardent face looked out of a broad silver frame, undoubtedly a gift from Leah and undoubtedly the most expensive object in Hennie's parlor.

A silent, sad recall filled the next few moments, until she broke the silence with deliberate cheerfulness.

"This won't happen again. This time the world's learned a final hard lesson. We have the U.N., and Russia wants peace as much as we do. Between the two of us, we'll keep it."

And the Russians made a pact with Hitler when it suited them, Paul thought, but didn't say.

Hennie mused, "We've seen a great deal, you and I, from the time I used to read Grimms' fairy tales to you."

Something in her tone, an echo, a sense of déjà vu, took hold of him, for she was sitting on the same old sofa with the same shabby carpet under it, and he was back in his despair over Anna before his wedding, pleading with Hennie for advice—advice that she had given and he had not taken. The room was suddenly too small and the walls closed in. He wanted to get out, to feel space and motion.

"The trick is to be busy," Hennie said. "The survivors are coming through now, and I get home tired every night, which is the best thing for me."

The survivors. Not Joachim and Elisabeth, not Ilse nor Mario.

"Where are they coming from?" he asked.

"Everywhere. They were all poured into Poland, into the camps, from the corners of Europe, Germany, Italy, Greece, everywhere."

"Who survived?"

"A few lucky ones, if you want to call them that. A few young men who slaved in the iron mines for the German war machine and managed to keep alive. A few mechanics, or doctors who were used in some way. Not many."

"You remember the doctor I told you about . . . the woman in Italy with her son?"

"The one you rescued?"

"I wonder whether it's possible that she's still alive."

Hennie threw out her hands in her old, typical gesture. "Anything's possible, Paul, but not very likely. But write her name for me and on Monday I'll see whether there's any trace of her."

Late on Monday afternoon, after a long day of working his way back into the world of banking, there came a call from Hennie. She sounded breathless.

"Paul! I sifted through file after file and finally I went to the resettlement lists—outside of New York, that means—and my God, I found her! Same name, a doctor, went from Italy to Auschwitz. It's got to be your Ilse!"

He was stunned. "She's here? In the United States?"

"Yes. She's been here a year. They sent her first to Minneapolis for retraining and now she's back in New York."

"And Mario?"

"Nothing about him."

"Have you got an address?"

"And a phone number. She works at a clinic downtown."

He hung up, forgetting even to say thank you. Putting aside the papers that lay before him, he thought how accidental, how haphazard everything was. Millions, the six million dead, and somehow Ilse still lived. And he thought, remembering their few swift days, the wind in the mountain woods, and the porcelain stove in the corner, that in other circumstances, had they not been born on different continents, then Ilse might possibly have been the one for him. Who could say? Haphazard, accidental, all of it . . .

And he picked up the telephone. The same dread that he had felt before the meeting with Leah a few days ago, now chilled him again. To go back and back through the calendar of lost time . . .

There was a pause—he could almost hear how startled it was—when he gave his name.

"Oh!" she said. "I thought you were dead."

"Why, whatever made you—"

"Because when I came last year, I called your office and they told me you had gone to the war and hadn't come home, so I took it to mean that—"

"No, no. I stayed over there because, well, because I thought I could be useful, and because I just didn't feel like coming home yet. But never mind me. I want to hear about you."

"How do I begin? When I got out of the camp, there was a committee. They cleaned us, got rid of the lice, and gave us clothes. And after a while they helped with our papers, so my number came on the quota. After so many years, so many dreadful years, they reached my number."

Afraid to ask because afraid of the answer, he managed to put the question. "Mario?"

"Dead. We were separated on the train. I never saw him again."

The flat simplicity of these words was more awful than a torrent of tears would have been. Paul's ears rang with the echo: Mario is dead. Dead. Dead.

"Oh," he said, "I want to see you, Ilse. When may I? Where?"

"I get off early tomorrow afternoon. Can you come for coffee? I have a little place in Washington Heights."

He felt a surge of something that was sad and also eager.

"I'll be there. Four o'clock."

There was a row of stores, a laundry, a butcher's, a barber's, and a tailor's, with apartments above. Paul climbed a flight of dark stairs and rang the bell. She must have been waiting for him, because the door opened at once.

"So it's you. So it's really you," she said, and put her arms around him.

He held her for a minute or two, comforting, stroking her hair. When she stepped back, her eyes were wet.

"You're the only human being left from the world I knew! The only one!"

"Nobody else from Europe? There are so many living in this neighborhood!"

"But no one I knew. So you see, it has really been a whole new beginning . . ." She wiped her eyes. "But enough of that. I have coffee and I baked a streusel cake last night. Sit down. I'll only be a minute."

While she was in the kitchenette, he looked about. The room was sparsely furnished with pieces that were obviously secondhand, but there were green, healthy plants on the windowsill and rows of books on the shelves. In this short time she had already begun to collect books.

"I had a funny feeling when I poured the coffee just now," she said, bringing in the tray. "I was remembering that the second time we met, you came to my house and had coffee. You looked around, the way you did just now, and you said something about Mario's photograph. Do you know, I haven't even got a picture of him anymore? Only what's in here." She touched her forehead.

What could he say? The young men. All the brave young men. Volumes would be written about what happened, but they would never be able to come anywhere near the truth.

"I have no words to offer you," Paul said.

"Sometimes I try to tell myself that it's better my son wasn't left to live out a miserable life. They ruined him in that camp, the first time. I think they did something to his head, something physical, I mean. He was never quite right, never able to take care of himself."

She had lived a thousand years to every ten of an ordinary life. . . . A fire engine clanged in the street below and children clattered up the stairs, recalling him to the present.

"You don't look any older in spite of everything."

Yet there were changes; it seemed to Paul that a certain something had been added to her face, something softer, less positive or sure of itself. Suffering, he thought. It chastens.

"How are things with you now, Paul?" she asked.

"The same."

"And your wife?"

"The same." And suddenly he blurted, "I can't end it, you see. She needs me. She loves me, in her way."

"Yes, we can love people who are wrong for us, and we for them."

He had a need to speak, to say things he had never said to anyone else. "She's weak . . . she has so many ailments . . . sinus and migraine and nerves."

"She can't help it. Believe me, people like that don't enjoy being the way they are."

"Spoken like a doctor."

"Well, I am a doctor. No, you can't destroy her. You harmed her enough when you married her without loving her."

"I know that very well."

"There's been enough pain in this world without inflicting any more."

"God knows that's true."

"Oh, Paul, I've thought about you so many times! There's so much I want to ask. The other woman, Anna? You don't mind that I ask?"

"I don't mind. But there's nothing to tell you. Nothing's changed."

"I'm sorry," Ilse said.

The little reply was enigmatic, and he let it go.

"Are we going to see each other?" she asked.

"Of course!"

"Whenever you're free. I understand that there are complications."

"Not at all. We both come and go pretty much as we please. So I'll call you in a day or two."

Some weeks later there came an afternoon of cool June sparkle. An organ-grinder played a Neapolitan song, people were buying potted geraniums, and ice-cream vendors tinkled their bells. All in all, it was a joyous day for a wedding, Paul thought, as he turned the last corner before the temple.

Nevertheless, he was a trifle anxious. "Are you sure you want to go?" he asked Ilse for the third time.

"Of course I am."

He looked down at her with approval. She was handsome in pearl-gray silk and a yellow-flowered hat. Her hair, still worn as she always had worn it, was drawn smoothly back from a forehead that had begun to regain some of its old serenity. And her dark eyes, slightly tilted, faintly Oriental, were cheerful.

He had recommended Leah's place for clothes. "But I don't

need anything," she had protested. "I wear a white coat five and a half days a week." Her first glance around Leah's establishment had shocked her. "This is no place for me. These things cost a fortune."

He had soothed her. "Leave it to me. The owner is a relative of mine."

He had hardly needed to say a word to Leah, who, knowing Ilse's story and with characteristic generosity, had already intended to provide her with a wardrobe at cost.

"Now, there's quality for you," she had reported to Paul by telephone. "Oh, I liked her, Paul, I really did."

And Paul had assented, with some amusement. Quality indeed. Marian would say you could always tell an upper-class person, especially one with a European education.

He said now, "I wonder how long they're going to take inside?"

Ilse's fingers felt his wrist. "Your pulse is wild. But why shouldn't it be?"

He had no intention of going in to watch the ceremony, although he could have slipped in unnoticed at the rear of the temple. But he did not want to run even the slightest risk of disconcerting either Anna or Iris on this day. He would simply stand on the sidewalk until the bride and groom had left in the limousine that was already waiting for them at the curb.

The doors of the square stone building where they stood were now firmly shut. He could only imagine the scene, the two young people before the open Ark, the beautiful old words, the groom's foot breaking the glass, the lifted veil and the kiss.

He was shut out. Clearly he understood that no matter what else might happen, there could never be truth between his daughter and himself. The man who had nurtured Iris and led her up the aisle this day was her father.

Glancing down when Ilse withdrew her hand, he saw, as

her sleeve fell back, the numbers stamped on her white arm. And he was reminded. . . . It was she who had really lost a child. In the presence of such loss he felt, almost, a little ashamed.

An instant later the doors opened, releasing a surge of exultant music from the great organ. And the bride appeared with a slender man in a tailcoat—Paul scarcely saw him, for what did he matter?—and she was laughing, her voice had a pure, high ring, the veil blew back over her head, she gathered her full skirts, they got into the long, black car and were gone.

God bless you, Iris. May you know peace and love as long as you live, he said, without making a sound.

The curious little crowd that always collects from nowhere to see a bride now mingled with the crowd that was coming out of the building. Among them Paul hid, waiting until Anna should come in sight.

Ah, there, there! She was following with her eyes the car that had taken Iris away. Once again she wore pink, with a twist of flowers in her bright hair. She looked like a girl, as young as her daughter.

Then he became aware of the man who stood next to her. He had his arm around her waist. And Anna looked up at him; even as far away as they were, Paul could see that they were smiling at each other. This is the first time I've ever seen them together, he thought queerly, but abruptly there came a sharp recall: It was not the first time, it was the second. . . . Years before, when Marian was not yet pregnant and Anna was, although he had not known she was, yes, yes, he had sat in his car and watched this man and this woman walk together toward the house where they lived when they were poor. . . . How he had trembled then, his heart staggering in his chest, with the discovery that he could not—because it was not in him to do such cruelty—could not tear down the man's roof . . . even if Anna had been willing . . . which she had not been!

He should have let her alone, really alone, since then. God knew he had meant to. . . .

Now they were saying something to each other. The man's head inclined toward hers, his very posture revealing his possession, his whole possession. They had a life, those two, a history of their own! What right had he to intervene, if only in his most extravagant, wasteful thoughts?

And something happened inside Paul's head, in his heart, something that darted like pain, and receded quickly with exquisite relief. Yes, yes. First love she had been and, in her most special way, perhaps the only one? But there were other ways, many ways. And he must wait no more.

"That's Anna, isn't it?" Ilse whispered and, answering his nod, "Charming, Paul. How charming!"

For a long moment he watched Anna and her husband get into their car. "Now," he said aloud.

Surprised, Ilse asked, "What, now?"

"Oh, a walk, and maybe dinner with me if you've nothing else you want to do, or no one else to see."

"There is nothing, and there is no one I'd like better."

When are you going to start living? asked Leah.

Now, he repeated to himself. It's time, and past time.

And they walked on hand in hand through the lowering summer day toward the avenue. It was a most ordinary thoroughfare, crowded with traffic, noisy with pushing, pulsing life and suddenly very, very beautiful.

The Middle East

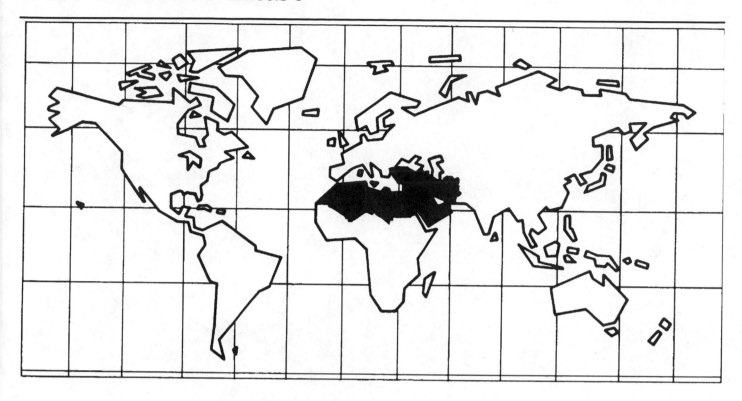

AUTHOR/EDITOR
Dr. William Spencer

The author/editor for *Global Studies: The Middle East* was formerly professor of history at Florida State University and has specialized in Middle East/North African affairs for more than 40 years. He is the author of many books on the region and, in addition to his university teaching, has traveled extensively on research, U.S. government, and United Nations assignments. Since retiring from Florida State, Dr. Spencer has continued to be active in his field, serving as visiting professor at various colleges and universities. In his teaching and service as a curriculum consultant, particularly to school systems and community colleges, Dr. Spencer has made his life's work helping U.S. educators develop a better understanding of this volatile region of the world.

CONSULTANT
Elizabeth Bouvier Spencer

Elizabeth Spencer is an artist and teacher who has traveled with her husband, Dr. William Spencer, to the Middle East on many research trips. She is responsible for much of the material in this book on home and family life, architecture, and housing, aside from her contributions as grammarian and amanuensis extraordinary.

SERIES CONSULTANT
H. Thomas Collins
Washington, D.C.